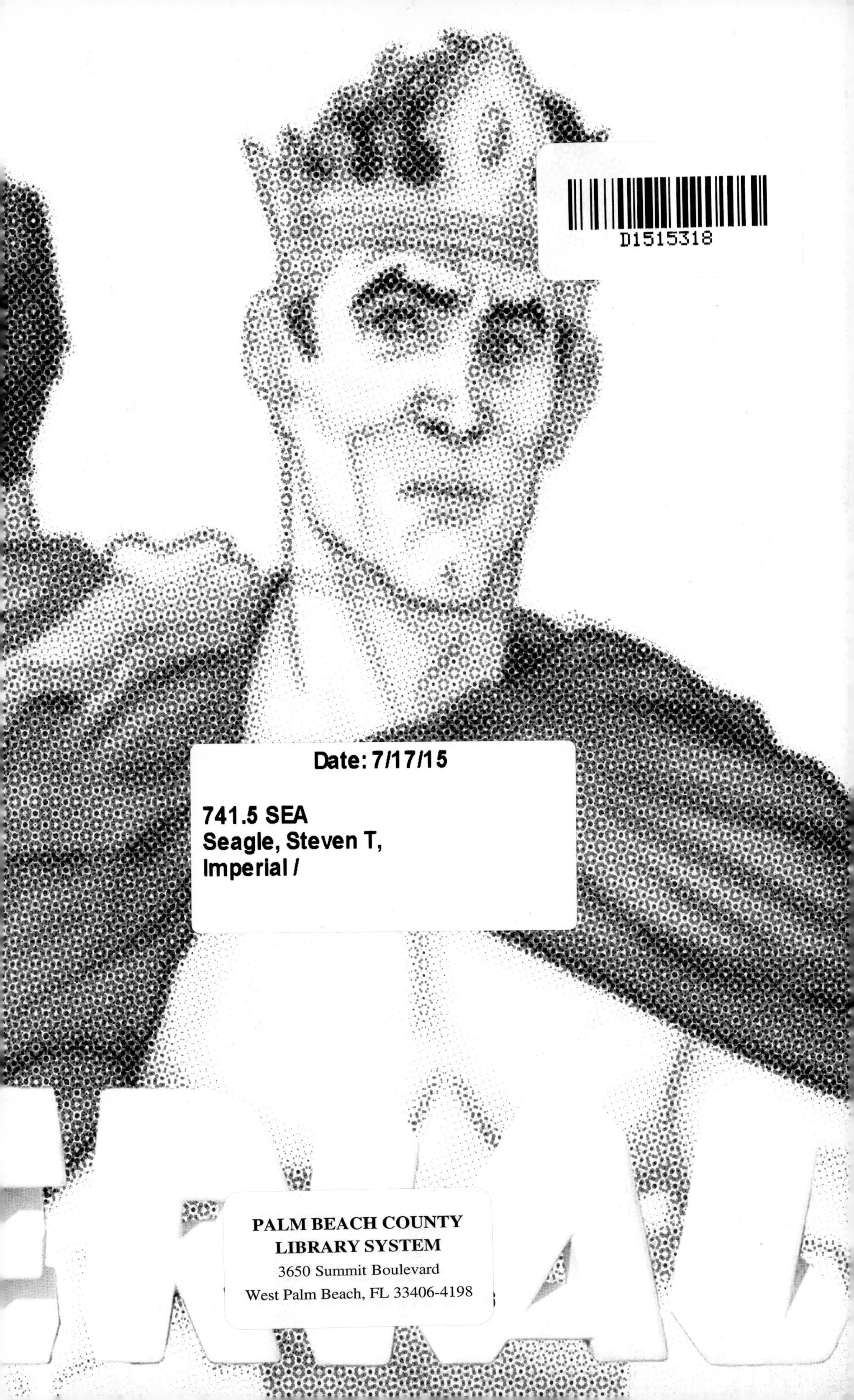

steven t.
seagle
writer + logo + design

mark
dos santos
penciller + inker

thomas
mauer
letterer

brad
simpson
colorist

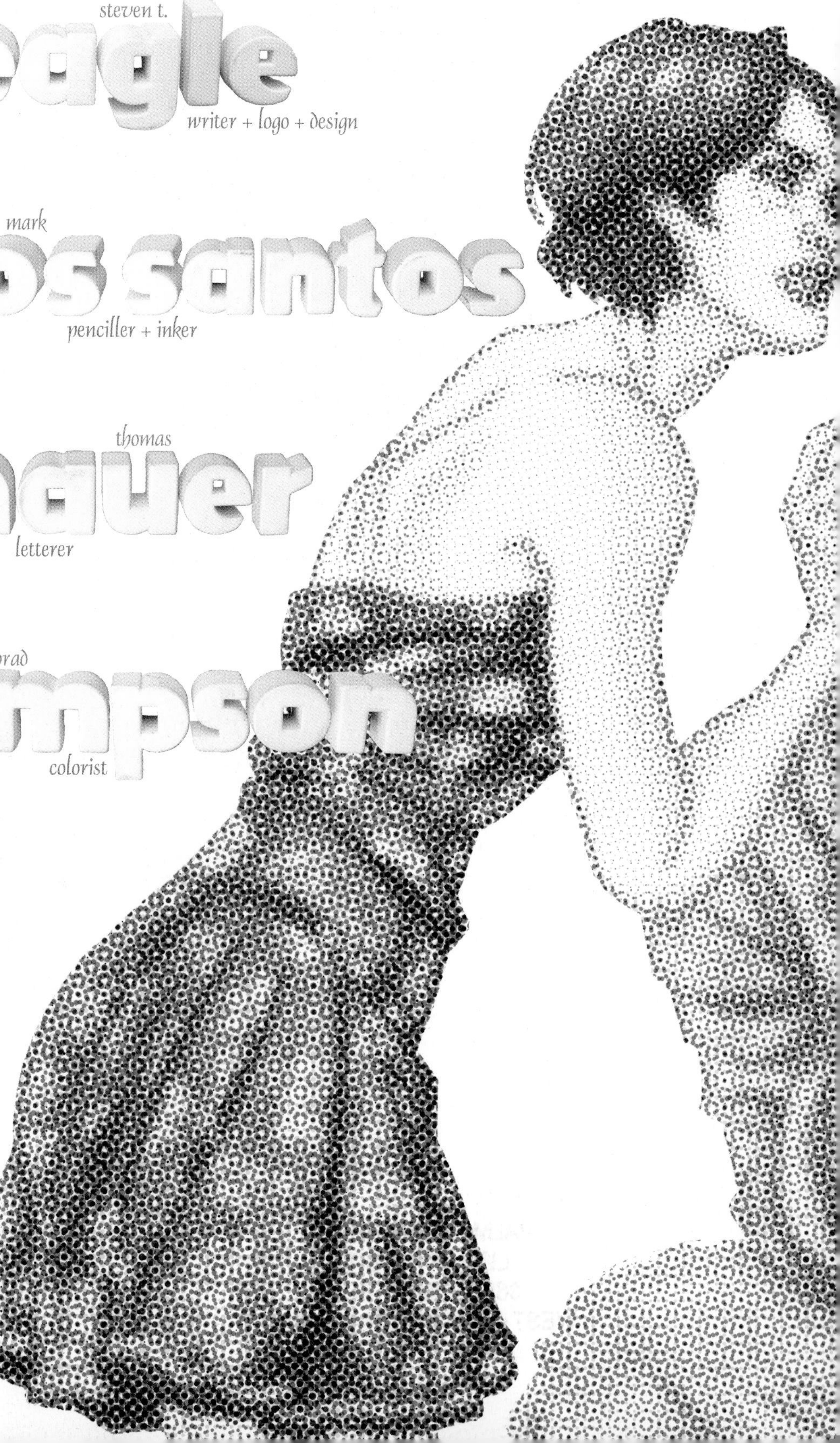

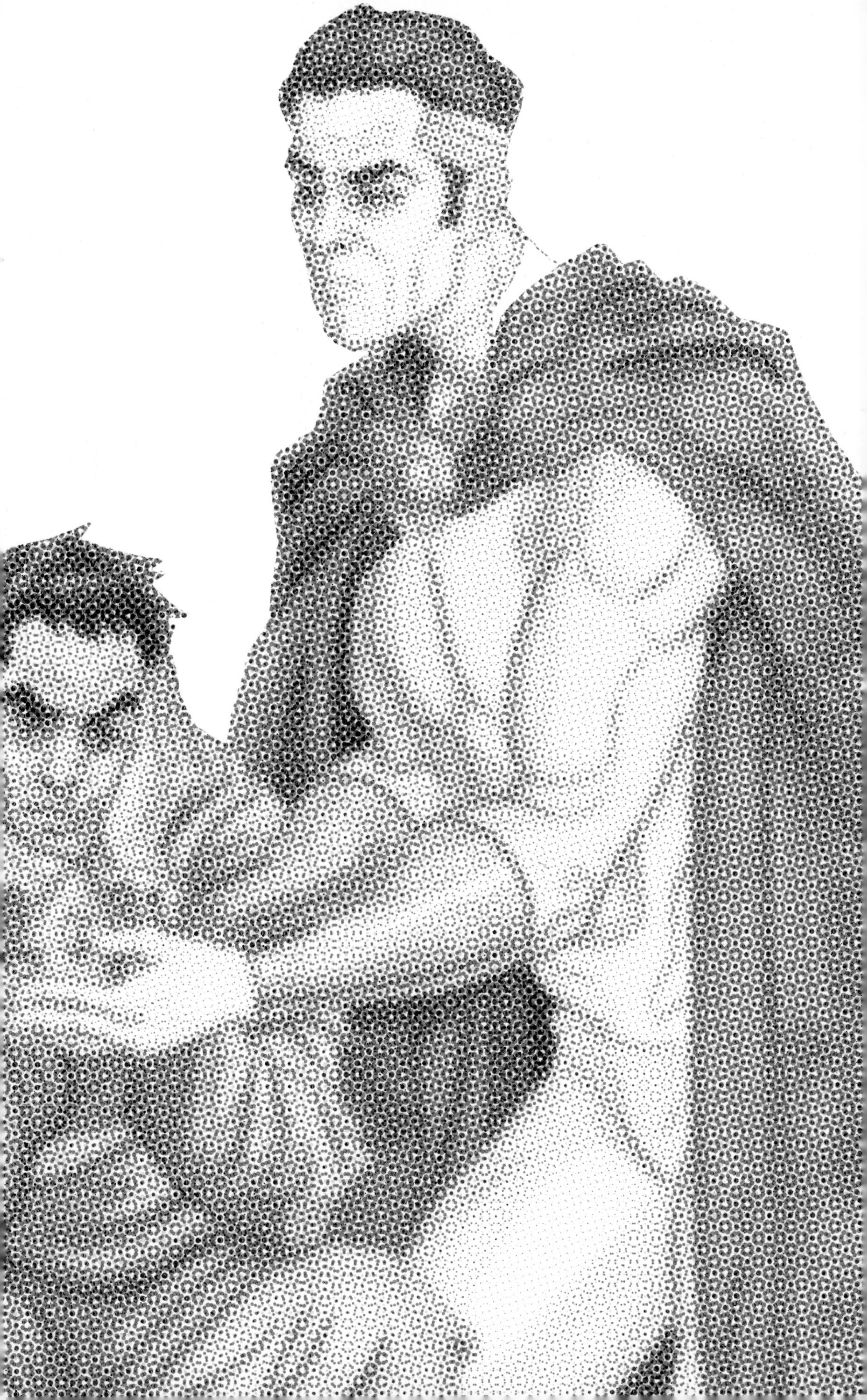

on the bride's side

Robert Kirkman - Chief Operating Officer + Erik Larsen - Chief Financial Officer + Todd McFarlane - President + Marc Silvestri - Chief Executive Officer + Jim Valentino Vice-President

Eric Stephenson - Publisher + Ron Richards - Director of Business Development + Jennifer de Guzman - Director of Trade Book Sales + Kat Salazar - Director of PR & Marketing + Corey Murphy - Director of Retail Sales + Jeremy Sullivan - Director of Digital Sales + Emilio Bautista - Sales Assistant + Brannwyn Bigglestone - Senior Accounts Manager + Emily Miller - Accounts Manager + Jessica Ambriz - Administrative Assistant + David Brothers - Content Manager + Jonathan Chan - Production Manager + Drew Gill - Art Director + Meredith Wallace - Print Manager + Vincent Kukua - Production Artist + Addison Duke - Production Artist + Tricia Ramos - Production Assistant
WWW.IMAGECOMICS.COM

on the groom's side

WWW.MANOFACTION.TV

for Imperial

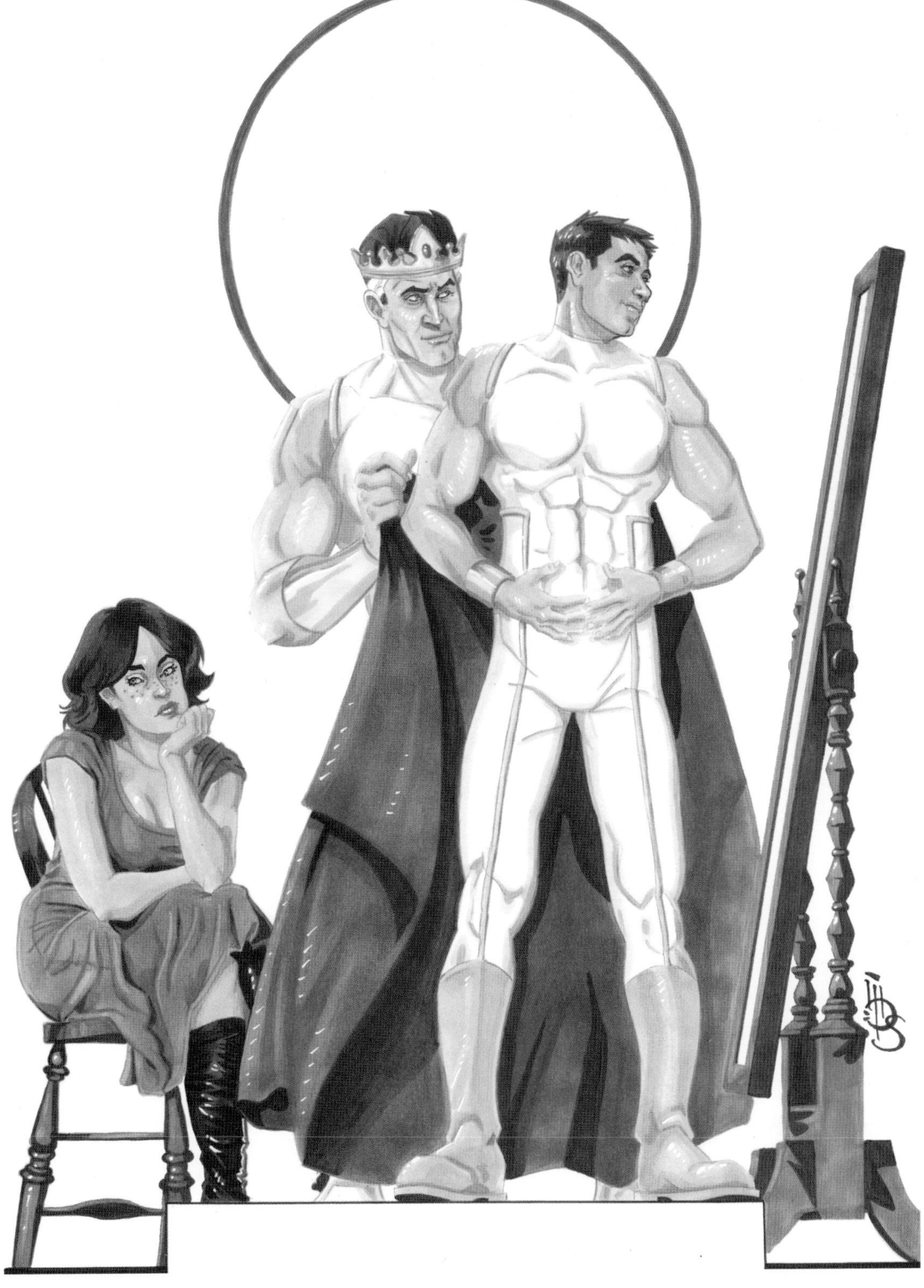

Dad's will said I had ta dump his ashes in the Colorado Rockies ta make him happy.

He picked that exact minute ta show up the first time--

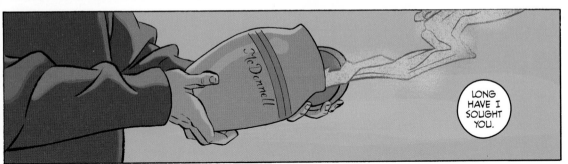

LONG HAVE I SOUGHT YOU.

I think he said "sought."

I've never, ever heard that word said out loud in my whole life, but I'm pretty sure he said it then.

MARK McDONNELL...?

Yeah, it was definitely "sought."

I wasn't, y'know, expectin' someone ta drop in from above like that...

Out in the middle a nowhere an' all...

So I kinda freaked a little.

GAAAAH!

Slung about an arm and two legs worth of dad dust all over that white uniform thing he wears.

Is it a uniform or is it a costume?

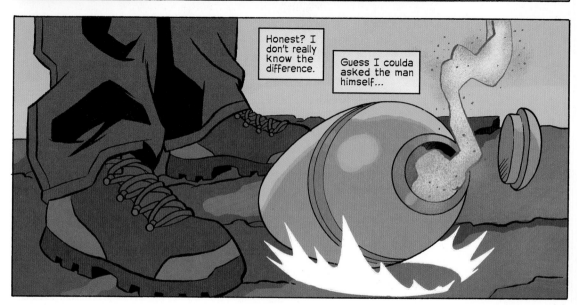

Honest? I don't really know the difference.

Guess I coulda asked the man himself...

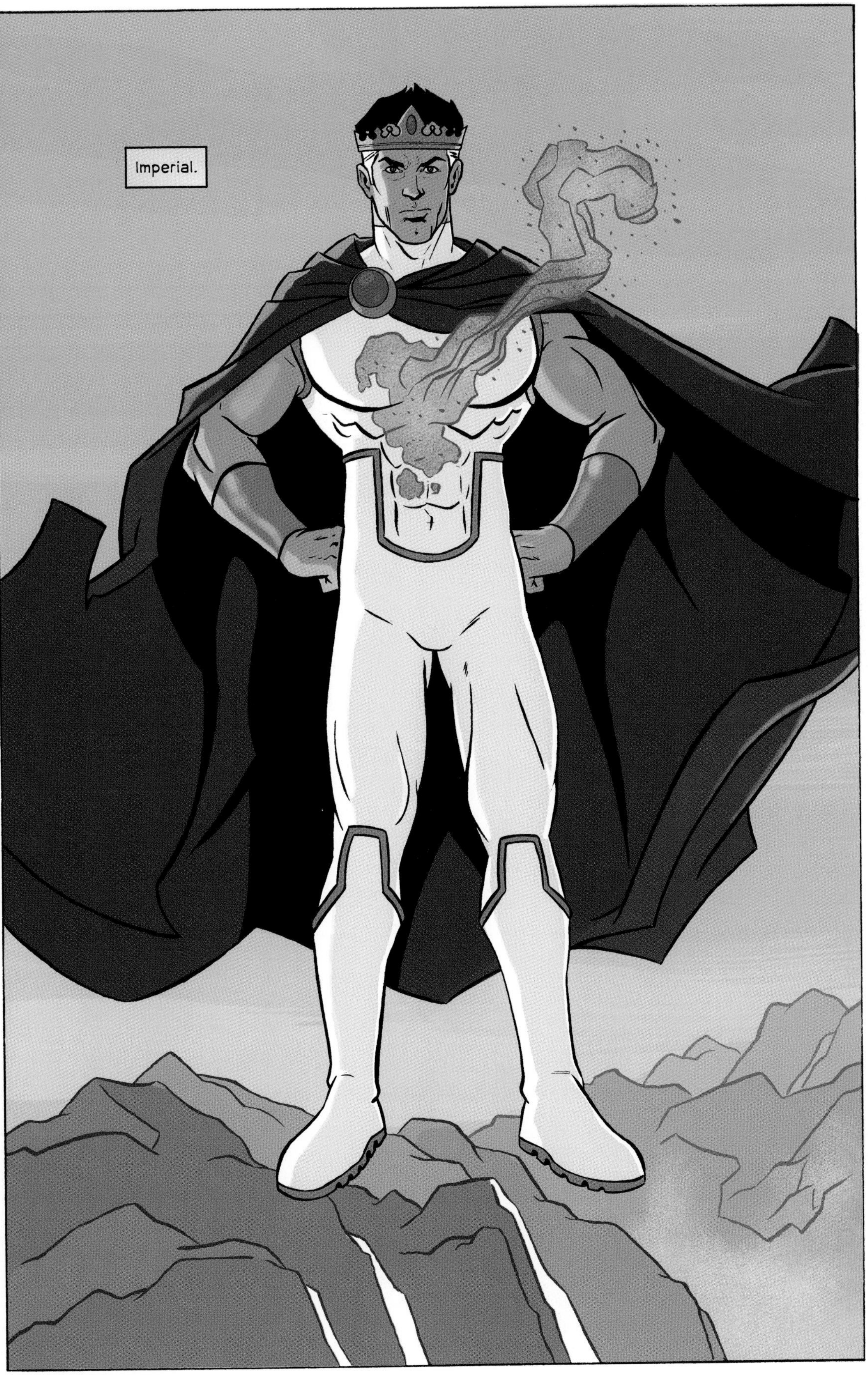
Imperial.

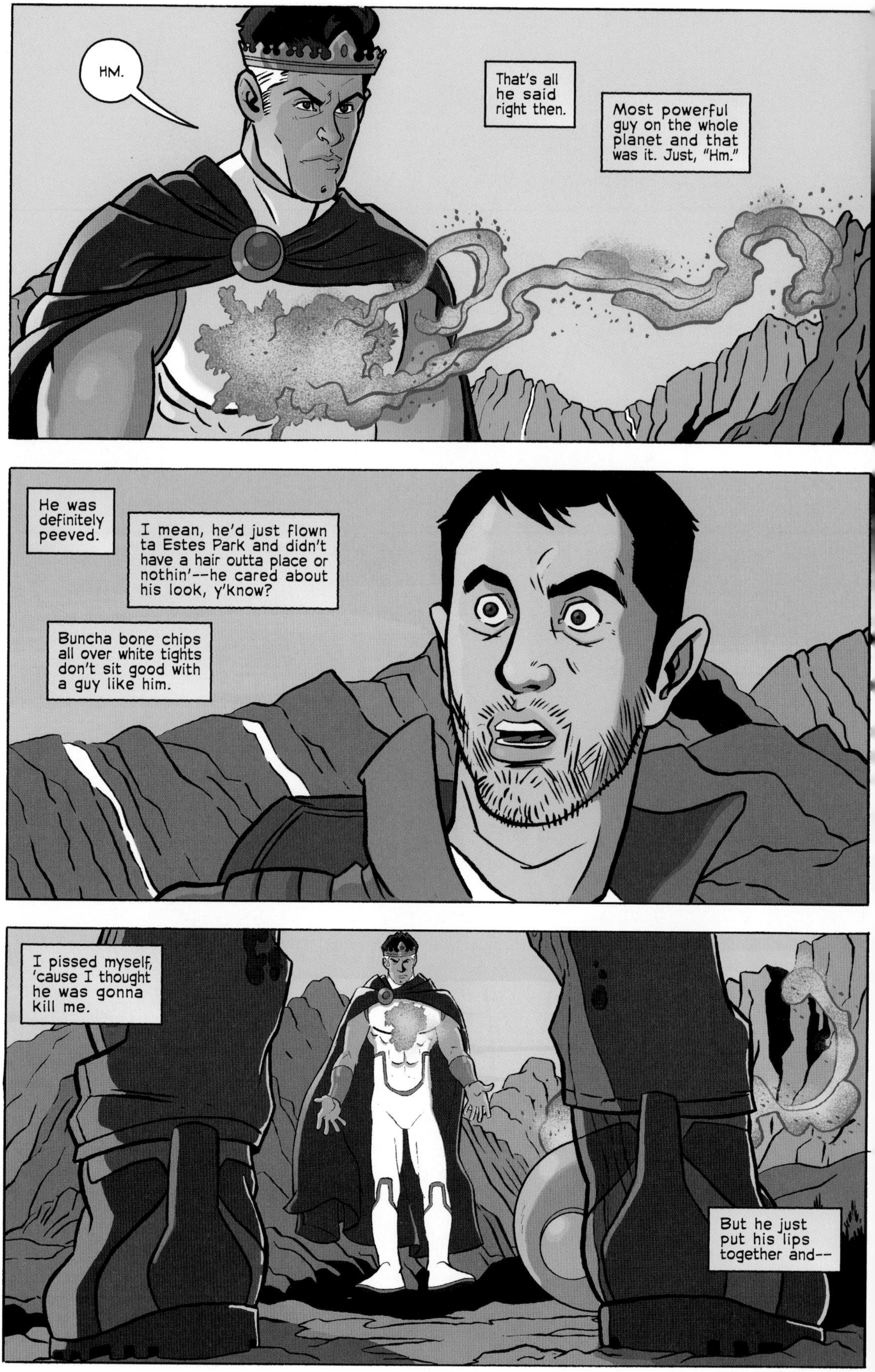
HM.
That's all he said right then.
Most powerful guy on the whole planet and that was it. Just, "Hm."
He was definitely peeved.
I mean, he'd just flown ta Estes Park and didn't have a hair outta place or nothin'--he cared about his look, y'know?
Buncha bone chips all over white tights don't sit good with a guy like him.
I pissed myself, 'cause I thought he was gonna kill me.
But he just put his lips together and--

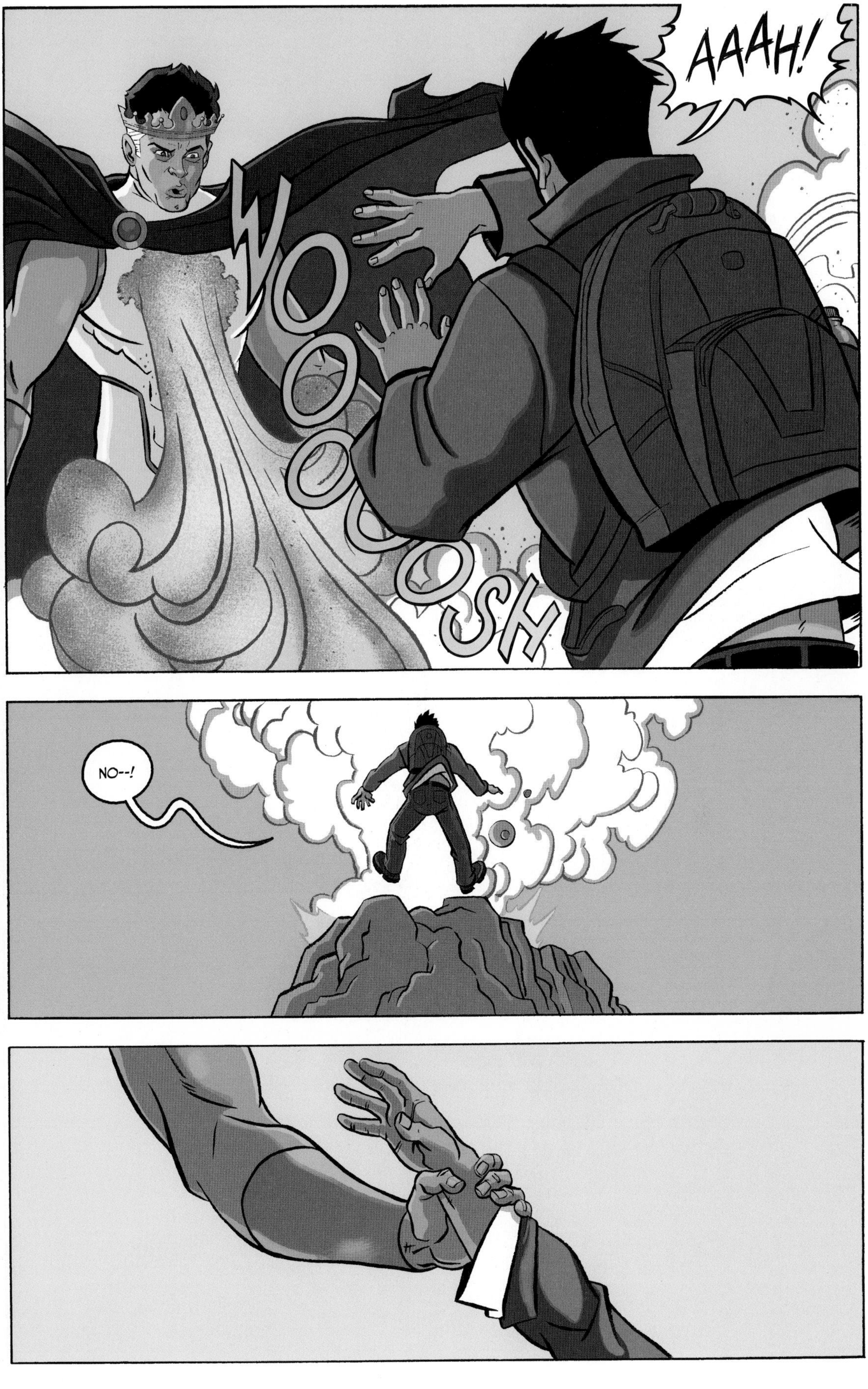
AAAH!
WOOOOOSH
NO--!

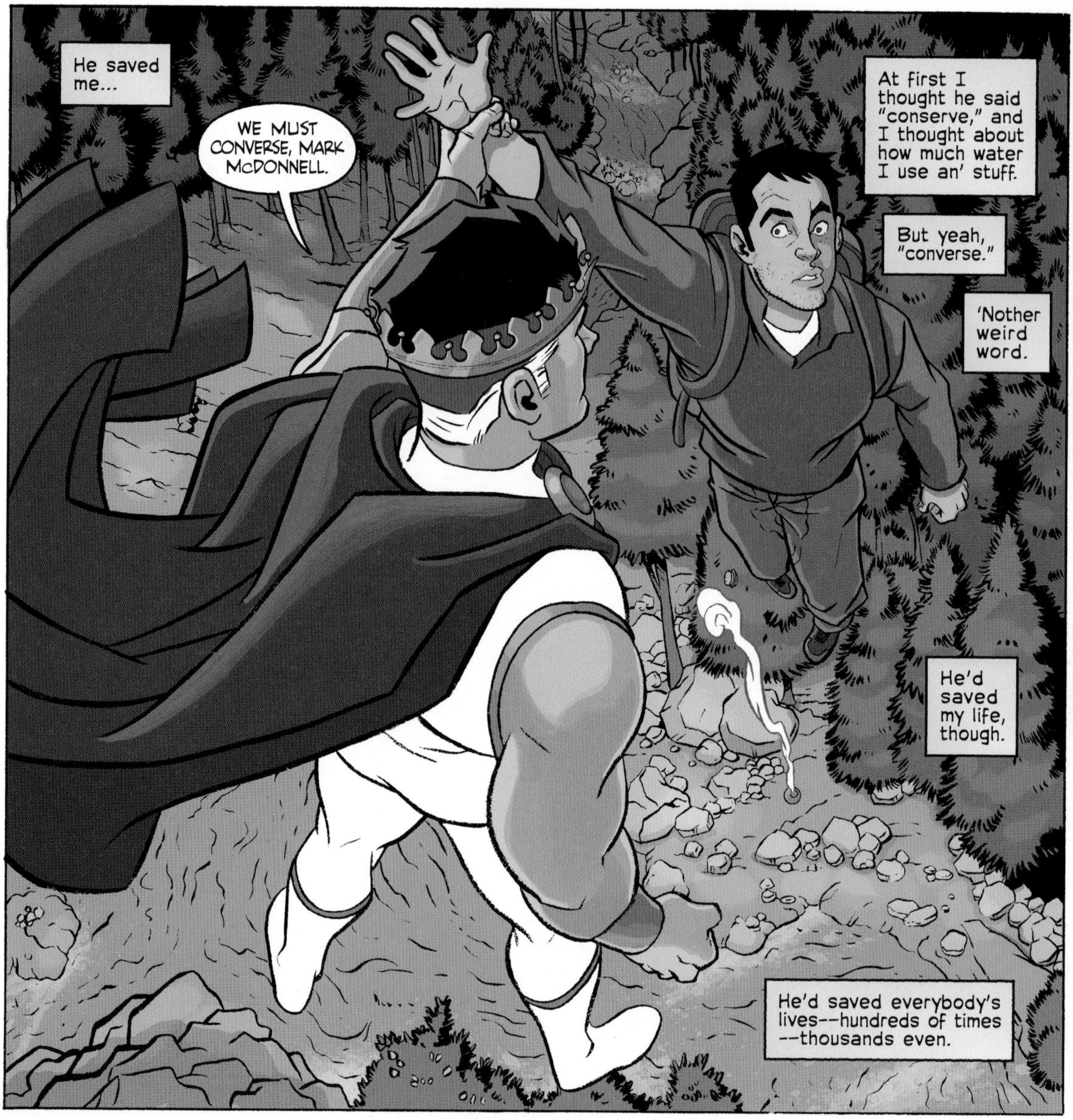
He saved me...
WE MUST CONVERSE, MARK McDONNELL.
At first I thought he said "conserve," and I thought about how much water I use an' stuff.
But yeah, "converse."
'Nother weird word.
He'd saved my life, though.
He'd saved everybody's lives--hundreds of times --thousands even.

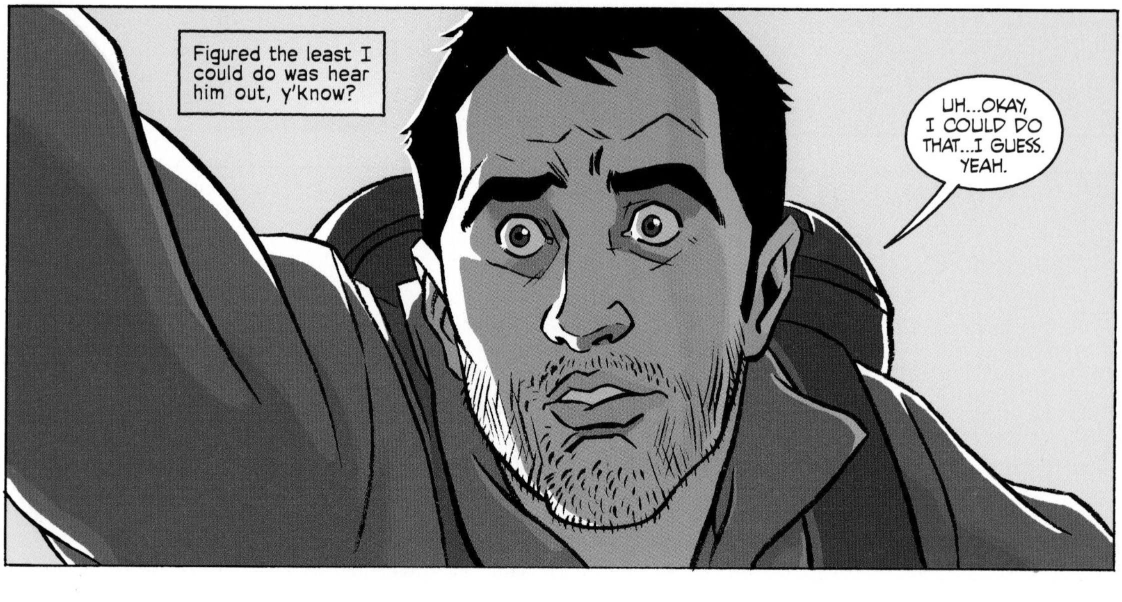
Figured the least I could do was hear him out, y'know?
UH...OKAY, I COULD DO THAT...I GUESS. YEAH.

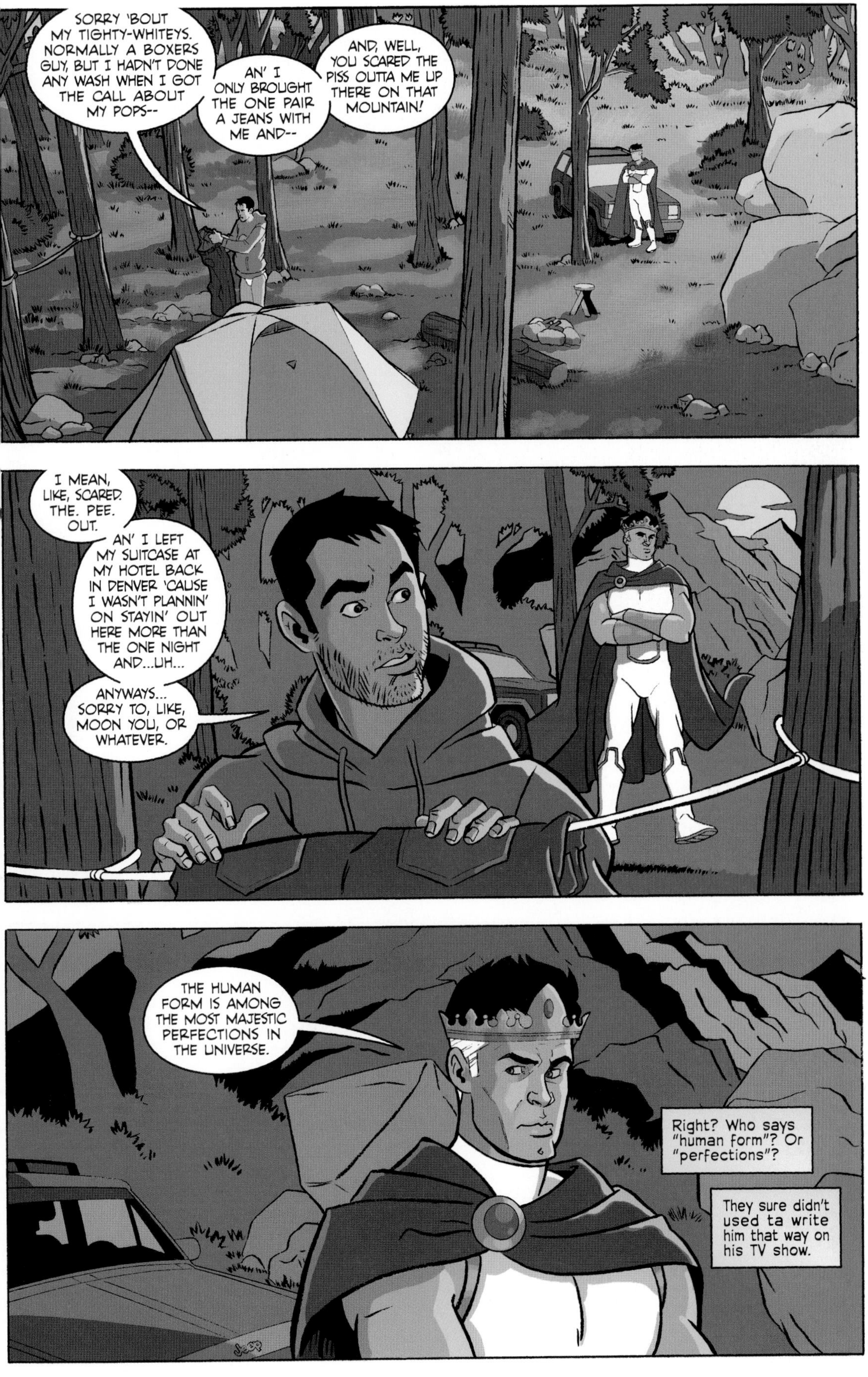

SORRY 'BOUT MY TIGHTY-WHITEYS. NORMALLY A BOXERS GUY, BUT I HADN'T DONE ANY WASH WHEN I GOT THE CALL ABOUT MY POPS--
AN' I ONLY BROUGHT THE ONE PAIR A JEANS WITH ME AND--
AND, WELL, YOU SCARED THE PISS OUTTA ME UP THERE ON THAT MOUNTAIN!
I MEAN, LIKE, SCARED. THE. PEE. OUT.
AN' I LEFT MY SUITCASE AT MY HOTEL BACK IN DENVER 'CAUSE I WASN'T PLANNIN' ON STAYIN' OUT HERE MORE THAN THE ONE NIGHT AND...UH...
ANYWAYS... SORRY TO, LIKE, MOON YOU, OR WHATEVER.
THE HUMAN FORM IS AMONG THE MOST MAJESTIC PERFECTIONS IN THE UNIVERSE.
Right? Who says "human form"? Or "perfections"?
They sure didn't used ta write him that way on his TV show.

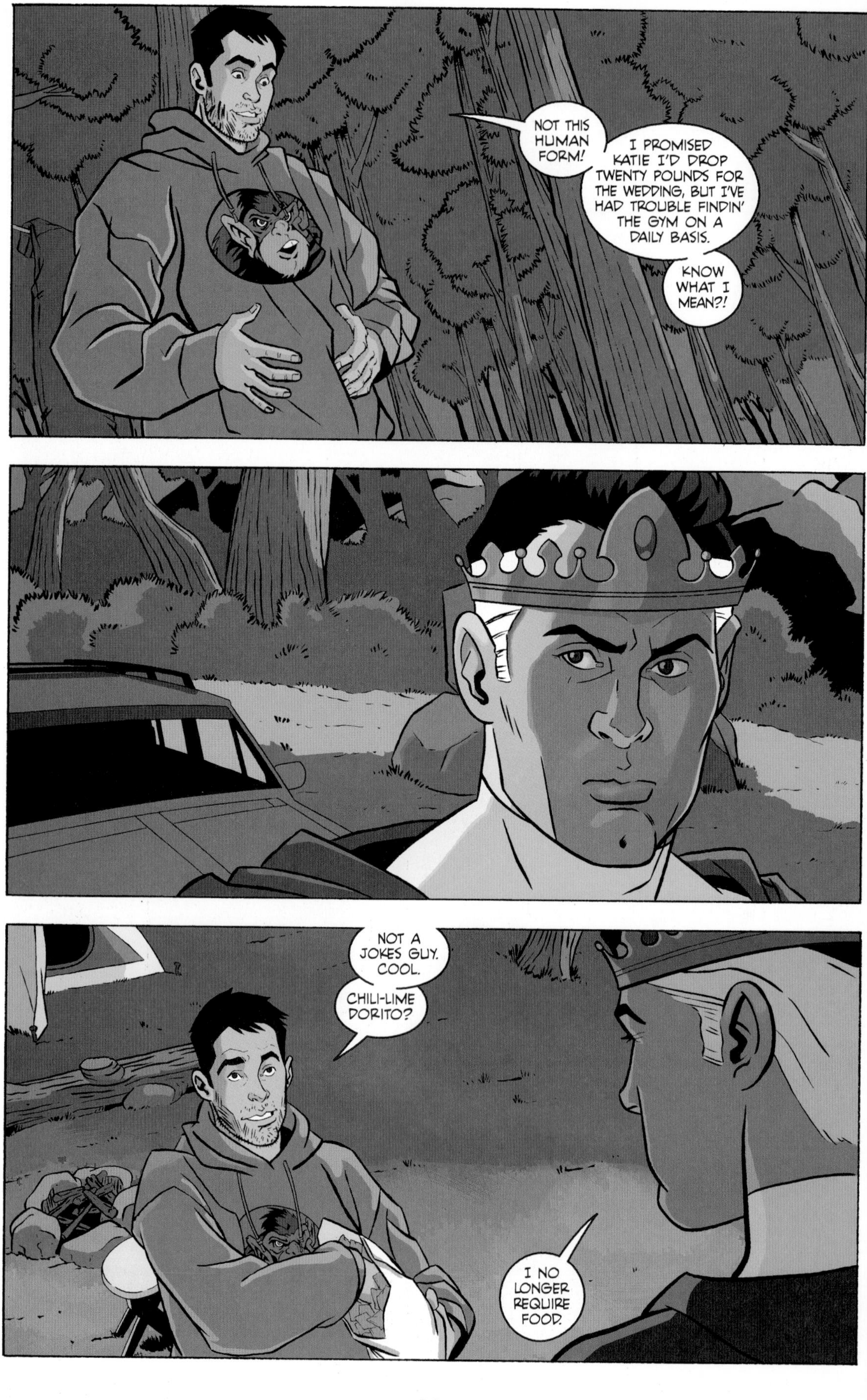
NOT THIS HUMAN FORM!
I PROMISED KATIE I'D DROP TWENTY POUNDS FOR THE WEDDING, BUT I'VE HAD TROUBLE FINDIN' THE GYM ON A DAILY BASIS.
KNOW WHAT I MEAN?!
NOT A JOKES GUY. COOL.
CHILI-LIME DORITO?
I NO LONGER REQUIRE FOOD.

OKAY, WEIRD.

SO, UH, YOU WANTED TO "CONVERSE"?

WITH ME...?

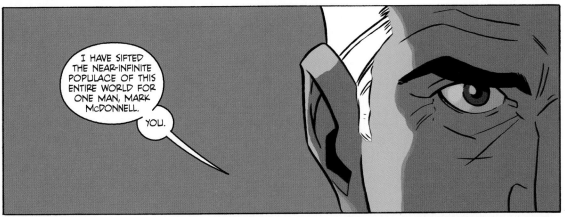

I HAVE SIFTED THE NEAR-INFINITE POPULACE OF THIS ENTIRE WORLD FOR ONE MAN, MARK McDONNELL.

YOU.

OH, CRAP! IS IT ABOUT THAT SPEEDIN' TICKET FROM KANSAS?

'CAUSE MY FRIEND TIM TOLD ME THAT IF YOU AIN'T A RESIDENT AN' NEVER PLAN ON GOIN' BACK, THEN YOU CAN PRETTY MUCH IGNORE 'EM.

AN' BELIEVE ME, I NEVER PLAN ON GOIN' BACK TA KANSAS.

OH, CRAP. YOU'RE FROM KANSAS, AREN'T YOU?

I'M NOT DISSIN' IT. I JUST LIKE MY STATES A LITTLE LESS...FLAT...

I'LL SHUT UP NOW.

15

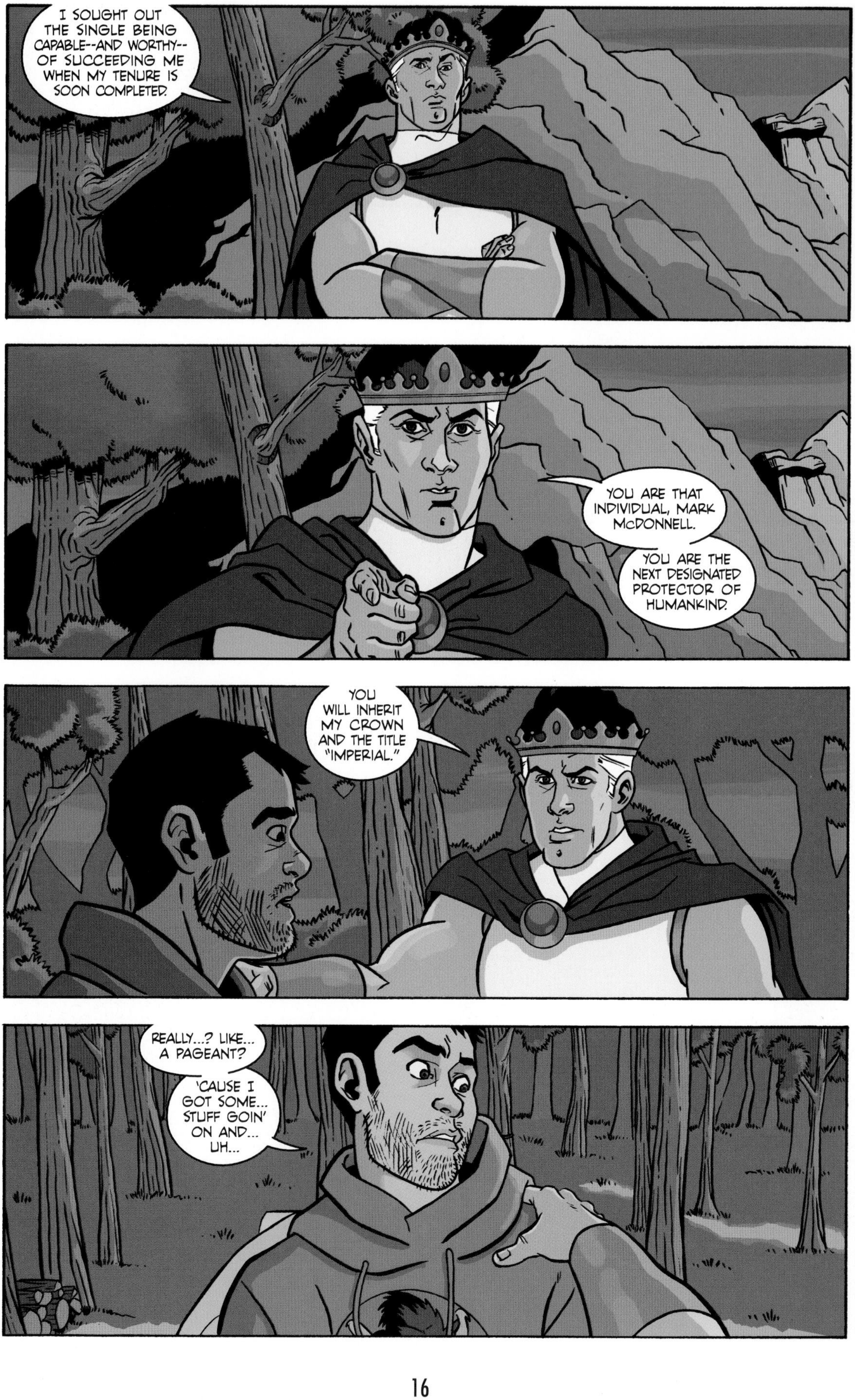
I SOUGHT OUT THE SINGLE BEING CAPABLE--AND WORTHY--OF SUCCEEDING ME WHEN MY TENURE IS SOON COMPLETED.
YOU ARE THAT INDIVIDUAL, MARK McDONNELL.
YOU ARE THE NEXT DESIGNATED PROTECTOR OF HUMANKIND.
YOU WILL INHERIT MY CROWN AND THE TITLE "IMPERIAL."
REALLY...? LIKE... A PAGEANT?
'CAUSE I GOT SOME... STUFF GOIN' ON AND... UH...

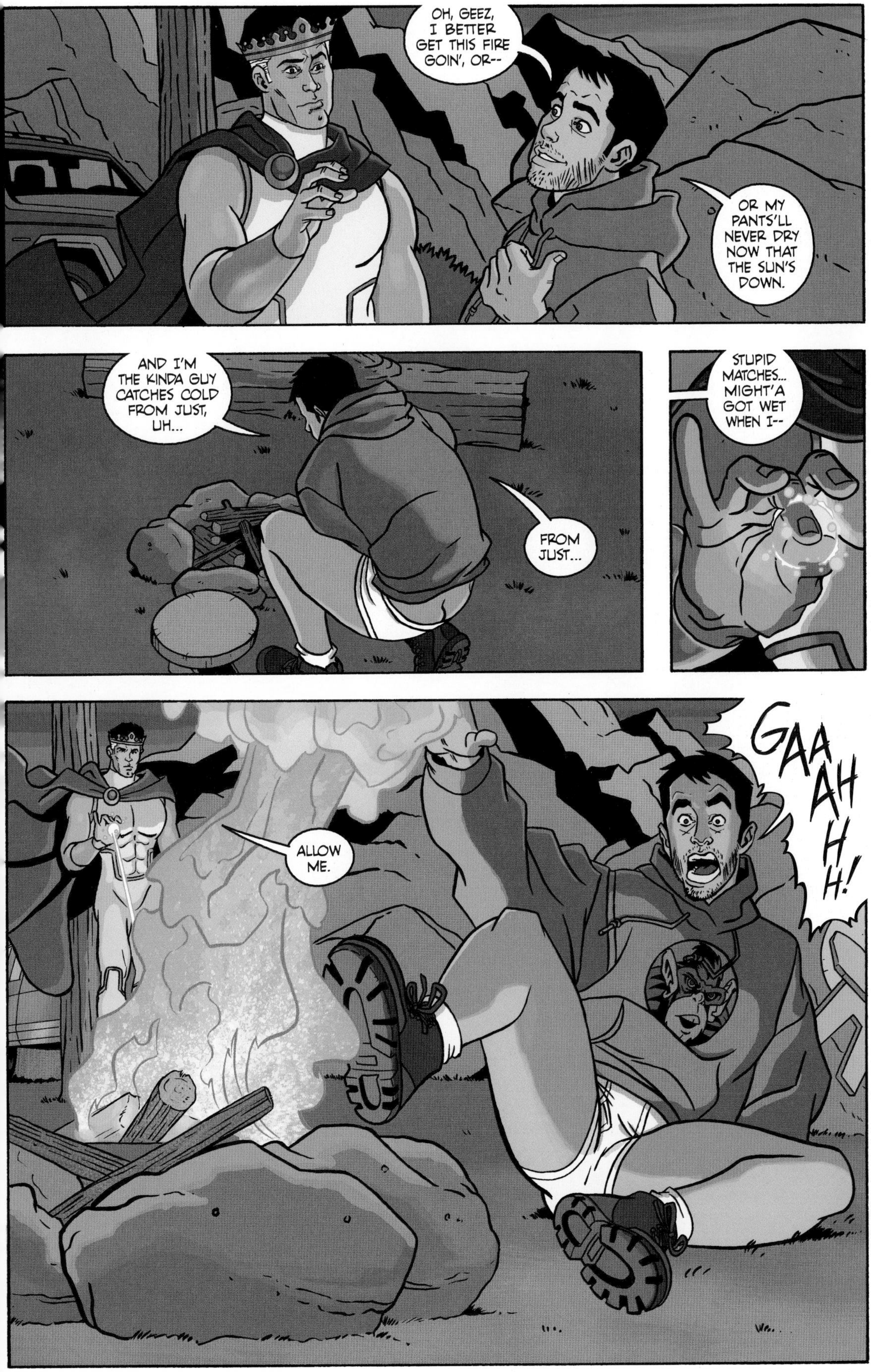
OH, GEEZ, I BETTER GET THIS FIRE GOIN', OR--
OR MY PANTS'LL NEVER DRY NOW THAT THE SUN'S DOWN.
AND I'M THE KINDA GUY CATCHES COLD FROM JUST, UH...
FROM JUST...
STUPID MATCHES... MIGHT'A GOT WET WHEN I--
ALLOW ME.
GAAAHHH!

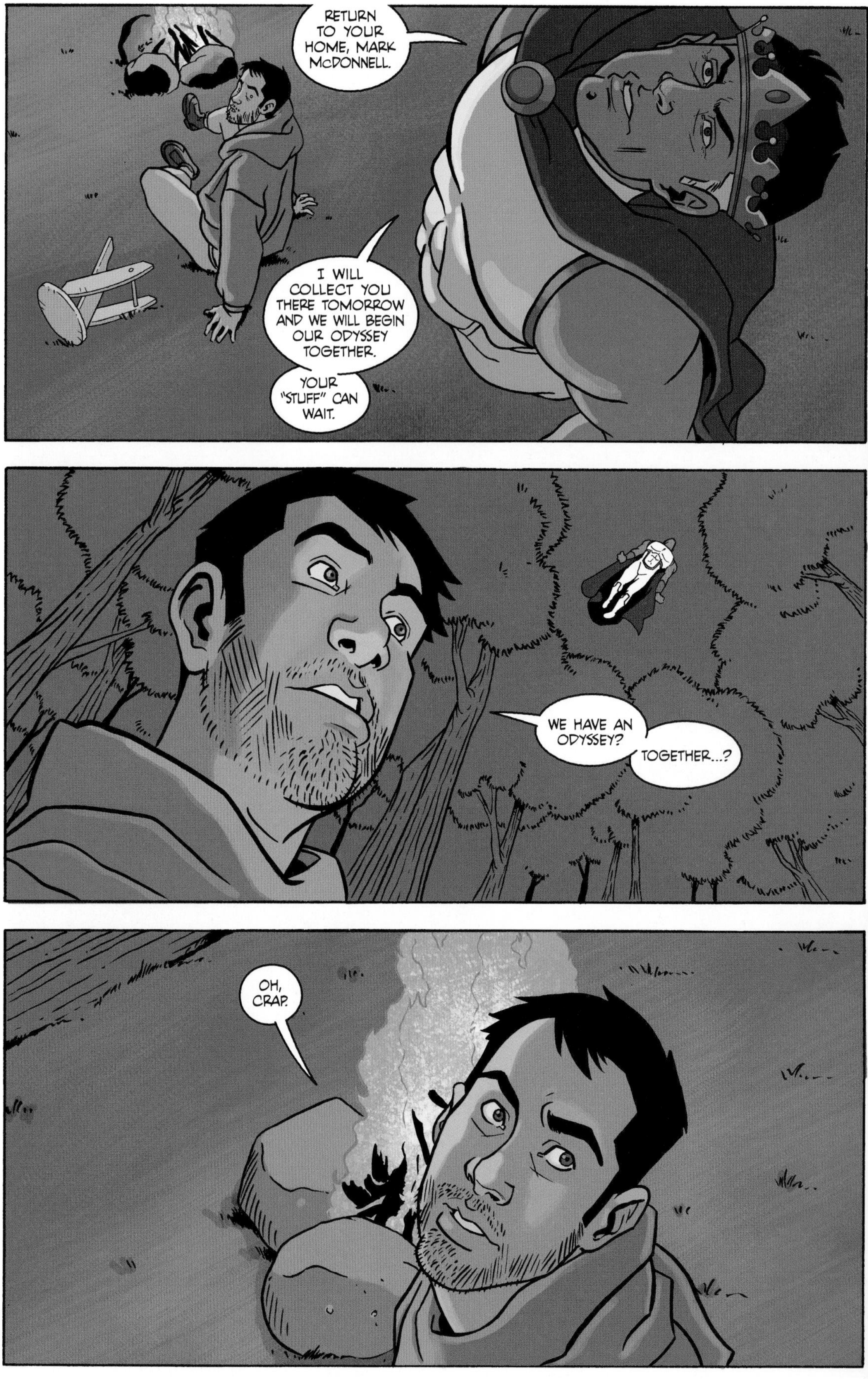
RETURN TO YOUR HOME, MARK McDONNELL.
I WILL COLLECT YOU THERE TOMORROW AND WE WILL BEGIN OUR ODYSSEY TOGETHER.
YOUR "STUFF" CAN WAIT.
WE HAVE AN ODYSSEY?
TOGETHER...?
OH, CRAP.

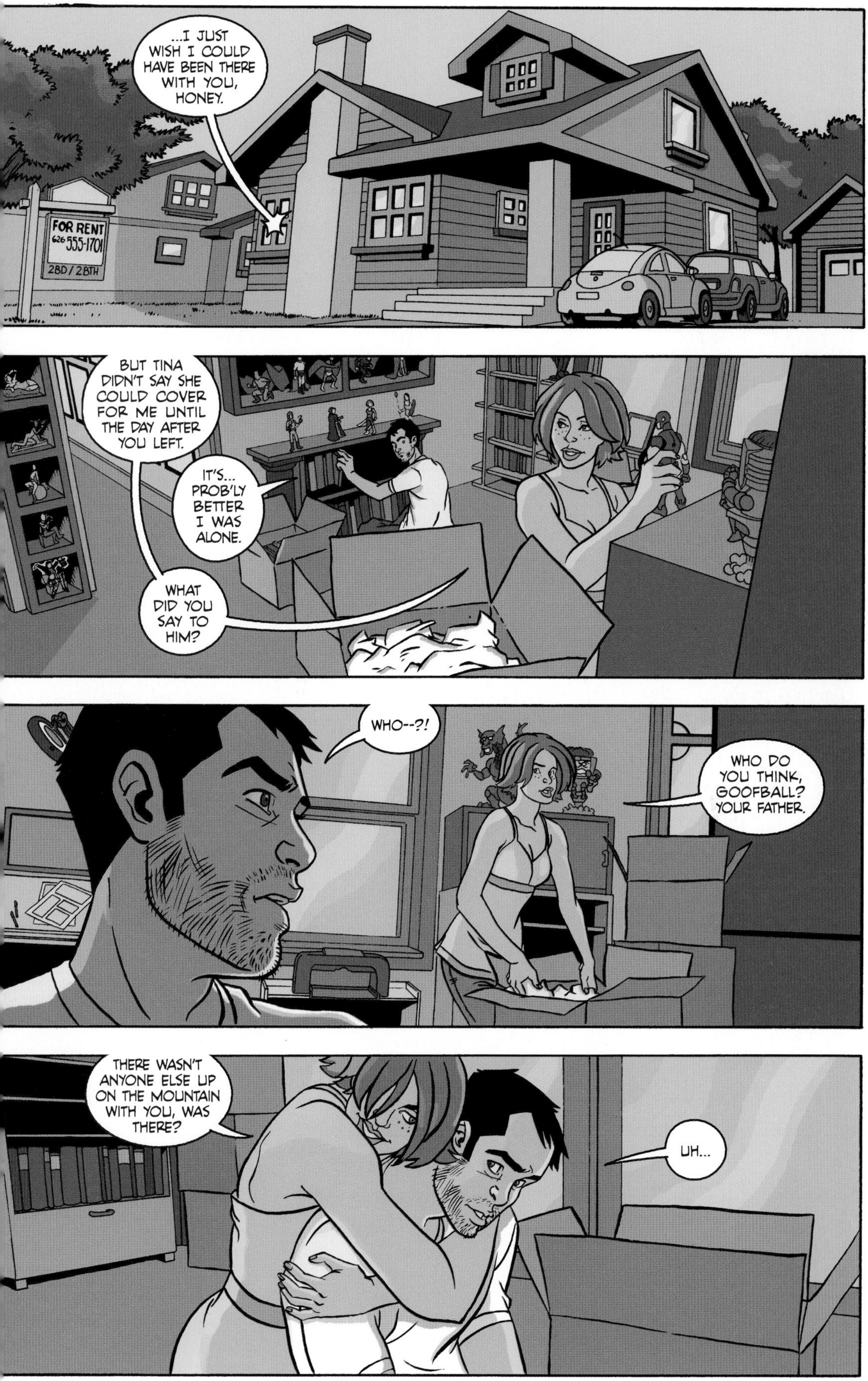
...I JUST WISH I COULD HAVE BEEN THERE WITH YOU, HONEY.
FOR RENT 626 555-1701 2BD / 2BTH
BUT TINA DIDN'T SAY SHE COULD COVER FOR ME UNTIL THE DAY AFTER YOU LEFT.
IT'S... PROB'LY BETTER I WAS ALONE.
WHAT DID YOU SAY TO HIM?
WHO--?!
WHO DO YOU THINK, GOOFBALL? YOUR FATHER.
THERE WASN'T ANYONE ELSE UP ON THE MOUNTAIN WITH YOU, WAS THERE?
UH...

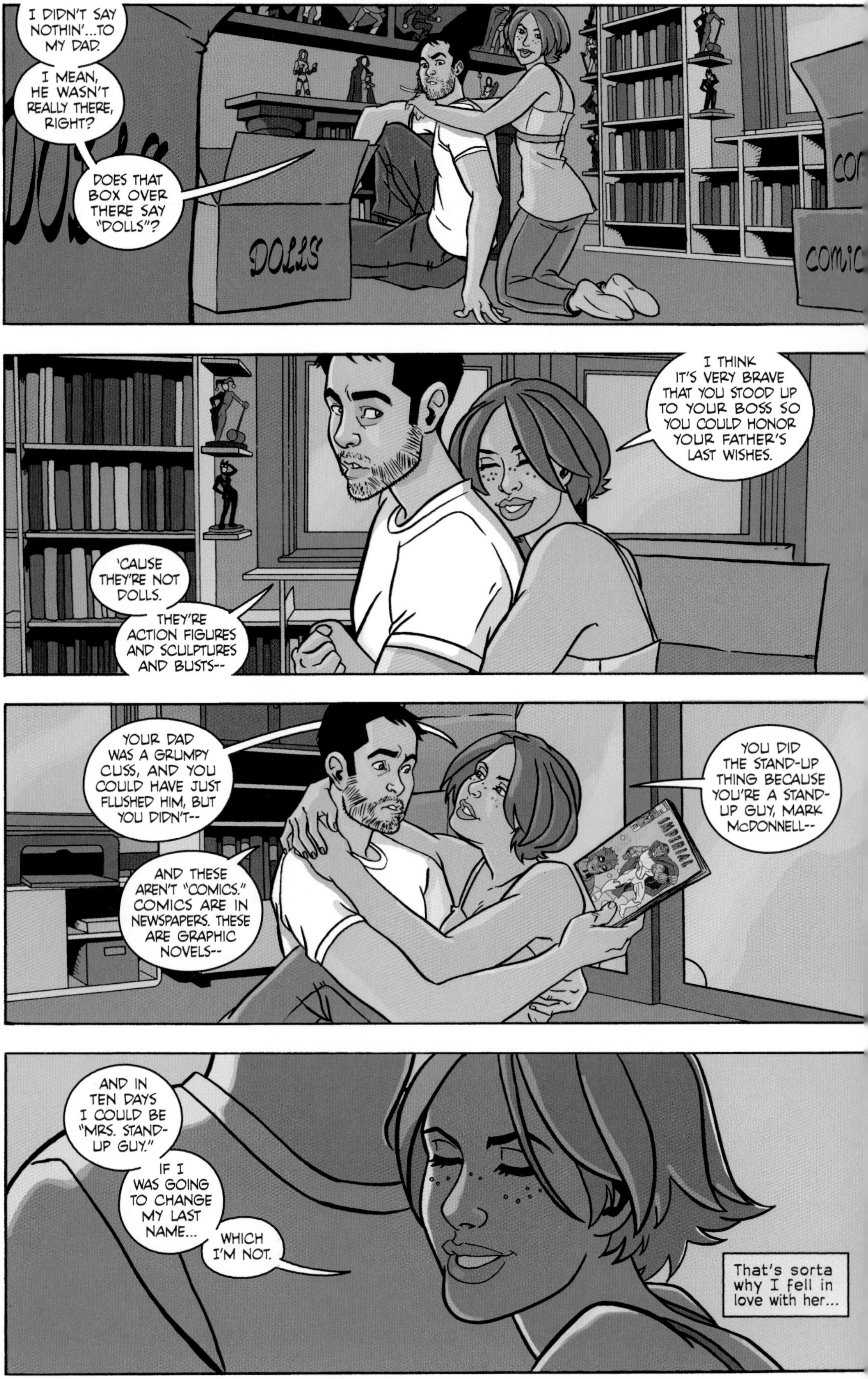
I DIDN'T SAY NOTHIN'...TO MY DAD.
I MEAN, HE WASN'T REALLY THERE, RIGHT?
DOES THAT BOX OVER THERE SAY "DOLLS"?
DOLLS
I THINK IT'S VERY BRAVE THAT YOU STOOD UP TO YOUR BOSS SO YOU COULD HONOR YOUR FATHER'S LAST WISHES.
'CAUSE THEY'RE NOT DOLLS.
THEY'RE ACTION FIGURES AND SCULPTURES AND BUSTS--
YOUR DAD WAS A GRUMPY CUSS, AND YOU COULD HAVE JUST FLUSHED HIM, BUT YOU DIDN'T--
YOU DID THE STAND-UP THING BECAUSE YOU'RE A STAND-UP GUY, MARK McDONNELL--
AND THESE AREN'T "COMICS." COMICS ARE IN NEWSPAPERS. THESE ARE GRAPHIC NOVELS--
IMPERIAL
AND IN TEN DAYS I COULD BE "MRS. STAND-UP GUY."
IF I WAS GOING TO CHANGE MY LAST NAME...
WHICH I'M NOT.
That's sorta why I fell in love with her...

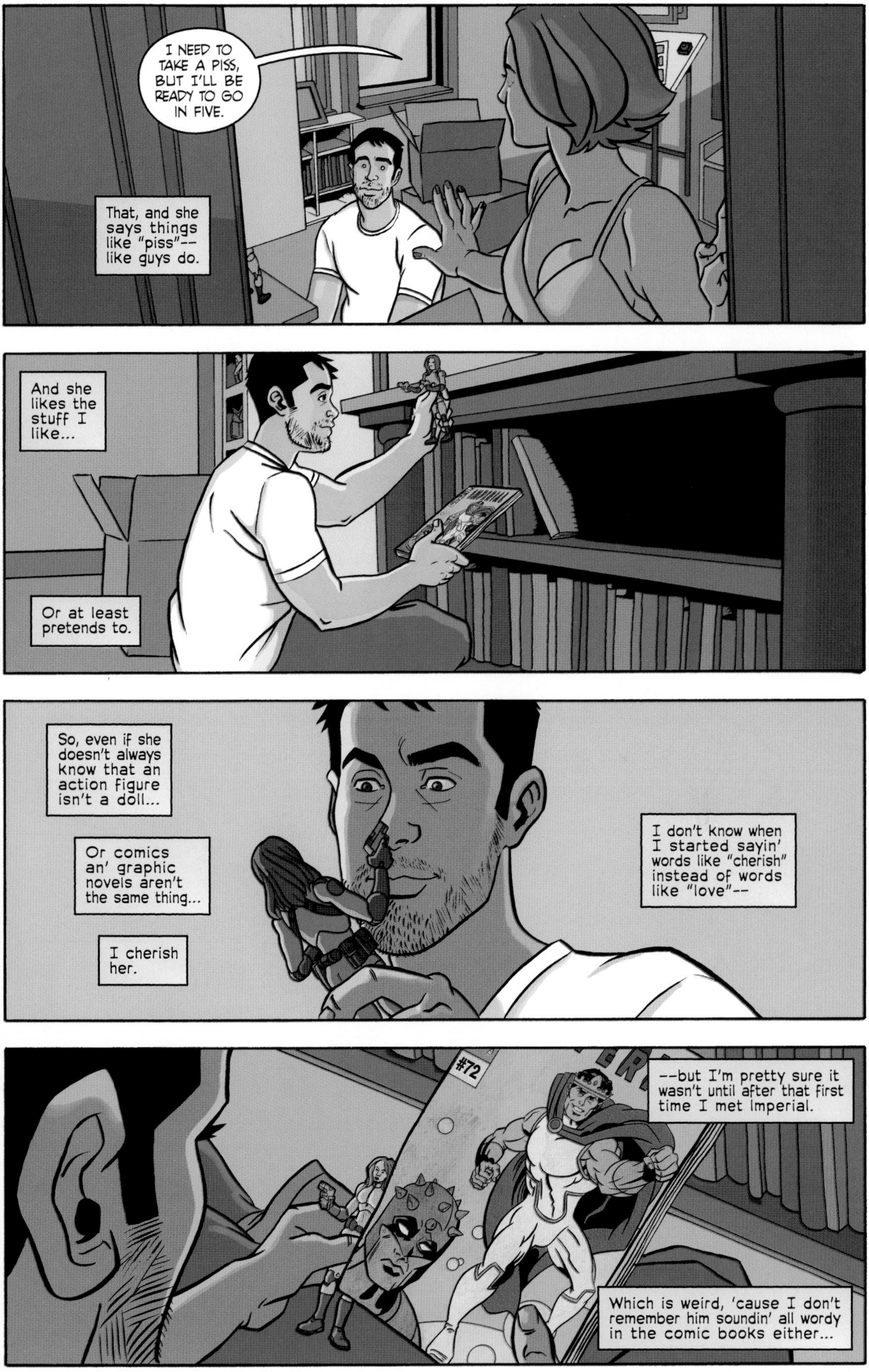

I NEED TO TAKE A PISS, BUT I'LL BE READY TO GO IN FIVE.
That, and she says things like "piss"-- like guys do.
And she likes the stuff I like...
Or at least pretends to.
So, even if she doesn't always know that an action figure isn't a doll...
Or comics an' graphic novels aren't the same thing...
I cherish her.
I don't know when I started sayin' words like "cherish" instead of words like "love"--
#72
--but I'm pretty sure it wasn't until after that first time I met Imperial.
Which is weird, 'cause I don't remember him soundin' all wordy in the comic books either...

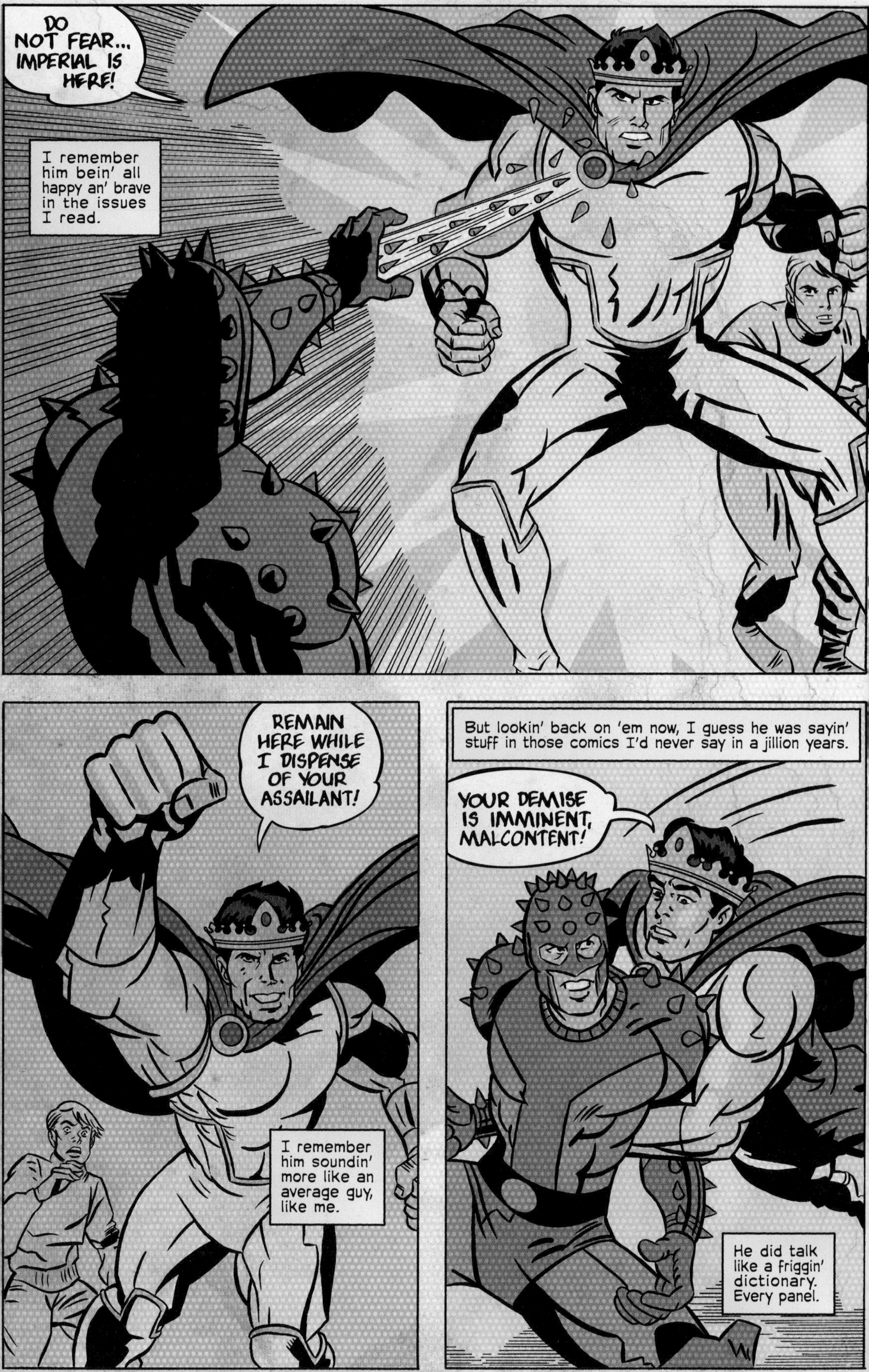
DO NOT FEAR... IMPERIAL IS HERE!
I remember him bein' all happy an' brave in the issues I read.
REMAIN HERE WHILE I DISPENSE OF YOUR ASSAILANT!
I remember him soundin' more like an average guy, like me.
But lookin' back on 'em now, I guess he was sayin' stuff in those comics I'd never say in a jillion years.
YOUR DEMISE IS IMMINENT, MALCONTENT!
He did talk like a friggin' dictionary. Every panel.

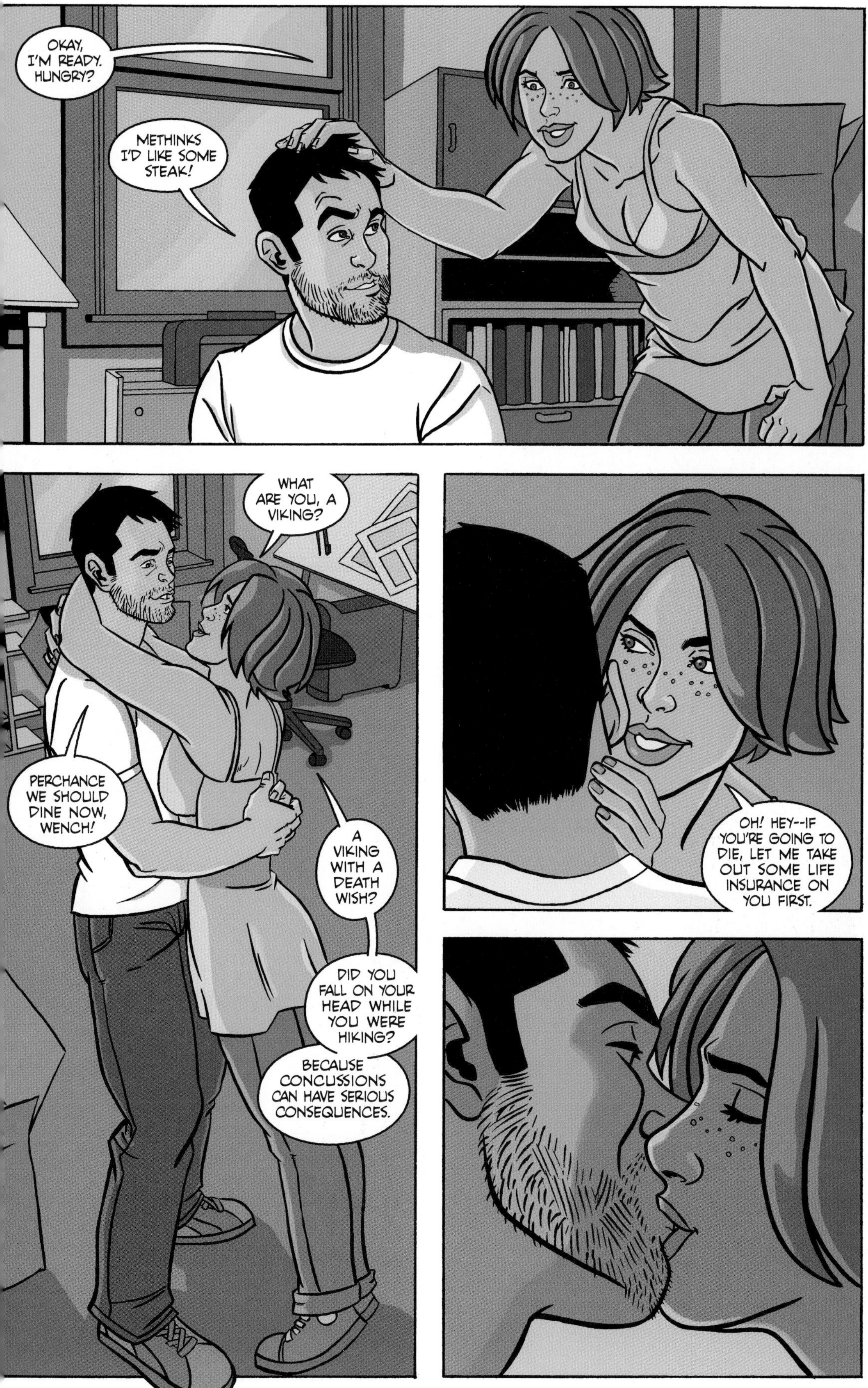
OKAY, I'M READY. HUNGRY?
METHINKS I'D LIKE SOME STEAK!
WHAT ARE YOU, A VIKING?
PERCHANCE WE SHOULD DINE NOW, WENCH!
A VIKING WITH A DEATH WISH?
DID YOU FALL ON YOUR HEAD WHILE YOU WERE HIKING?
BECAUSE CONCUSSIONS CAN HAVE SERIOUS CONSEQUENCES.
OH! HEY--IF YOU'RE GOING TO DIE, LET ME TAKE OUT SOME LIFE INSURANCE ON YOU FIRST.

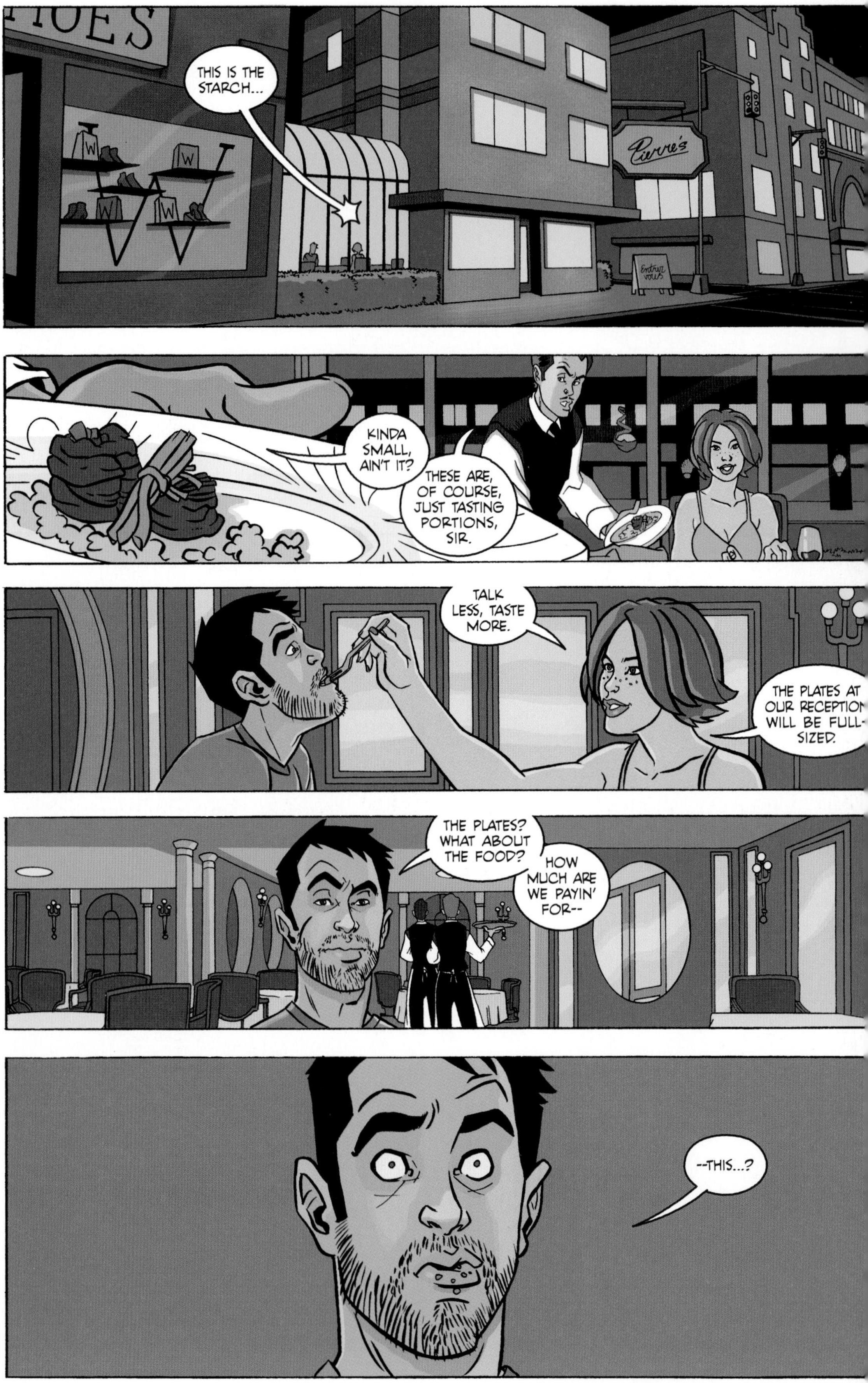
HOES
THIS IS THE STARCH...
W
Pierre's
Entrez vous
KINDA SMALL, AIN'T IT?
THESE ARE, OF COURSE, JUST TASTING PORTIONS, SIR.
TALK LESS, TASTE MORE.
THE PLATES AT OUR RECEPTION WILL BE FULL-SIZED.
THE PLATES? WHAT ABOUT THE FOOD?
HOW MUCH ARE WE PAYIN' FOR--
--THIS...?

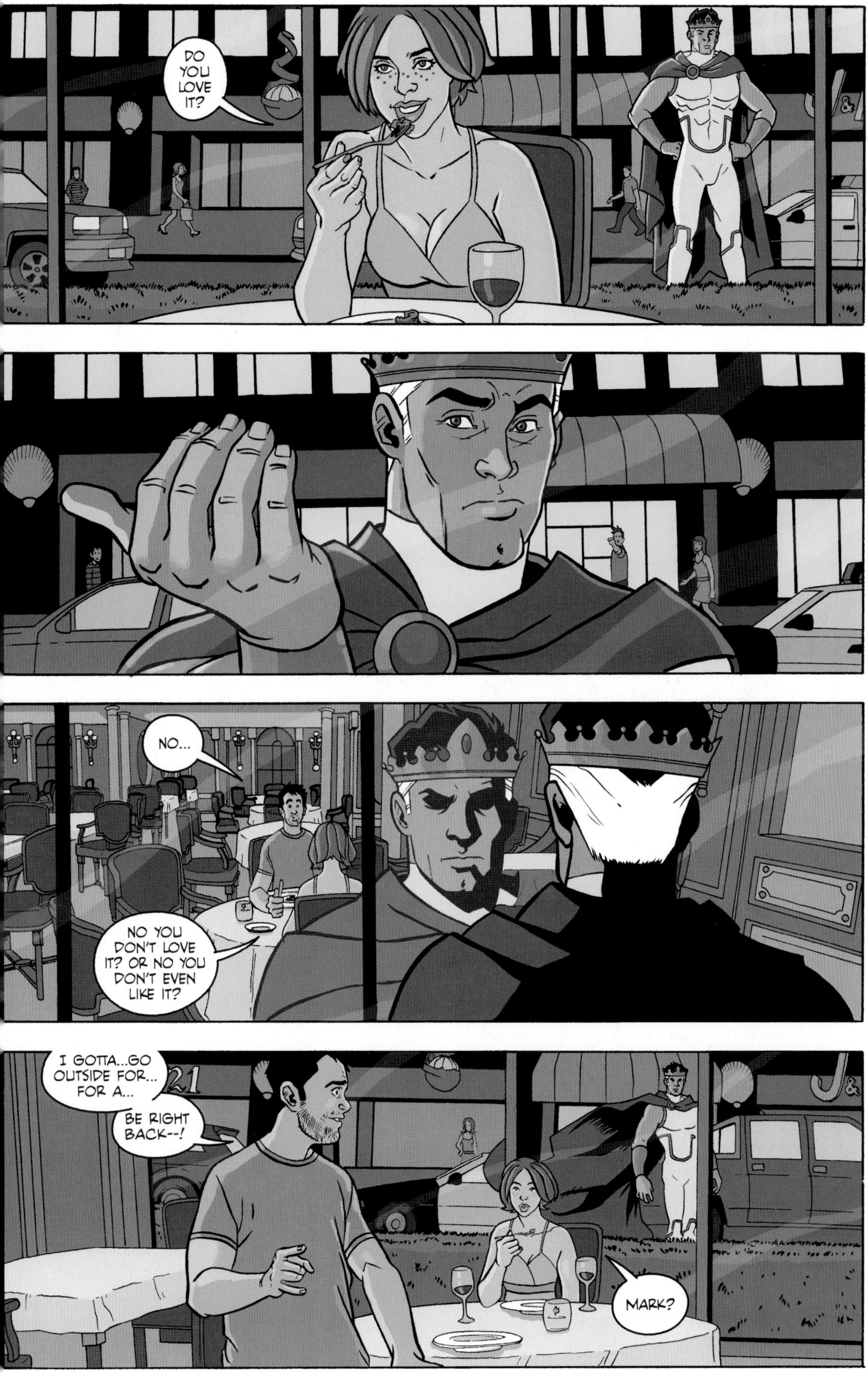
DO YOU LOVE IT?
NO...
NO YOU DON'T LOVE IT? OR NO YOU DON'T EVEN LIKE IT?
I GOTTA...GO OUTSIDE FOR... FOR A...
BE RIGHT BACK--!
MARK?

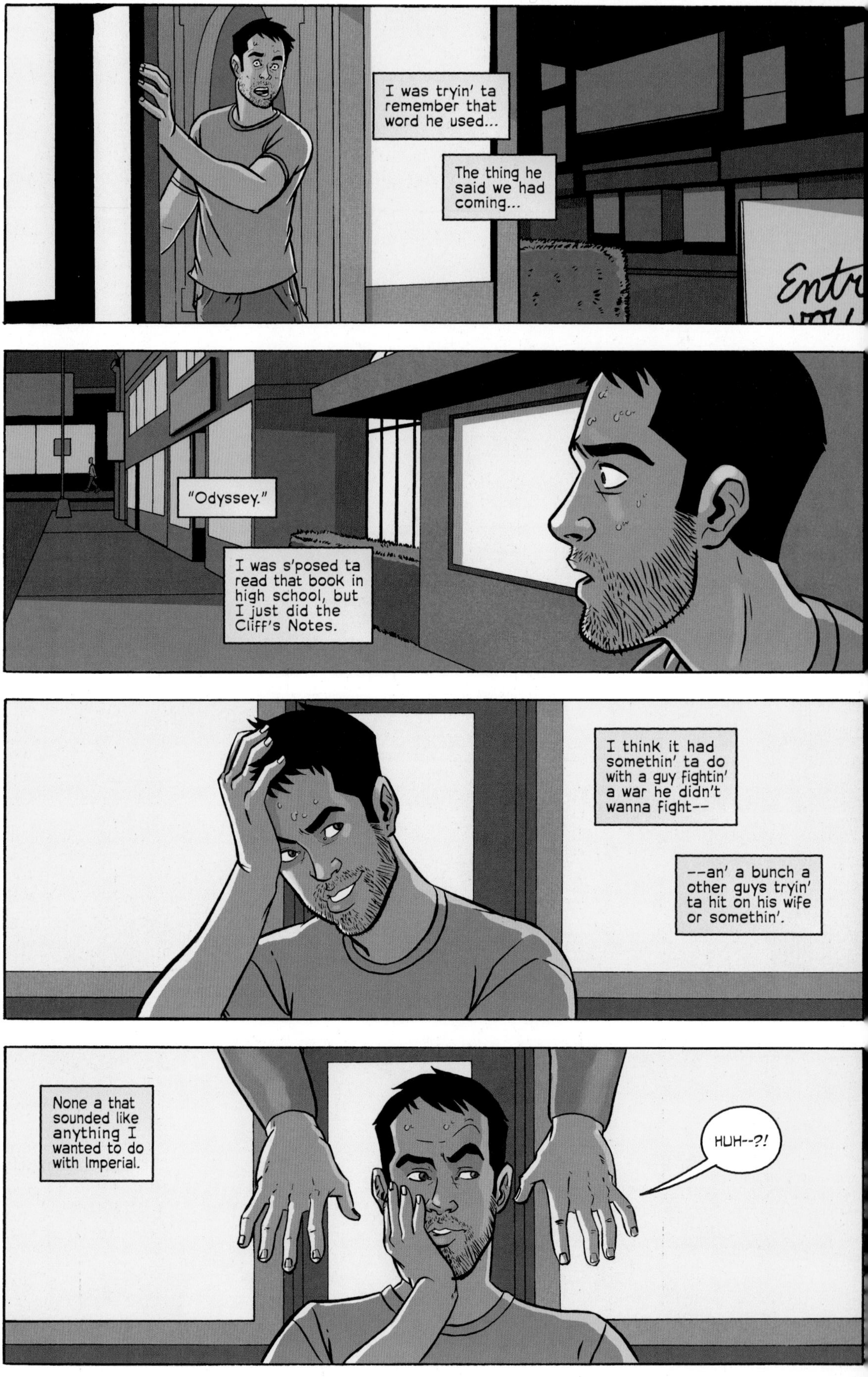
I was tryin' ta remember that word he used...
The thing he said we had coming...
"Odyssey."
I was s'posed ta read that book in high school, but I just did the Cliff's Notes.
I think it had somethin' ta do with a guy fightin' a war he didn't wanna fight--
--an' a bunch a other guys tryin' ta hit on his wife or somethin'.
None a that sounded like anything I wanted to do with Imperial.
HUH--?!

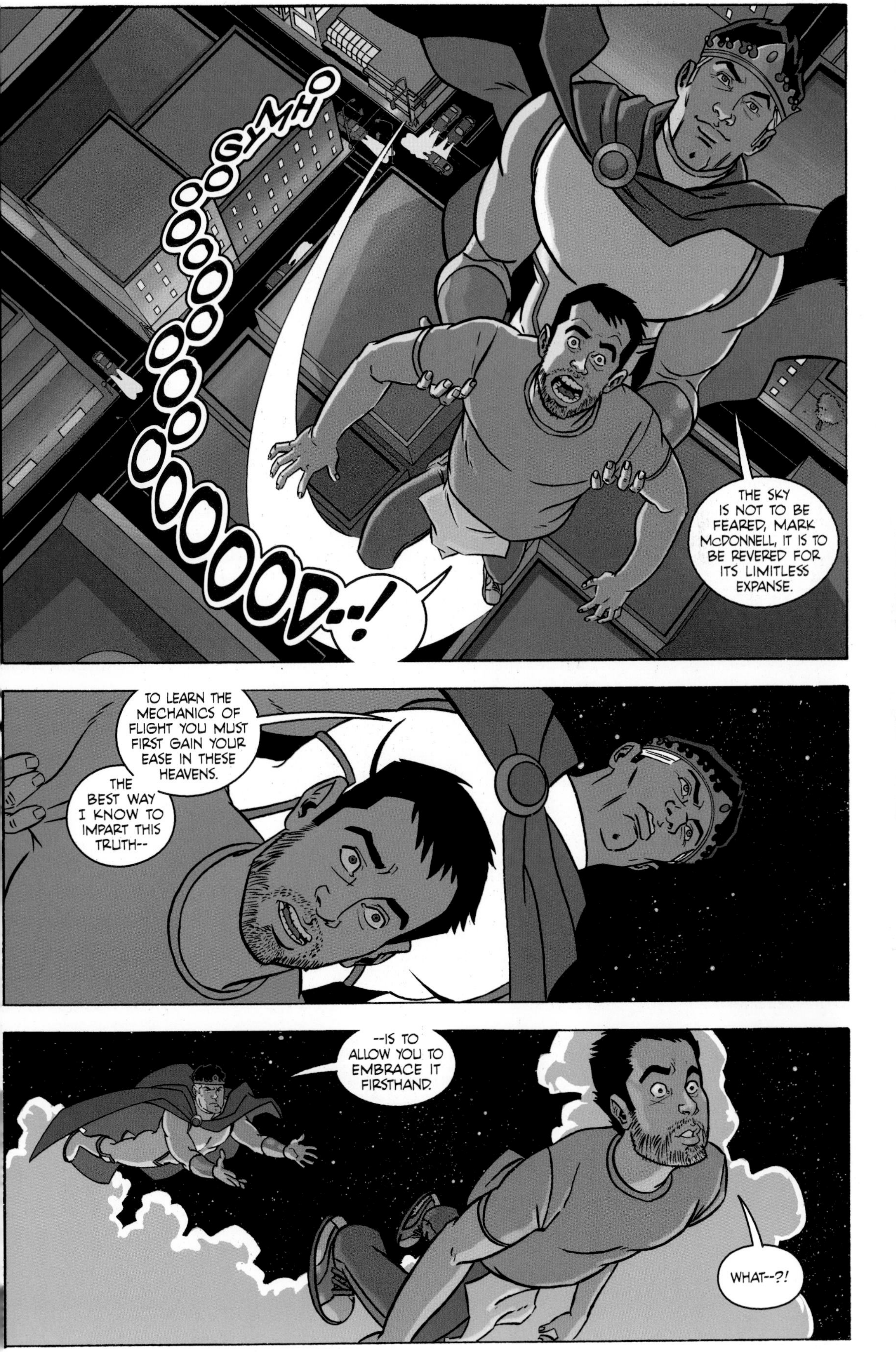
OHMYGOOOOOOOOOOOOOOOOD--!
THE SKY IS NOT TO BE FEARED, MARK McDONNELL, IT IS TO BE REVERED FOR ITS LIMITLESS EXPANSE.
TO LEARN THE MECHANICS OF FLIGHT YOU MUST FIRST GAIN YOUR EASE IN THESE HEAVENS.
THE BEST WAY I KNOW TO IMPART THIS TRUTH--
--IS TO ALLOW YOU TO EMBRACE IT FIRSTHAND.
WHAT--?!

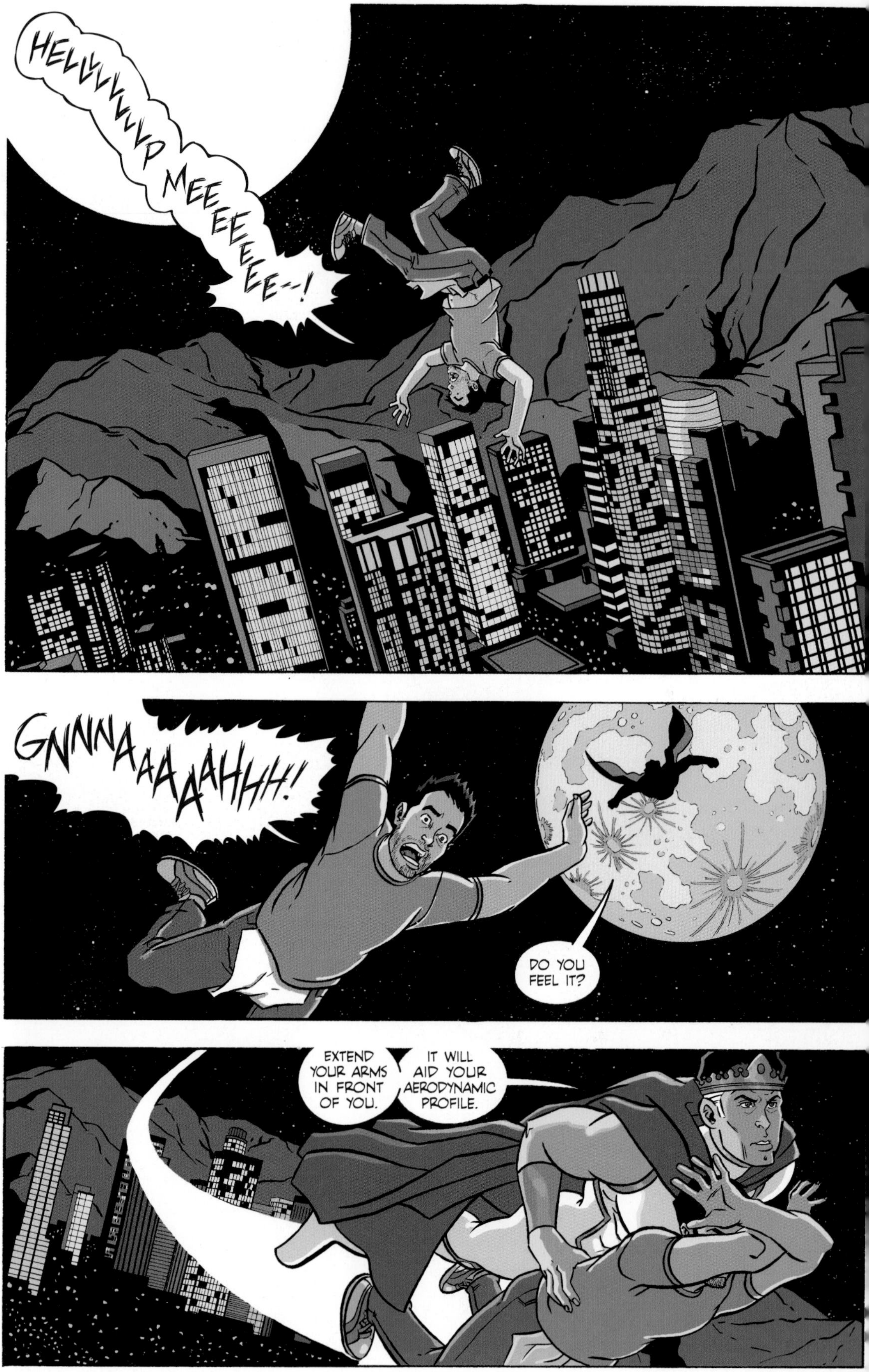
HELLLLLLLLP MEEEEEEEE--!
GNNNAAAAAHHH!
DO YOU FEEL IT?
EXTEND YOUR ARMS IN FRONT OF YOU.
IT WILL AID YOUR AERODYNAMIC PROFILE.

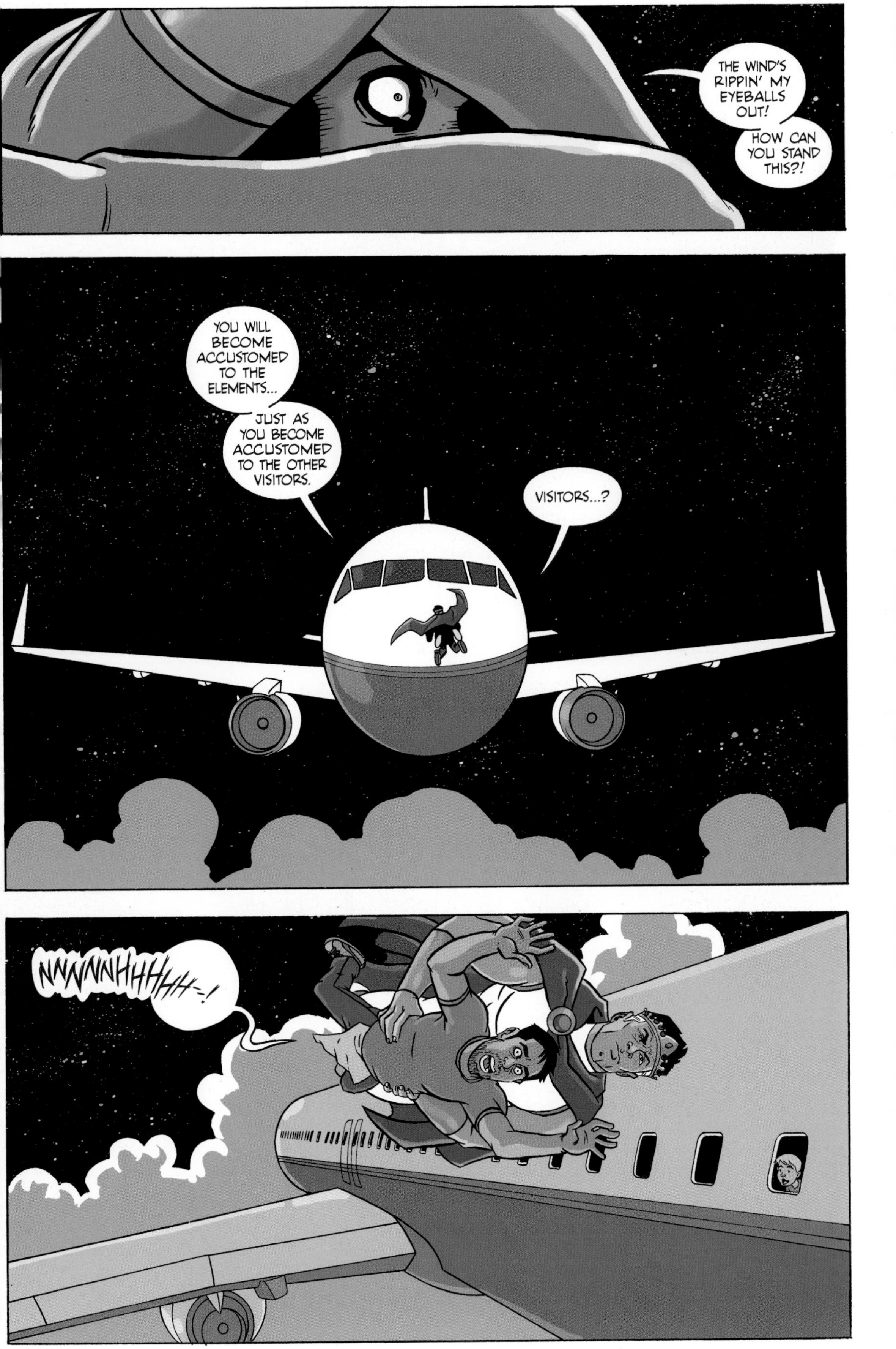
THE WIND'S RIPPIN' MY EYEBALLS OUT!
HOW CAN YOU STAND THIS?!
YOU WILL BECOME ACCUSTOMED TO THE ELEMENTS...
JUST AS YOU BECOME ACCUSTOMED TO THE OTHER VISITORS.
VISITORS...?
NNNNNHHHHH--!

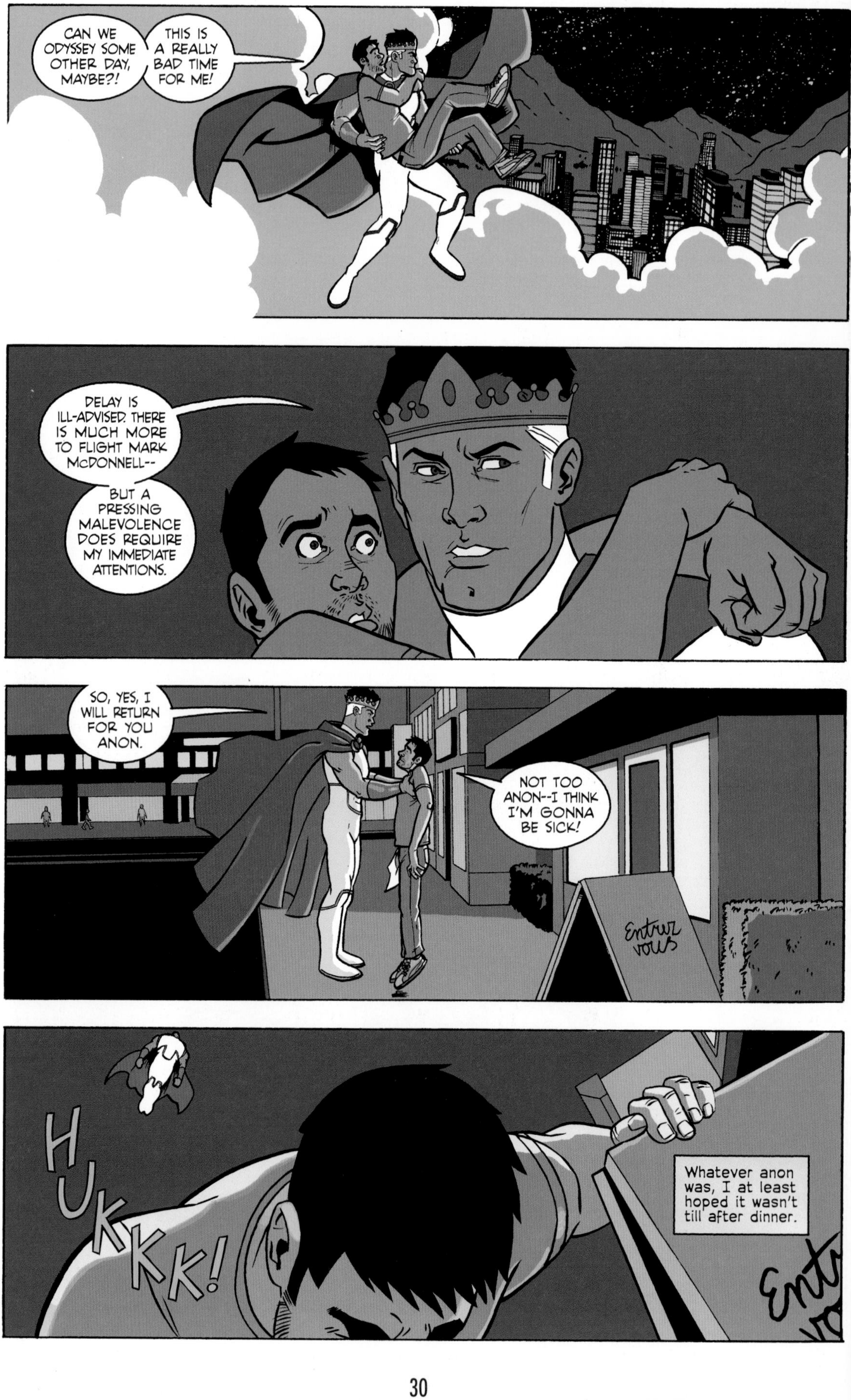
CAN WE ODYSSEY SOME OTHER DAY, MAYBE?!
THIS IS A REALLY BAD TIME FOR ME!
DELAY IS ILL-ADVISED. THERE IS MUCH MORE TO FLIGHT MARK McDONNELL--
BUT A PRESSING MALEVOLENCE DOES REQUIRE MY IMMEDIATE ATTENTIONS.
SO, YES, I WILL RETURN FOR YOU ANON.
NOT TOO ANON--I THINK I'M GONNA BE SICK!
Entrez vous
HUKKK!
Whatever anon was, I at least hoped it wasn't till after dinner.

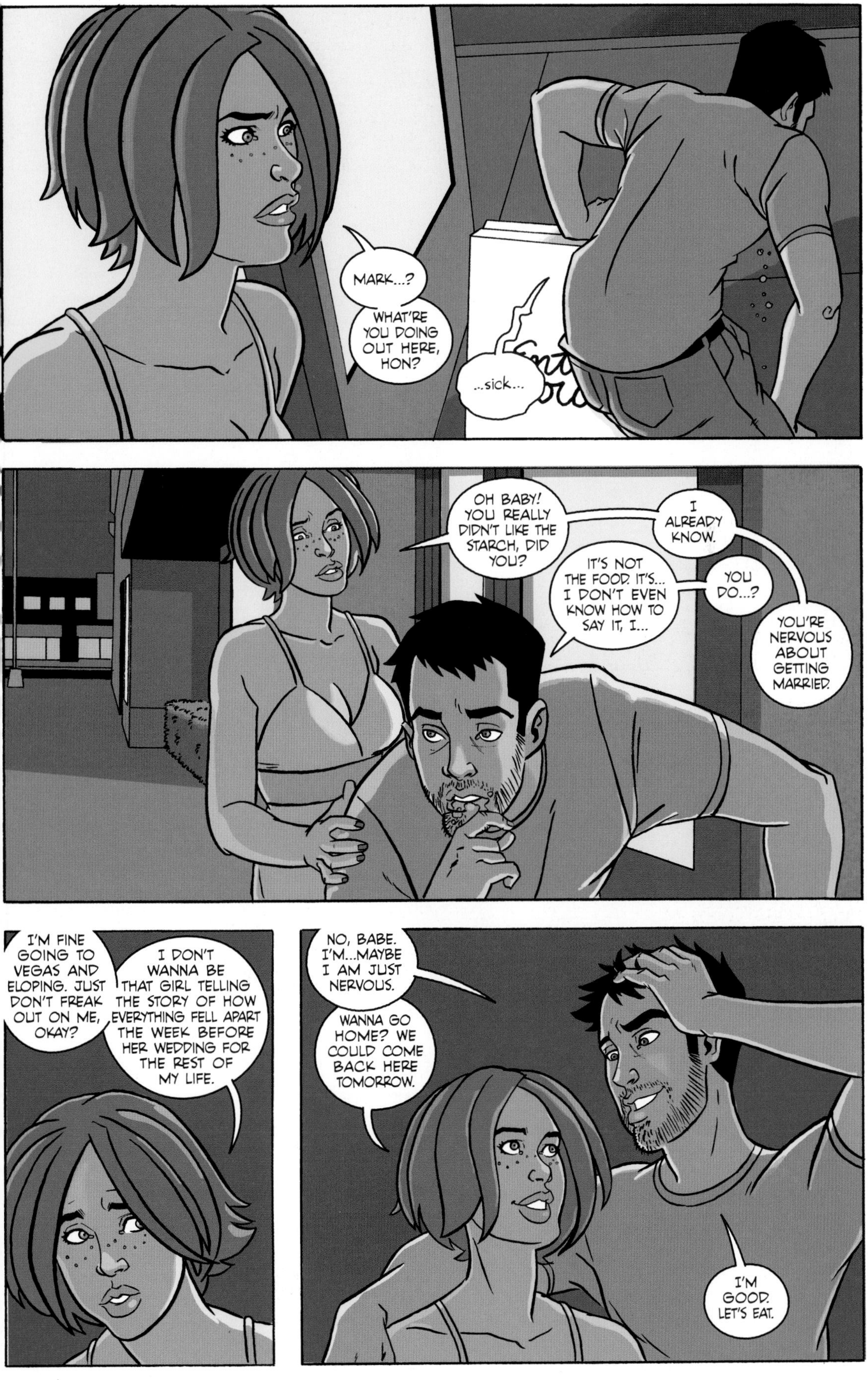
MARK...?
WHAT'RE YOU DOING OUT HERE, HON?
...sick...
OH BABY! YOU REALLY DIDN'T LIKE THE STARCH, DID YOU?
IT'S NOT THE FOOD. IT'S... I DON'T EVEN KNOW HOW TO SAY IT, I...
I ALREADY KNOW.
YOU DO...?
YOU'RE NERVOUS ABOUT GETTING MARRIED.
I'M FINE GOING TO VEGAS AND ELOPING. JUST DON'T FREAK OUT ON ME, OKAY?
I DON'T WANNA BE THAT GIRL TELLING THE STORY OF HOW EVERYTHING FELL APART THE WEEK BEFORE HER WEDDING FOR THE REST OF MY LIFE.
NO, BABE. I'M...MAYBE I AM JUST NERVOUS.
WANNA GO HOME? WE COULD COME BACK HERE TOMORROW.
I'M GOOD. LET'S EAT.

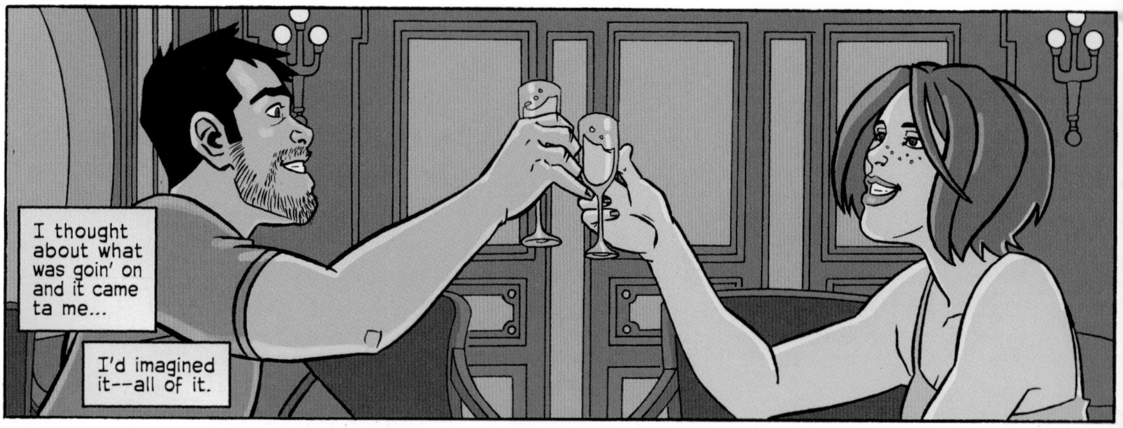
I thought about what was goin' on and it came ta me...
I'd imagined it--all of it.

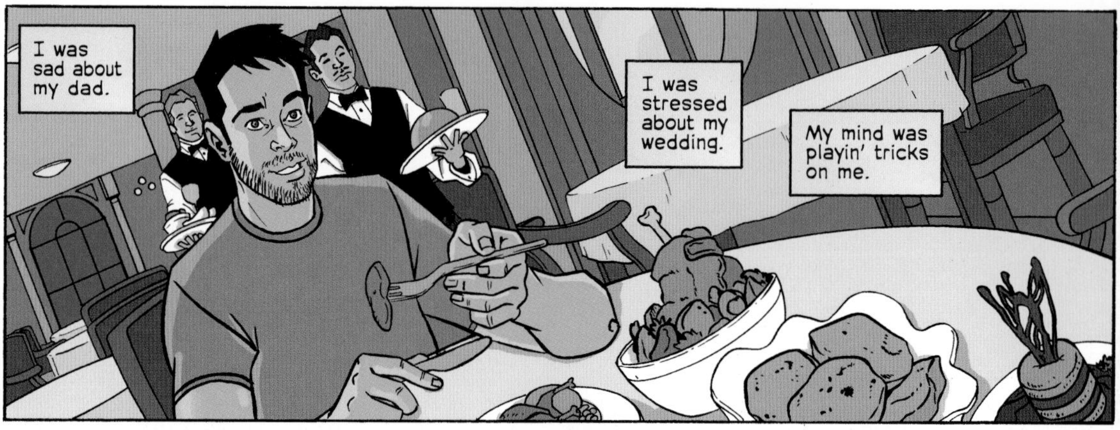
I was sad about my dad.
I was stressed about my wedding.
My mind was playin' tricks on me.

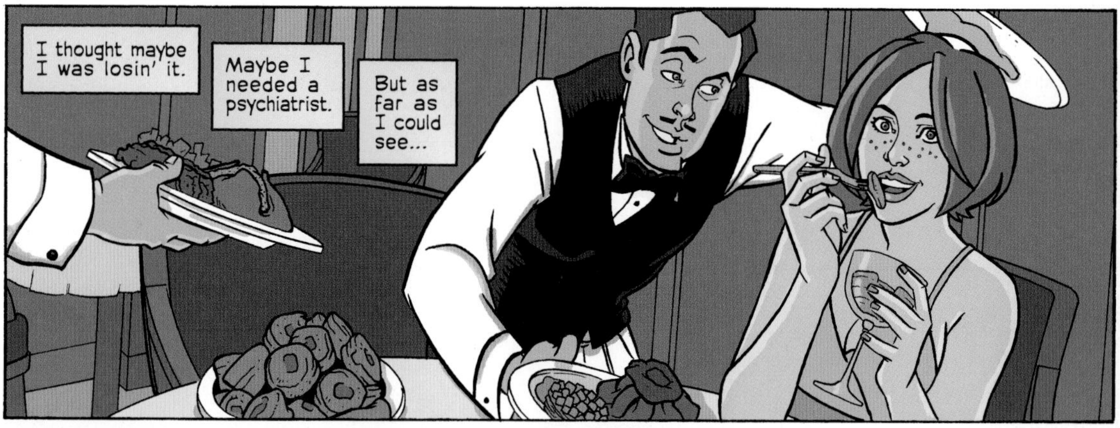
I thought maybe I was losin' it.
Maybe I needed a psychiatrist.
But as far as I could see...

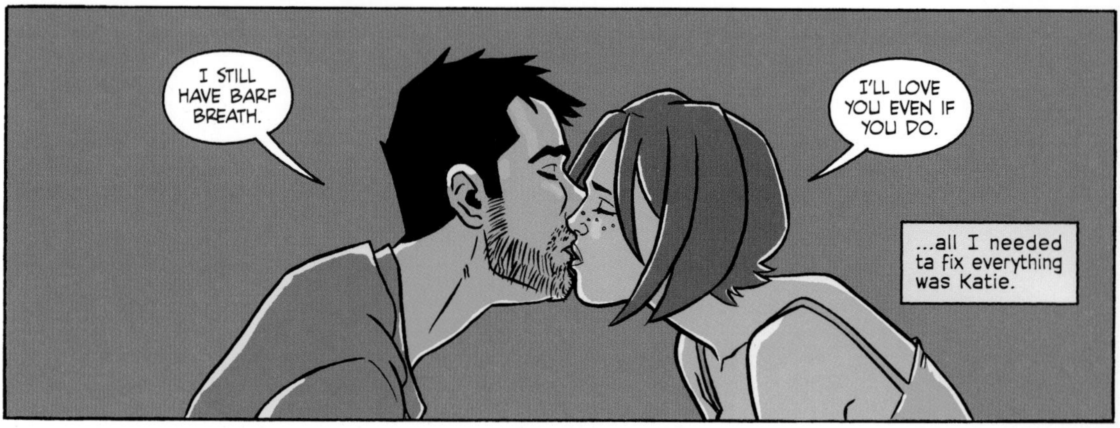
I STILL HAVE BARF BREATH.
I'LL LOVE YOU EVEN IF YOU DO.
...all I needed ta fix everything was Katie.

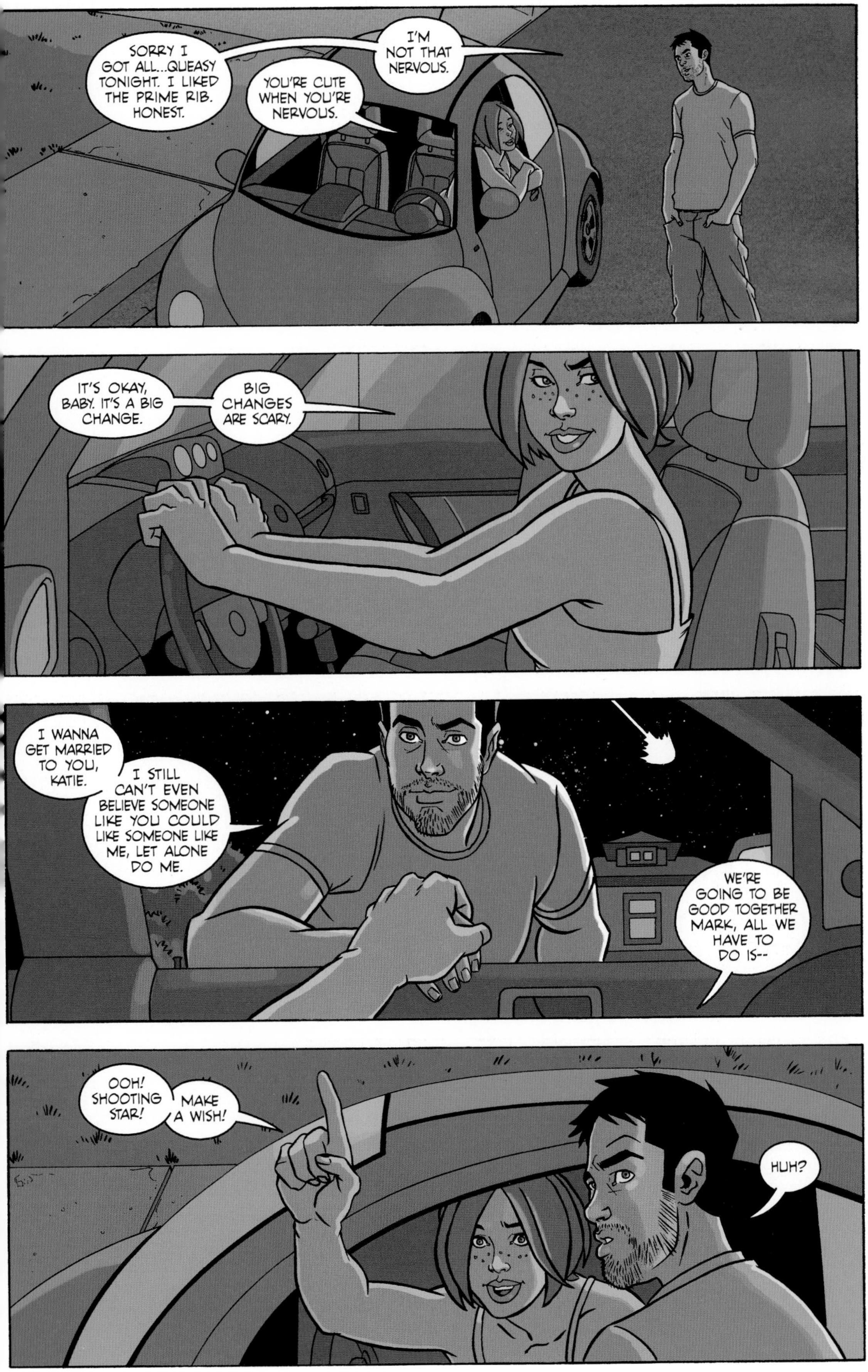
SORRY I GOT ALL...QUEASY TONIGHT. I LIKED THE PRIME RIB. HONEST.
I'M NOT THAT NERVOUS.
YOU'RE CUTE WHEN YOU'RE NERVOUS.
IT'S OKAY, BABY. IT'S A BIG CHANGE.
BIG CHANGES ARE SCARY.
I WANNA GET MARRIED TO YOU, KATIE.
I STILL CAN'T EVEN BELIEVE SOMEONE LIKE YOU COULD LIKE SOMEONE LIKE ME, LET ALONE DO ME.
WE'RE GOING TO BE GOOD TOGETHER MARK, ALL WE HAVE TO DO IS--
OOH! SHOOTING STAR!
MAKE A WISH!
HUH?

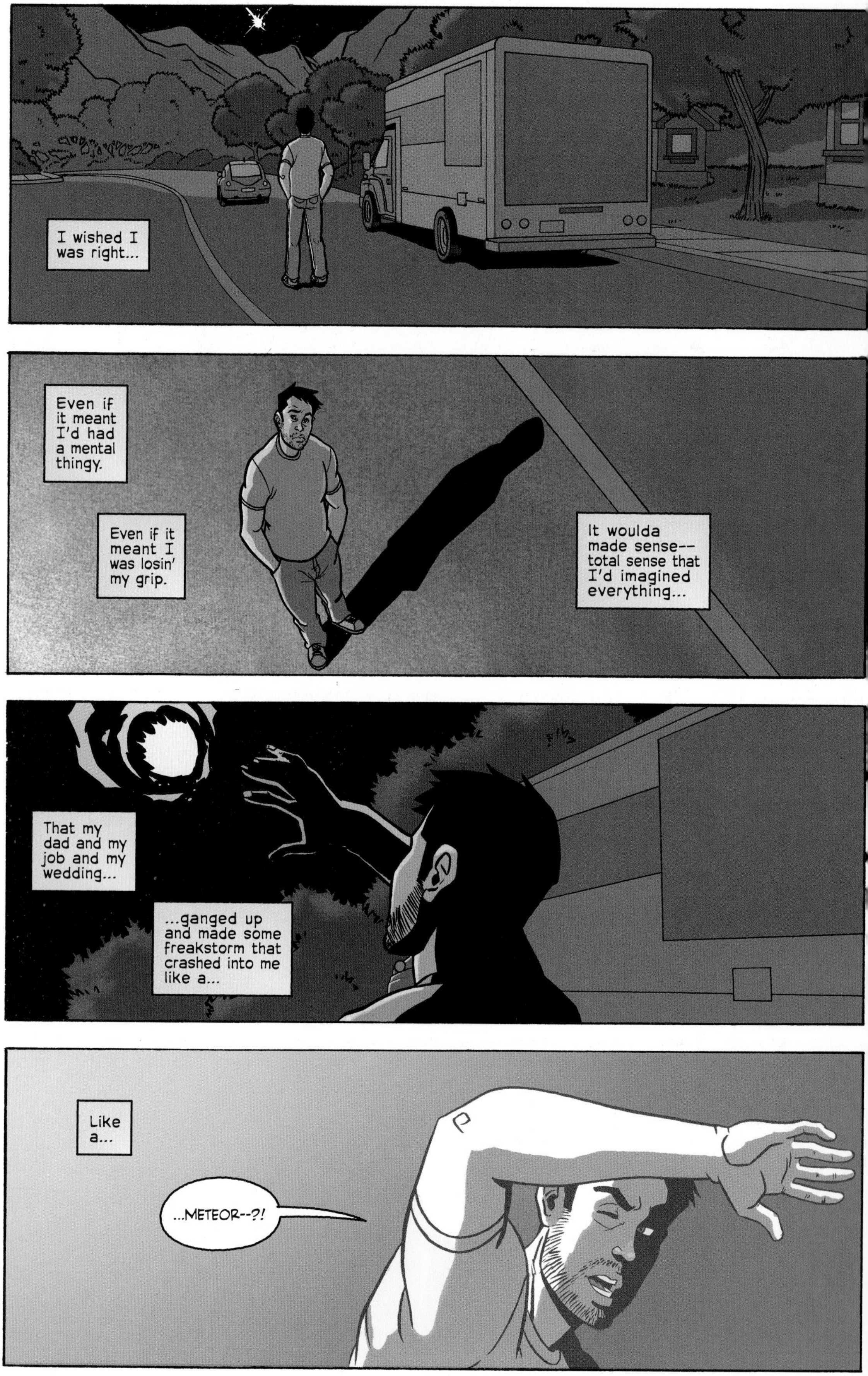
I wished I was right...
Even if it meant I'd had a mental thingy.
Even if it meant I was losin' my grip.
It woulda made sense--total sense that I'd imagined everything...
That my dad and my job and my wedding...
...ganged up and made some freakstorm that crashed into me like a...
Like a...
...METEOR--?!

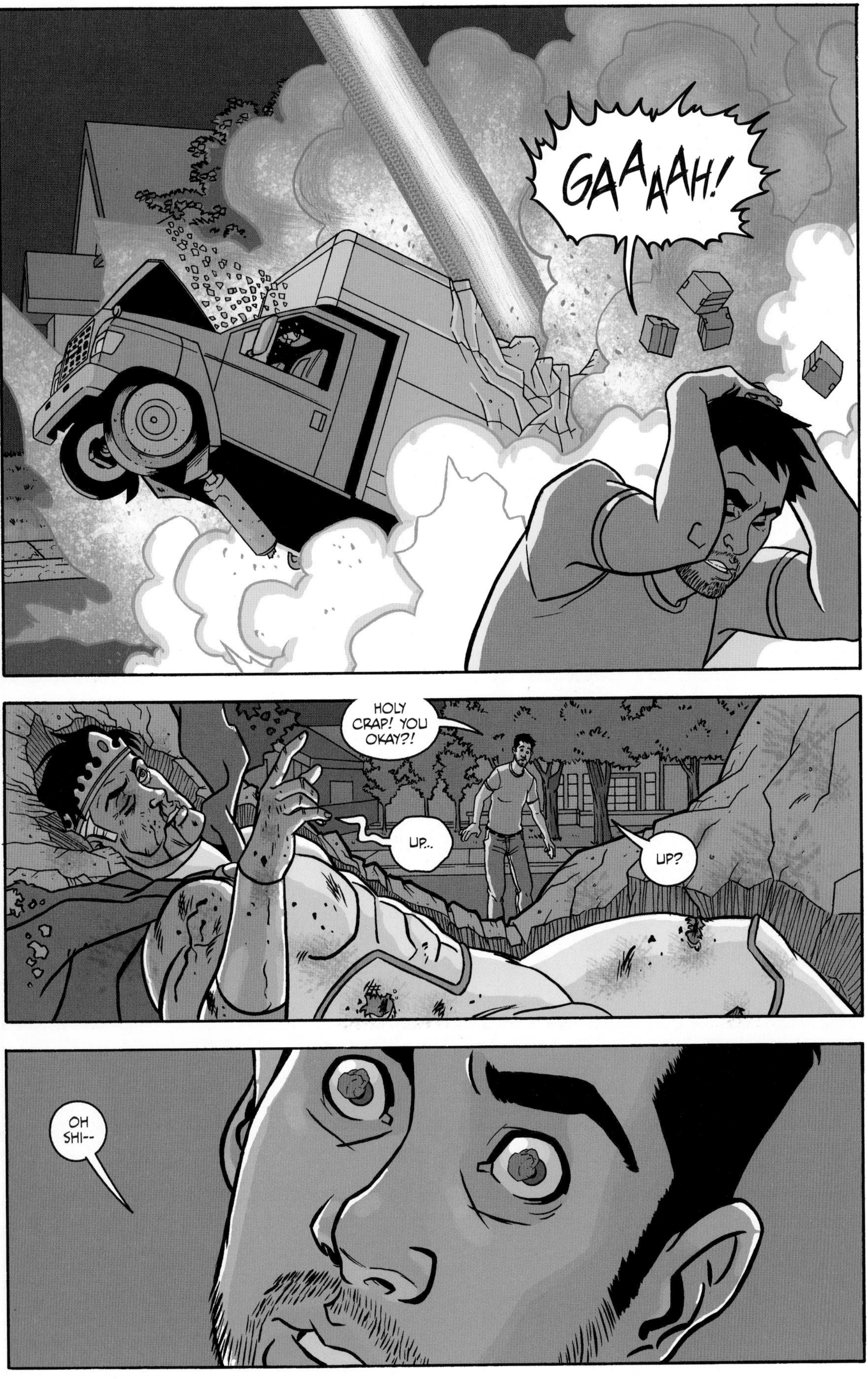
GAAAAH!
HOLY CRAP! YOU OKAY?!
UP..
UP?
OH SHI--

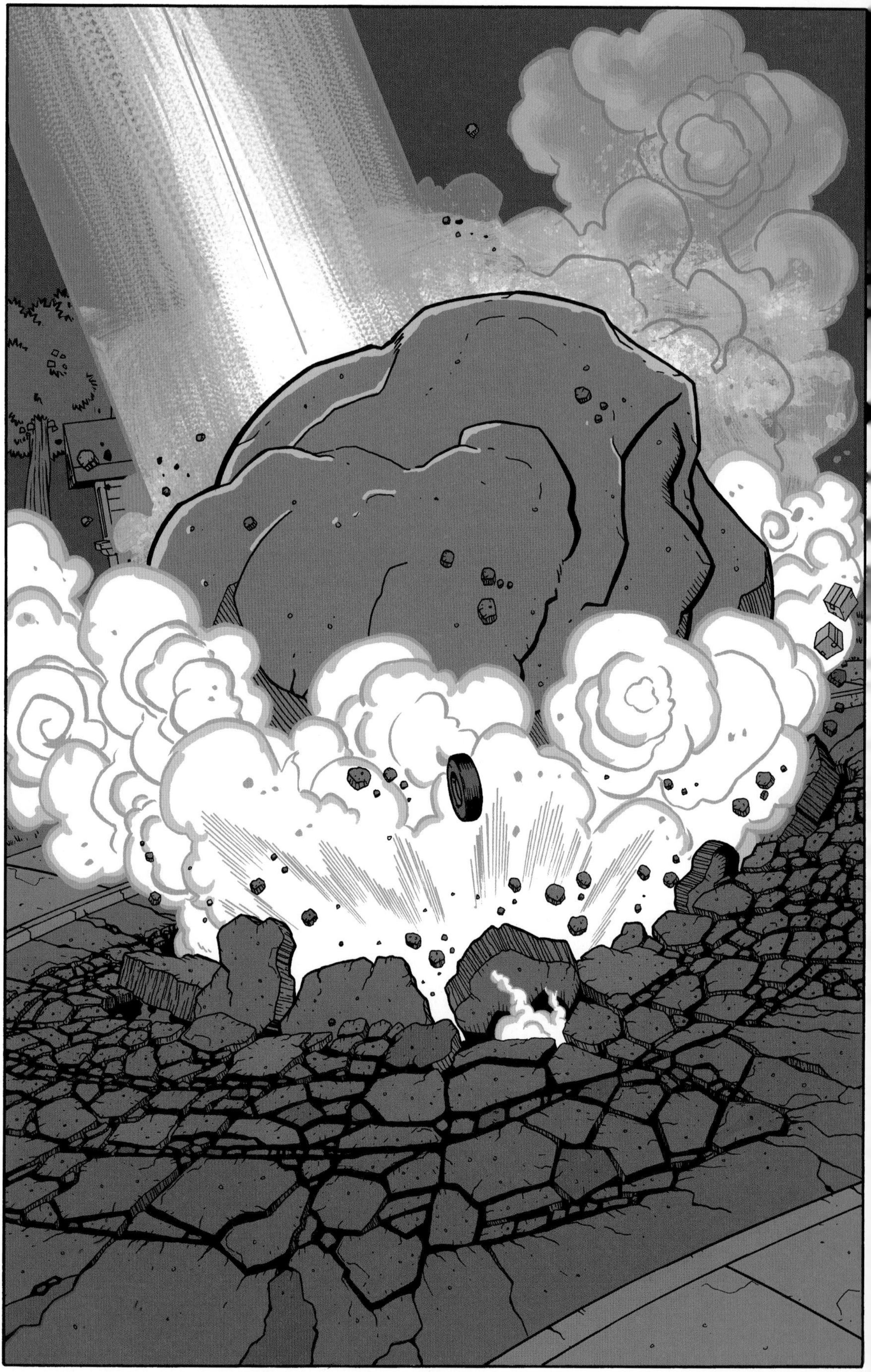

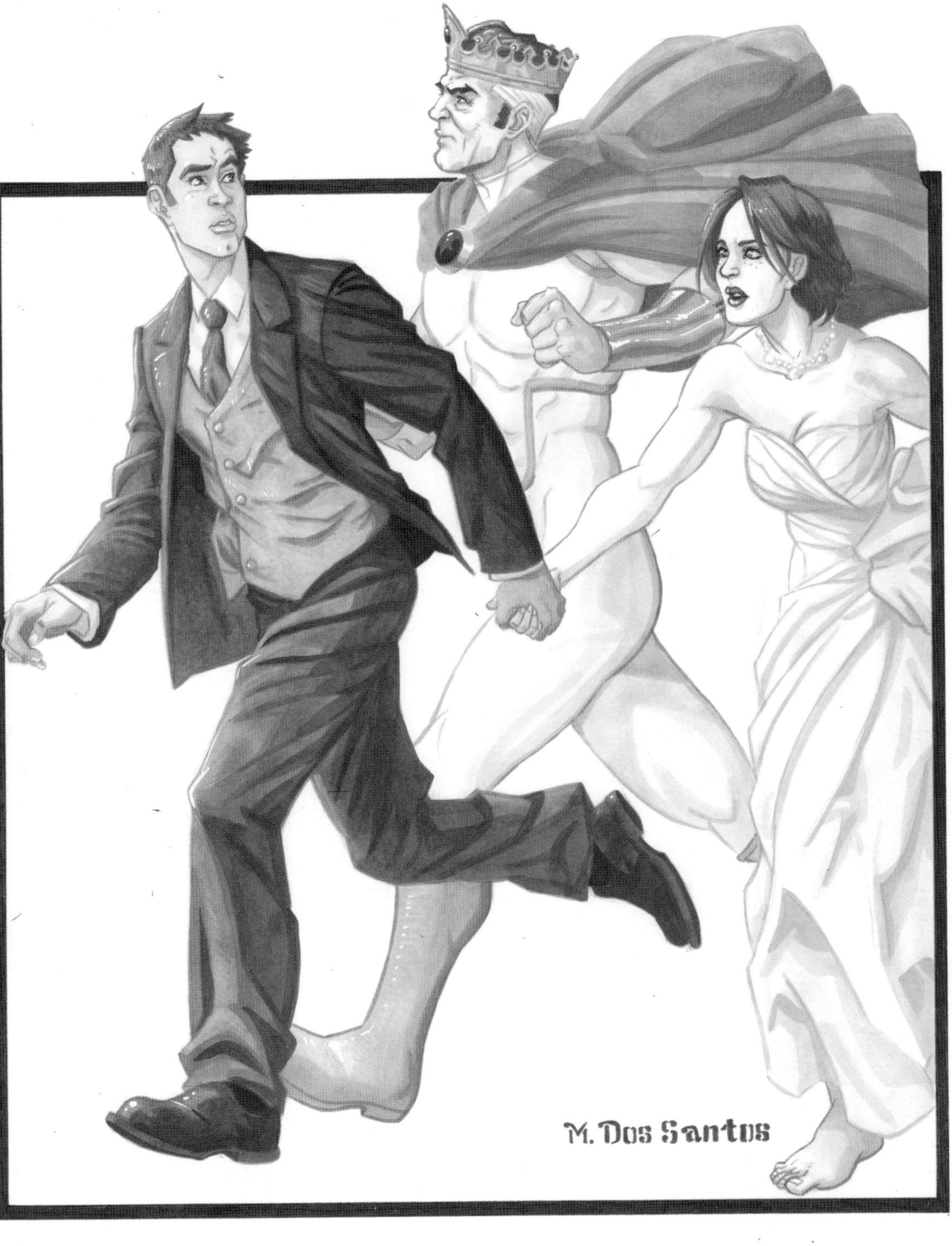
M. Dos Santos

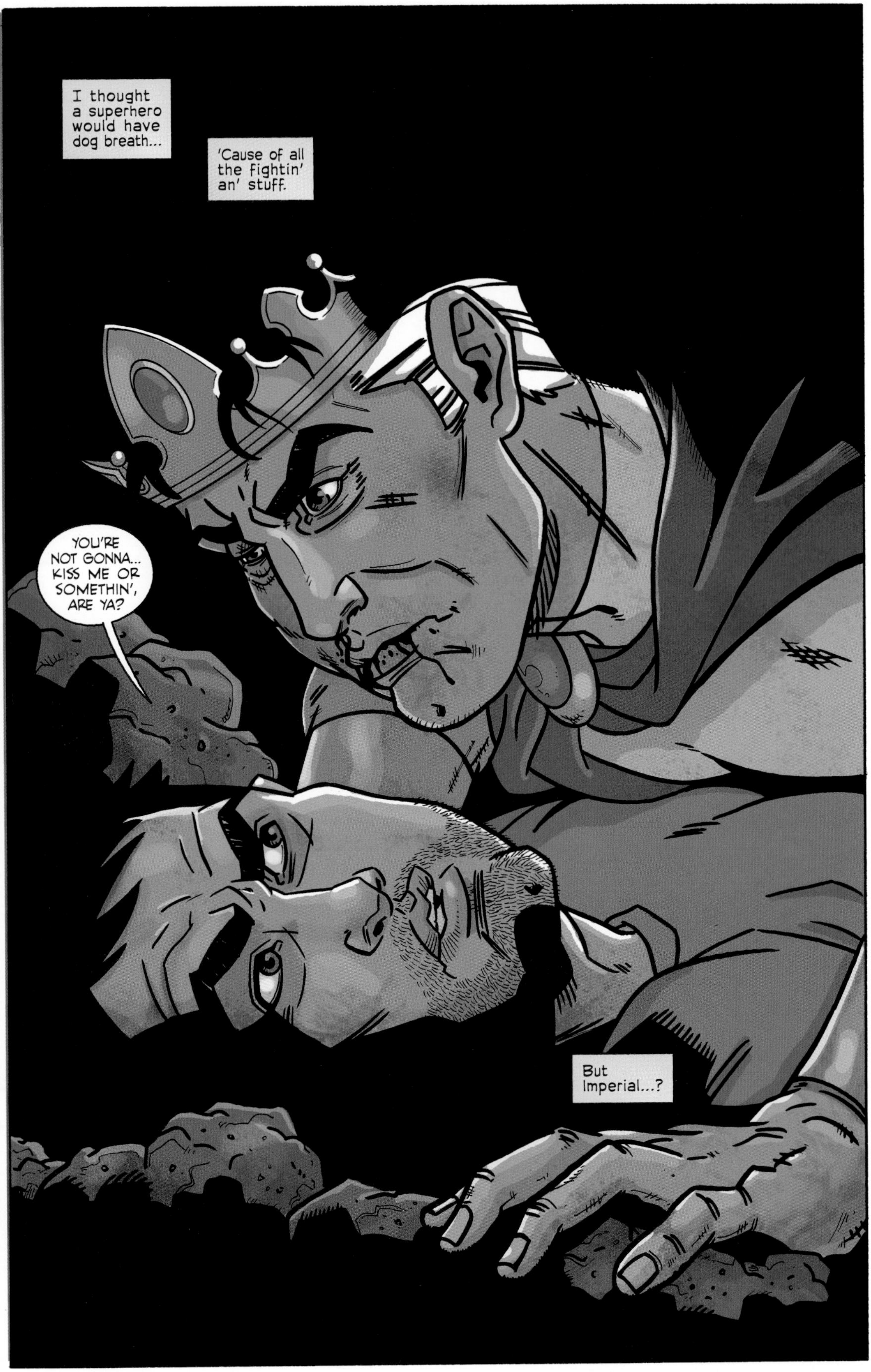

I thought a superhero would have dog breath...
'Cause of all the fightin' an' stuff.
YOU'RE NOT GONNA... KISS ME OR SOMETHIN', ARE YA?
But Imperial...?

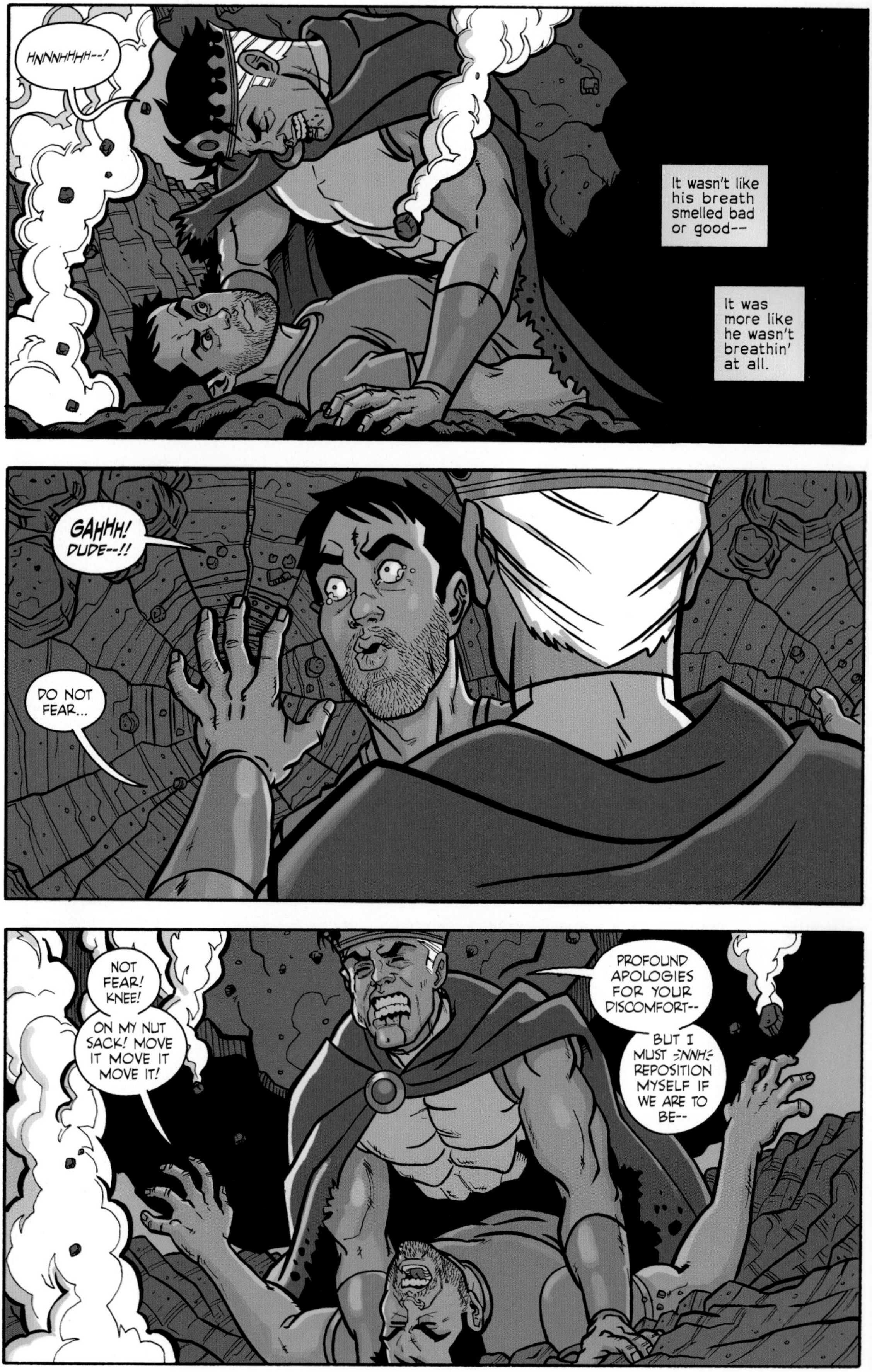
HNNNHHHH--!
It wasn't like his breath smelled bad or good--
It was more like he wasn't breathin' at all.
GAHHH! DUDE--!!
DO NOT FEAR...
NOT FEAR! KNEE!
ON MY NUT SACK! MOVE IT MOVE IT MOVE IT!
PROFOUND APOLOGIES FOR YOUR DISCOMFORT--
BUT I MUST =NNH= REPOSITION MYSELF IF WE ARE TO BE--

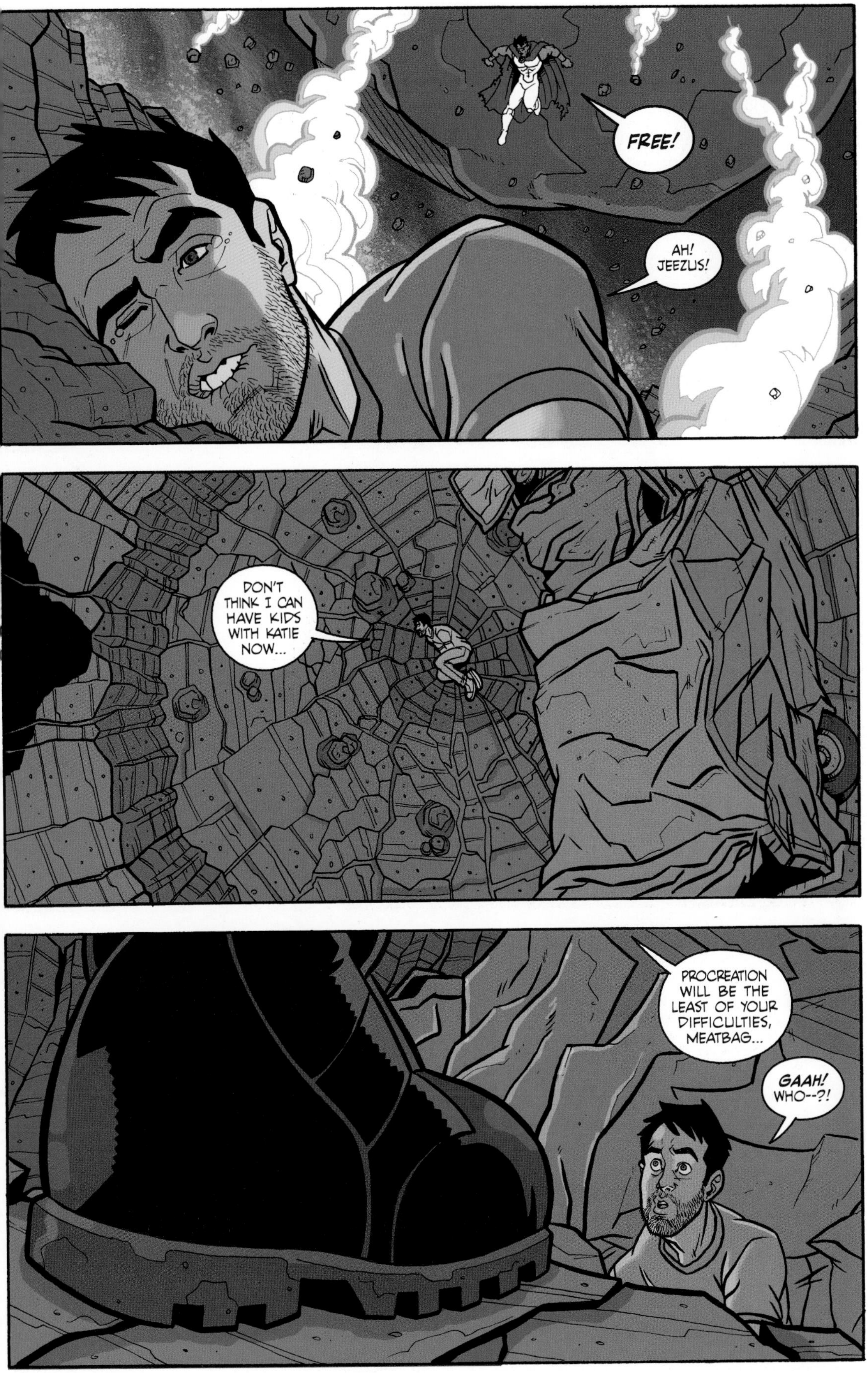
FREE!
AH! JEEZUS!
DON'T THINK I CAN HAVE KIDS WITH KATIE NOW...
PROCREATION WILL BE THE LEAST OF YOUR DIFFICULTIES, MEATBAG...
GAAH! WHO--?!

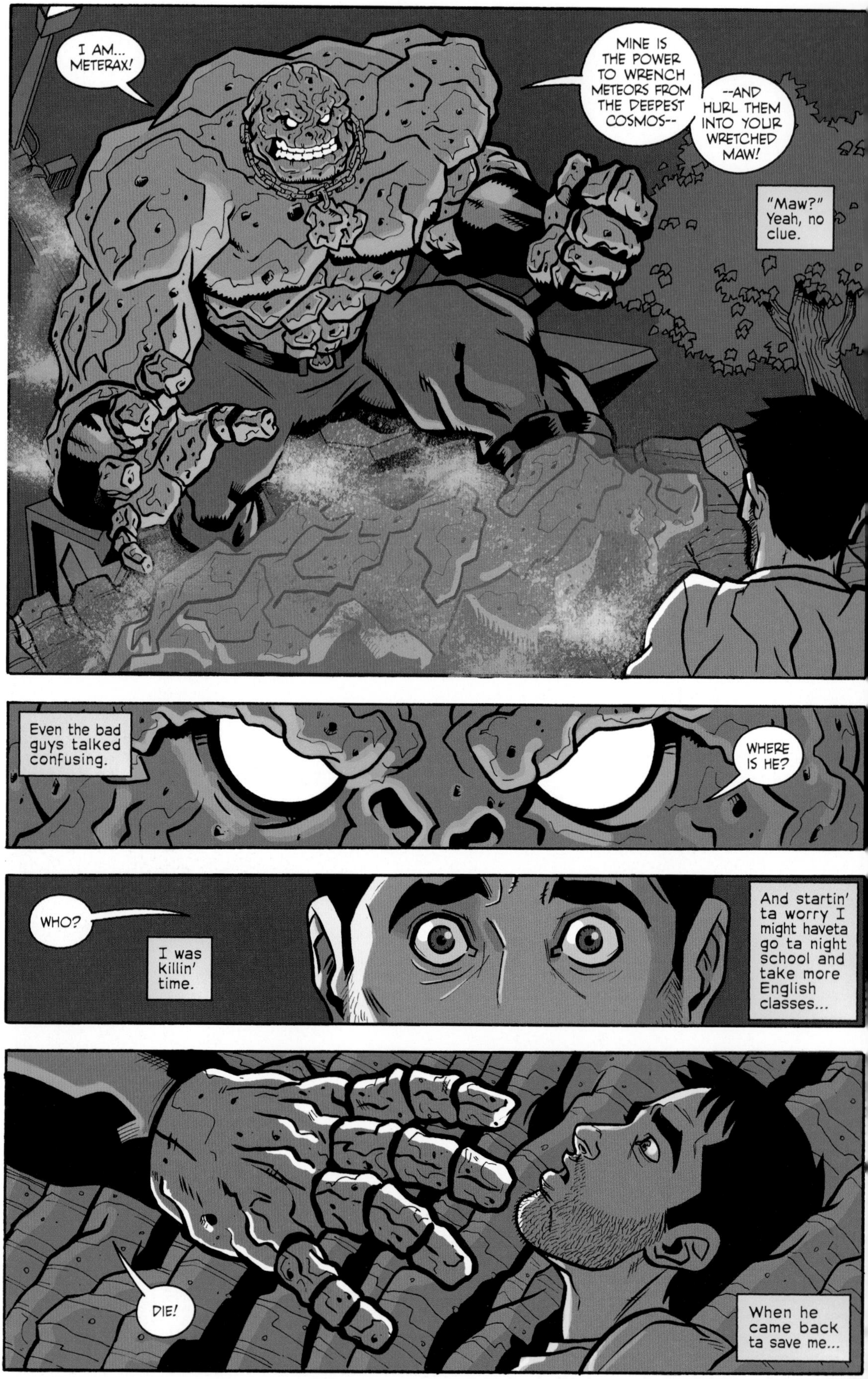
I AM... METERAX!
MINE IS THE POWER TO WRENCH METEORS FROM THE DEEPEST COSMOS--
--AND HURL THEM INTO YOUR WRETCHED MAW!
"Maw?" Yeah, no clue.
Even the bad guys talked confusing.
WHERE IS HE?
WHO?
I was killin' time.
And startin' ta worry I might haveta go ta night school and take more English classes...
DIE!
When he came back ta save me...

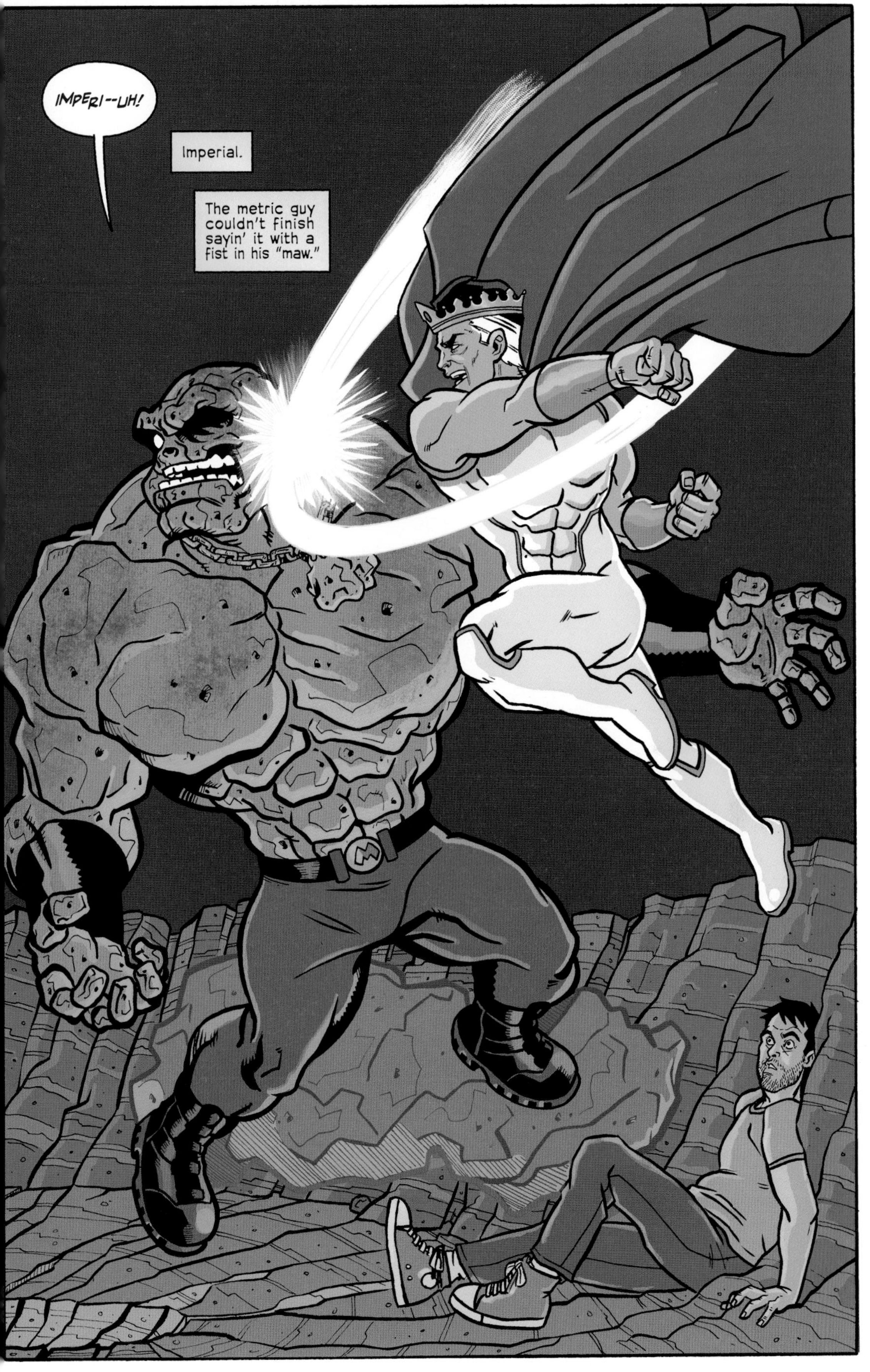
IMPERI--UH!
Imperial.
The metric guy couldn't finish sayin' it with a fist in his "maw."

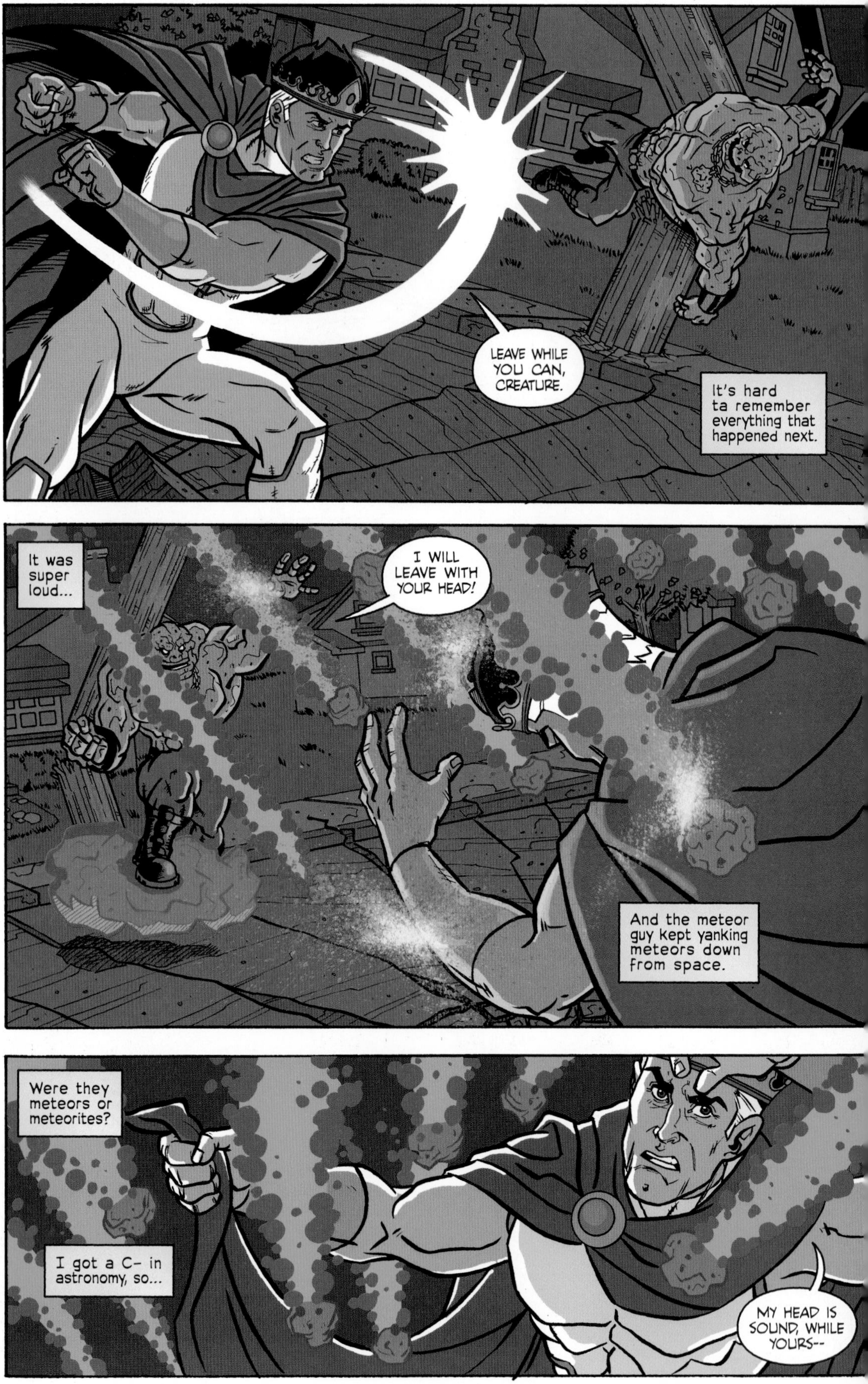
LEAVE WHILE YOU CAN, CREATURE.
It's hard ta remember everything that happened next.
It was super loud...
I WILL LEAVE WITH YOUR HEAD!
And the meteor guy kept yanking meteors down from space.
Were they meteors or meteorites?
I got a C- in astronomy, so...
MY HEAD IS SOUND, WHILE YOURS--

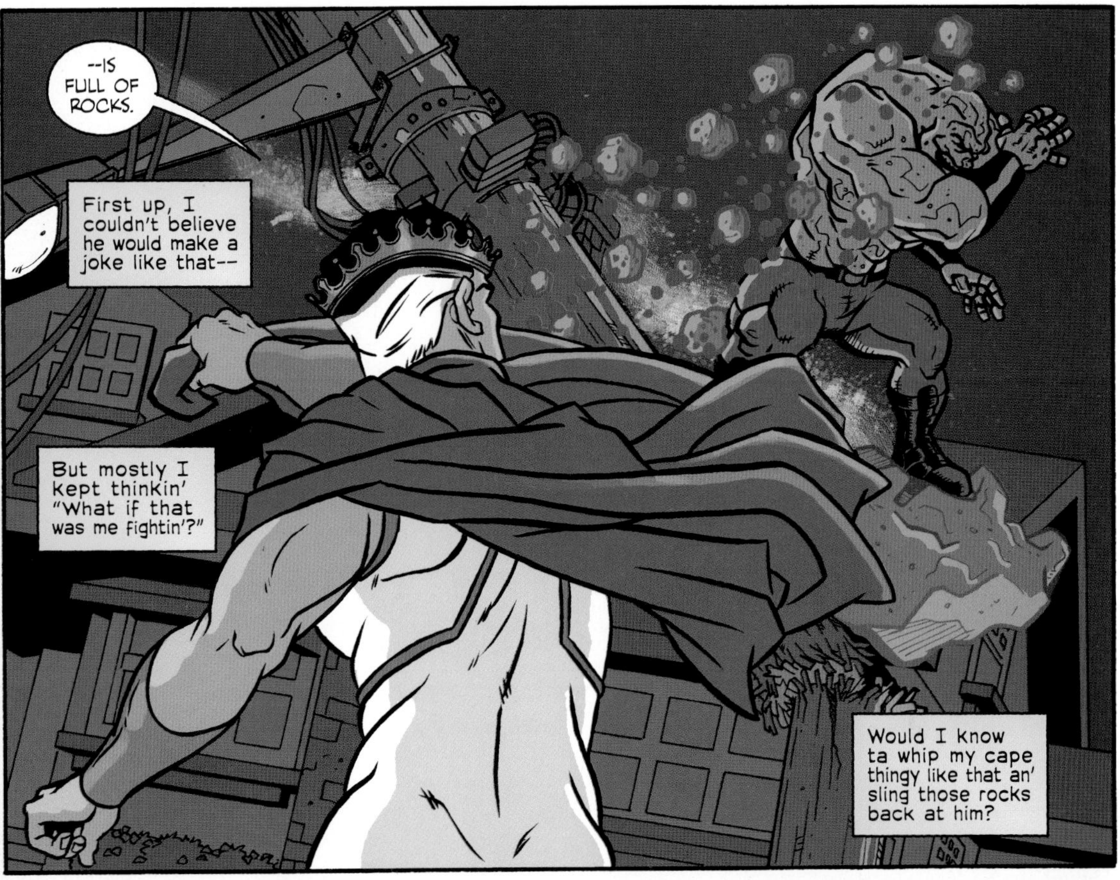
--IS FULL OF ROCKS.
First up, I couldn't believe he would make a joke like that--
But mostly I kept thinkin' "What if that was me fightin'?"
Would I know ta whip my cape thingy like that an' sling those rocks back at him?

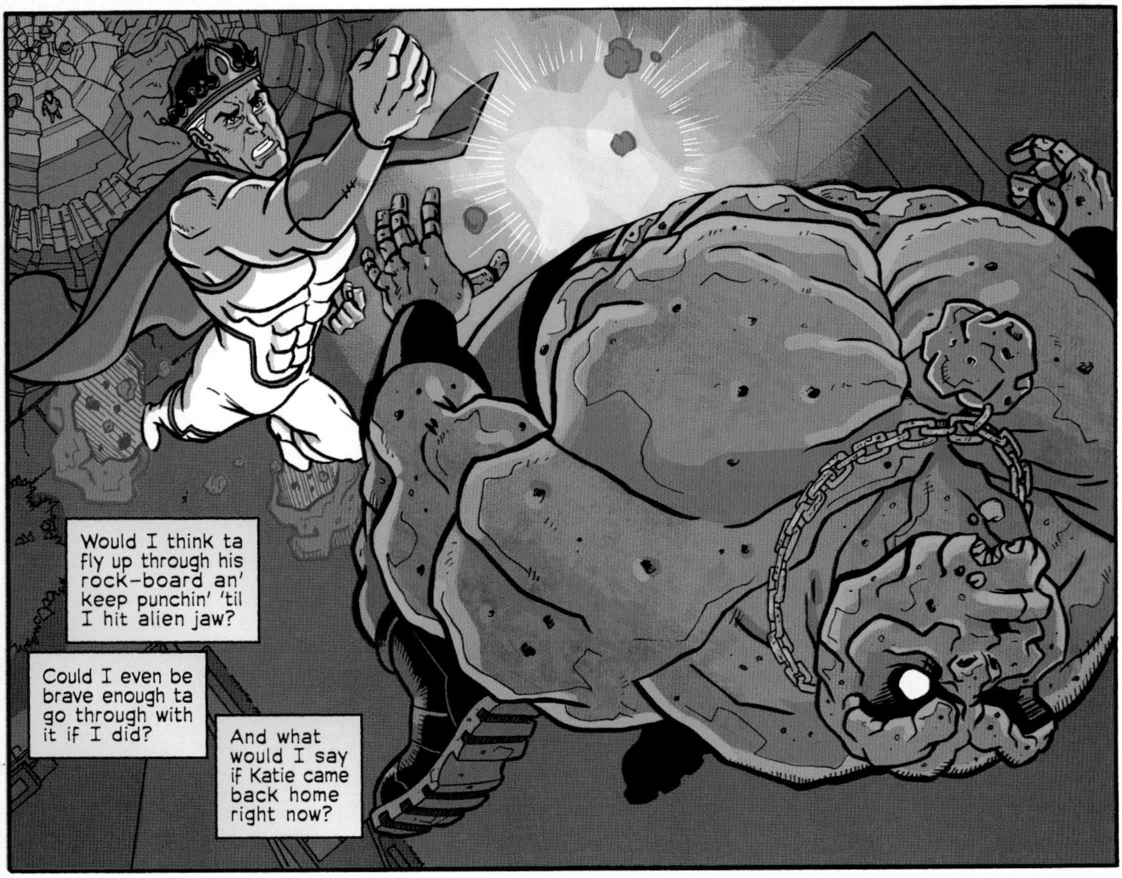
Would I think ta fly up through his rock-board an' keep punchin' 'til I hit alien jaw?
Could I even be brave enough ta go through with it if I did?
And what would I say if Katie came back home right now?

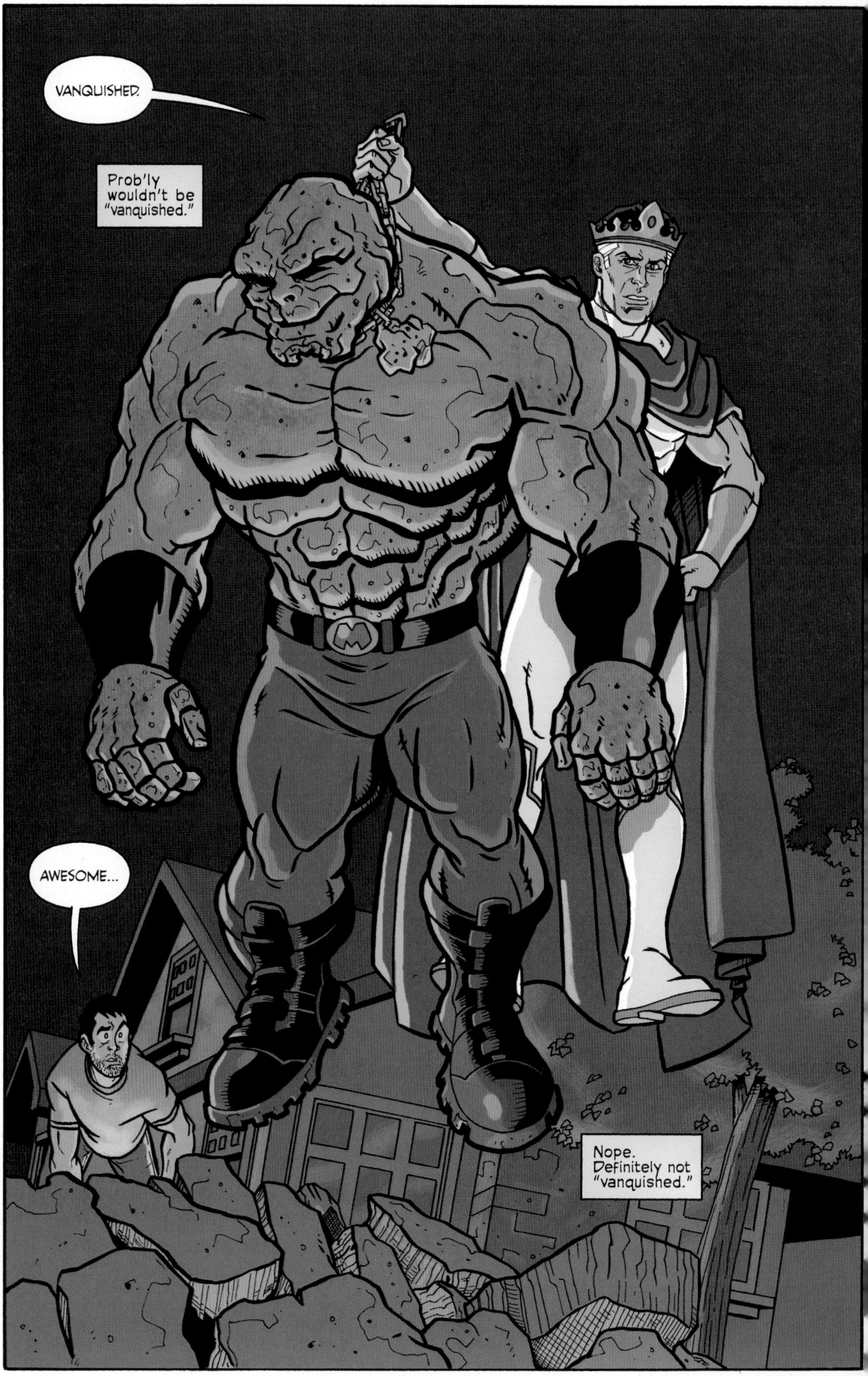
VANQUISHED.
Prob'ly wouldn't be "vanquished."
AWESOME...
Nope. Definitely not "vanquished."

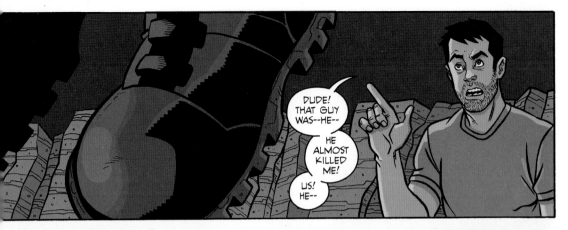

DUDE! THAT GUY WAS--HE--

HE ALMOST KILLED ME!

US! HE--

HE IS A MINOR THREAT, NOTHING MORE.

THAT'S "MINOR?!"

I COULD NEVER HANDLE SOMEONE LIKE HIM! I'D WIND UP S'MORES!

"S'MORES?"

HERSHEY BAR... MARSHMALLOW... GRAHAM CRACKER...?

YOU NEED TA GET OUT MORE.

ME? I HAVE SEEN THE RINGS OF SATURN WITH MY OWN EYES.

YEAH? WELL, I DOUBT THEY'RE AS GOOD AS S'MORES.

47

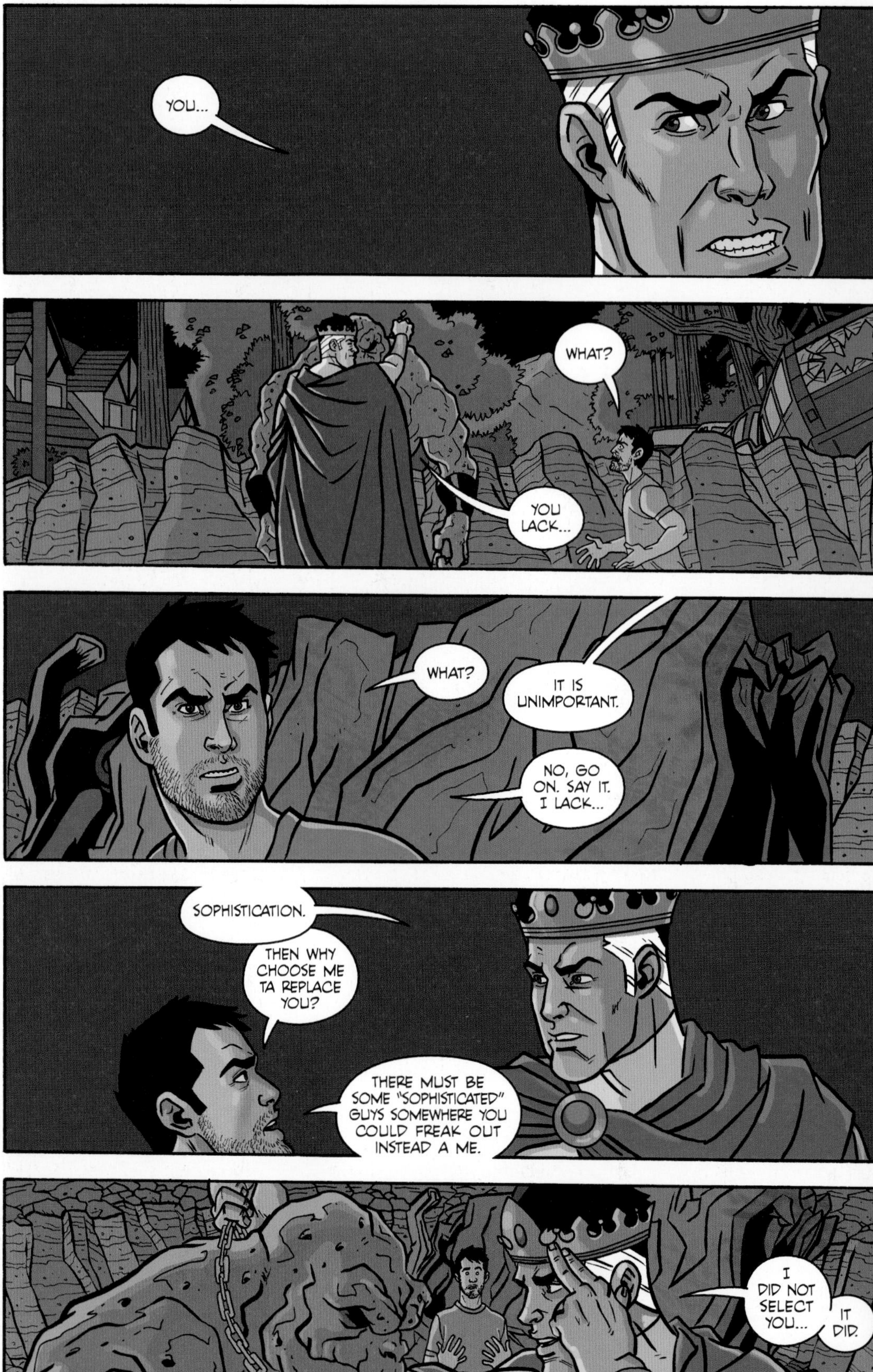
YOU...
WHAT?
YOU LACK...
WHAT?
IT IS UNIMPORTANT.
NO, GO ON. SAY IT. I LACK...
SOPHISTICATION.
THEN WHY CHOOSE ME TA REPLACE YOU?
THERE MUST BE SOME "SOPHISTICATED" GUYS SOMEWHERE YOU COULD FREAK OUT INSTEAD A ME.
I DID NOT SELECT YOU...
IT DID.

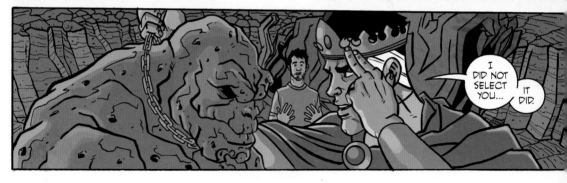

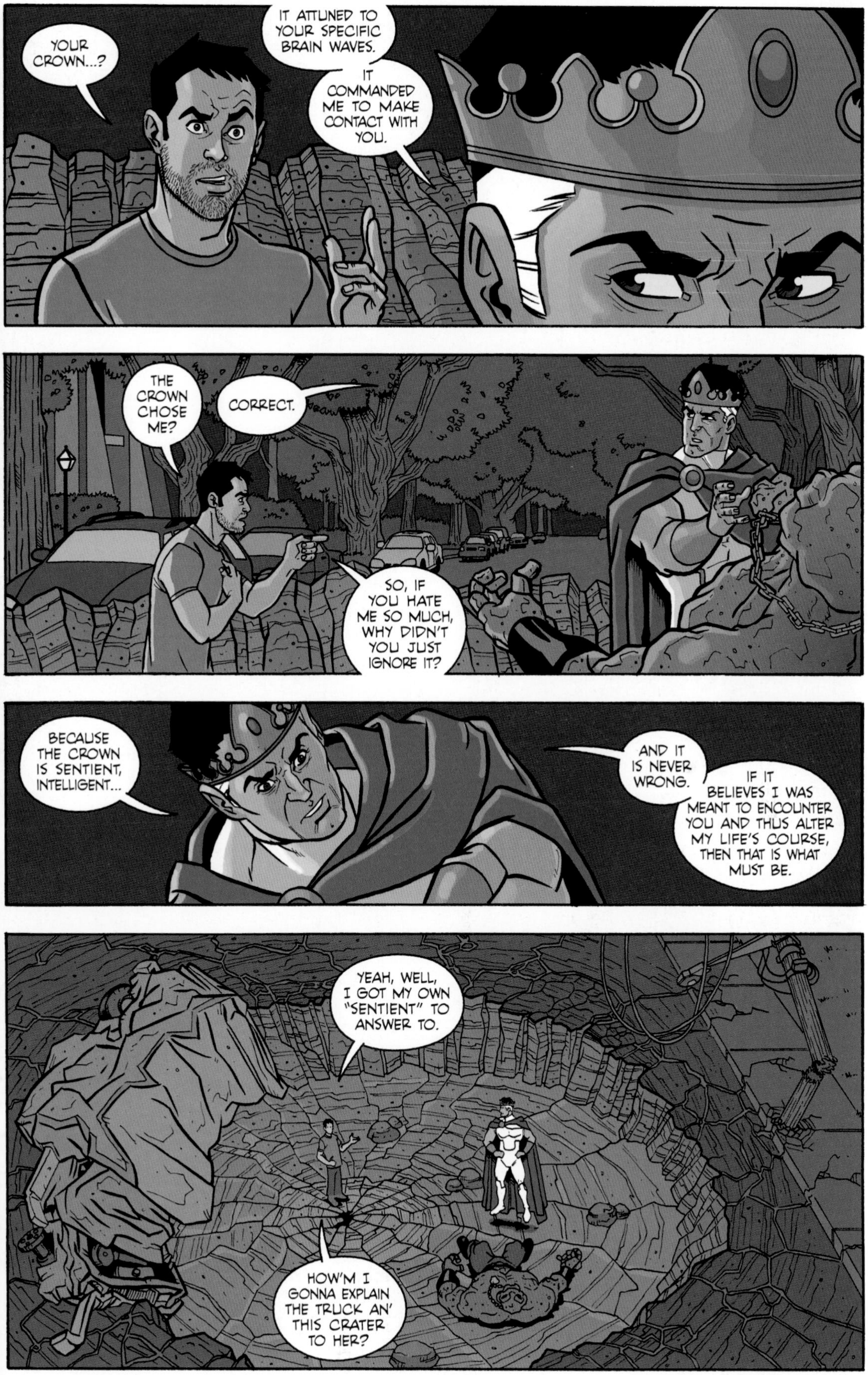
YOUR CROWN...?
IT ATTUNED TO YOUR SPECIFIC BRAIN WAVES.
IT COMMANDED ME TO MAKE CONTACT WITH YOU.
THE CROWN CHOSE ME?
CORRECT.
SO, IF YOU HATE ME SO MUCH, WHY DIDN'T YOU JUST IGNORE IT?
BECAUSE THE CROWN IS SENTIENT, INTELLIGENT...
AND IT IS NEVER WRONG.
IF IT BELIEVES I WAS MEANT TO ENCOUNTER YOU AND THUS ALTER MY LIFE'S COURSE, THEN THAT IS WHAT MUST BE.
YEAH, WELL, I GOT MY OWN "SENTIENT" TO ANSWER TO.
HOW'M I GONNA EXPLAIN THE TRUCK AN' THIS CRATER TO HER?

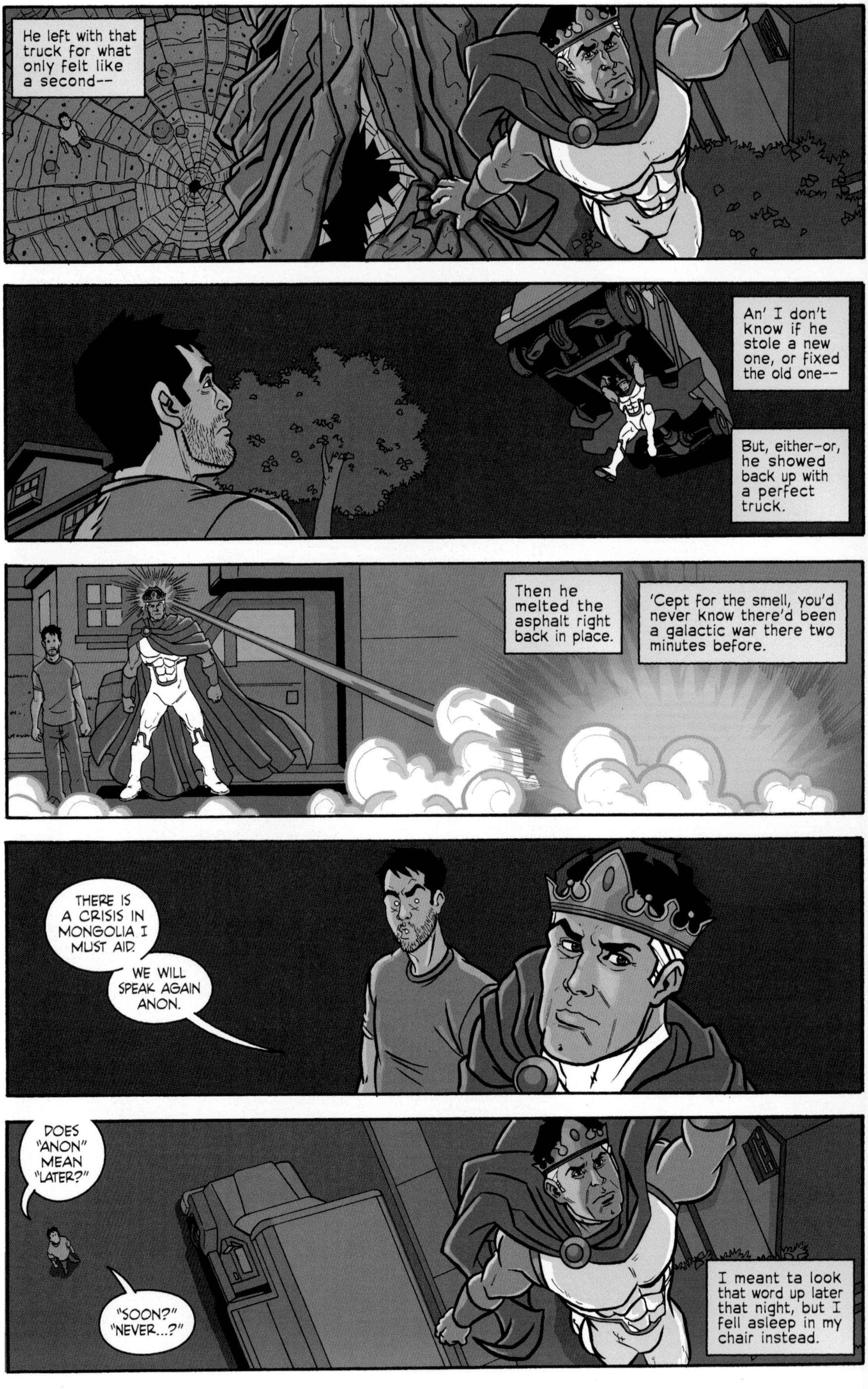
He left with that truck for what only felt like a second--
An' I don't know if he stole a new one, or fixed the old one--
But, either-or, he showed back up with a perfect truck.
Then he melted the asphalt right back in place.
'Cept for the smell, you'd never know there'd been a galactic war there two minutes before.
THERE IS A CRISIS IN MONGOLIA I MUST AID.
WE WILL SPEAK AGAIN ANON.
DOES "ANON" MEAN "LATER?"
"SOON?" "NEVER...?"
I meant ta look that word up later that night, but I fell asleep in my chair instead.

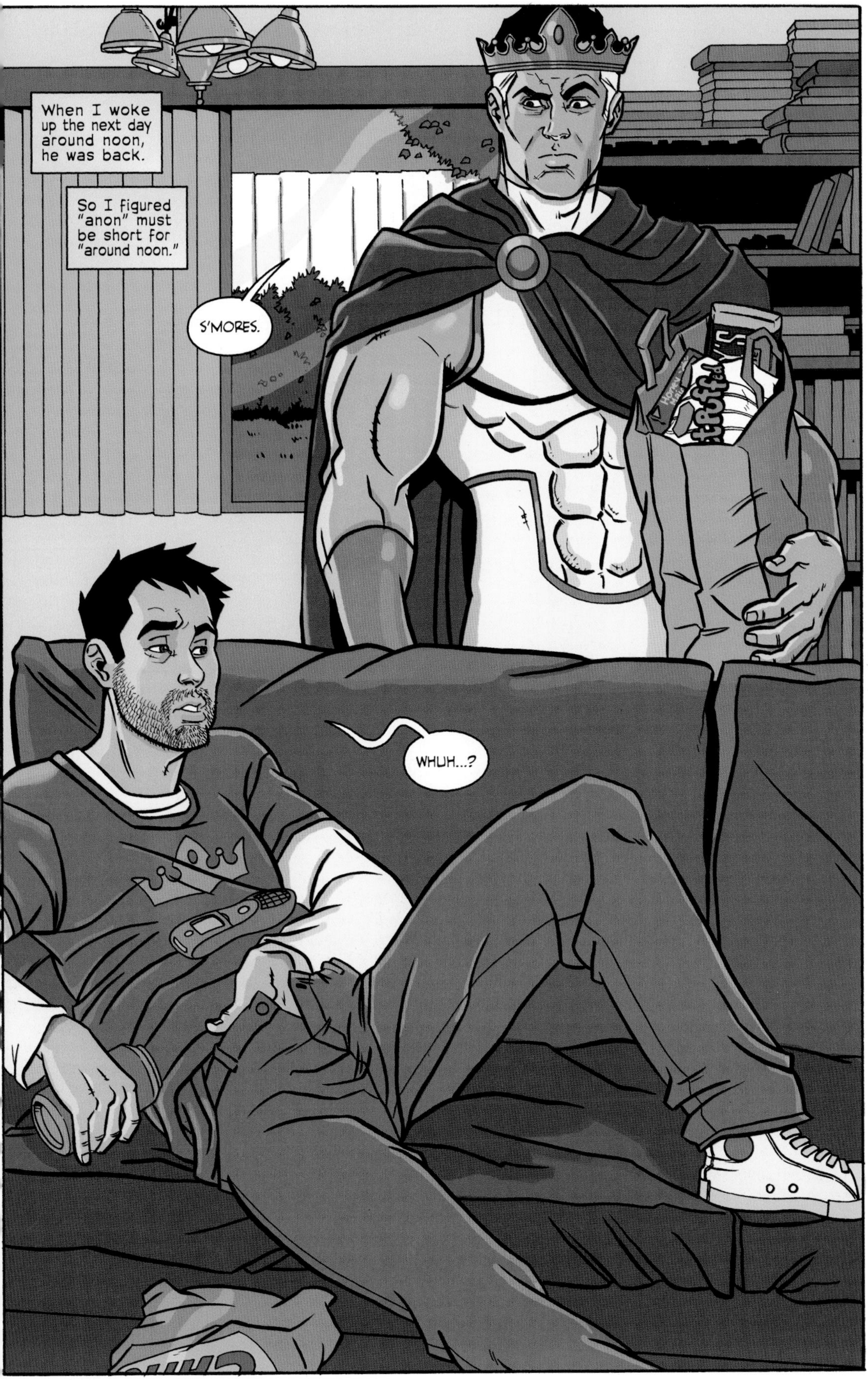

When I woke up the next day around noon, he was back.
So I figured "anon" must be short for "around noon."
S'MORES.
WHUH...?

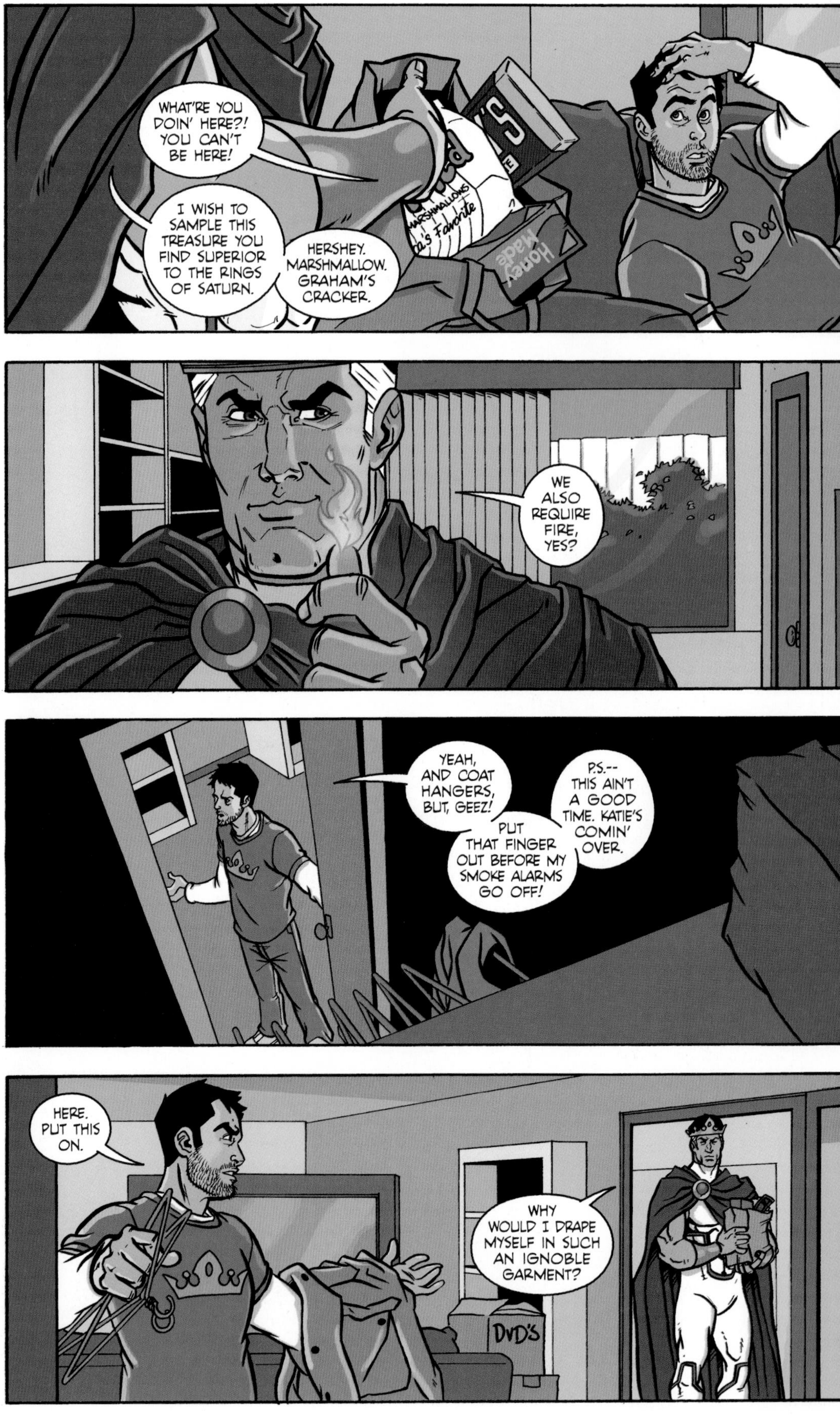
WHAT'RE YOU DOIN' HERE?! YOU CAN'T BE HERE!
I WISH TO SAMPLE THIS TREASURE YOU FIND SUPERIOR TO THE RINGS OF SATURN.
HERSHEY. MARSHMALLOW. GRAHAM'S CRACKER.
MARSHMALLOWS
Honey Made
WE ALSO REQUIRE FIRE, YES?
YEAH, AND COAT HANGERS, BUT, GEEZ!
PUT THAT FINGER OUT BEFORE MY SMOKE ALARMS GO OFF!
P.S.-- THIS AIN'T A GOOD TIME. KATIE'S COMIN' OVER.
HERE. PUT THIS ON.
WHY WOULD I DRAPE MYSELF IN SUCH AN IGNOBLE GARMENT?
DVD'S

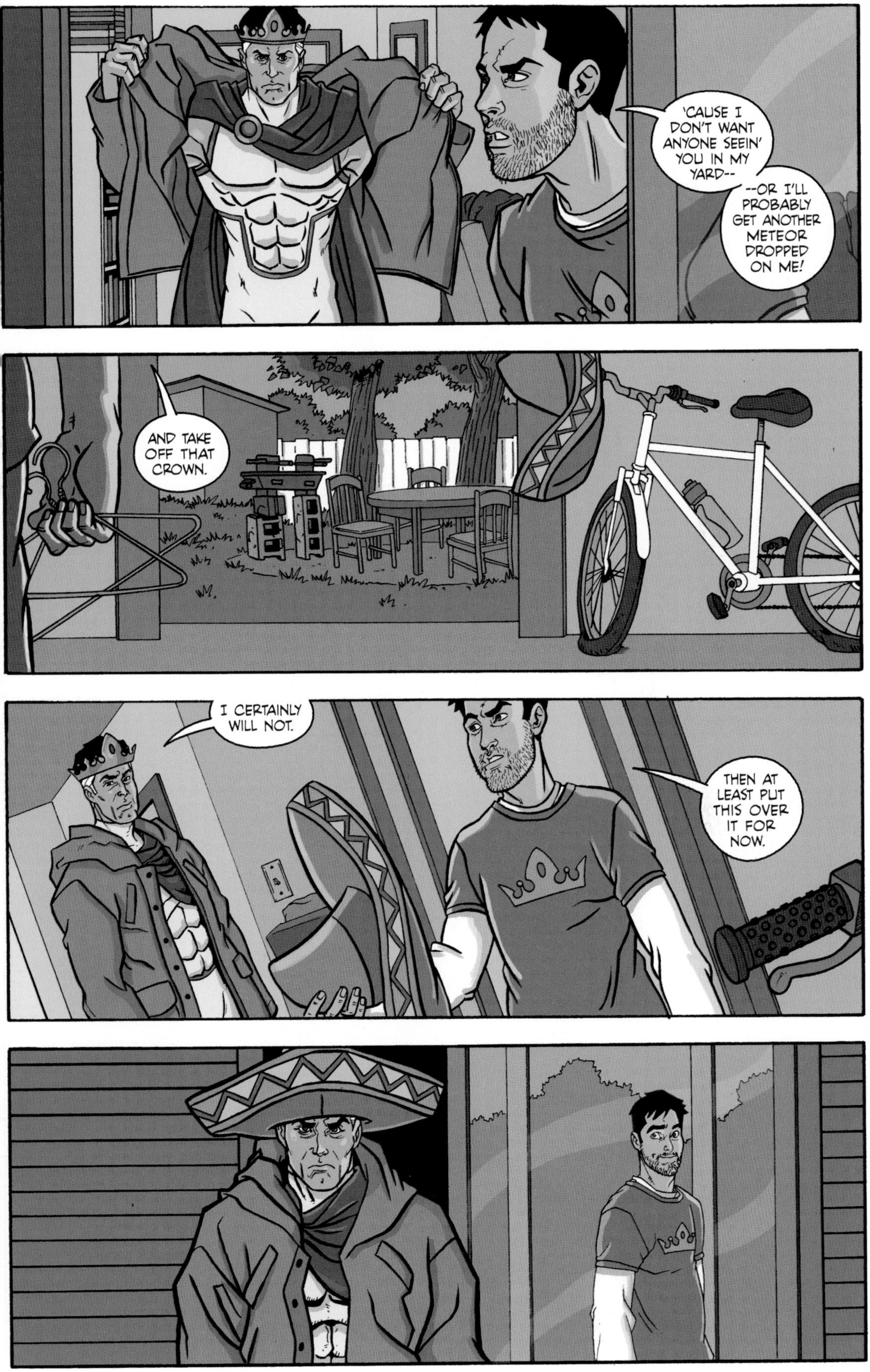
'CAUSE I DON'T WANT ANYONE SEEIN' YOU IN MY YARD--
--OR I'LL PROBABLY GET ANOTHER METEOR DROPPED ON ME!
AND TAKE OFF THAT CROWN.
I CERTAINLY WILL NOT.
THEN AT LEAST PUT THIS OVER IT FOR NOW.

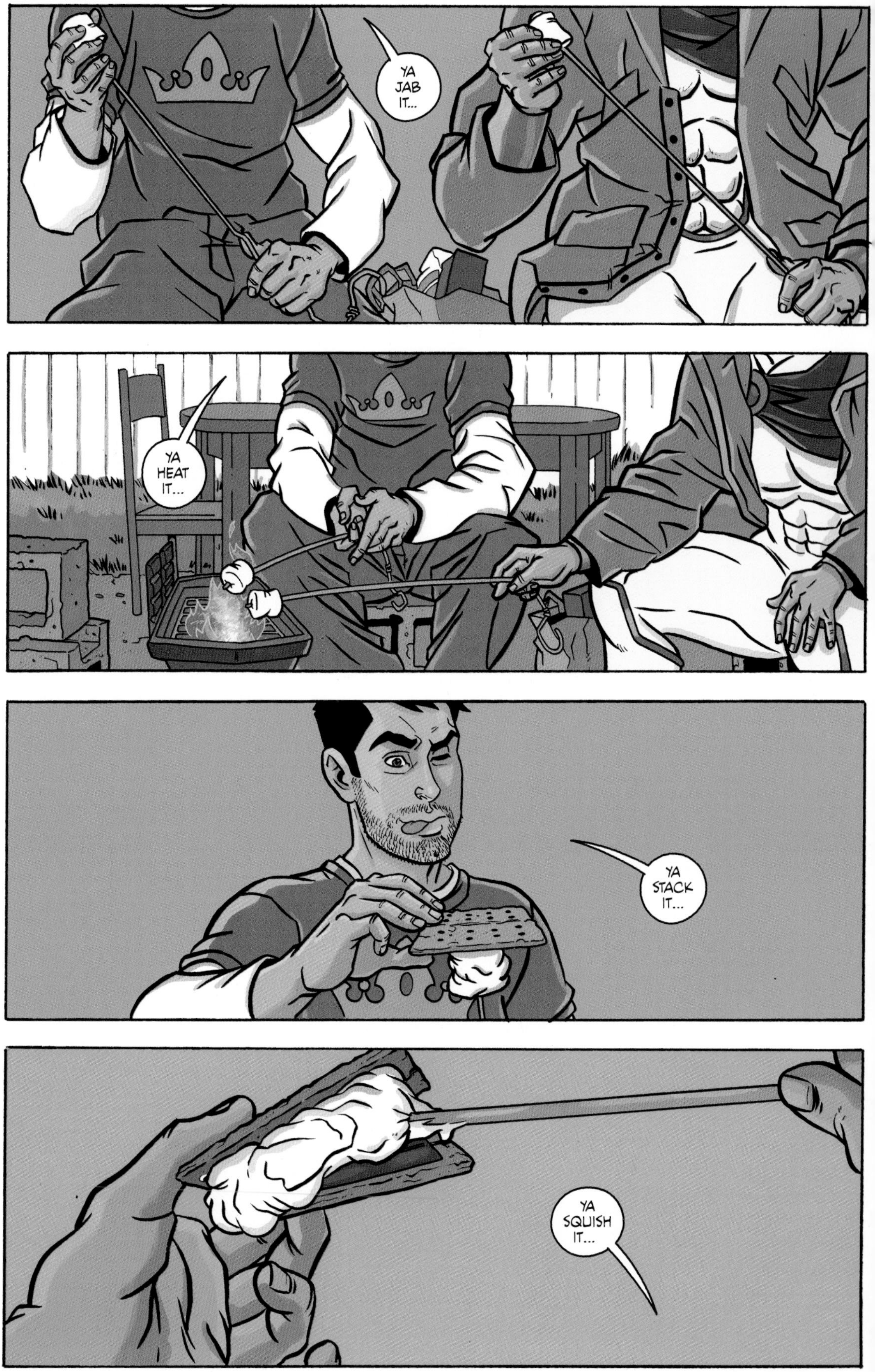
YA JAB IT...
YA HEAT IT...
YA STACK IT...
YA SQUISH IT...

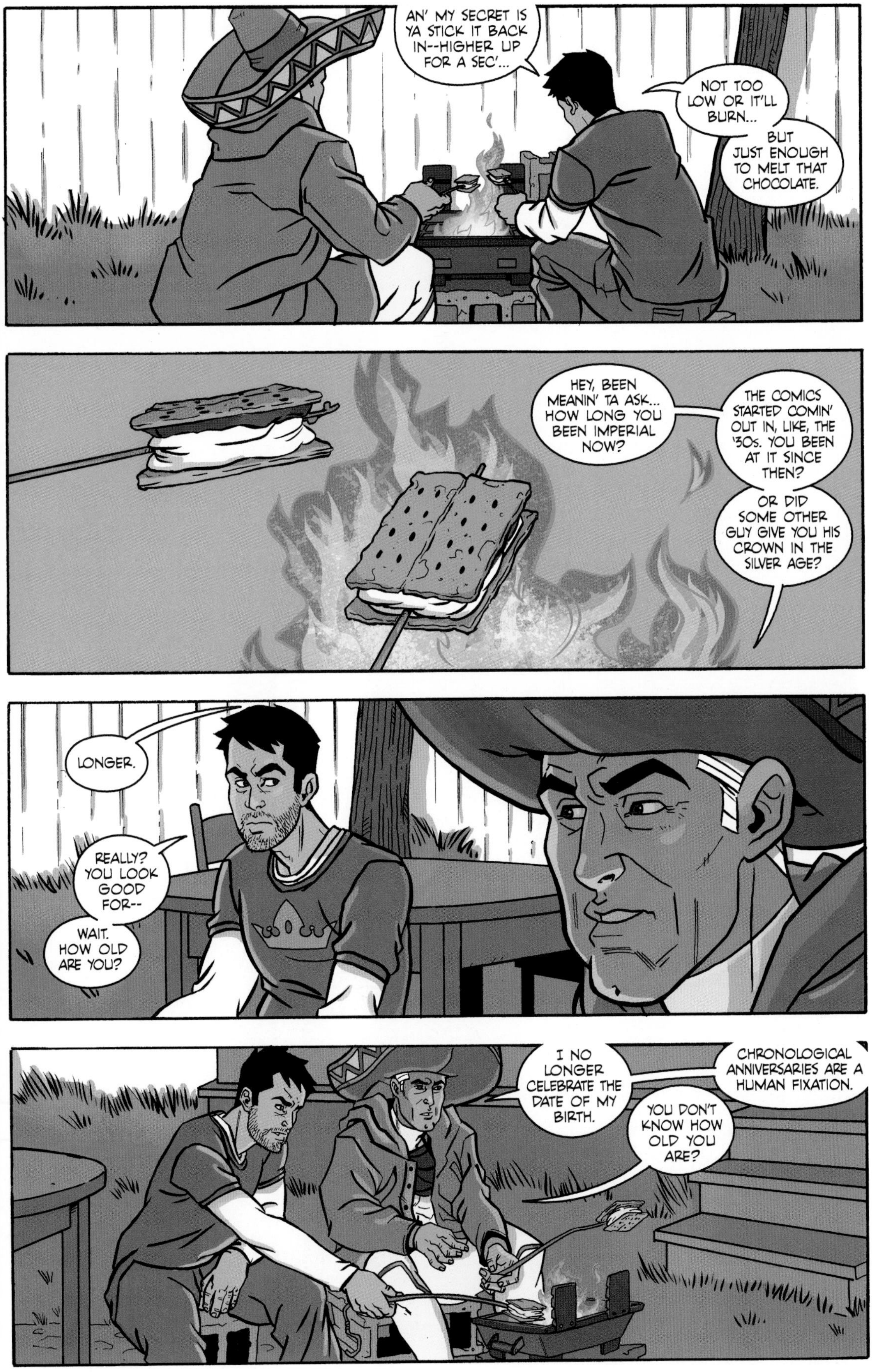
AN' MY SECRET IS YA STICK IT BACK IN--HIGHER UP FOR A SEC'...
NOT TOO LOW OR IT'LL BURN...
BUT JUST ENOUGH TO MELT THAT CHOCOLATE.
HEY, BEEN MEANIN' TA ASK... HOW LONG YOU BEEN IMPERIAL NOW?
THE COMICS STARTED COMIN' OUT IN, LIKE, THE '30s. YOU BEEN AT IT SINCE THEN?
OR DID SOME OTHER GUY GIVE YOU HIS CROWN IN THE SILVER AGE?
LONGER.
REALLY? YOU LOOK GOOD FOR--
WAIT. HOW OLD ARE YOU?
I NO LONGER CELEBRATE THE DATE OF MY BIRTH.
CHRONOLOGICAL ANNIVERSARIES ARE A HUMAN FIXATION.
YOU DON'T KNOW HOW OLD YOU ARE?

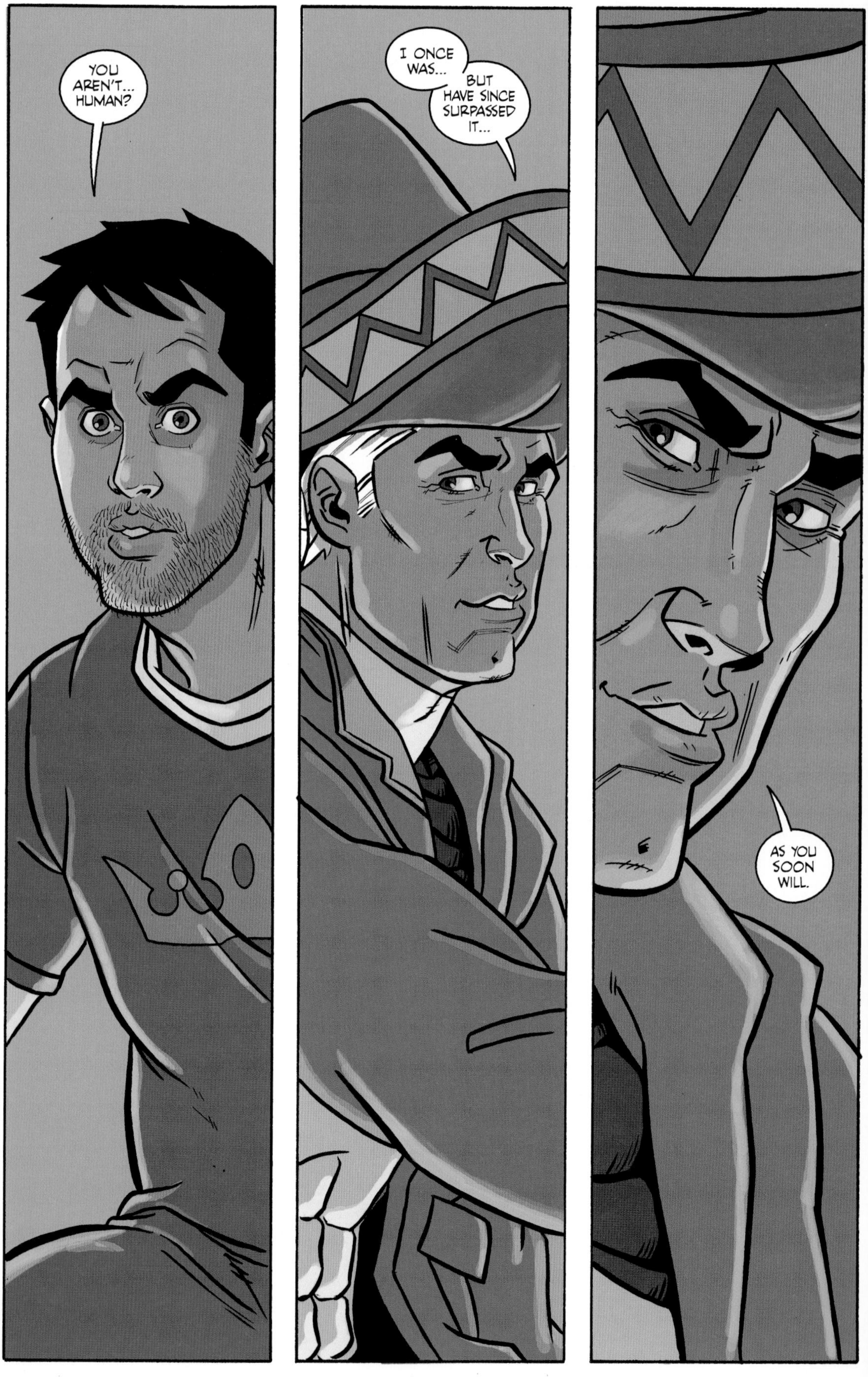
YOU ARE'T... HUMAN?
I ONCE WAS...
BUT HAVE SINCE SURPASSED IT...
AS YOU SOON WILL.

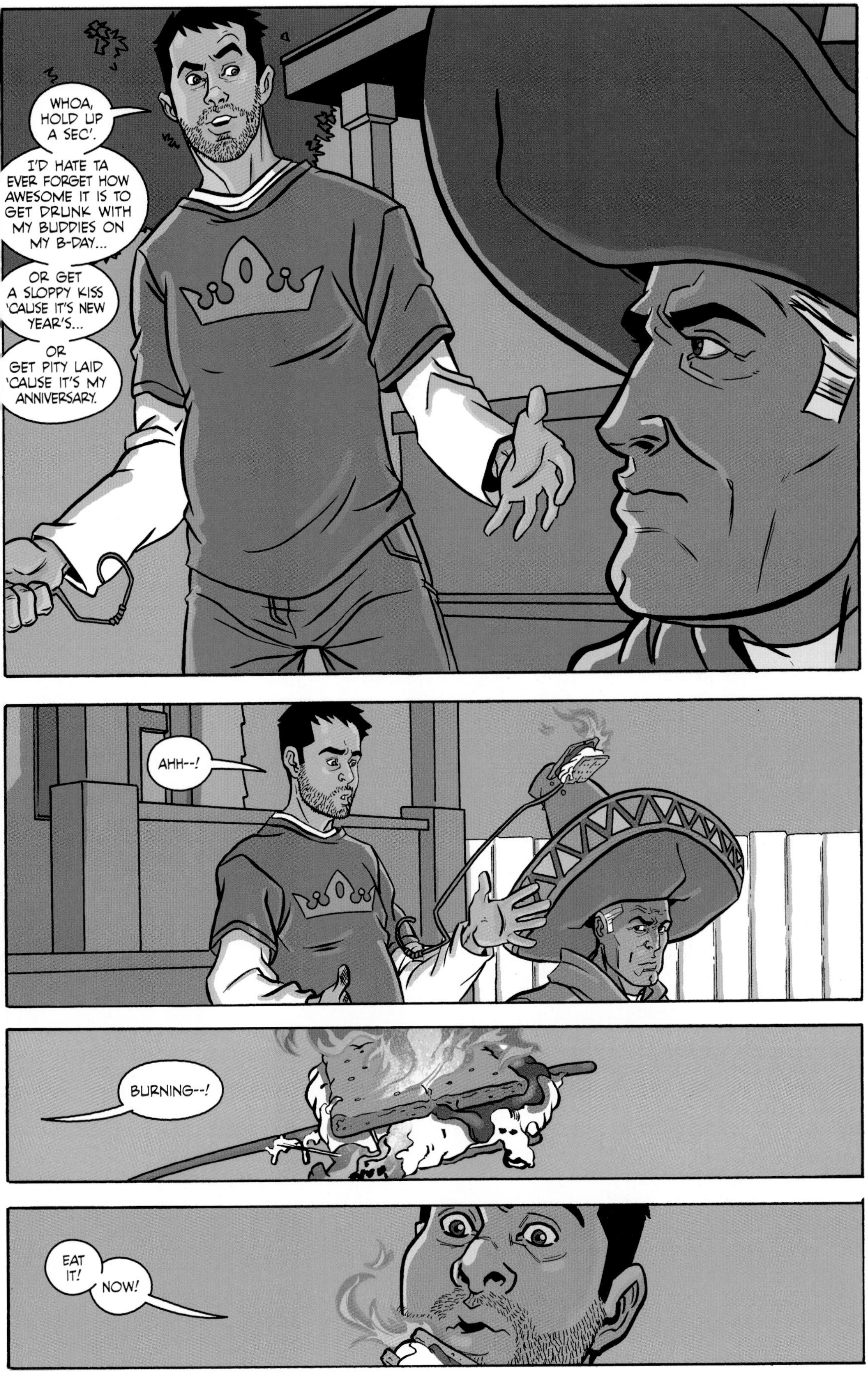

WHOA, HOLD UP A SEC'.
I'D HATE TA EVER FORGET HOW AWESOME IT IS TO GET DRUNK WITH MY BUDDIES ON MY B-DAY...
OR GET A SLOPPY KISS 'CAUSE IT'S NEW YEAR'S...
OR GET PITY LAID 'CAUSE IT'S MY ANNIVERSARY.
AHH--!
BURNING--!
EAT IT!
NOW!

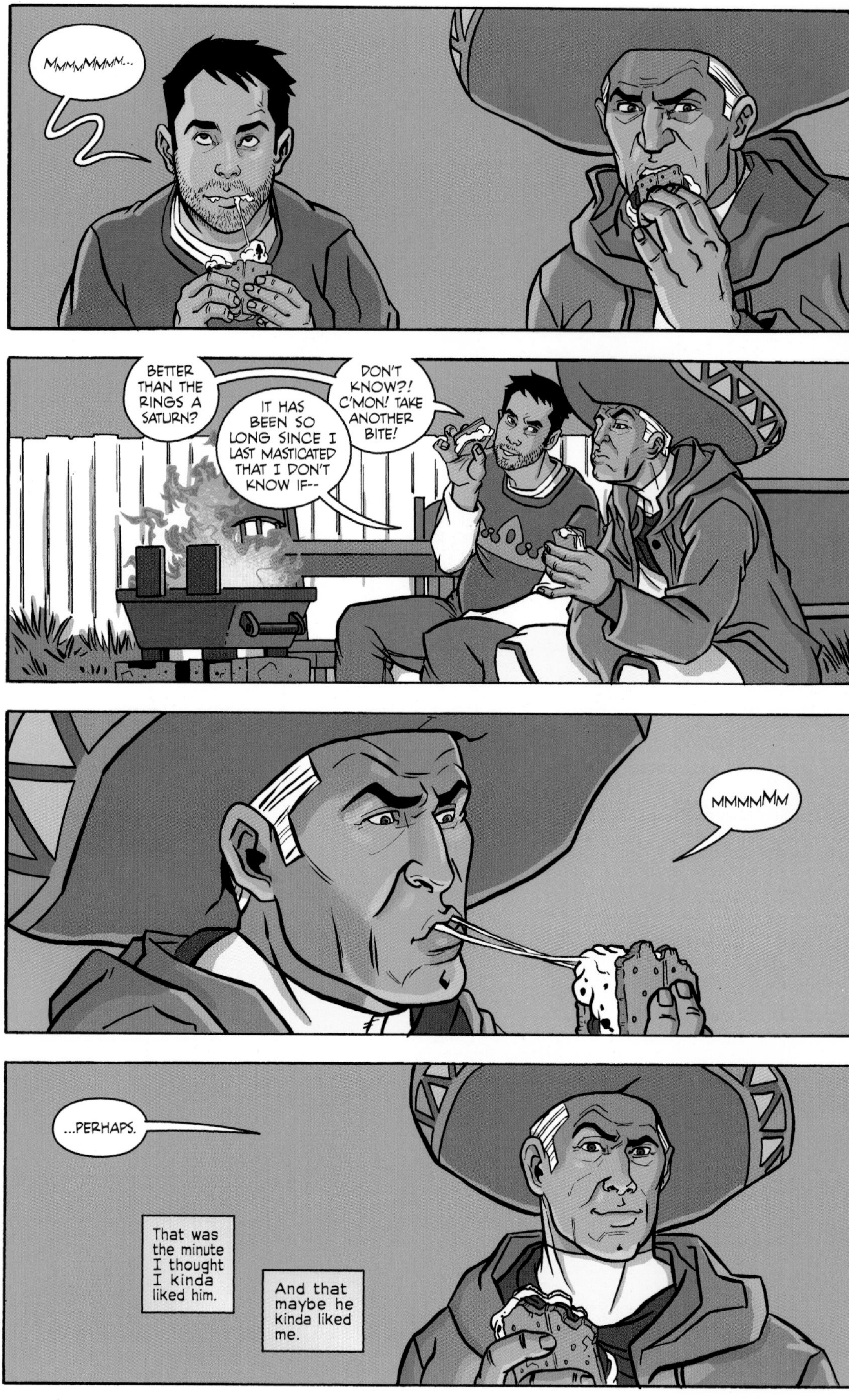
MMMMMMM...
BETTER THAN THE RINGS A SATURN?
IT HAS BEEN SO LONG SINCE I LAST MASTICATED THAT I DON'T KNOW IF--
DON'T KNOW?! C'MON! TAKE ANOTHER BITE!
MMMMMM
...PERHAPS.
That was the minute I thought I kinda liked him.
And that maybe he kinda liked me.

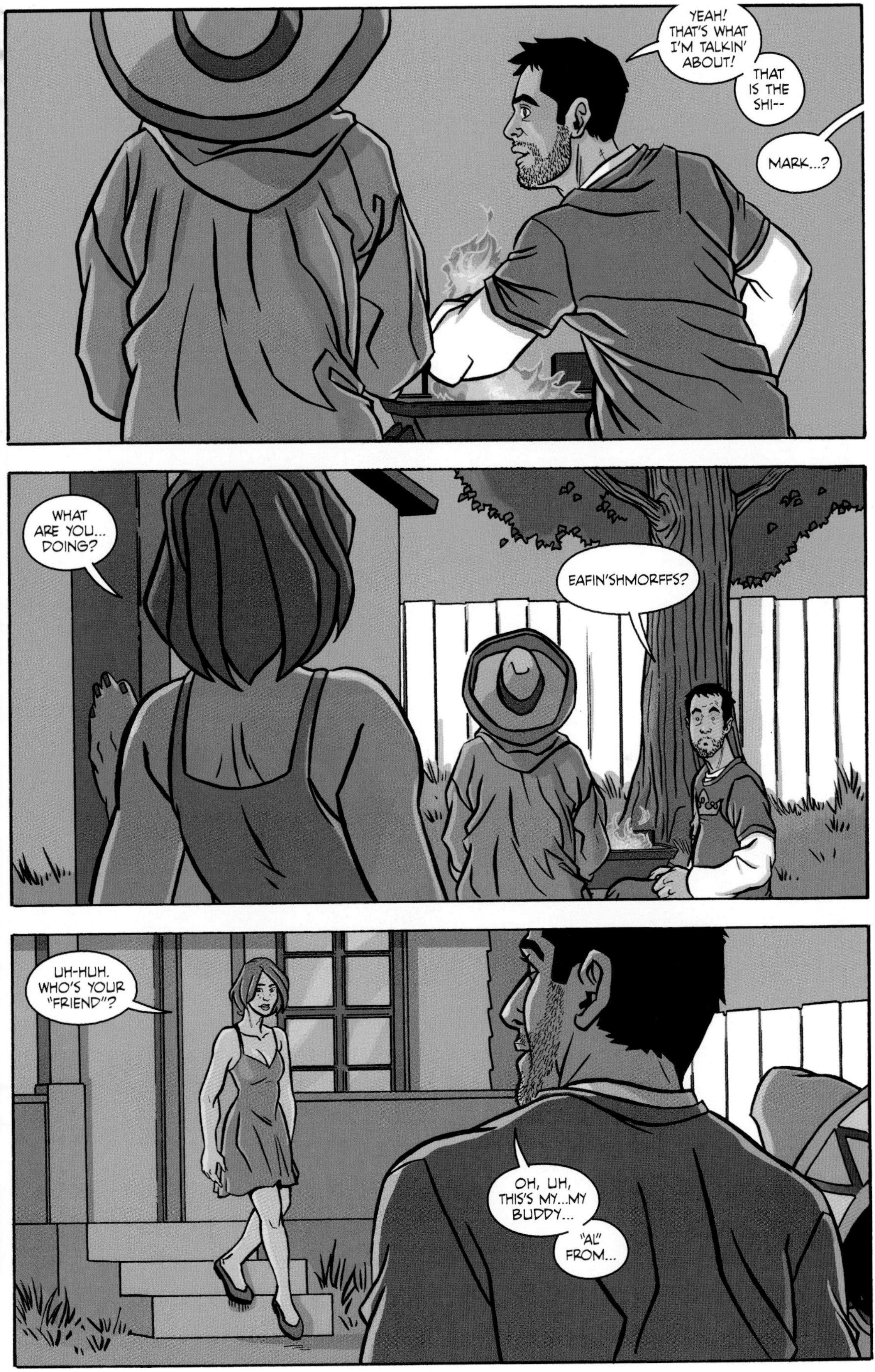
YEAH! THAT'S WHAT I'M TALKIN' ABOUT!
THAT IS THE SHI--
MARK...?
WHAT ARE YOU... DOING?
EAFIN'SHMORFFS?
UH-HUH. WHO'S YOUR "FRIEND"?
OH, UH, THIS'S MY...MY BUDDY...
"AL" FROM...

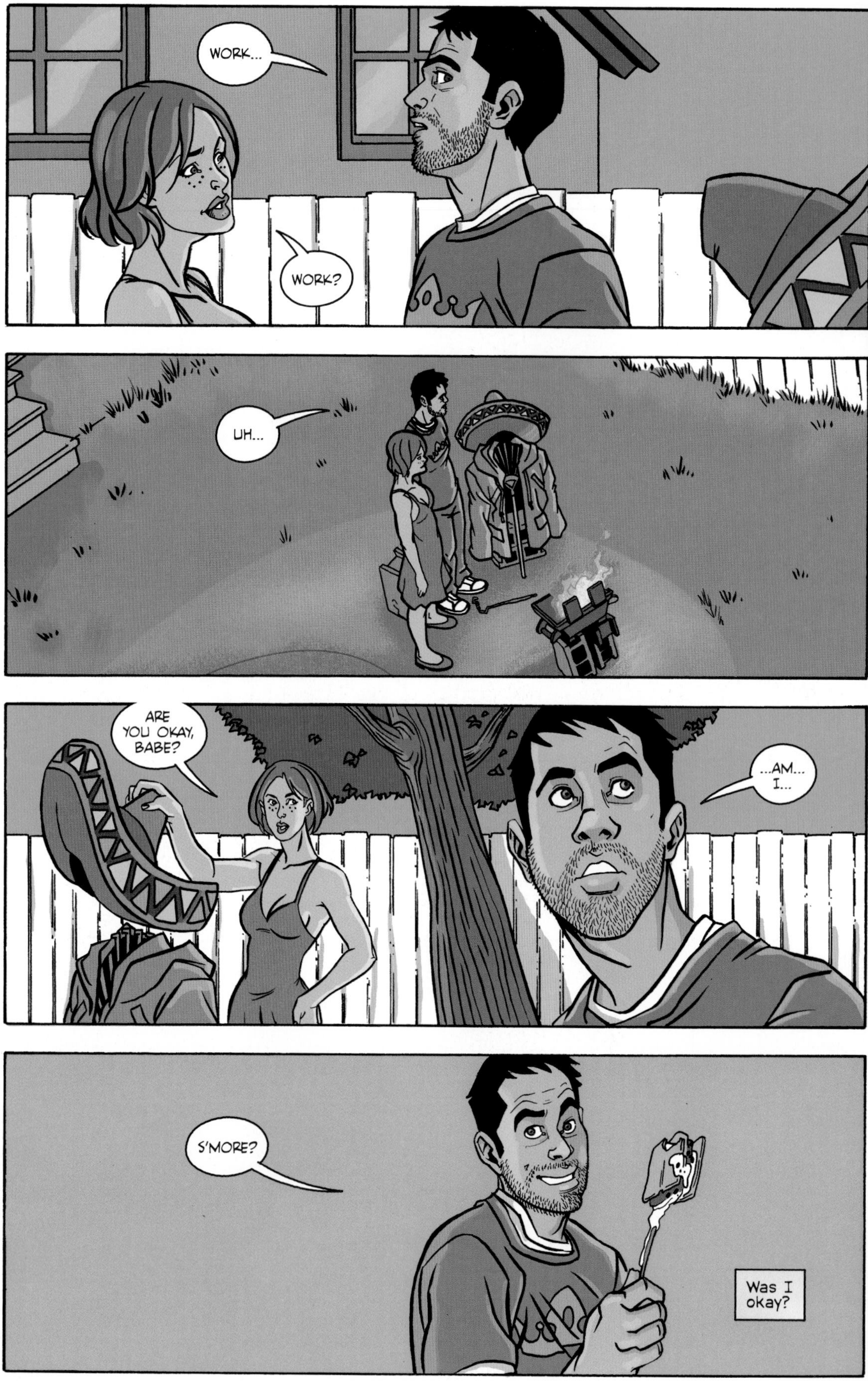
WORK...
WORK?
UH...
ARE YOU OKAY, BABE?
...AM... I...
S'MORE?
Was I okay?

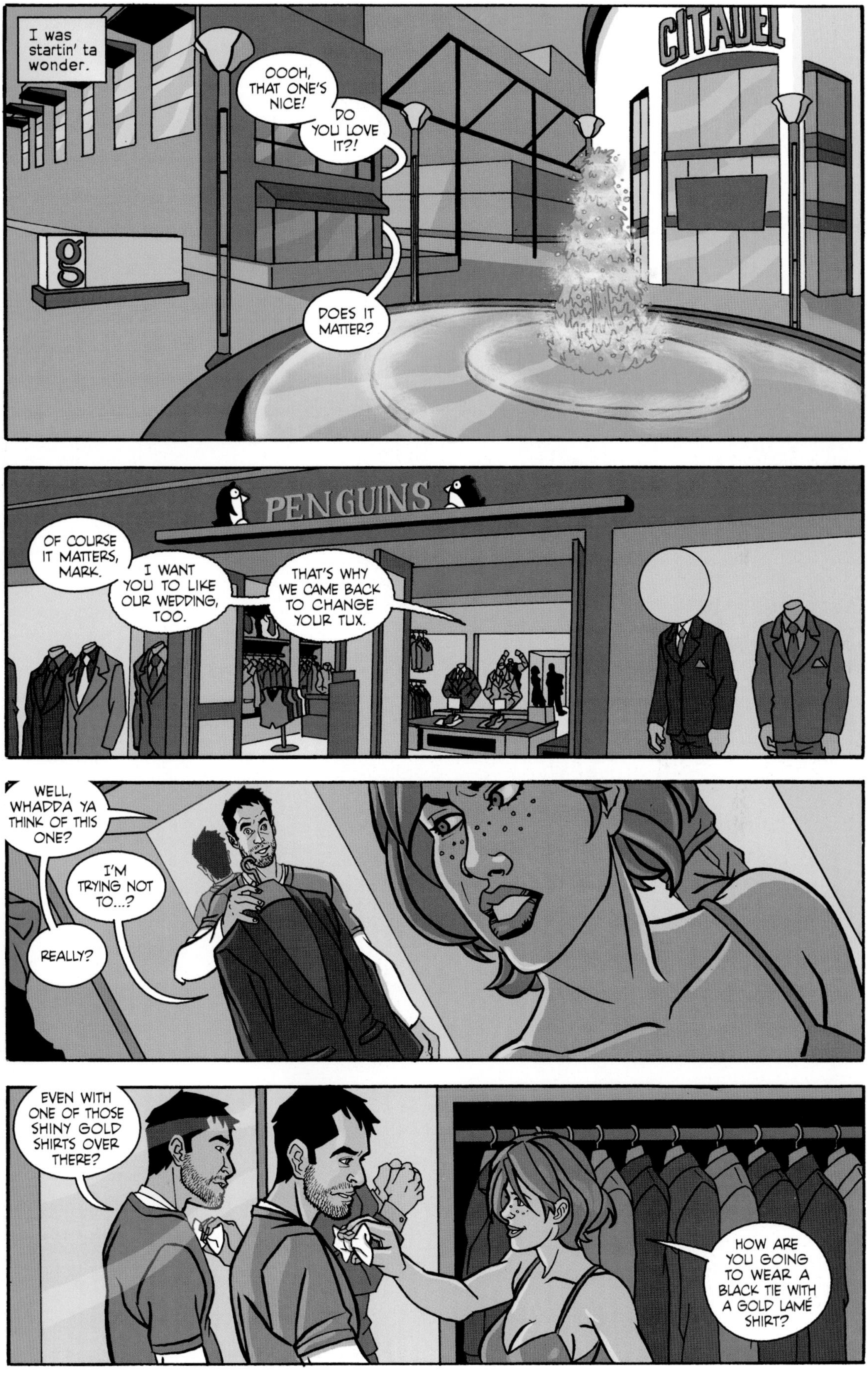
I was startin' ta wonder.
OOOH, THAT ONE'S NICE!
DO YOU LOVE IT?!
DOES IT MATTER?
CITADEL
PENGUINS
OF COURSE IT MATTERS, MARK.
I WANT YOU TO LIKE OUR WEDDING, TOO.
THAT'S WHY WE CAME BACK TO CHANGE YOUR TUX.
WELL, WHADDA YA THINK OF THIS ONE?
I'M TRYING NOT TO...?
REALLY?
EVEN WITH ONE OF THOSE SHINY GOLD SHIRTS OVER THERE?
HOW ARE YOU GOING TO WEAR A BLACK TIE WITH A GOLD LAMÉ SHIRT?

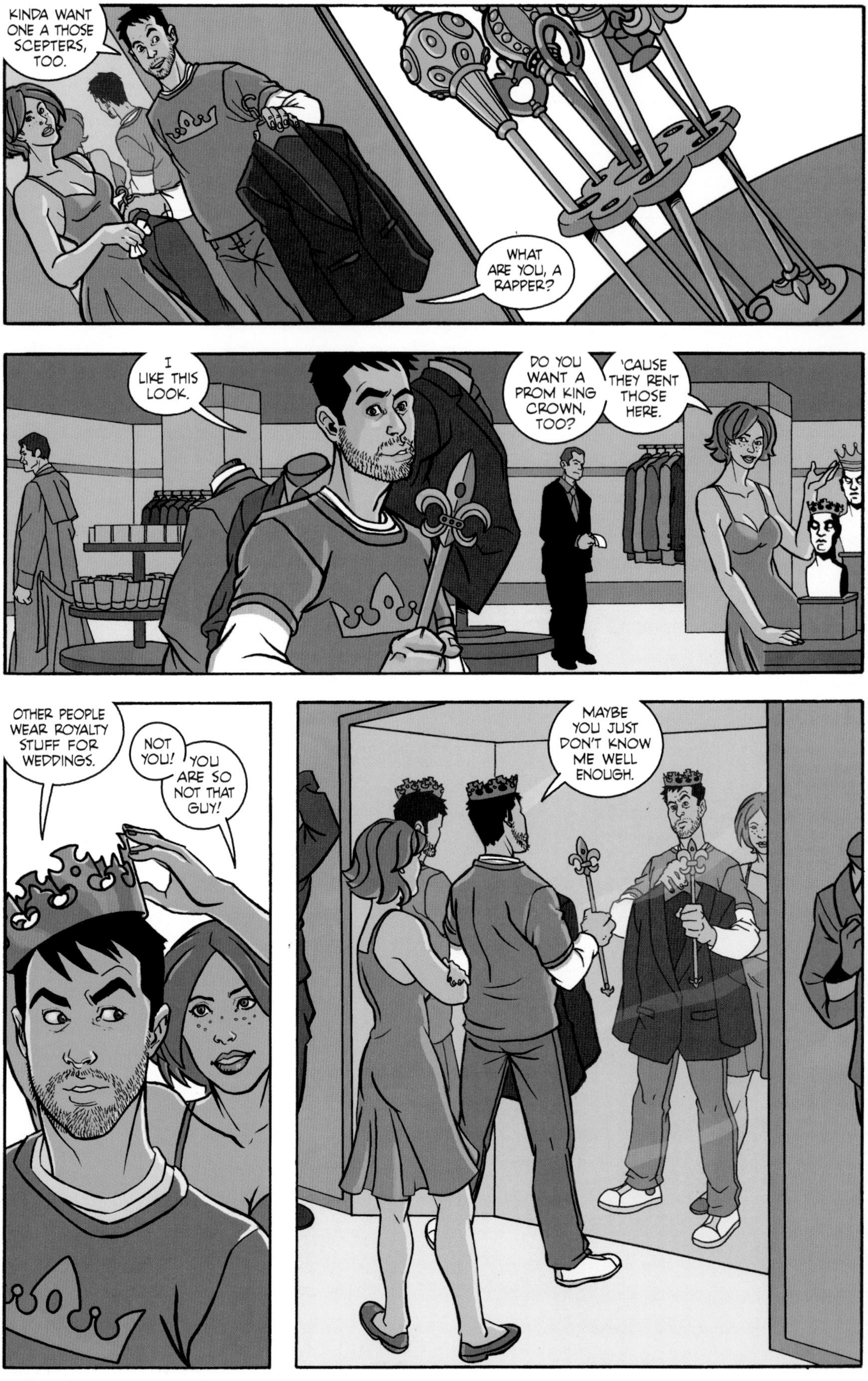
KINDA WANT ONE A THOSE SCEPTERS, TOO.
WHAT ARE YOU, A RAPPER?
I LIKE THIS LOOK.
DO YOU WANT A PROM KING CROWN, TOO?
'CAUSE THEY RENT THOSE HERE.
OTHER PEOPLE WEAR ROYALTY STUFF FOR WEDDINGS.
NOT YOU!
YOU ARE SO NOT THAT GUY!
MAYBE YOU JUST DON'T KNOW ME WELL ENOUGH.

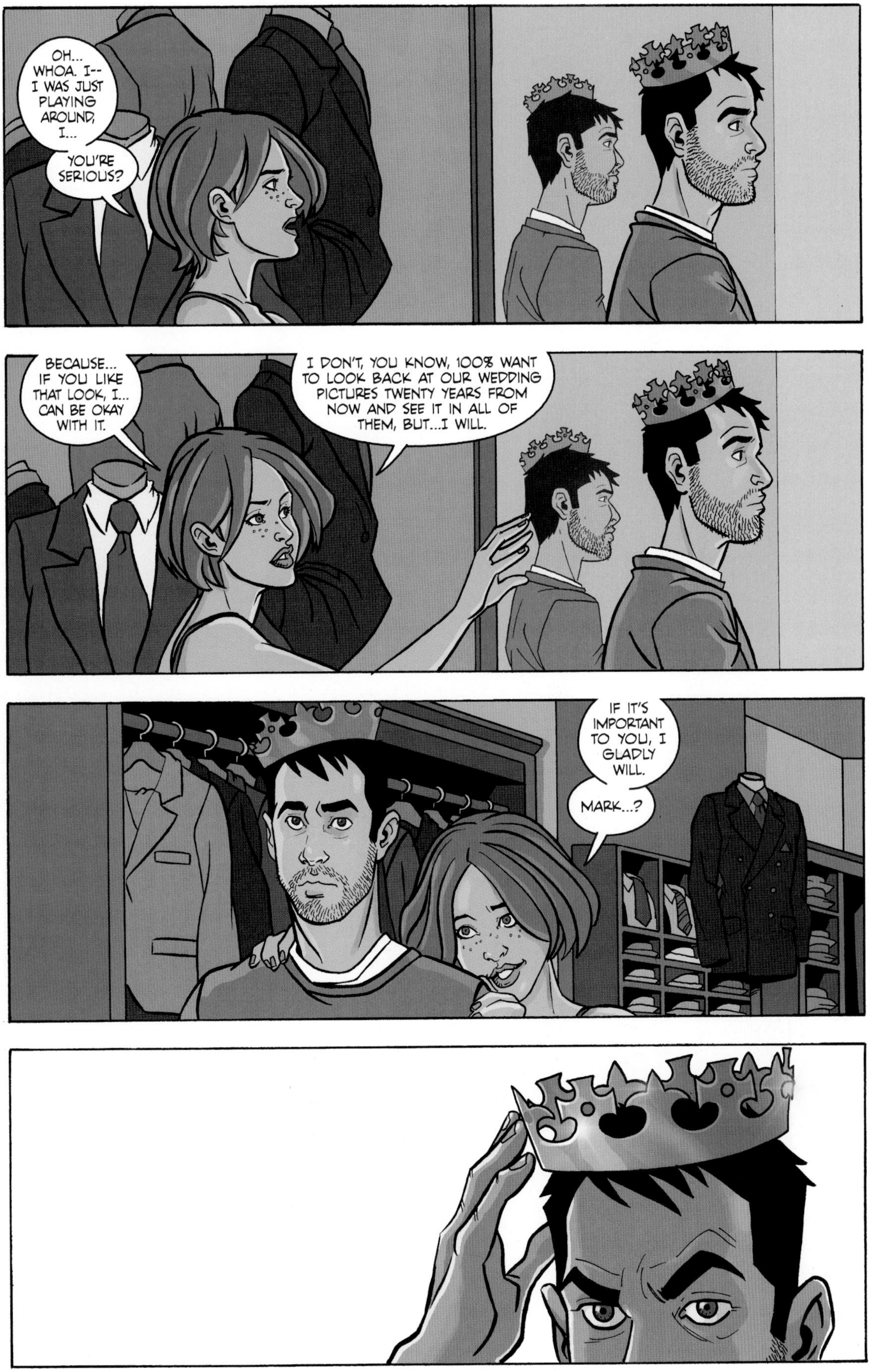
OH... WHOA. I-- I WAS JUST PLAYING AROUND, I...
YOU'RE SERIOUS?
BECAUSE... IF YOU LIKE THAT LOOK, I... CAN BE OKAY WITH IT.
I DON'T, YOU KNOW, 100% WANT TO LOOK BACK AT OUR WEDDING PICTURES TWENTY YEARS FROM NOW AND SEE IT IN ALL OF THEM, BUT...I WILL.
IF IT'S IMPORTANT TO YOU, I GLADLY WILL.
MARK...?

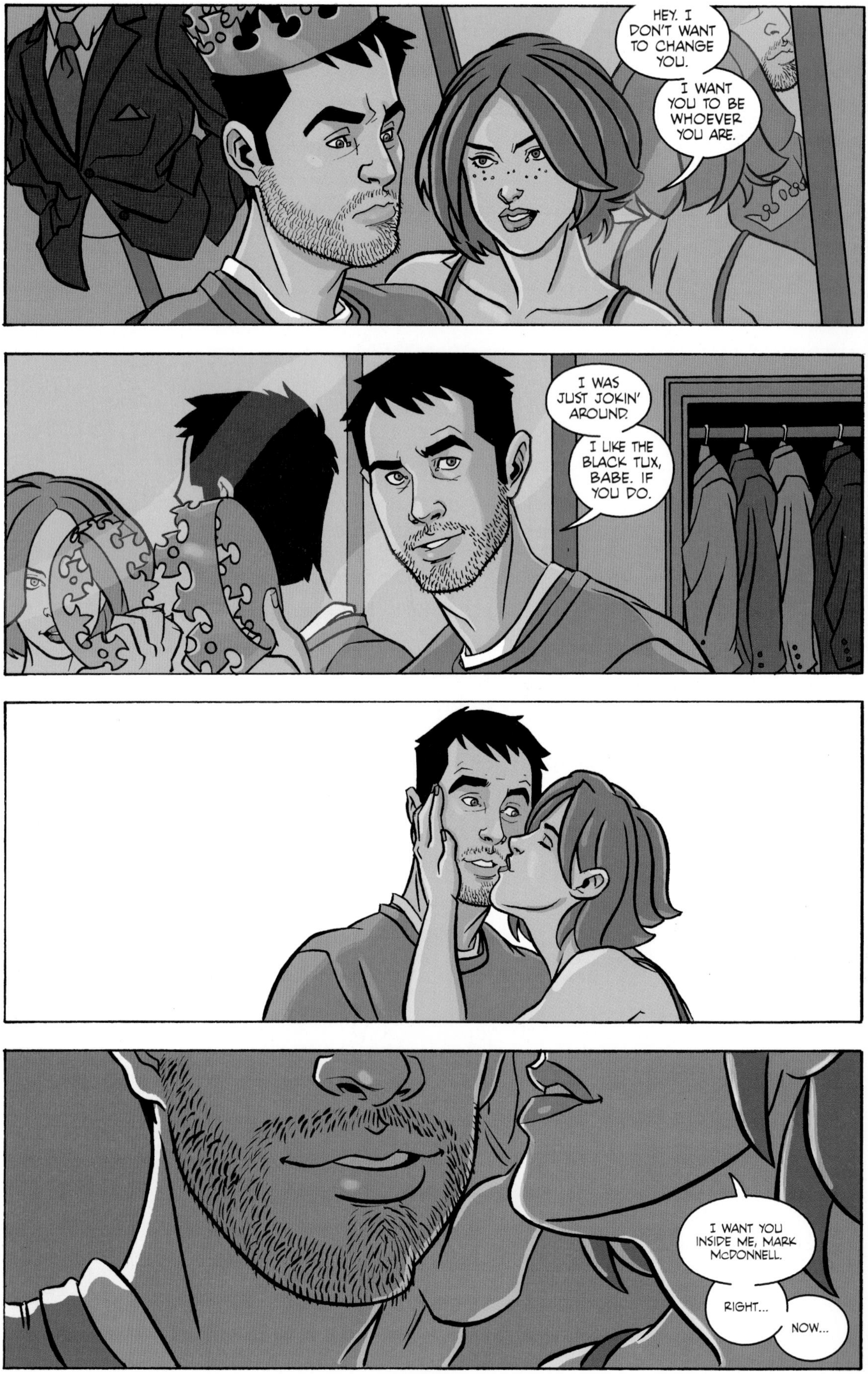
HEY. I DON'T WANT TO CHANGE YOU.
I WANT YOU TO BE WHOEVER YOU ARE.
I WAS JUST JOKIN' AROUND.
I LIKE THE BLACK TUX, BABE. IF YOU DO.
I WANT YOU INSIDE ME, MARK McDONNELL.
RIGHT...
NOW...

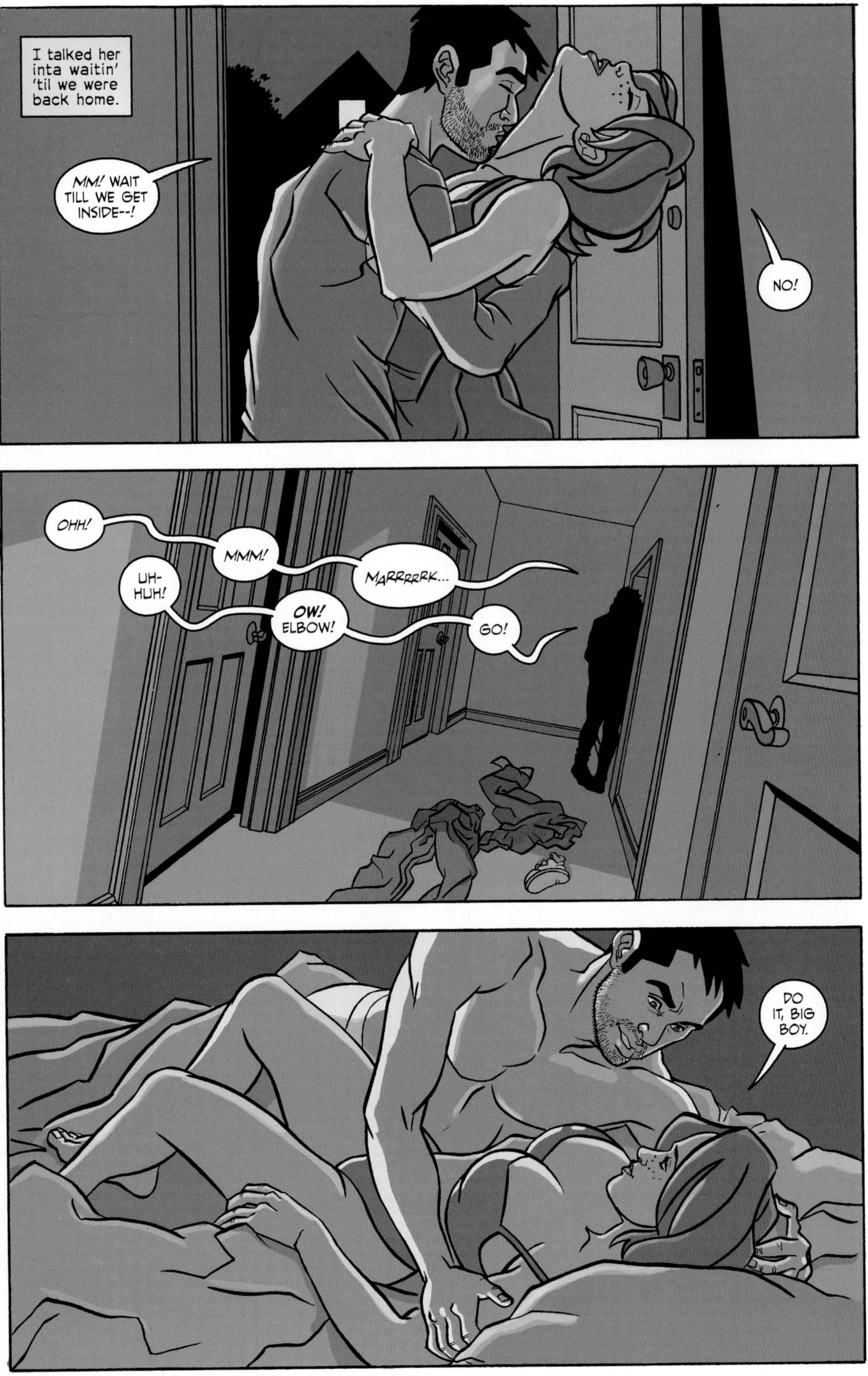
I talked her inta waitin' 'til we were back home.
MM! WAIT TILL WE GET INSIDE--!
NO!
OHH!
MMM!
MARRRRRK...
UH-HUH!
OW! ELBOW!
GO!
DO IT, BIG BOY.

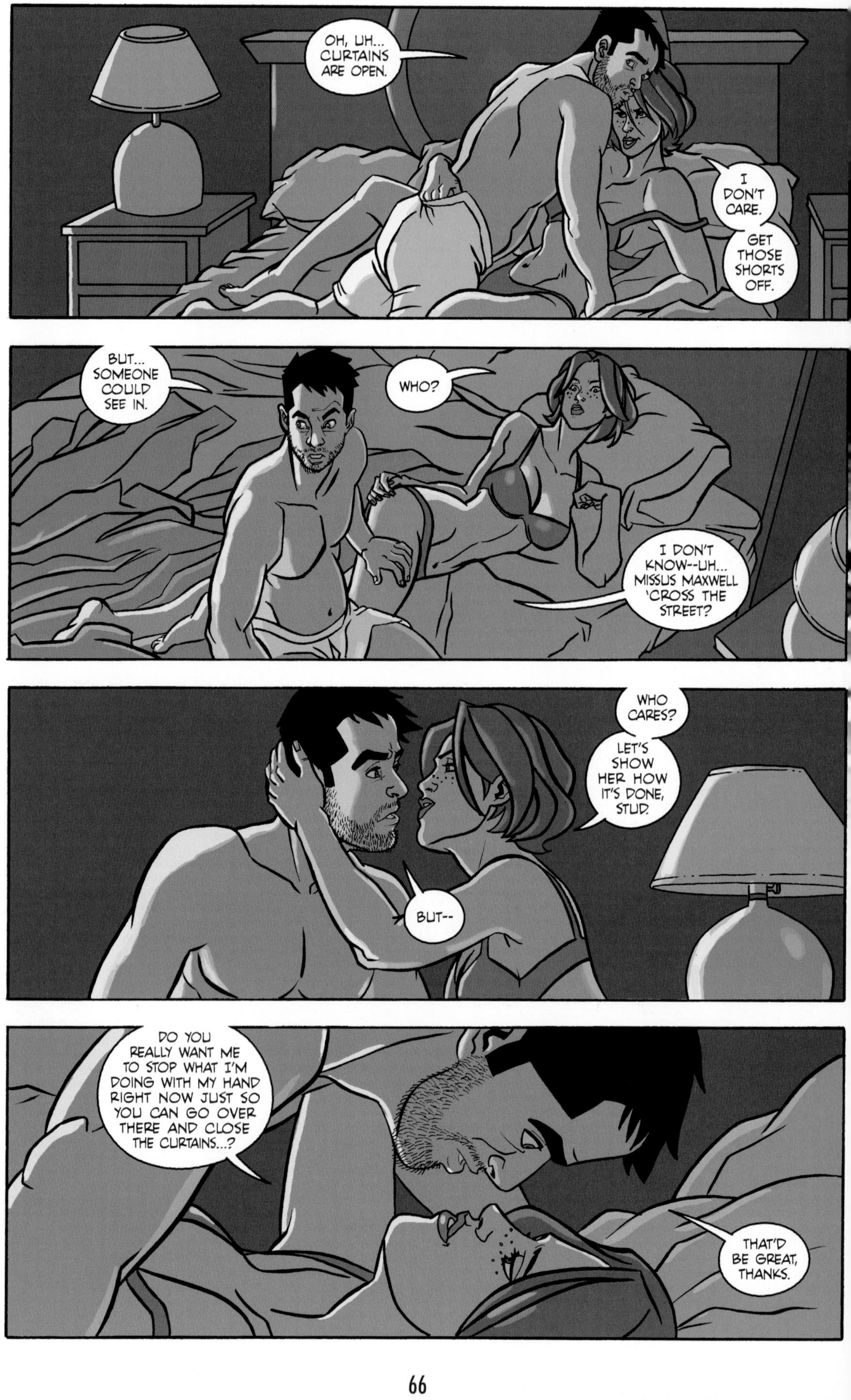
OH, UH... CURTAINS ARE OPEN.
I DON'T CARE.
GET THOSE SHORTS OFF.
BUT... SOMEONE COULD SEE IN.
WHO?
I DON'T KNOW--UH... MISSUS MAXWELL 'CROSS THE STREET?
WHO CARES?
LET'S SHOW HER HOW IT'S DONE, STUD.
BUT--
DO YOU REALLY WANT ME TO STOP WHAT I'M DOING WITH MY HAND RIGHT NOW JUST SO YOU CAN GO OVER THERE AND CLOSE THE CURTAINS...?
THAT'D BE GREAT, THANKS.

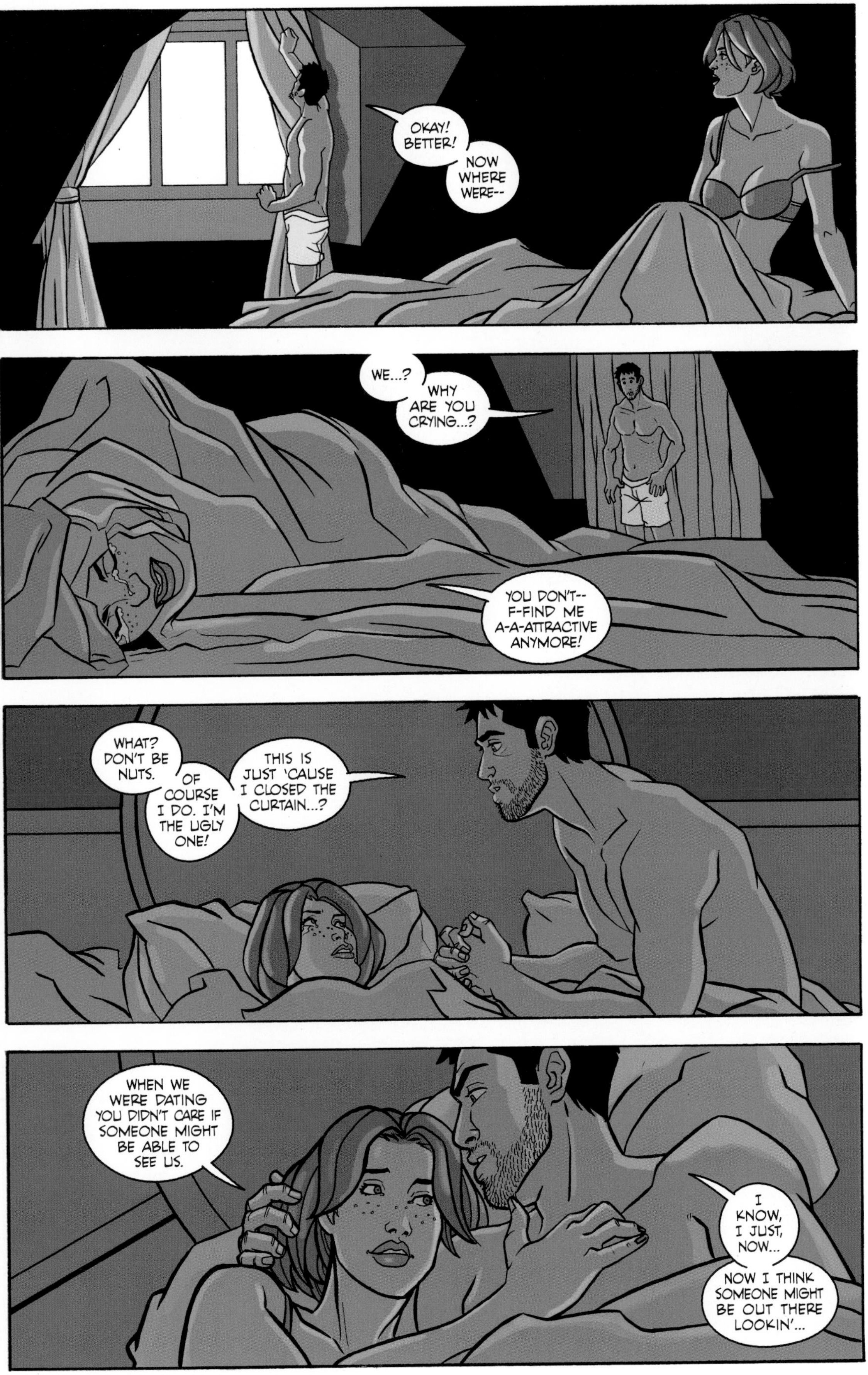
OKAY! BETTER!
NOW WHERE WERE--
WE...?
WHY ARE YOU CRYING...?
YOU DON'T-- F-FIND ME A-A-ATTRACTIVE ANYMORE!
WHAT? DON'T BE NUTS.
OF COURSE I DO. I'M THE UGLY ONE!
THIS IS JUST 'CAUSE I CLOSED THE CURTAIN...?
WHEN WE WERE DATING YOU DIDN'T CARE IF SOMEONE MIGHT BE ABLE TO SEE US.
I KNOW, I JUST, NOW...
NOW I THINK SOMEONE MIGHT BE OUT THERE LOOKIN'...

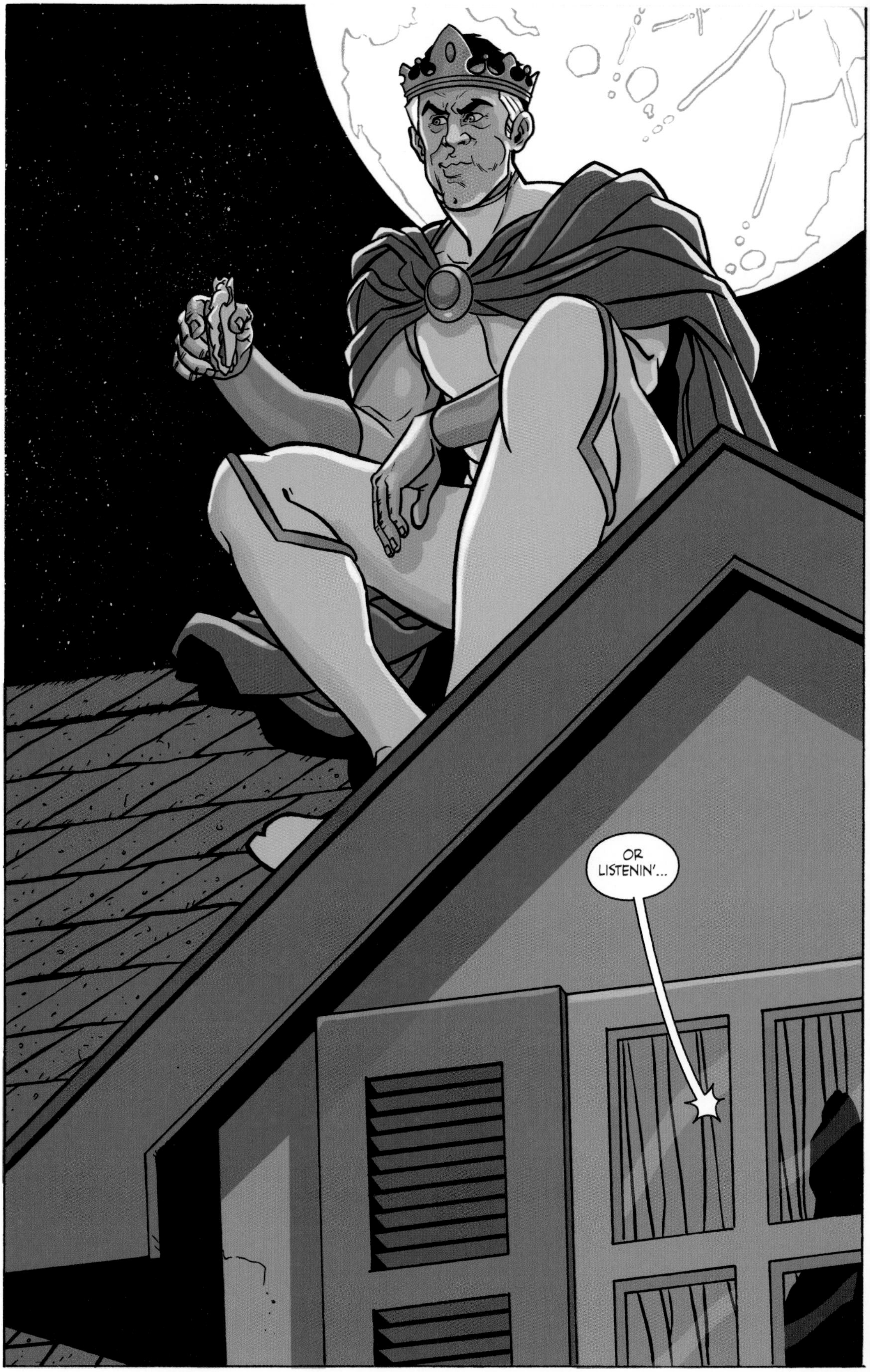
OR LISTENIN'...

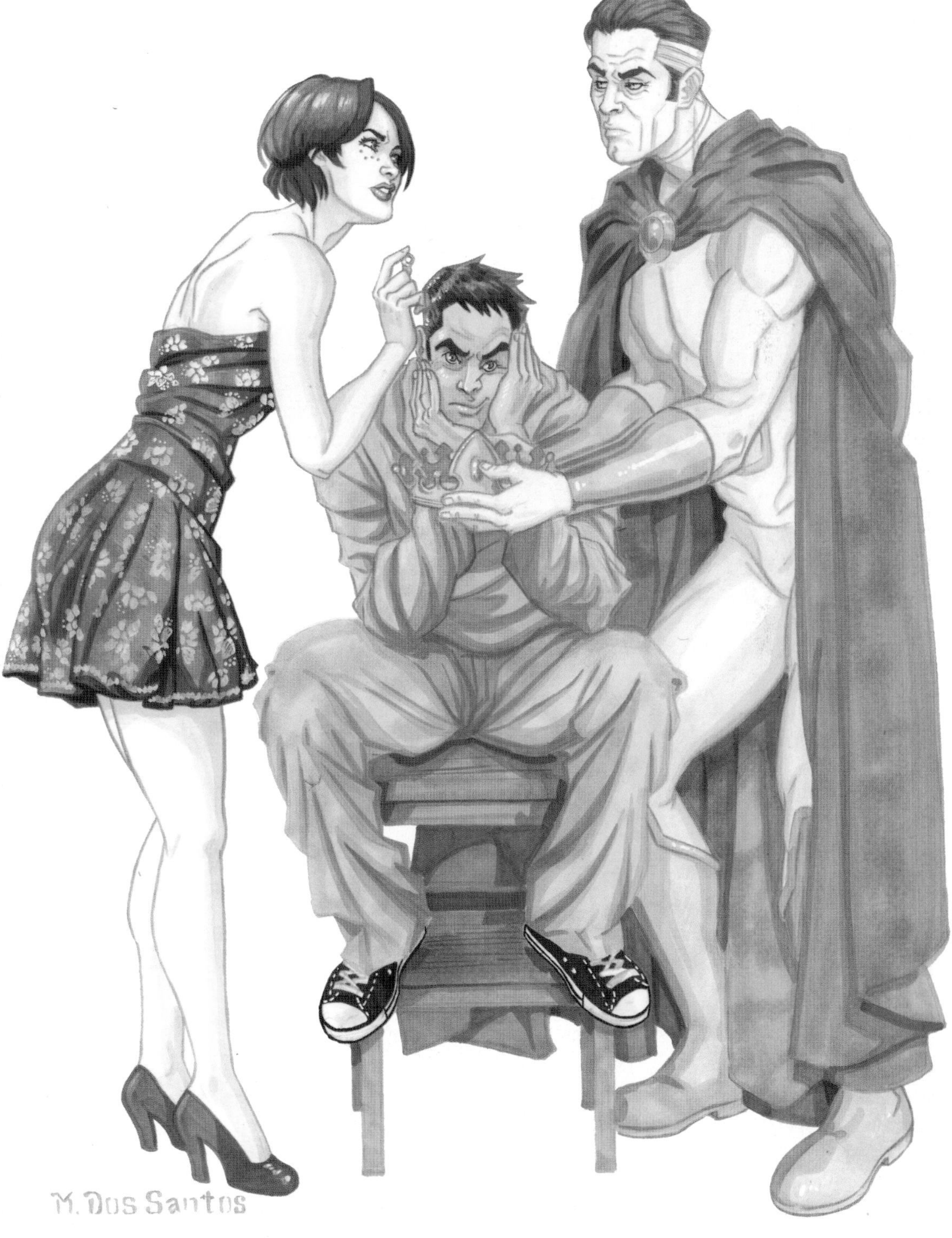
M. Dos Santos

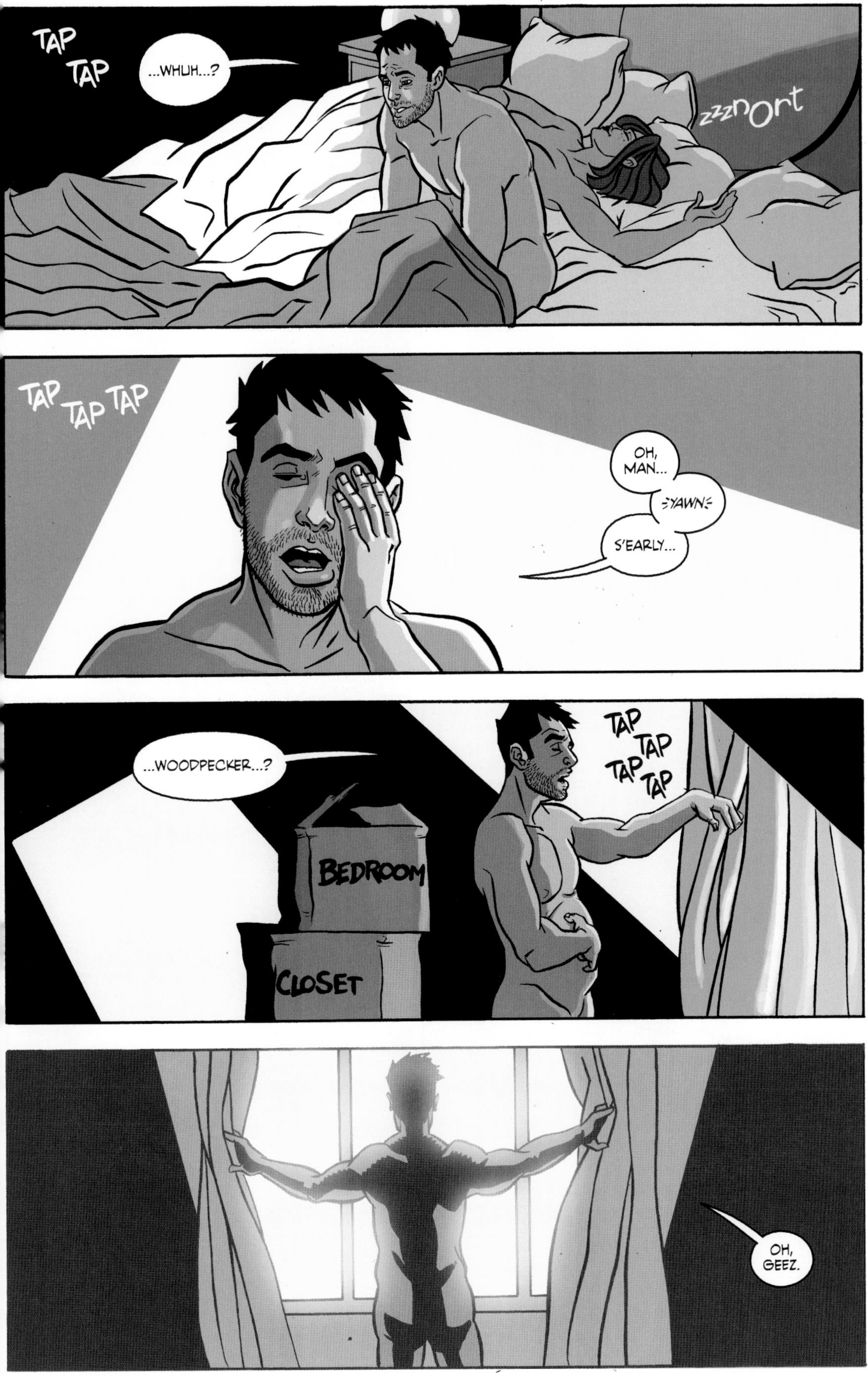
TAP
TAP
...WHUH...?
zzznOrt
TAP TAP TAP
OH, MAN...
YAWN
S'EARLY...
...WOODPECKER...?
TAP TAP TAP TAP
BEDROOM
CLOSET
OH, GEEZ.

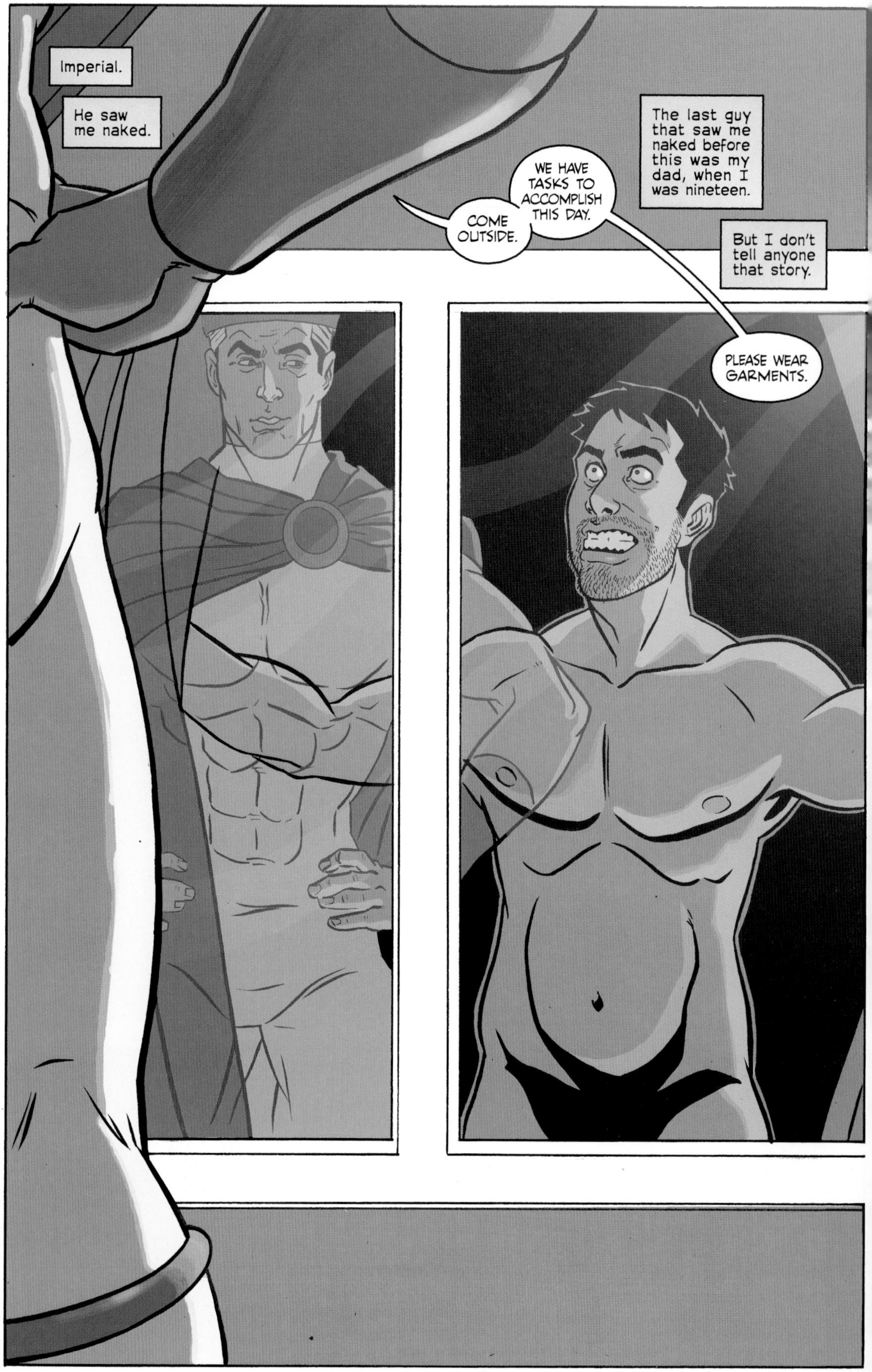
Imperial.
He saw me naked.
The last guy that saw me naked before this was my dad, when I was nineteen.
WE HAVE TASKS TO ACCOMPLISH THIS DAY.
COME OUTSIDE.
But I don't tell anyone that story.
PLEASE WEAR GARMENTS.

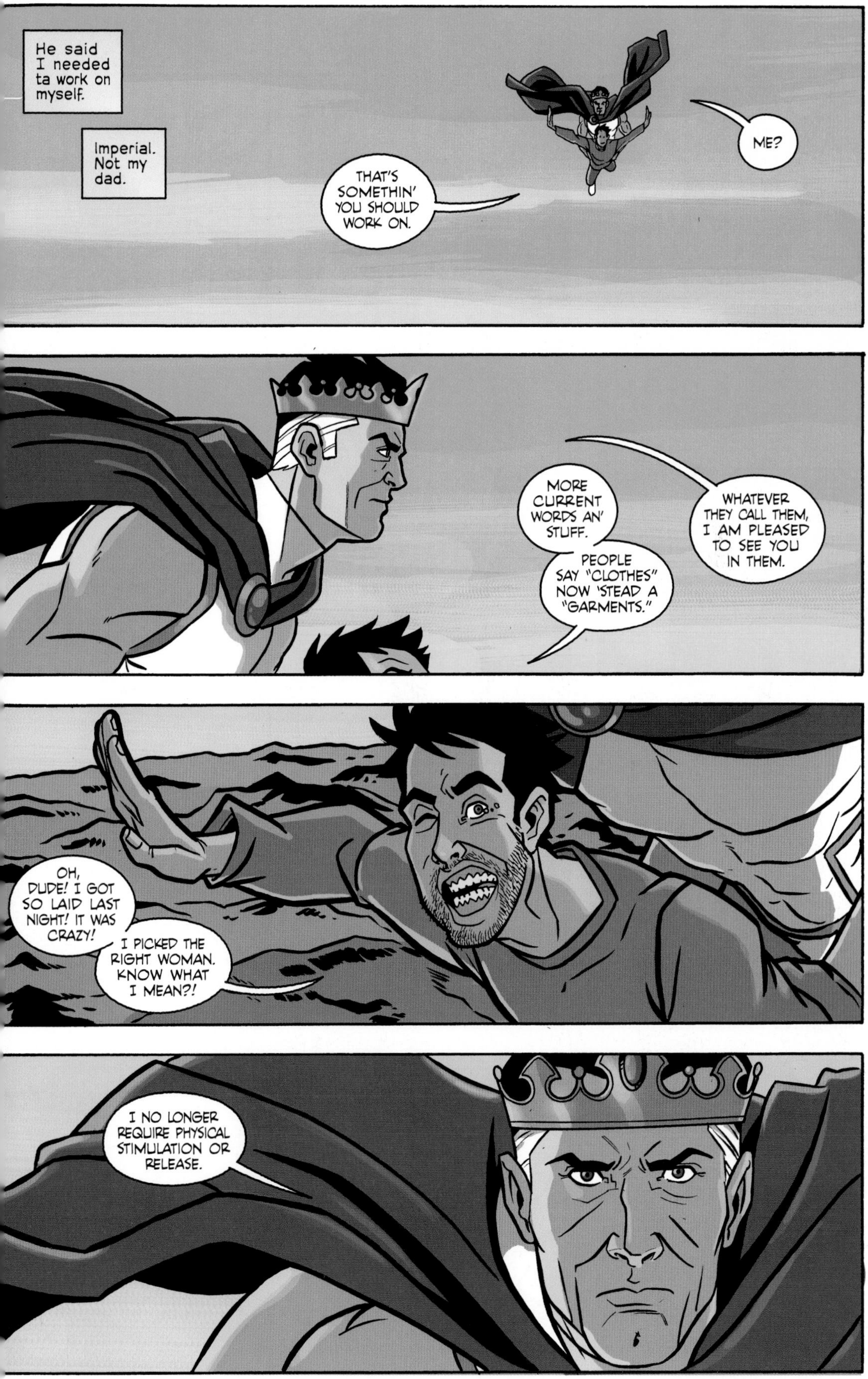

He said I needed ta work on myself.
Imperial. Not my dad.
ME?
THAT'S SOMETHIN' YOU SHOULD WORK ON.
MORE CURRENT WORDS AN' STUFF.
PEOPLE SAY "CLOTHES" NOW 'STEAD A "GARMENTS."
WHATEVER THEY CALL THEM, I AM PLEASED TO SEE YOU IN THEM.
OH, DUDE! I GOT SO LAID LAST NIGHT! IT WAS CRAZY!
I PICKED THE RIGHT WOMAN. KNOW WHAT I MEAN?!
I NO LONGER REQUIRE PHYSICAL STIMULATION OR RELEASE.

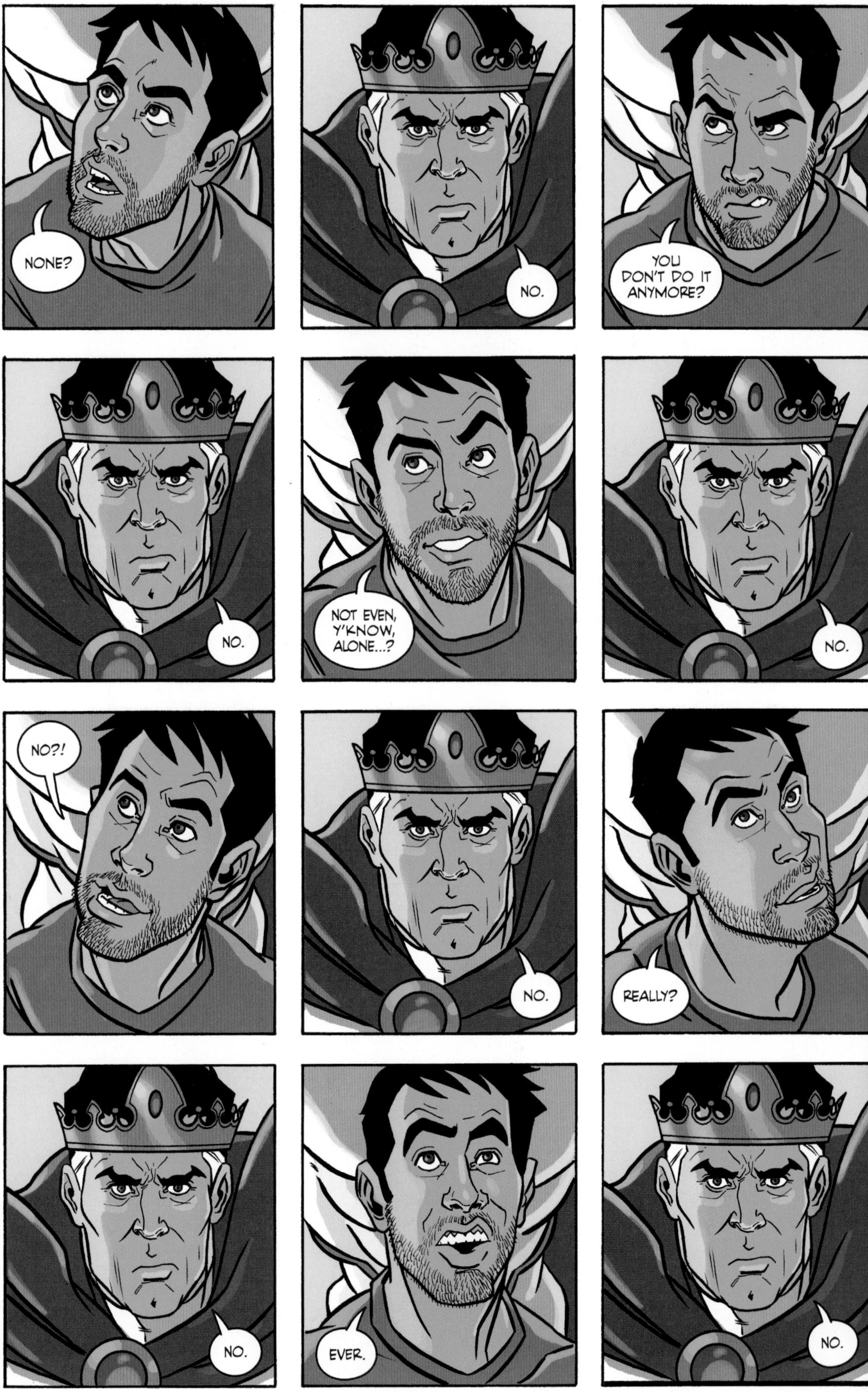
NONE?
NO.
YOU DON'T DO IT ANYMORE?
NO.
NOT EVEN, Y'KNOW, ALONE...?
NO.
NO?!
NO.
REALLY?
NO.
EVER.
NO.

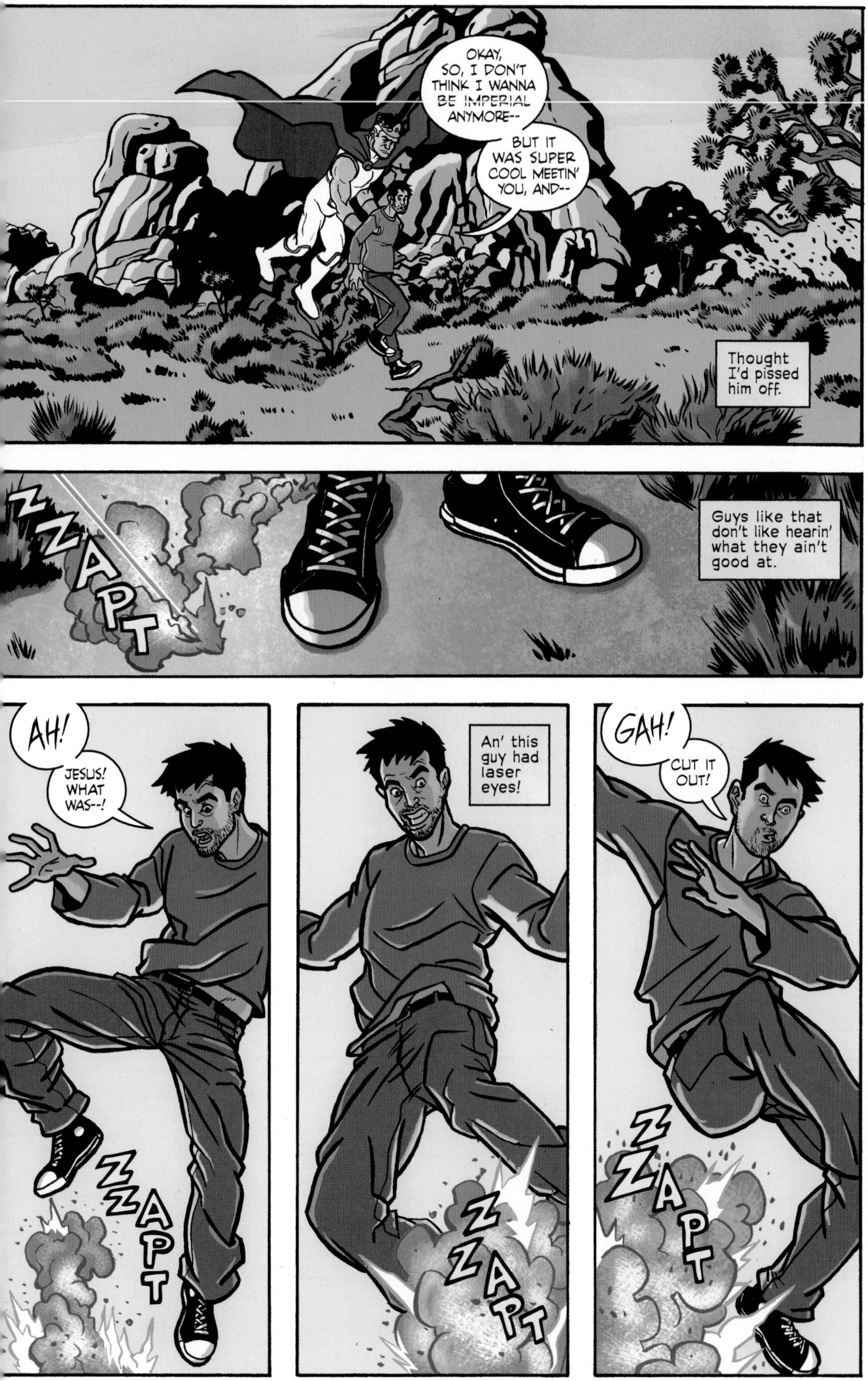
OKAY, SO, I DON'T THINK I WANNA BE IMPERIAL ANYMORE--
BUT IT WAS SUPER COOL MEETIN' YOU, AND--
Thought I'd pissed him off.
ZZAPT
Guys like that don't like hearin' what they ain't good at.
AH!
JESUS! WHAT WAS--!
ZZAPT
An' this guy had laser eyes!
ZZAPT
GAH!
CUT IT OUT!
ZZAPT

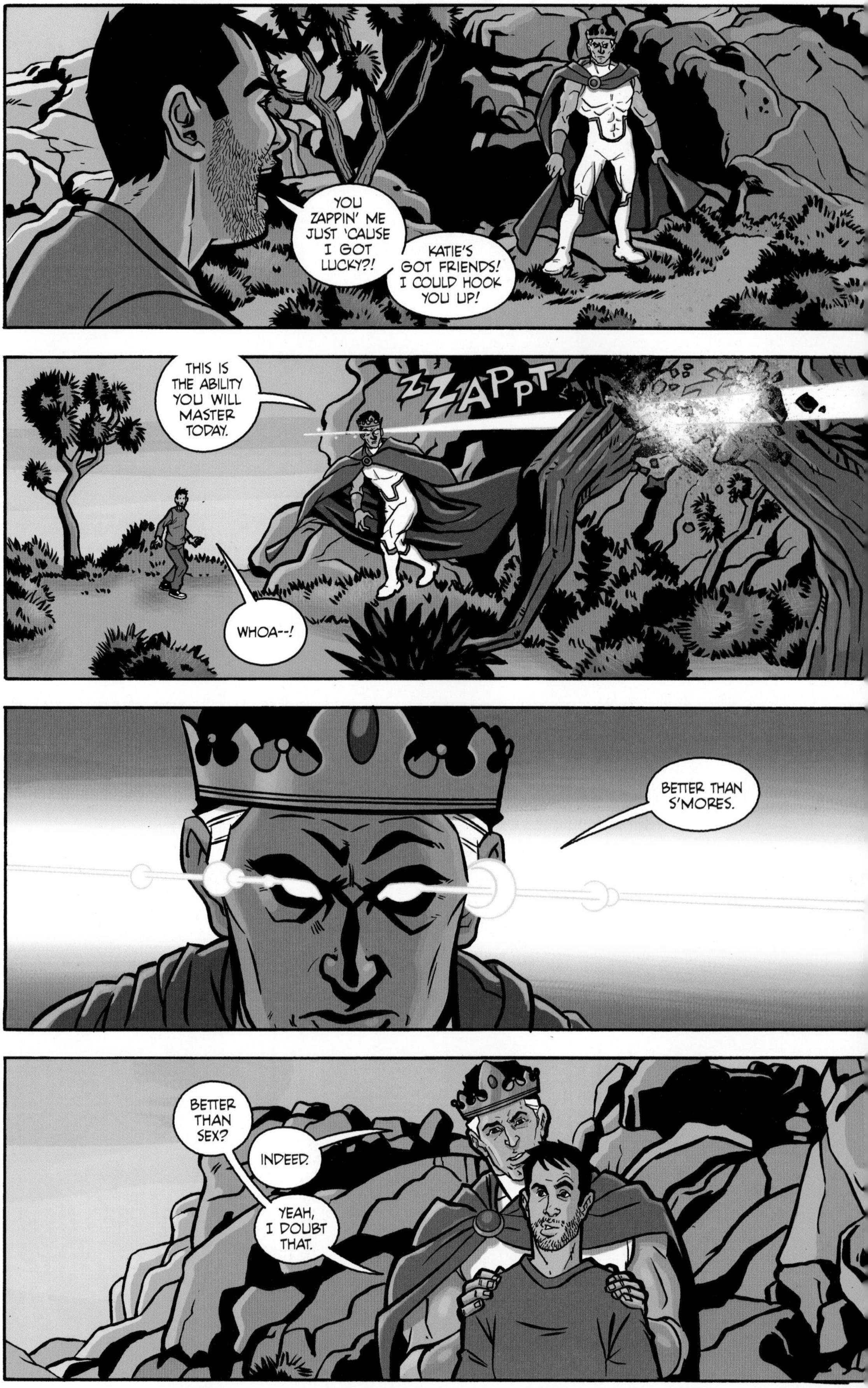
YOU ZAPPIN' ME JUST 'CAUSE I GOT LUCKY?!
KATIE'S GOT FRIENDS! I COULD HOOK YOU UP!
THIS IS THE ABILITY YOU WILL MASTER TODAY.
ZZAPPT
WHOA--!
BETTER THAN S'MORES.
BETTER THAN SEX?
INDEED.
YEAH, I DOUBT THAT.

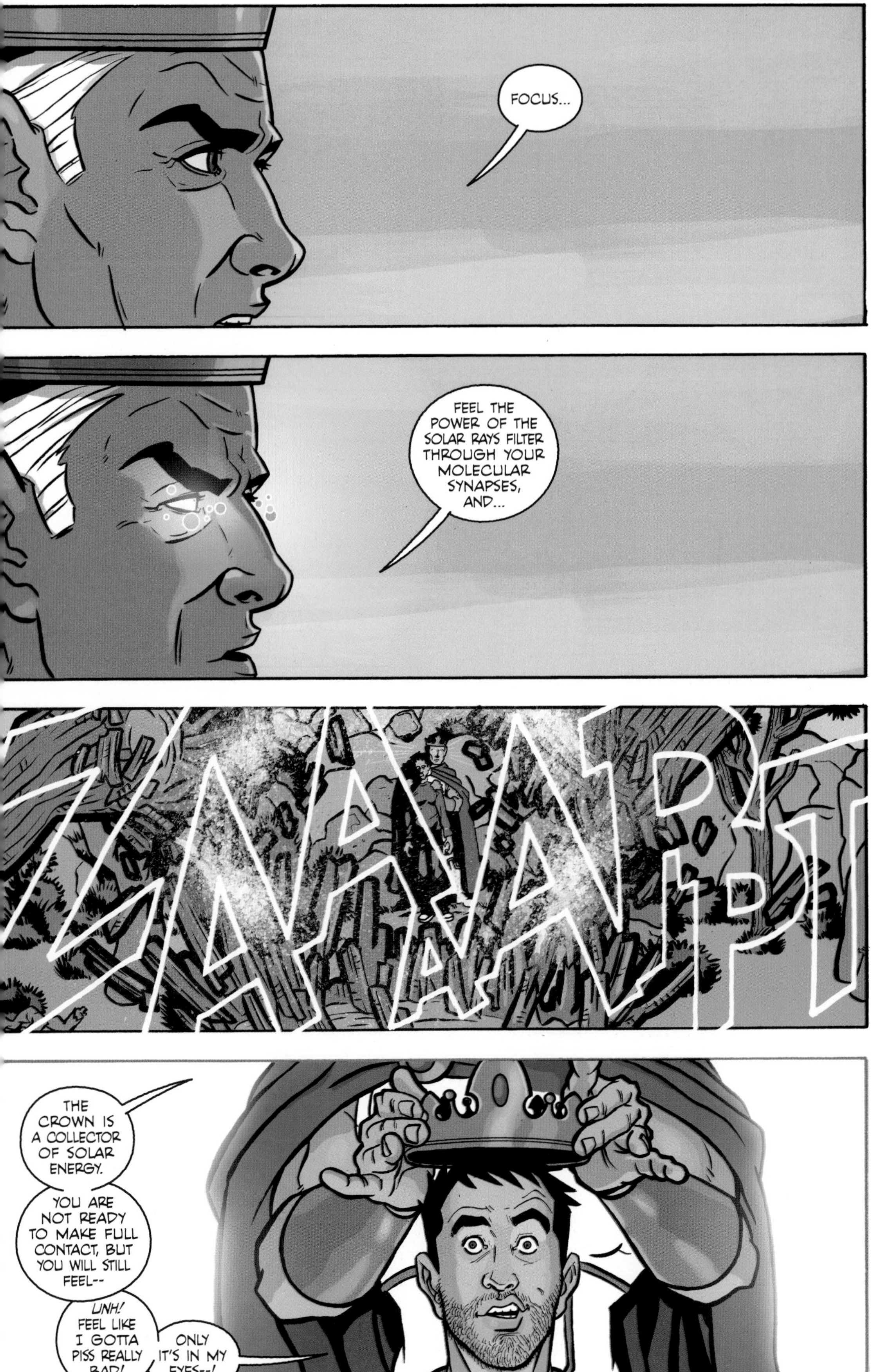
FOCUS...
FEEL THE POWER OF THE SOLAR RAYS FILTER THROUGH YOUR MOLECULAR SYNAPSES, AND...
ZAAAP!
THE CROWN IS A COLLECTOR OF SOLAR ENERGY.
YOU ARE NOT READY TO MAKE FULL CONTACT, BUT YOU WILL STILL FEEL--
UNH! FEEL LIKE I GOTTA PISS REALLY BAD!
ONLY IT'S IN MY EYES--!

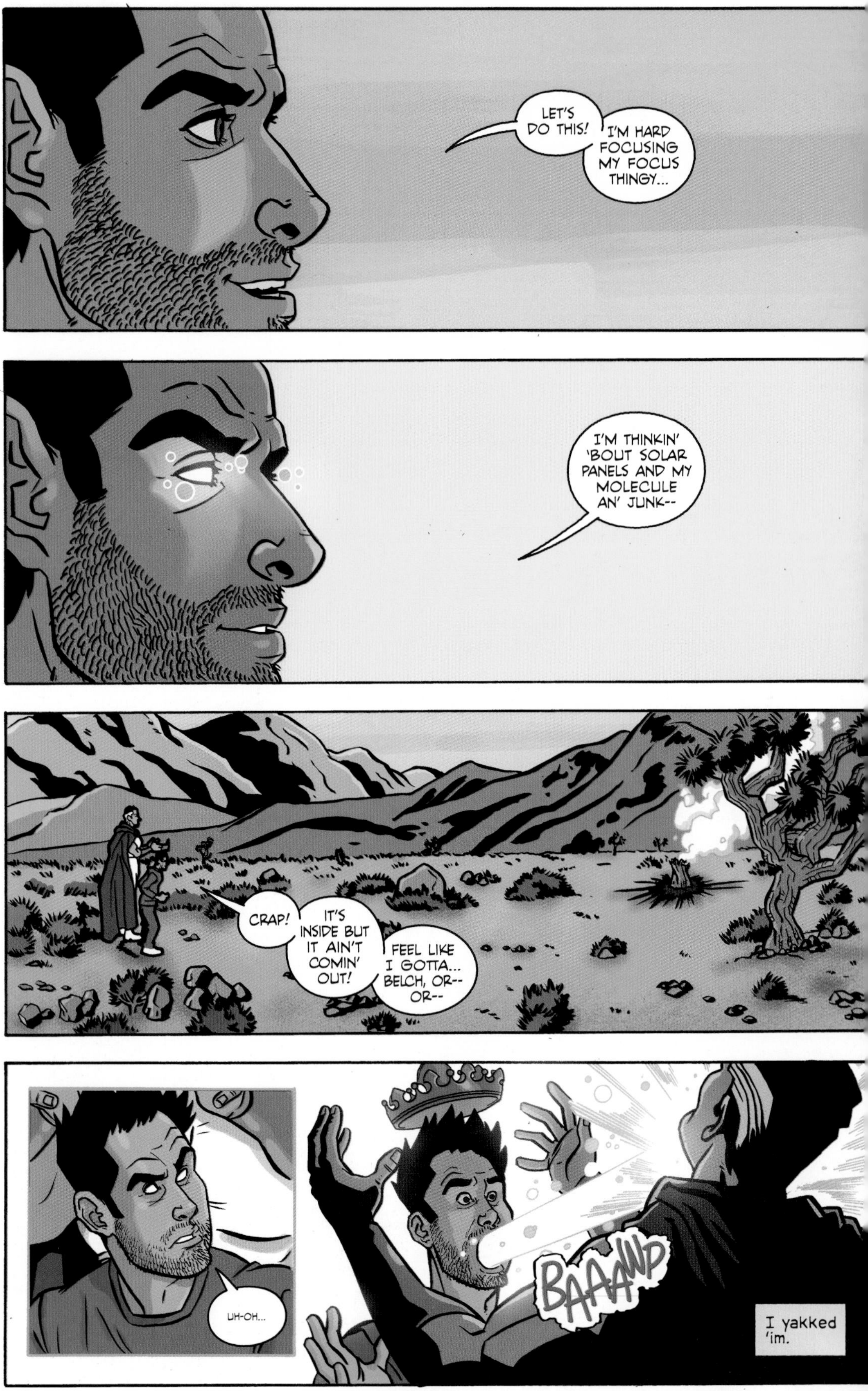
LET'S DO THIS!
I'M HARD FOCUSING MY FOCUS THINGY...
I'M THINKIN' 'BOUT SOLAR PANELS AN' MY MOLECULE AN' JUNK--
CRAP!
IT'S INSIDE BUT IT AIN'T COMIN' OUT!
FEEL LIKE I GOTTA... BELCH, OR-- OR--
UH-OH...
BAAAWP
I yakked 'im.

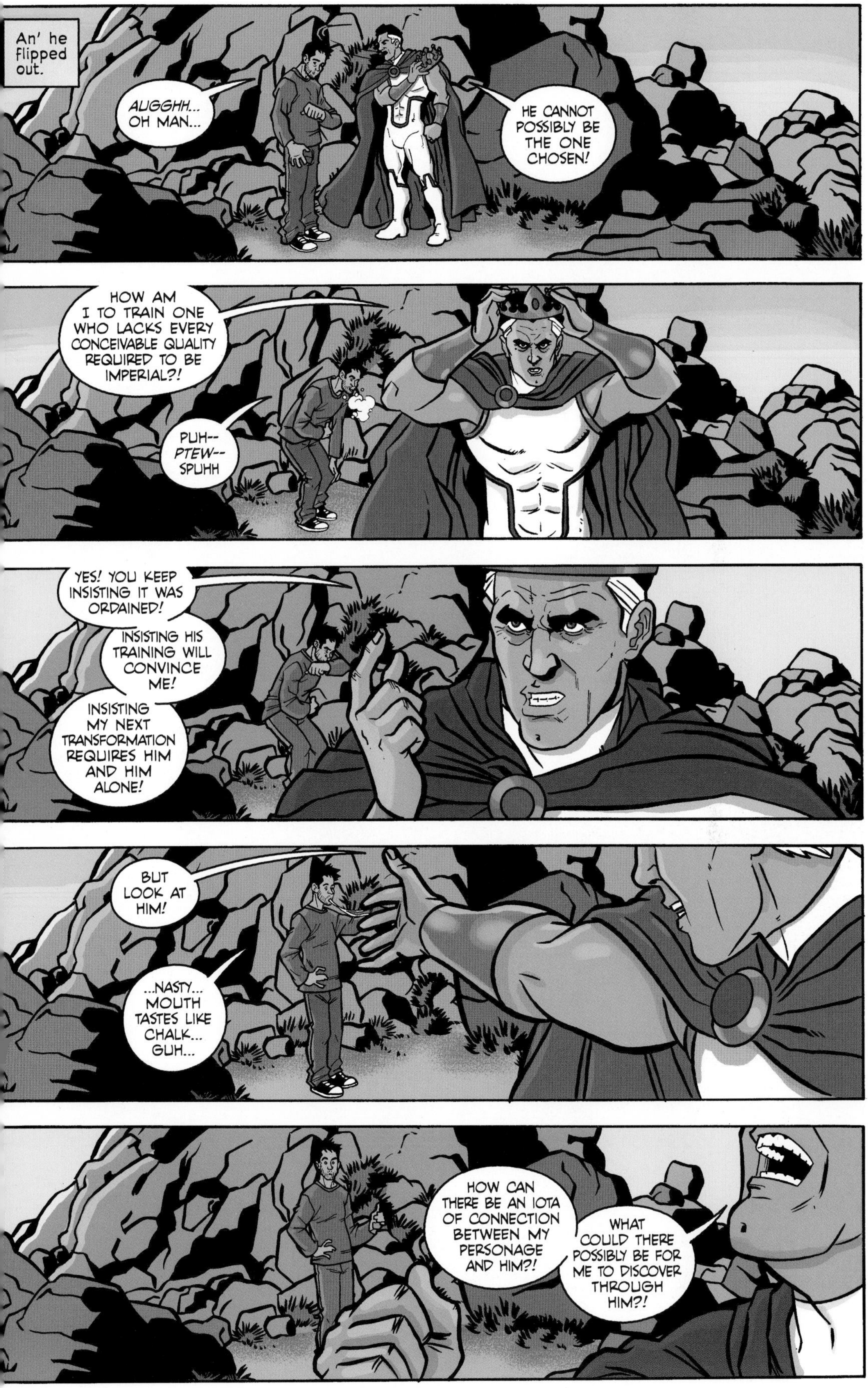
An' he flipped out.
AUGGHH... OH MAN...
HE CANNOT POSSIBLY BE THE ONE CHOSEN!
HOW AM I TO TRAIN ONE WHO LACKS EVERY CONCEIVABLE QUALITY REQUIRED TO BE IMPERIAL?!
PUH-- PTEW-- SPUHH
YES! YOU KEEP INSISTING IT WAS ORDAINED!
INSISTING HIS TRAINING WILL CONVINCE ME!
INSISTING MY NEXT TRANSFORMATION REQUIRES HIM AND HIM ALONE!
BUT LOOK AT HIM!
...NASTY... MOUTH TASTES LIKE CHALK... GUH...
HOW CAN THERE BE AN IOTA OF CONNECTION BETWEEN MY PERSONAGE AND HIM?!
WHAT COULD THERE POSSIBLY BE FOR ME TO DISCOVER THROUGH HIM?!

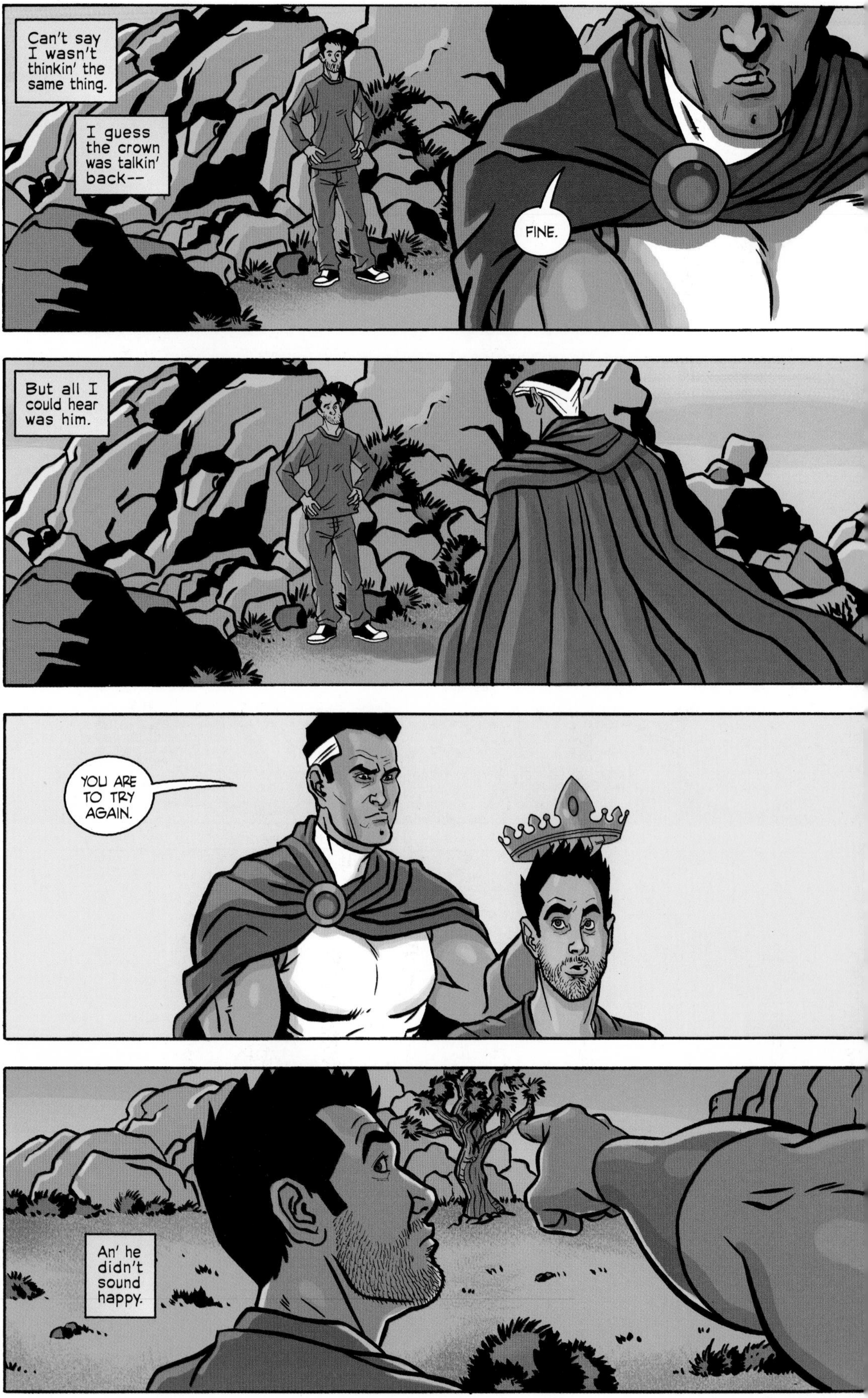
Can't say I wasn't thinkin' the same thing.
I guess the crown was talkin' back--
FINE.
But all I could hear was him.
YOU ARE TO TRY AGAIN.
An' he didn't sound happy.

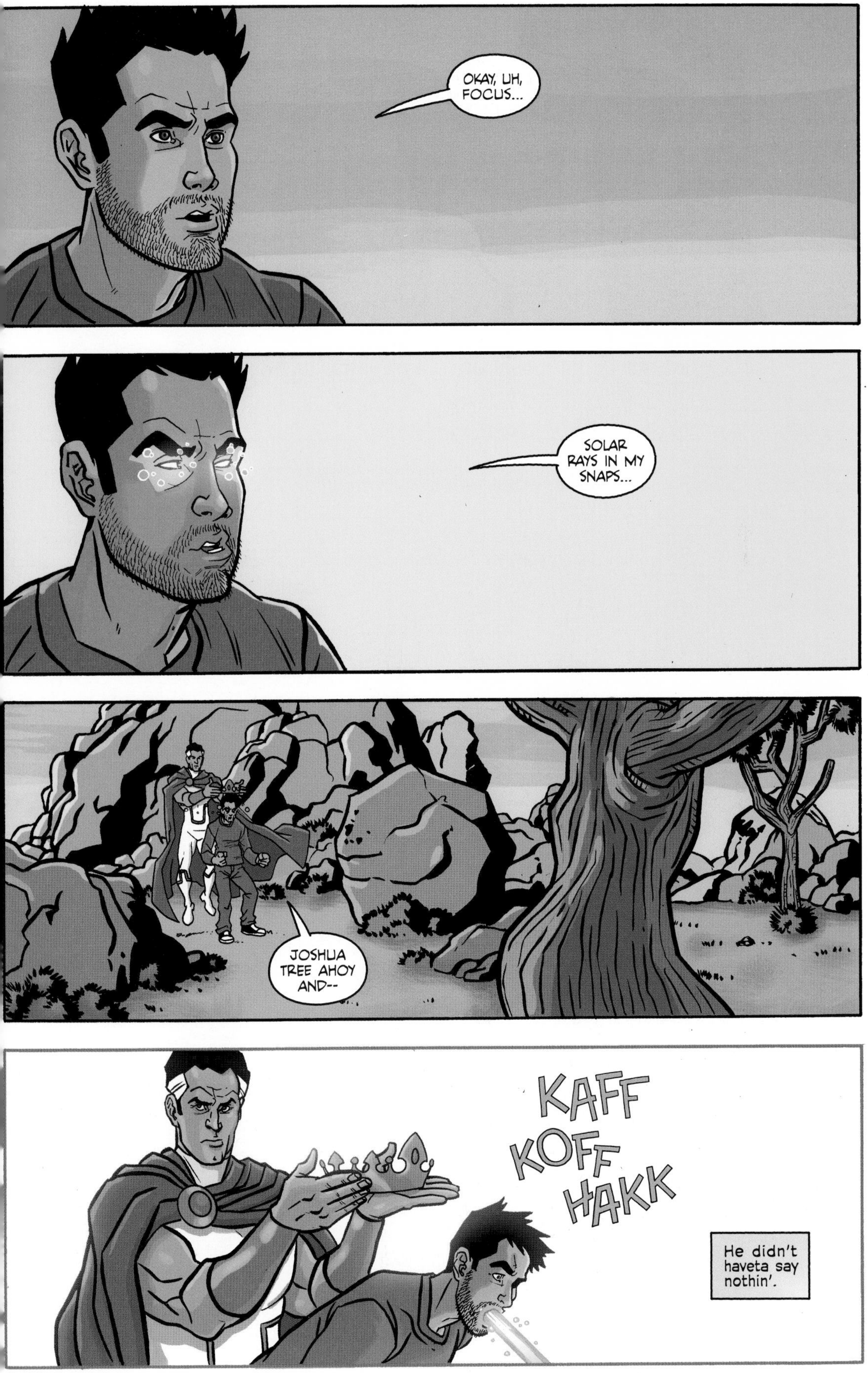
OKAY, UH, FOCUS...
SOLAR RAYS IN MY SNAPS...
JOSHUA TREE AHOY AND--
KAFF KOFF HAKK
He didn't haveta say nothin'.

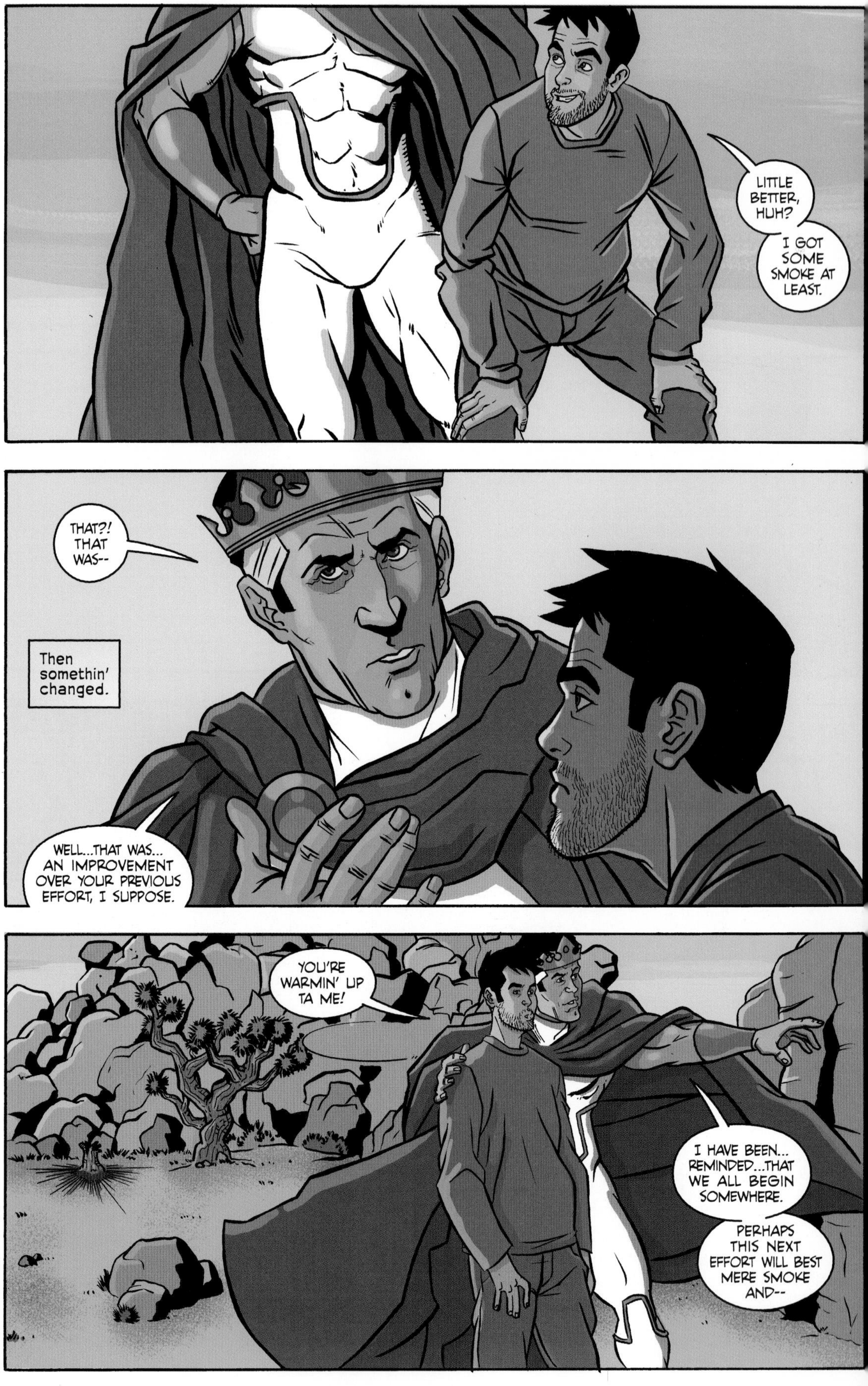
LITTLE BETTER, HUH?
I GOT SOME SMOKE AT LEAST.
THAT?! THAT WAS--
Then somethin' changed.
WELL...THAT WAS... AN IMPROVEMENT OVER YOUR PREVIOUS EFFORT, I SUPPOSE.
YOU'RE WARMIN' UP TA ME!
I HAVE BEEN... REMINDED...THAT WE ALL BEGIN SOMEWHERE.
PERHAPS THIS NEXT EFFORT WILL BEST MERE SMOKE AND--

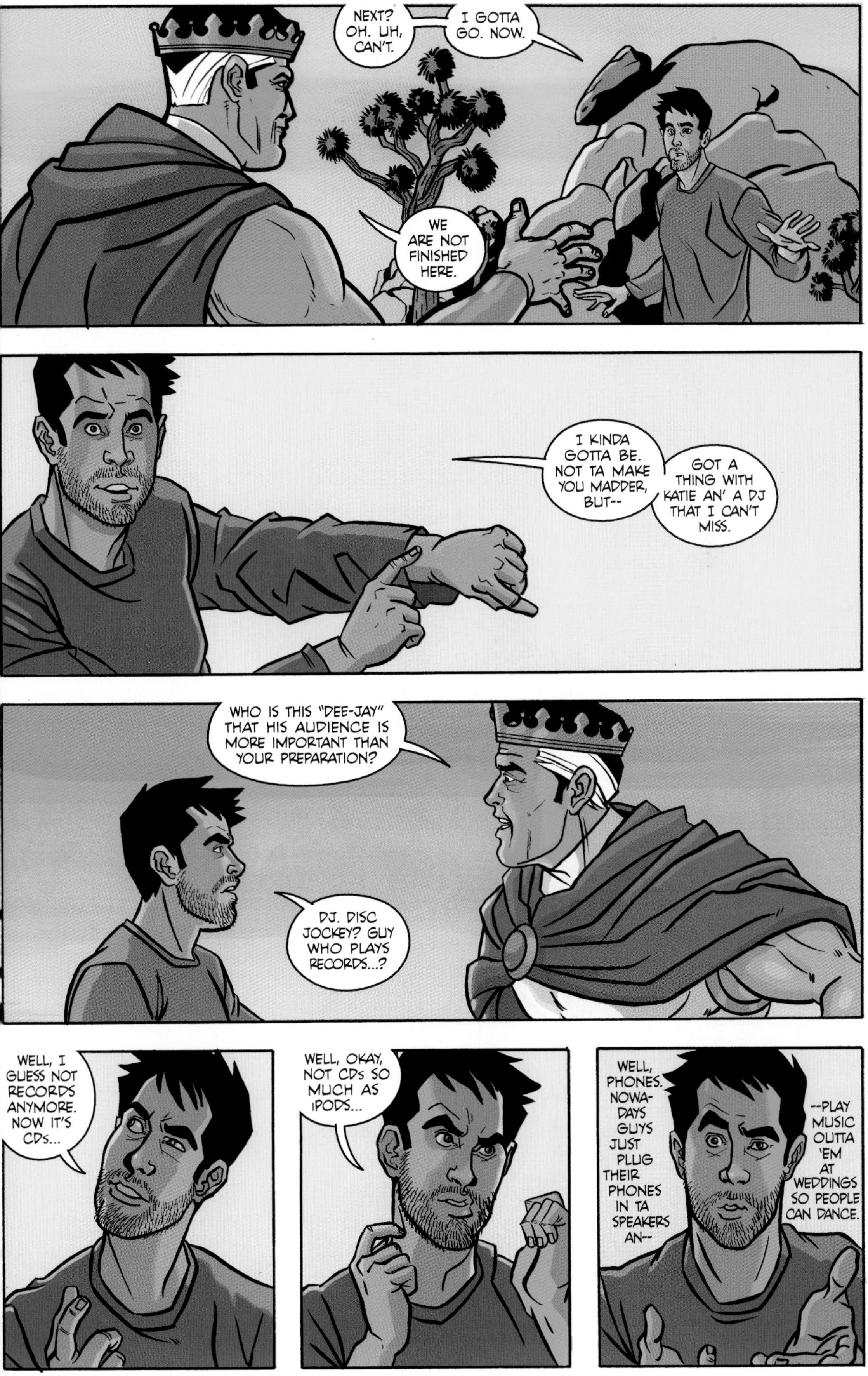
NEXT? OH. UH, CAN'T.
I GOTTA GO. NOW.
WE ARE NOT FINISHED HERE.
I KINDA GOTTA BE. NOT TA MAKE YOU MADDER, BUT--
GOT A THING WITH KATIE AN' A DJ THAT I CAN'T MISS.
WHO IS THIS "DEE-JAY" THAT HIS AUDIENCE IS MORE IMPORTANT THAN YOUR PREPARATION?
DJ. DISC JOCKEY? GUY WHO PLAYS RECORDS...?
WELL, I GUESS NOT RECORDS ANYMORE. NOW IT'S CDs...
WELL, OKAY, NOT CDs SO MUCH AS iPODS...
WELL, PHONES. NOWA-DAYS GUYS JUST PLUG THEIR PHONES IN TA SPEAKERS AN--
--PLAY MUSIC OUTTA 'EM AT WEDDINGS SO PEOPLE CAN DANCE.

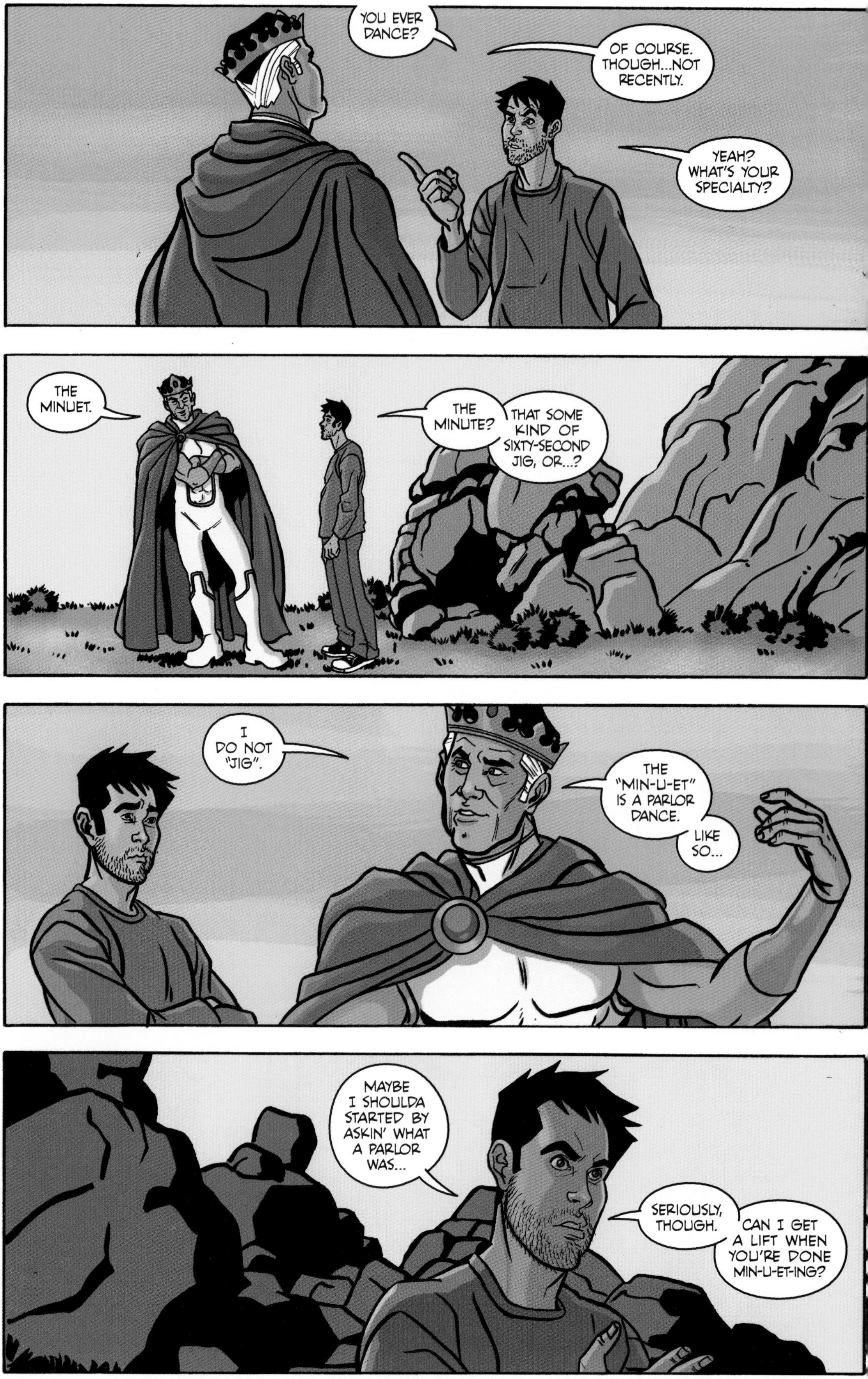
YOU EVER DANCE?
OF COURSE. THOUGH...NOT RECENTLY.
YEAH? WHAT'S YOUR SPECIALTY?
THE MINUET.
THE MINUTE?
THAT SOME KIND OF SIXTY-SECOND JIG, OR...?
I DO NOT "JIG".
THE "MIN-U-ET" IS A PARLOR DANCE.
LIKE SO...
MAYBE I SHOULDA STARTED BY ASKIN' WHAT A PARLOR WAS...
SERIOUSLY, THOUGH.
CAN I GET A LIFT WHEN YOU'RE DONE MIN-U-ET-ING?

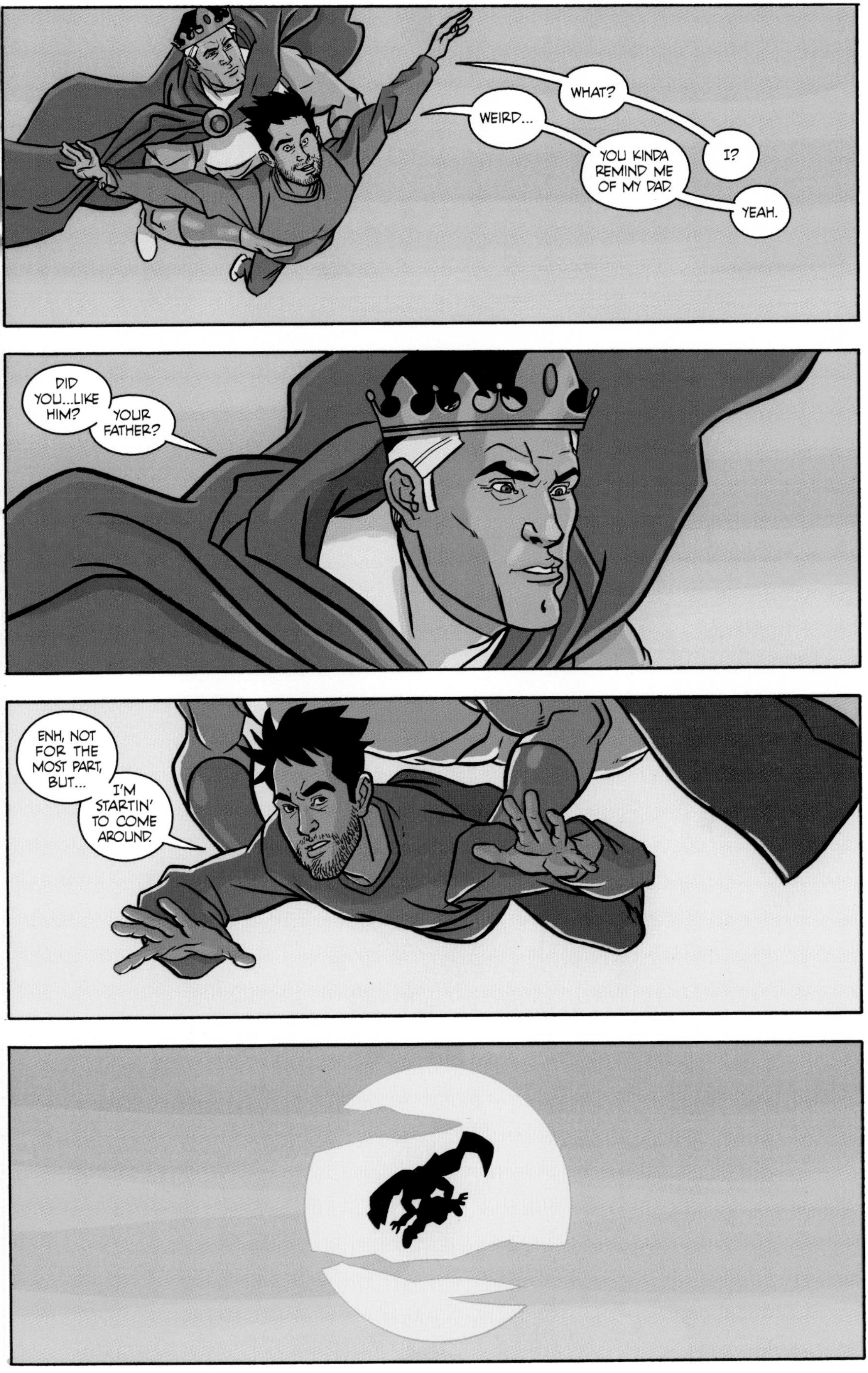
WEIRD...
WHAT?
YOU KINDA REMIND ME OF MY DAD.
I?
YEAH.
DID YOU...LIKE HIM?
YOUR FATHER?
ENH, NOT FOR THE MOST PART, BUT...
I'M STARTIN' TO COME AROUND.

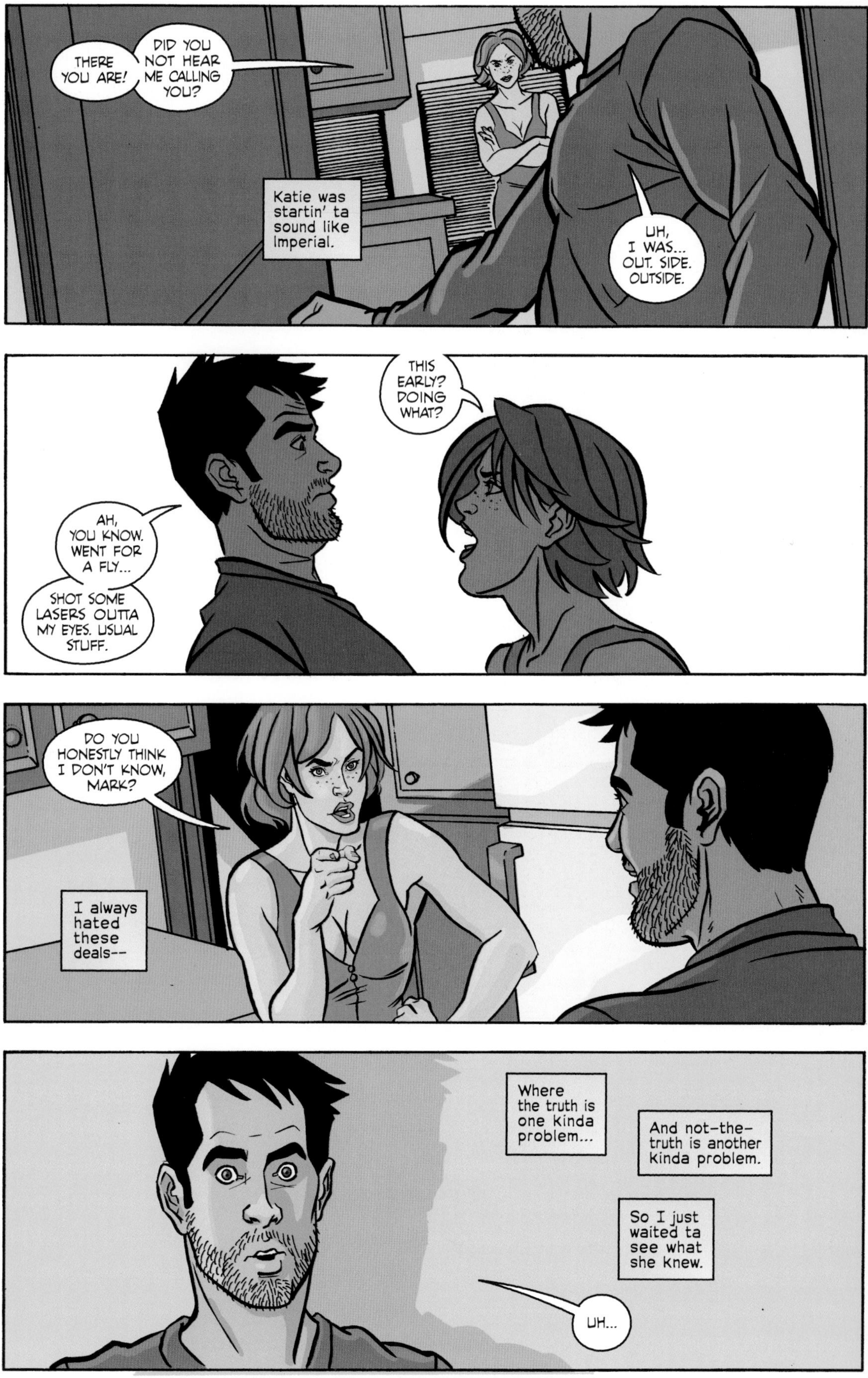
THERE YOU ARE!
DID YOU NOT HEAR ME CALLING YOU?
Katie was startin' ta sound like Imperial.
UH, I WAS... OUT. SIDE. OUTSIDE.
THIS EARLY? DOING WHAT?
AH, YOU KNOW. WENT FOR A FLY...
SHOT SOME LASERS OUTTA MY EYES. USUAL STUFF.
DO YOU HONESTLY THINK I DON'T KNOW, MARK?
I always hated these deals--
Where the truth is one kinda problem...
And not-the-truth is another kinda problem.
So I just waited ta see what she knew.
UH...

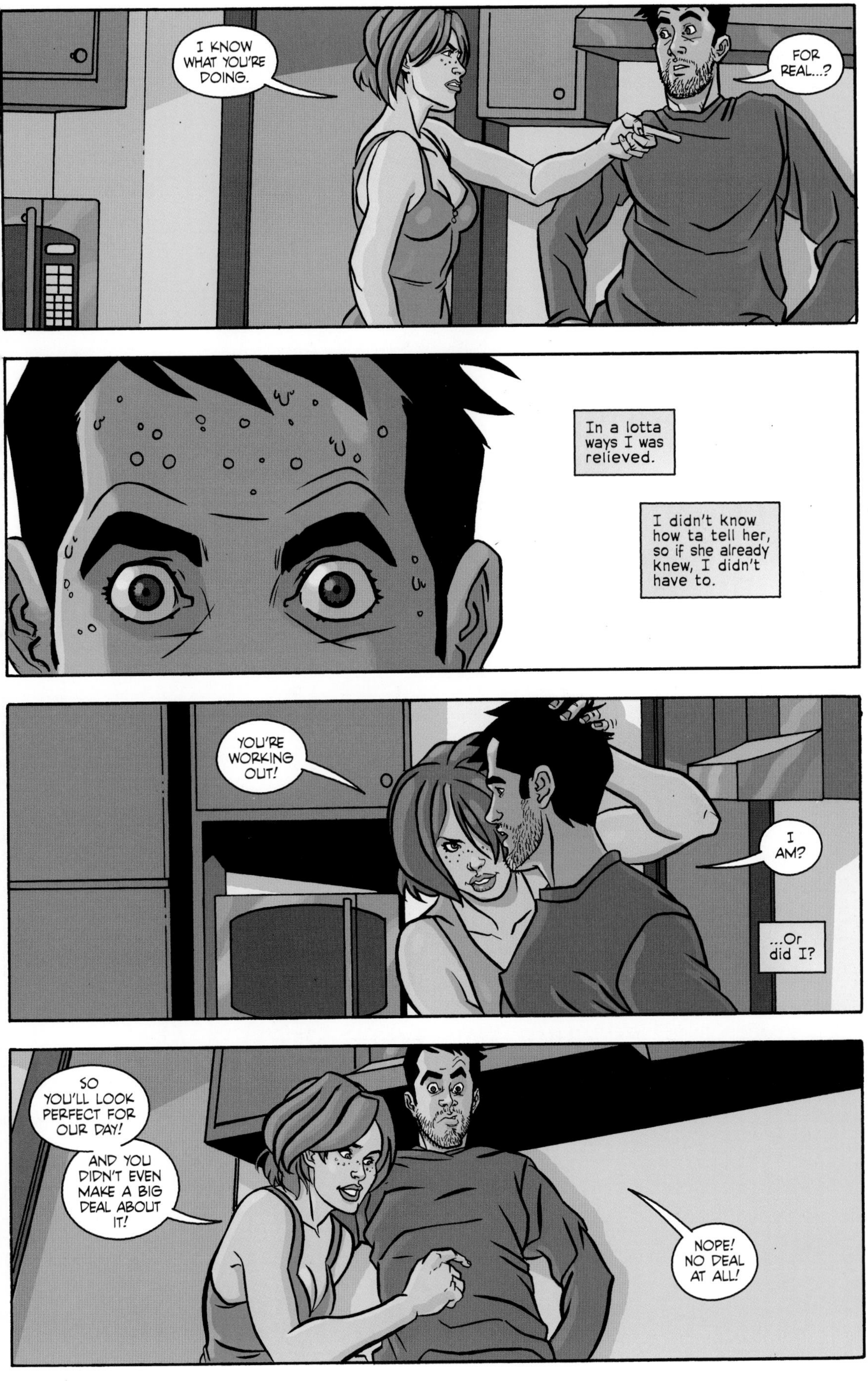
I KNOW WHAT YOU'RE DOING.
FOR REAL...?
In a lotta ways I was relieved.
I didn't know how ta tell her, so if she already knew, I didn't have to.
YOU'RE WORKING OUT!
I AM?
...Or did I?
SO YOU'LL LOOK PERFECT FOR OUR DAY!
AND YOU DIDN'T EVEN MAKE A BIG DEAL ABOUT IT!
NOPE! NO DEAL AT ALL!

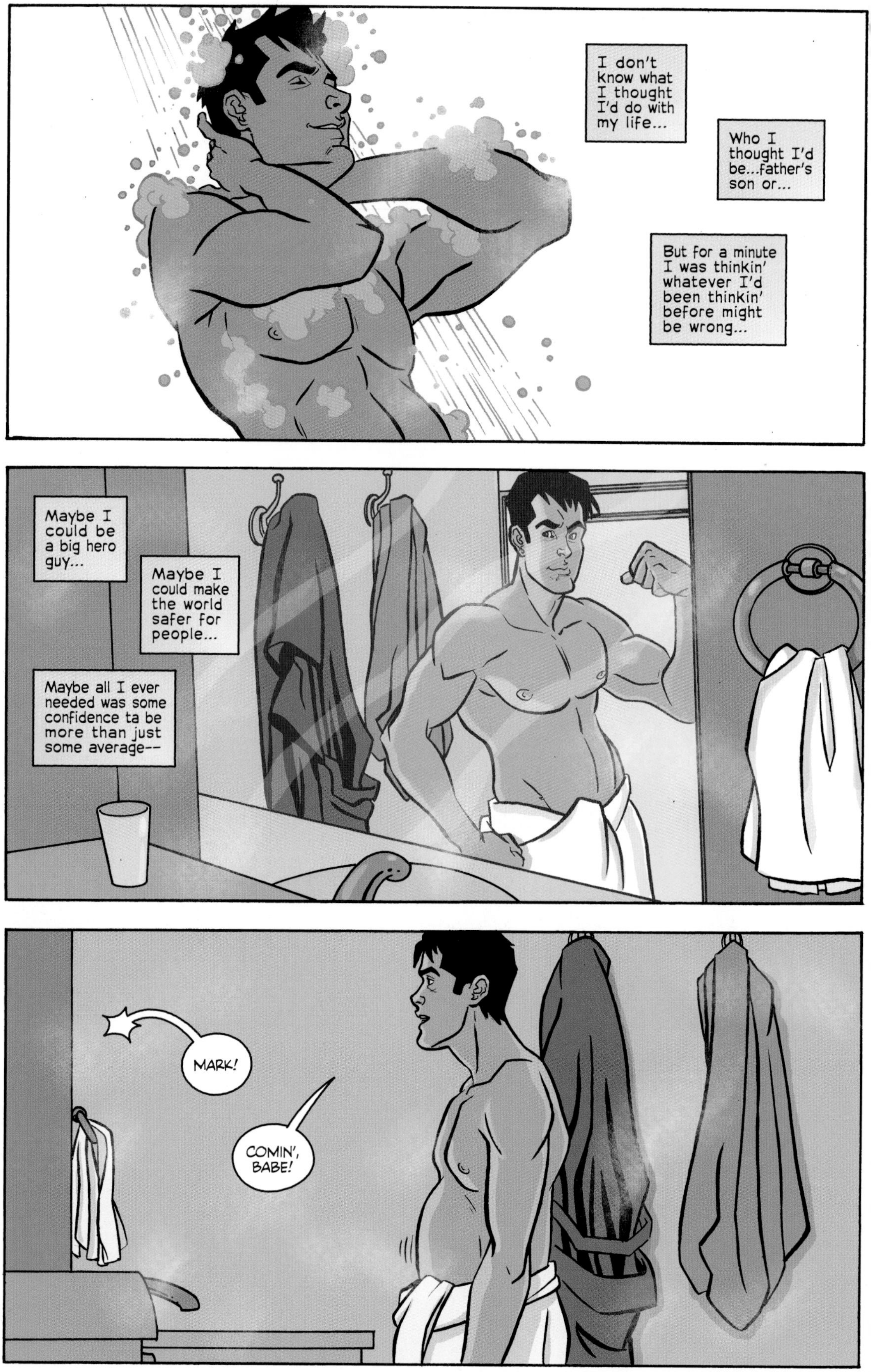
I don't know what I thought I'd do with my life...
Who I thought I'd be...father's son or...
But for a minute I was thinkin' whatever I'd been thinkin' before might be wrong...
Maybe I could be a big hero guy...
Maybe I could make the world safer for people...
Maybe all I ever needed was some confidence ta be more than just some average--
MARK!
COMIN', BABE!

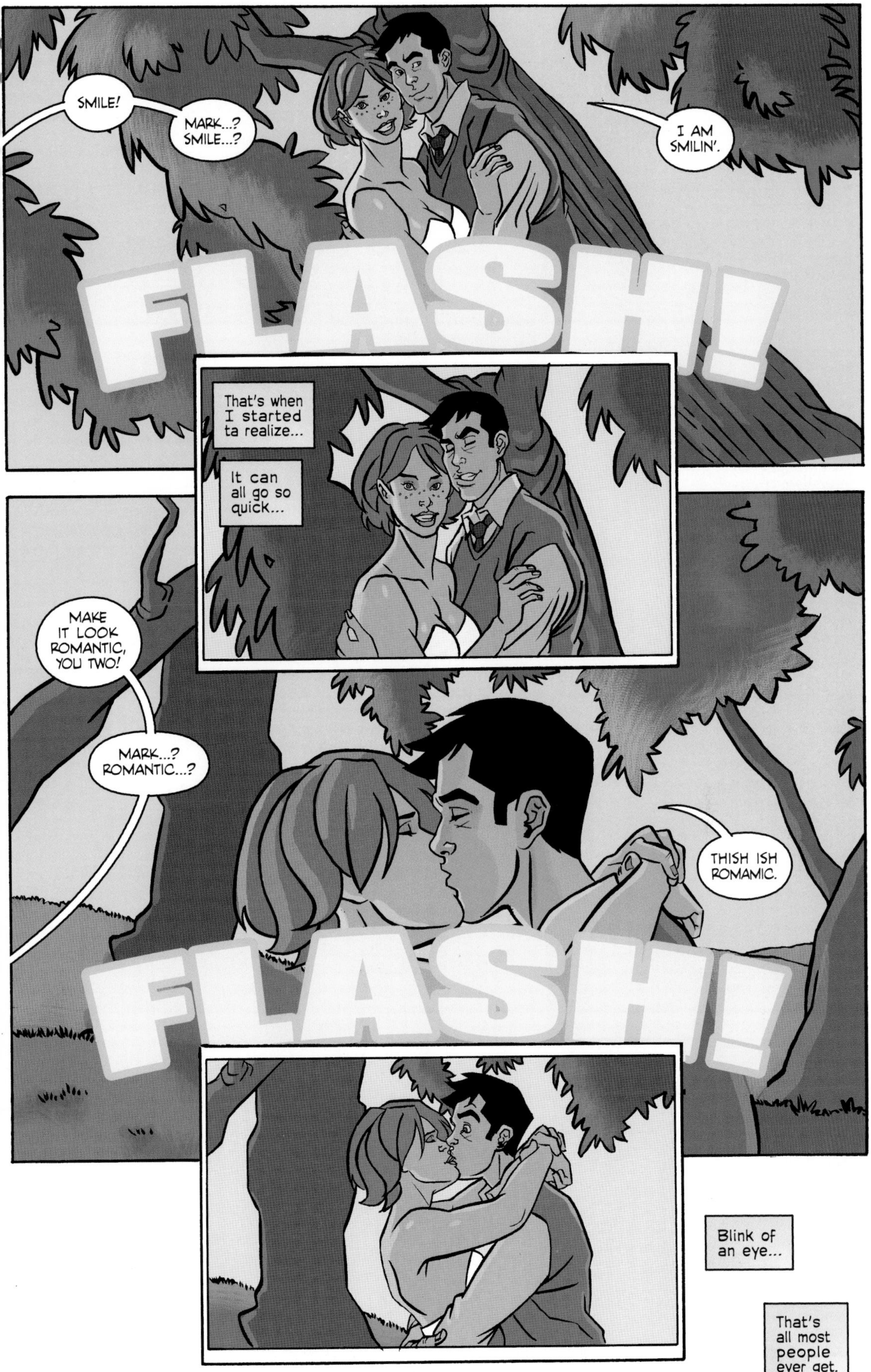
SMILE!
MARK...? SMILE...?
I AM SMILIN'.
FLASH!
That's when I started ta realize...
It can all go so quick...
MAKE IT LOOK ROMANTIC, YOU TWO!
MARK...? ROMANTIC...?
THISH ISH ROMAMIC.
FLASH!
Blink of an eye...
That's all most people ever get.

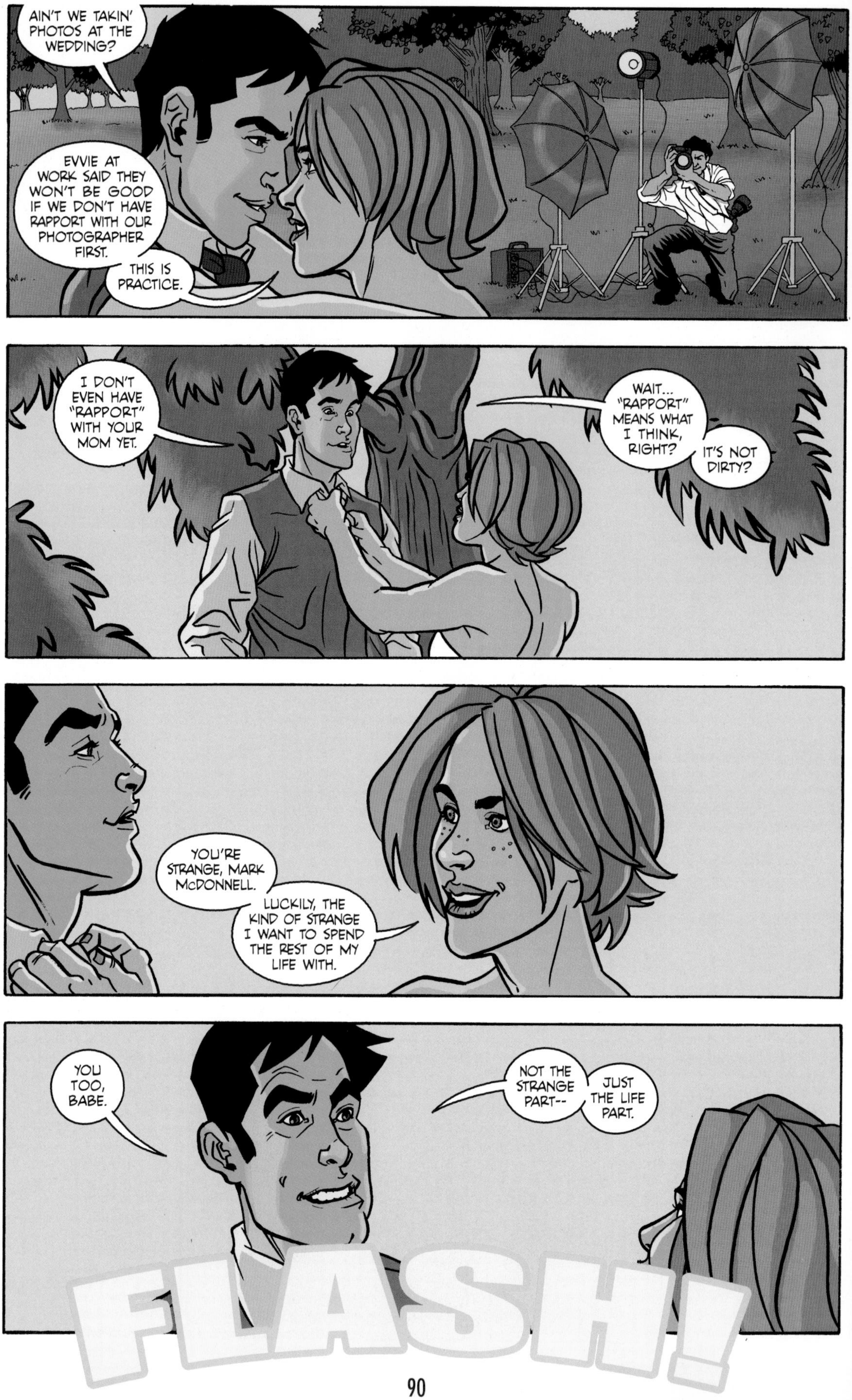
AIN'T WE TAKIN' PHOTOS AT THE WEDDING?
EVVIE AT WORK SAID THEY WON'T BE GOOD IF WE DON'T HAVE RAPPORT WITH OUR PHOTOGRAPHER FIRST.
THIS IS PRACTICE.
I DON'T EVEN HAVE "RAPPORT" WITH YOUR MOM YET.
WAIT... "RAPPORT" MEANS WHAT I THINK, RIGHT?
IT'S NOT DIRTY?
YOU'RE STRANGE, MARK McDONNELL.
LUCKILY, THE KIND OF STRANGE I WANT TO SPEND THE REST OF MY LIFE WITH.
YOU TOO, BABE.
NOT THE STRANGE PART--
JUST THE LIFE PART.
FLASH!

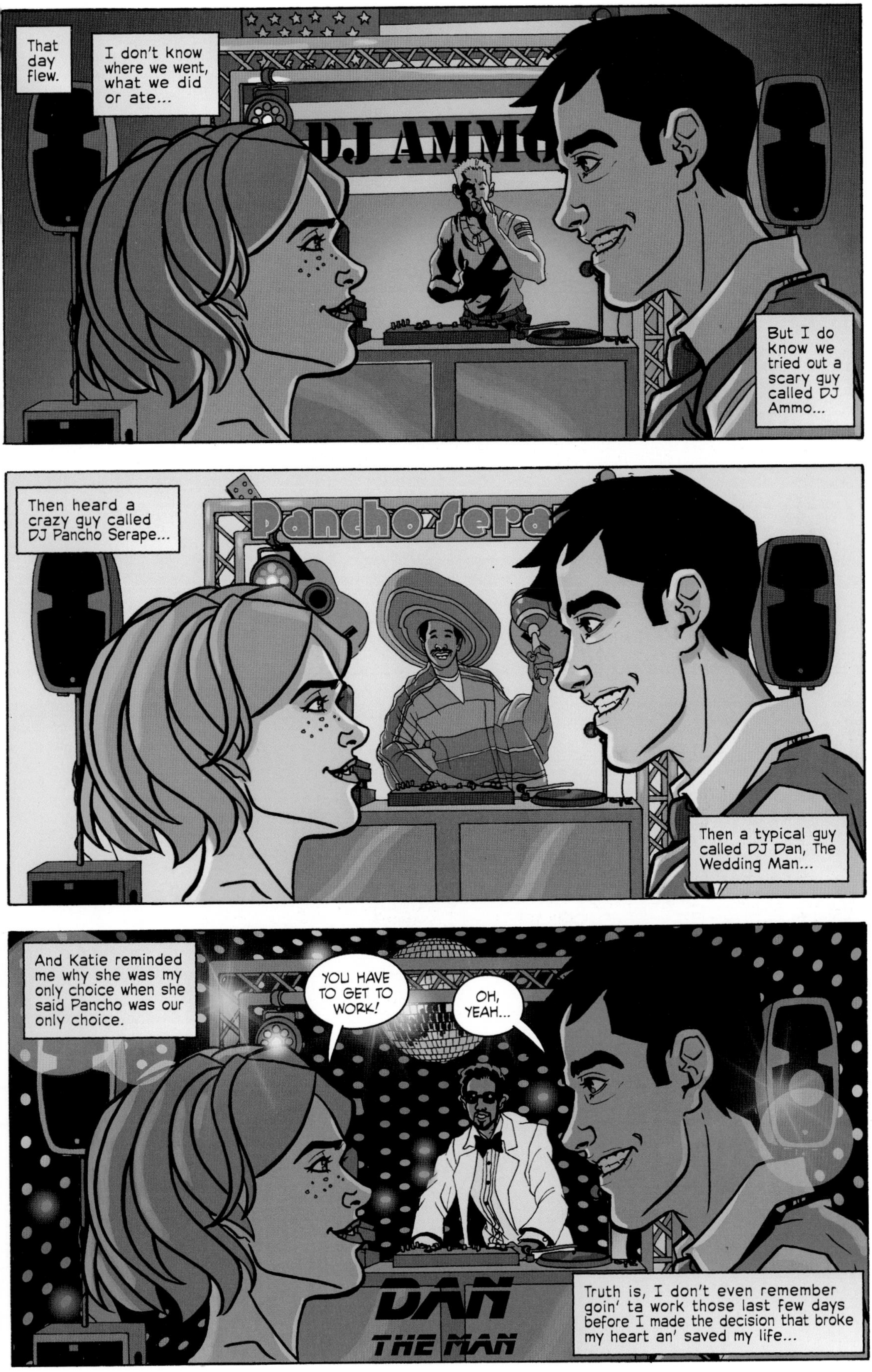
That day flew.
I don't know where we went, what we did or ate...
But I do know we tried out a scary guy called DJ Ammo...
Then heard a crazy guy called DJ Pancho Serape...
Then a typical guy called DJ Dan, The Wedding Man...
And Katie reminded me why she was my only choice when she said Pancho was our only choice.
YOU HAVE TO GET TO WORK!
OH, YEAH...
DAN THE MAN
Truth is, I don't even remember goin' ta work those last few days before I made the decision that broke my heart an' saved my life...

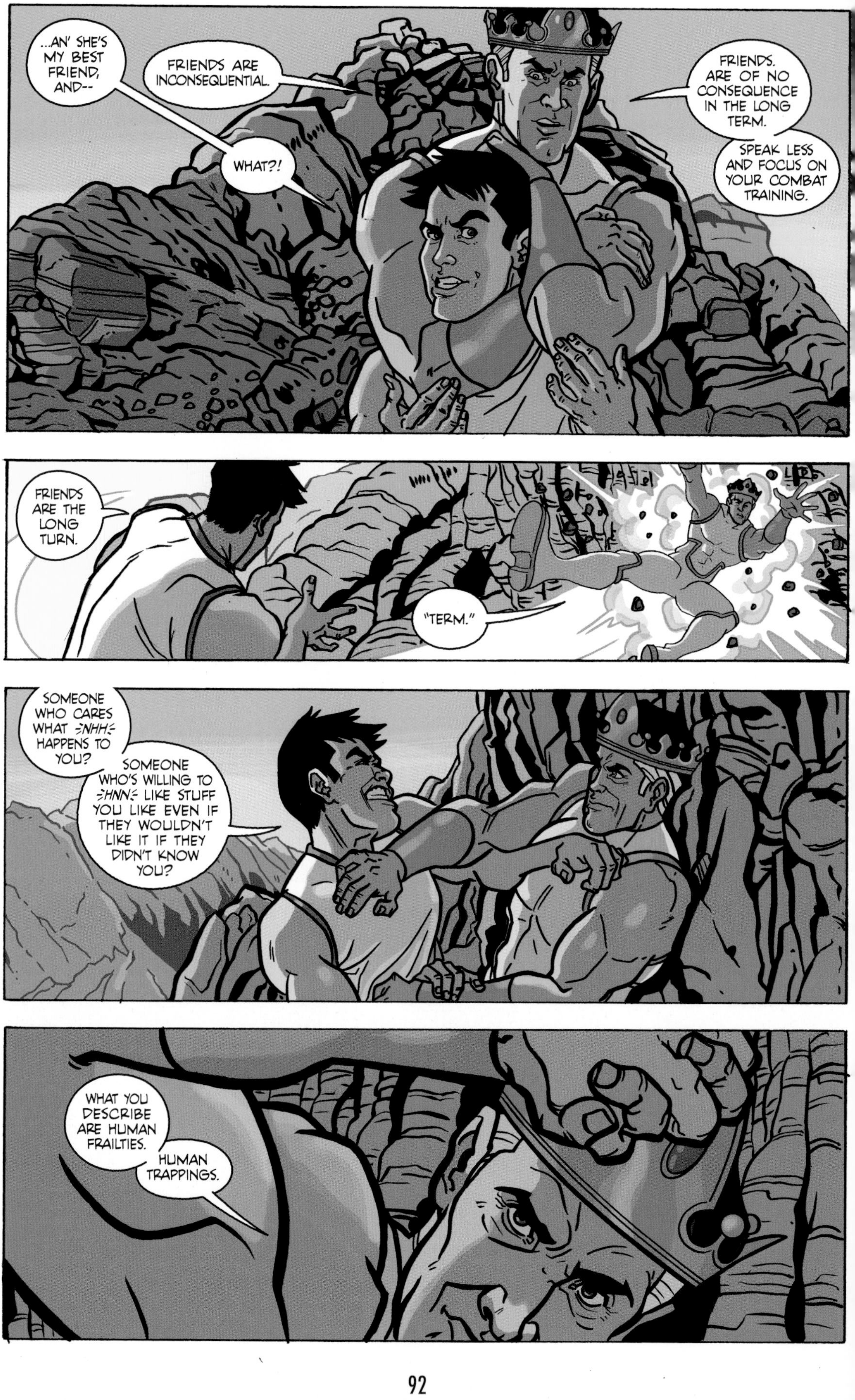
...AN' SHE'S MY BEST FRIEND, AND--
FRIENDS ARE INCONSEQUENTIAL.
WHAT?!
FRIENDS. ARE OF NO CONSEQUENCE IN THE LONG TERM.
SPEAK LESS AND FOCUS ON YOUR COMBAT TRAINING.
FRIENDS ARE THE LONG TURN.
"TERM."
SOMEONE WHO CARES WHAT =NHH= HAPPENS TO YOU?
SOMEONE WHO'S WILLING TO =HNN= LIKE STUFF YOU LIKE EVEN IF THEY WOULDN'T LIKE IT IF THEY DIDN'T KNOW YOU?
WHAT YOU DESCRIBE ARE HUMAN FRAILTIES.
HUMAN TRAPPINGS.

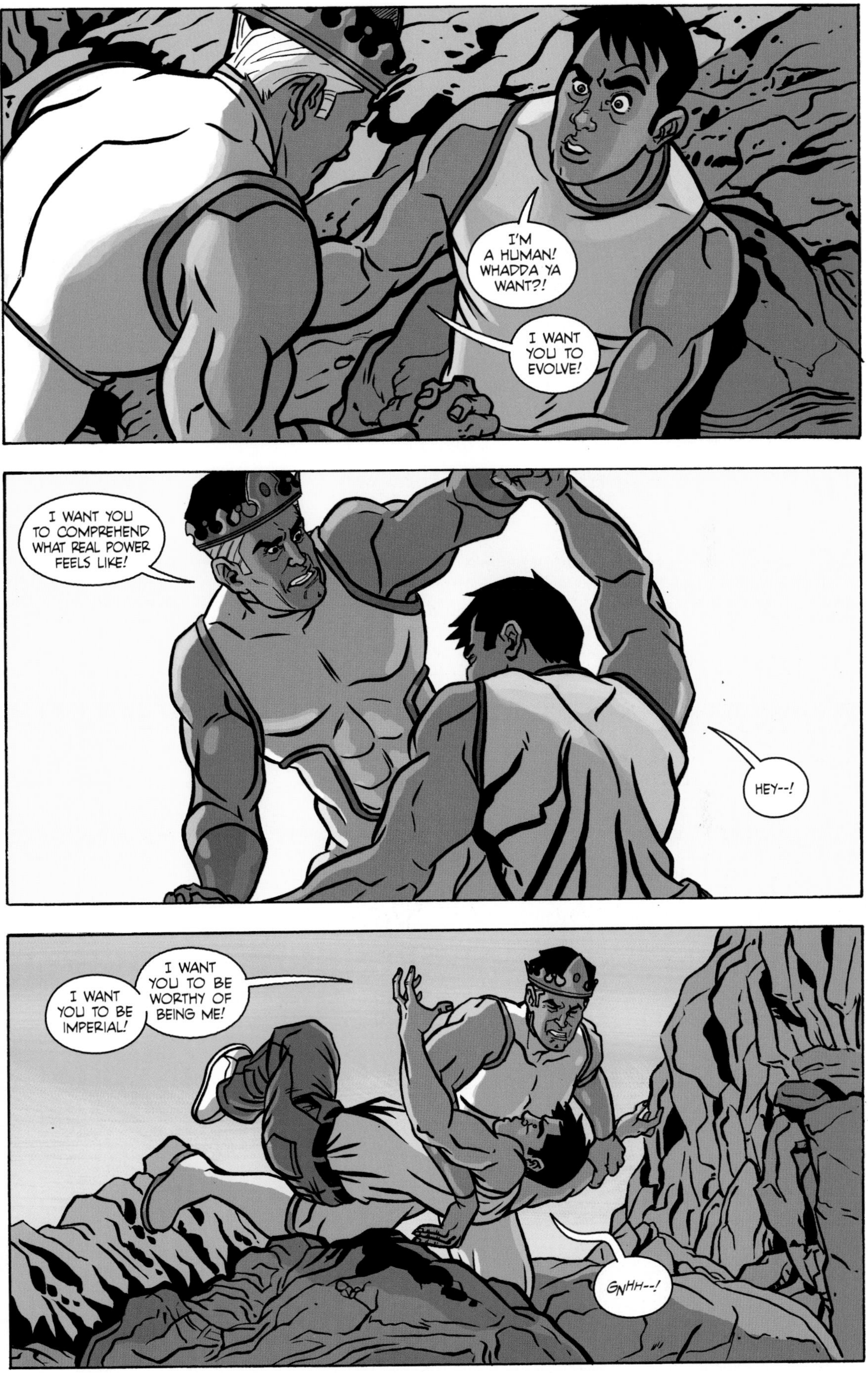
I'M A HUMAN! WHADDA YA WANT?!
I WANT YOU TO EVOLVE!
I WANT YOU TO COMPREHEND WHAT REAL POWER FEELS LIKE!
HEY--!
I WANT YOU TO BE IMPERIAL!
I WANT YOU TO BE WORTHY OF BEING ME!
GNHH--!

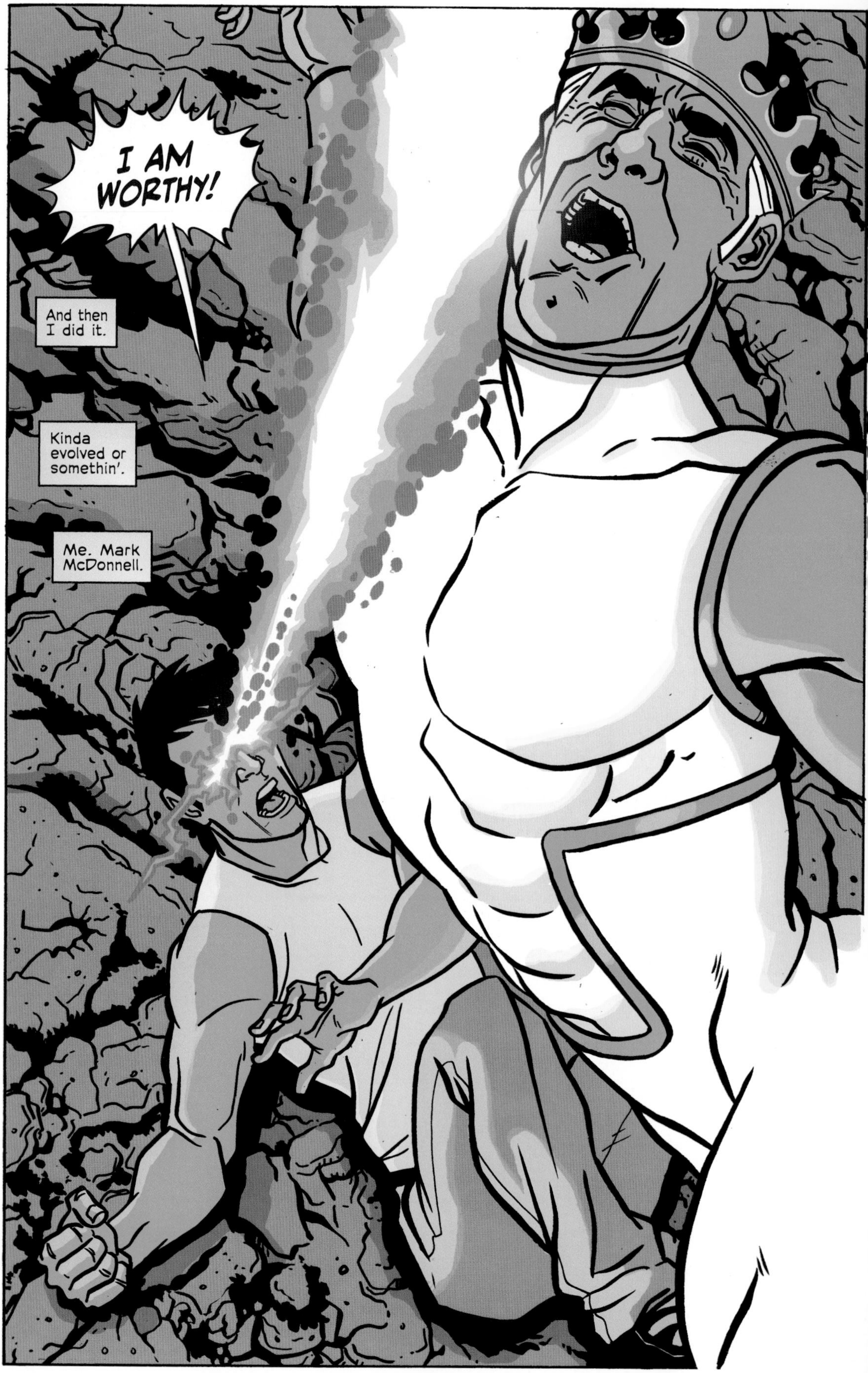
I AM WORTHY!
And then I did it.
Kinda evolved or somethin'.
Me. Mark McDonnell.

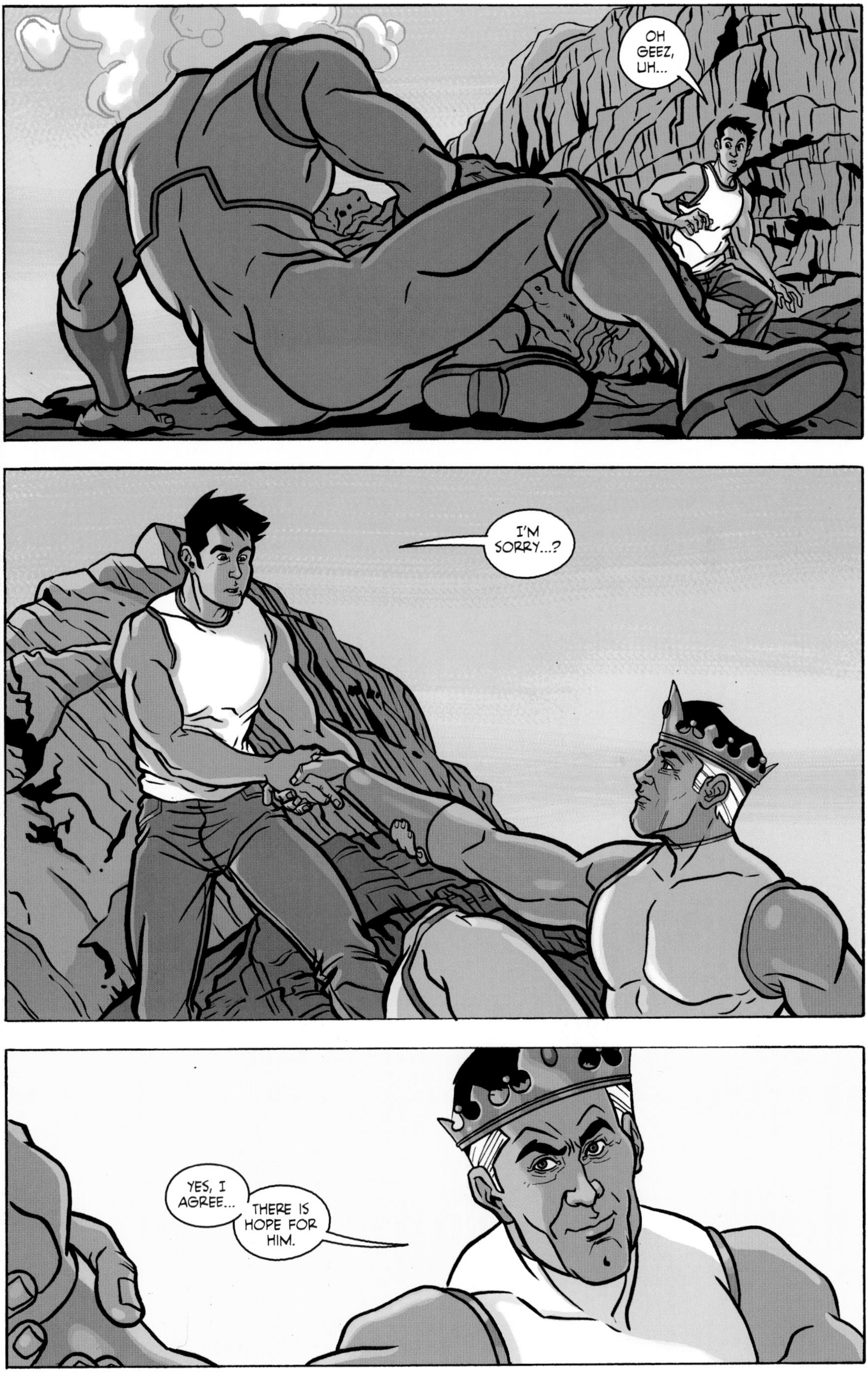
OH GEEZ, UH...
I'M SORRY...?
YES, I AGREE...
THERE IS HOPE FOR HIM.

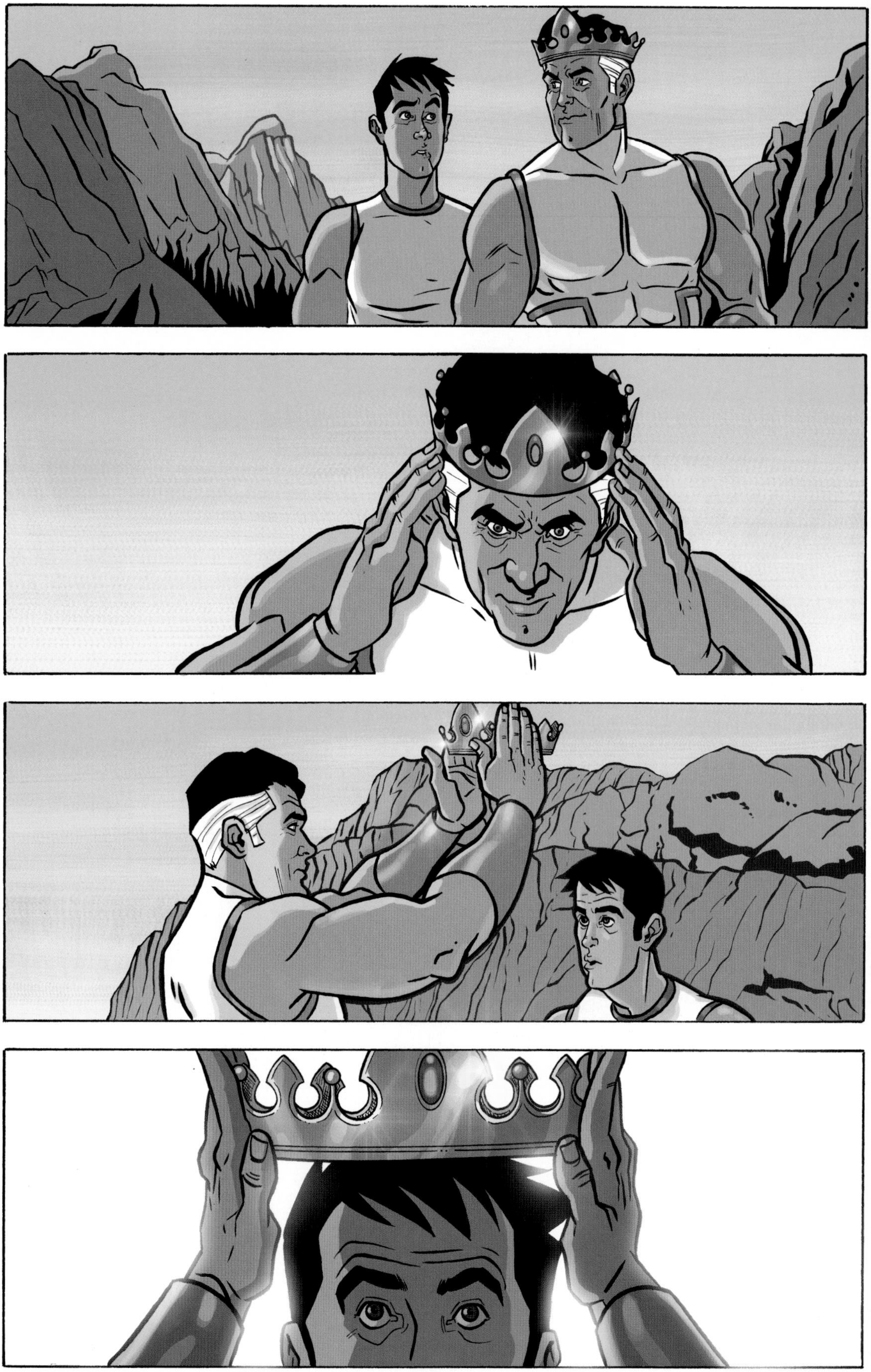

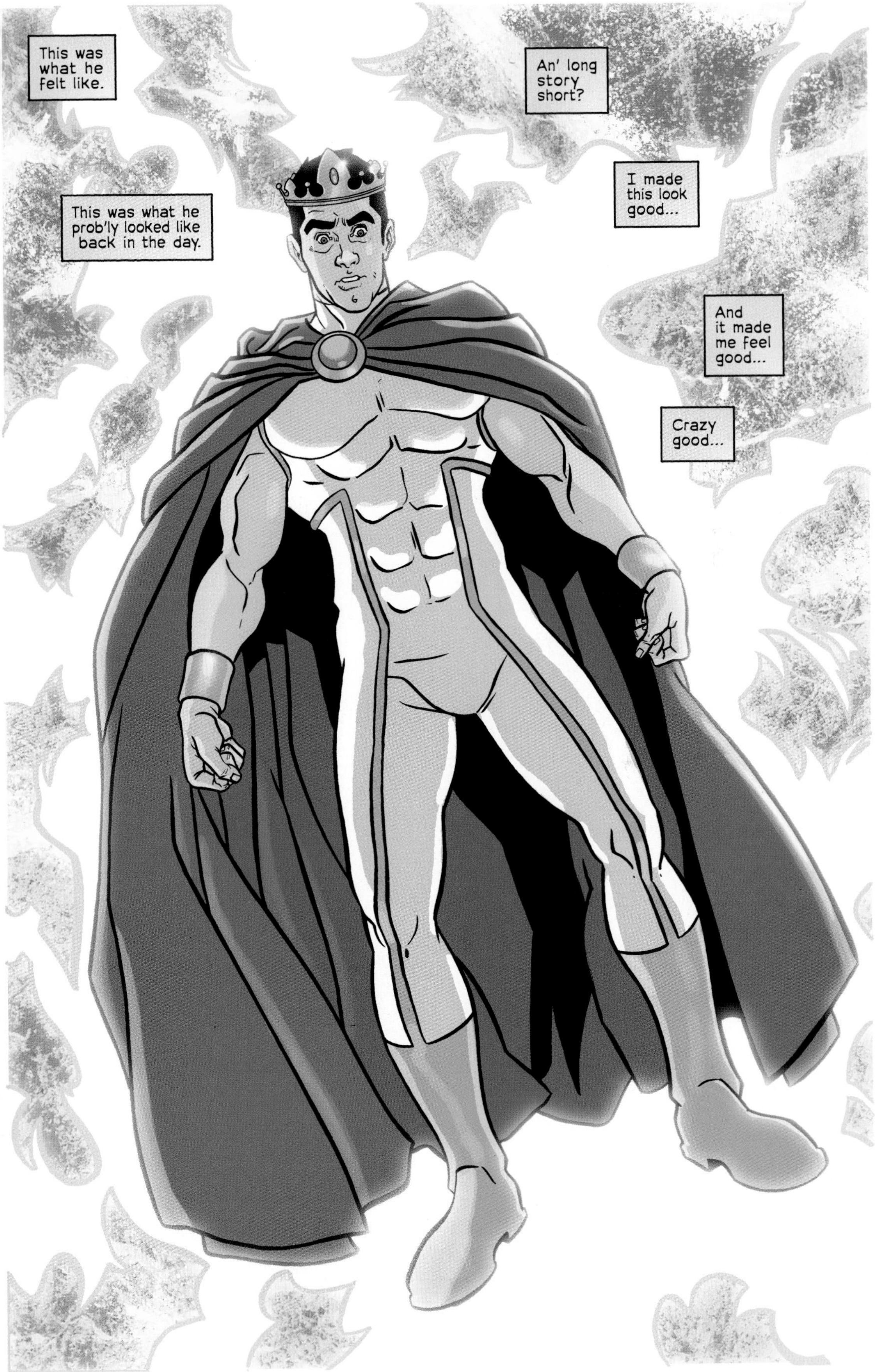
This was what he felt like.
This was what he prob'ly looked like back in the day.
An' long story short?
I made this look good...
And it made me feel good...
Crazy good...

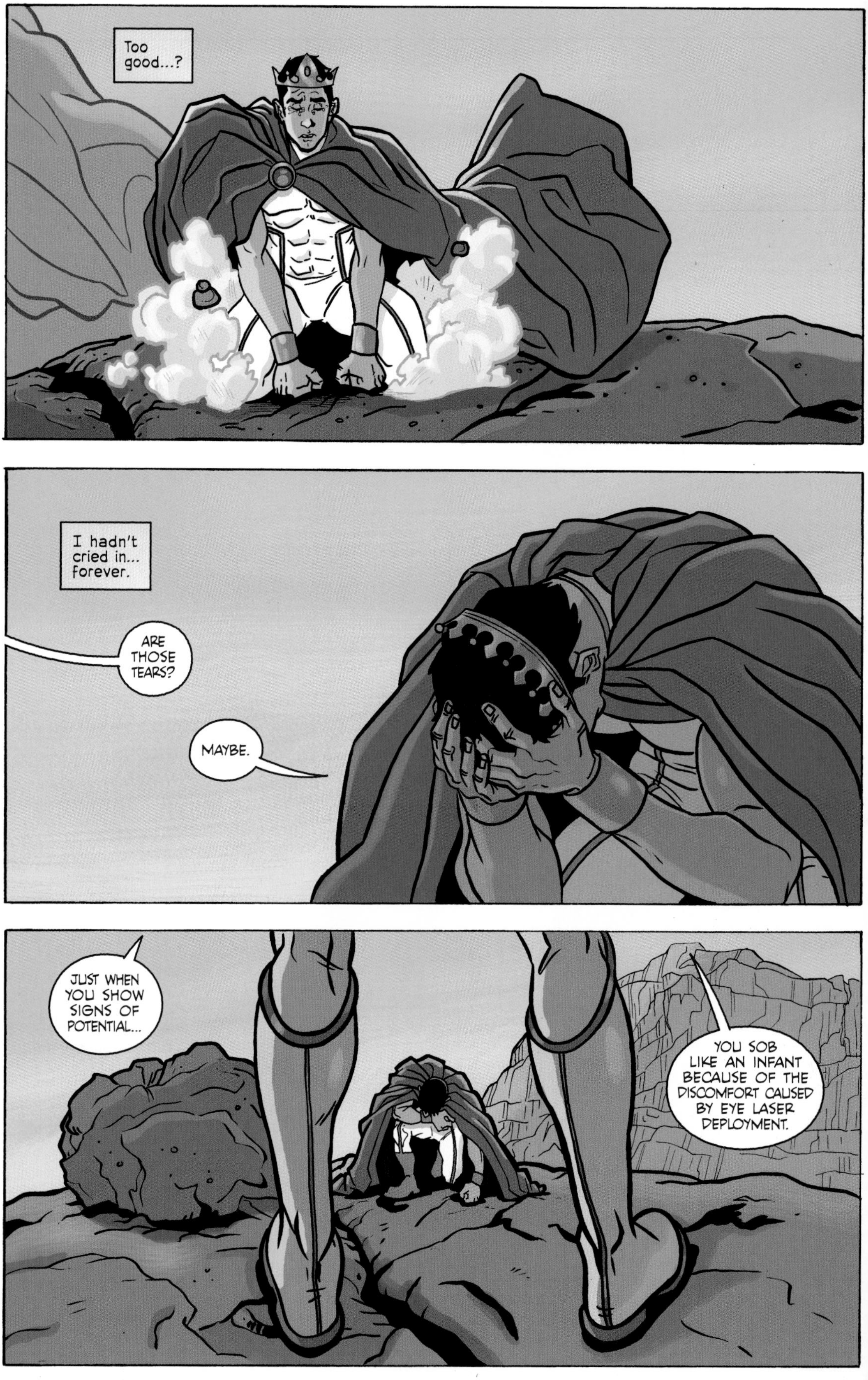
Too good...?
I hadn't cried in... forever.
ARE THOSE TEARS?
MAYBE.
JUST WHEN YOU SHOW SIGNS OF POTENTIAL...
YOU SOB LIKE AN INFANT BECAUSE OF THE DISCOMFORT CAUSED BY EYE LASER DEPLOYMENT.

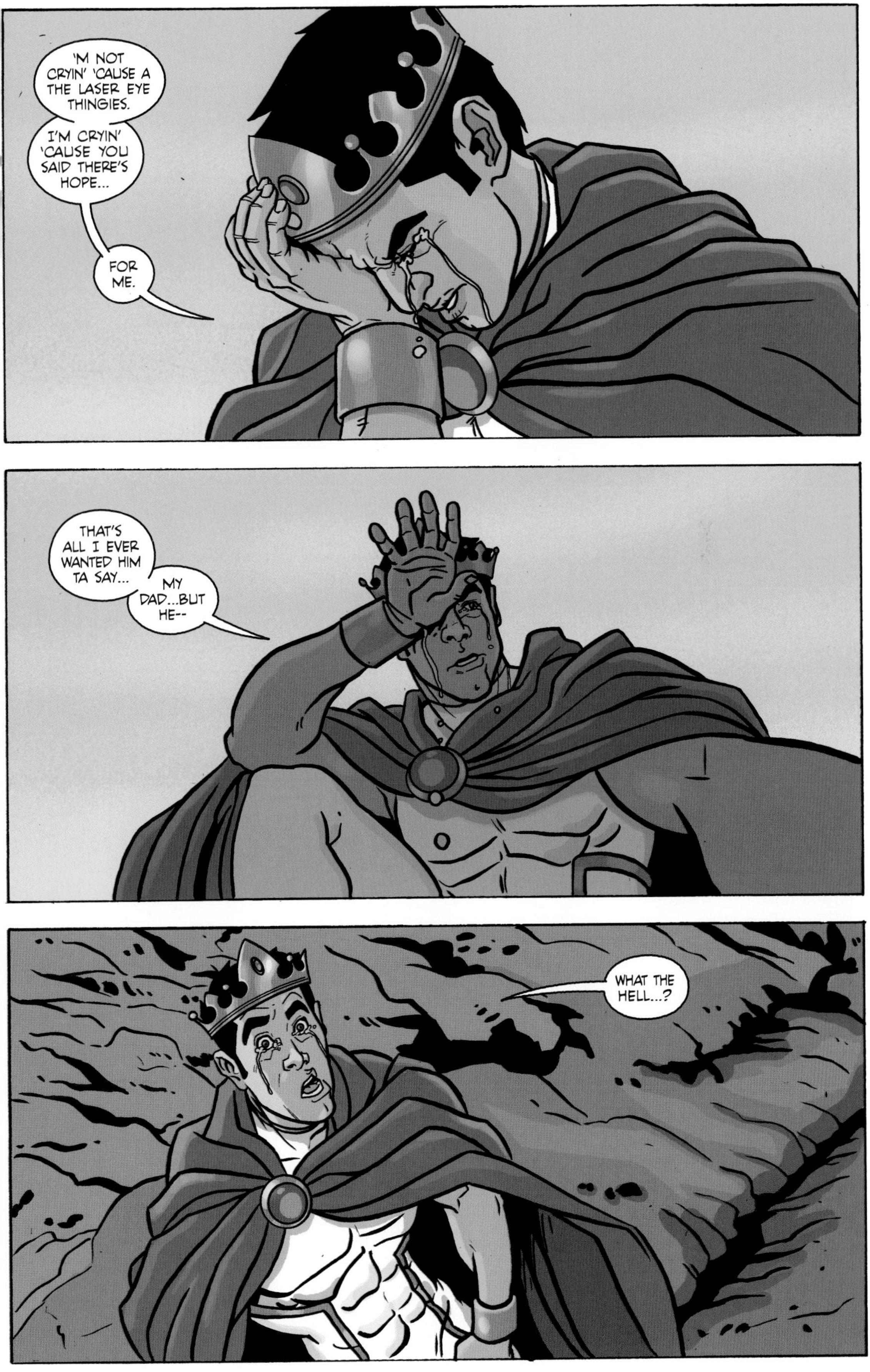
'M NOT CRYIN' 'CAUSE A THE LASER EYE THINGIES.
I'M CRYIN' 'CAUSE YOU SAID THERE'S HOPE...
FOR ME.
THAT'S ALL I EVER WANTED HIM TA SAY...
MY DAD...BUT HE--
WHAT THE HELL...?

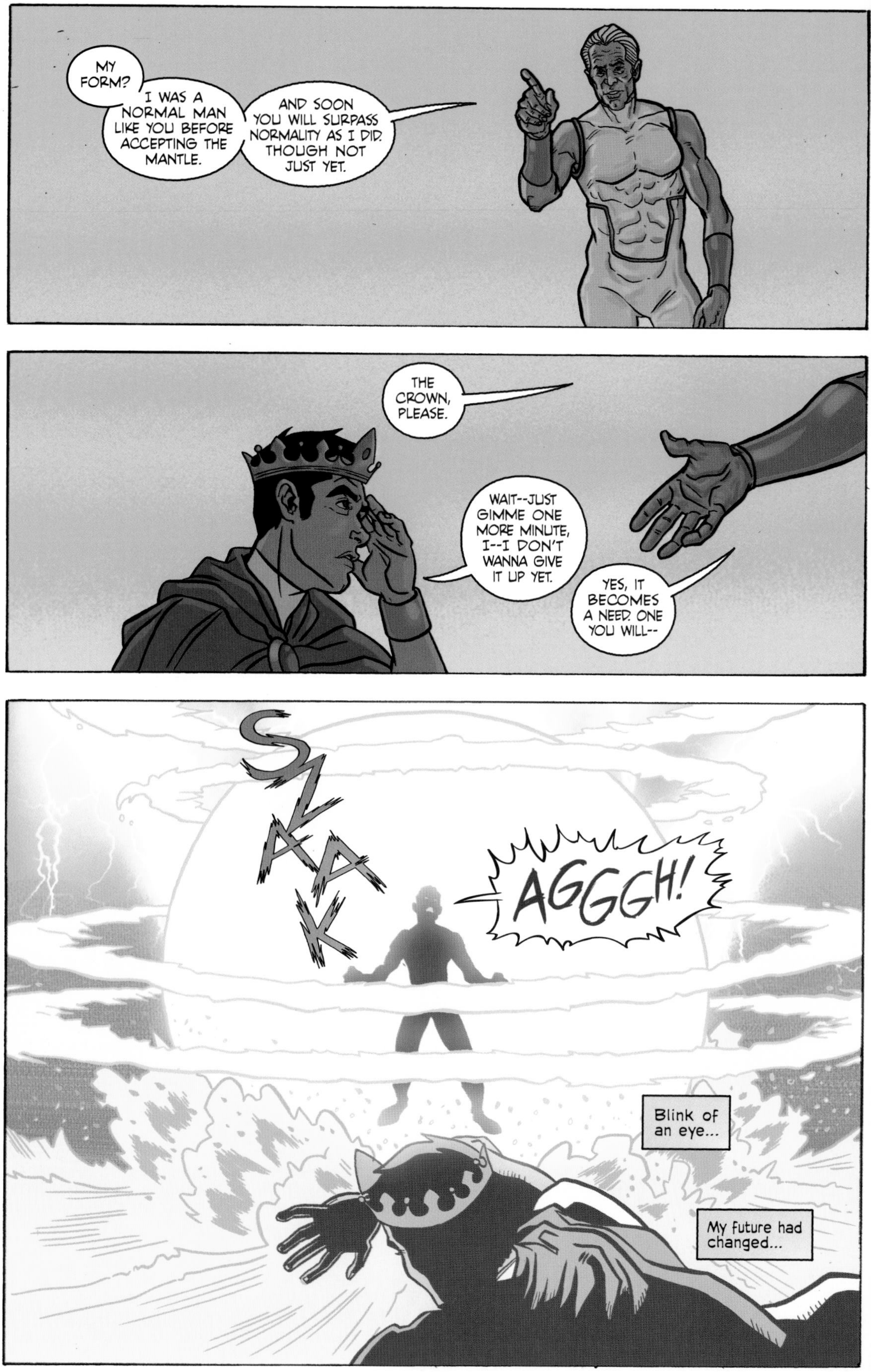
MY FORM?
I WAS A NORMAL MAN LIKE YOU BEFORE ACCEPTING THE MANTLE.
AND SOON YOU WILL SURPASS NORMALITY AS I DID. THOUGH NOT JUST YET.
THE CROWN, PLEASE.
WAIT--JUST GIMME ONE MORE MINUTE, I--I DON'T WANNA GIVE IT UP YET.
YES, IT BECOMES A NEED. ONE YOU WILL--
SNAAK
AGGGH!
Blink of an eye...
My future had changed...

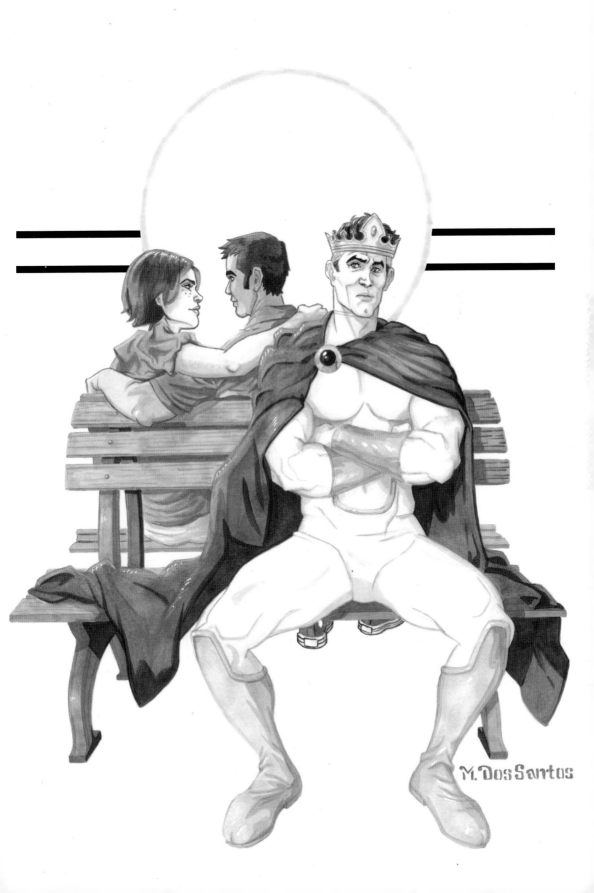

M. Dos Santos

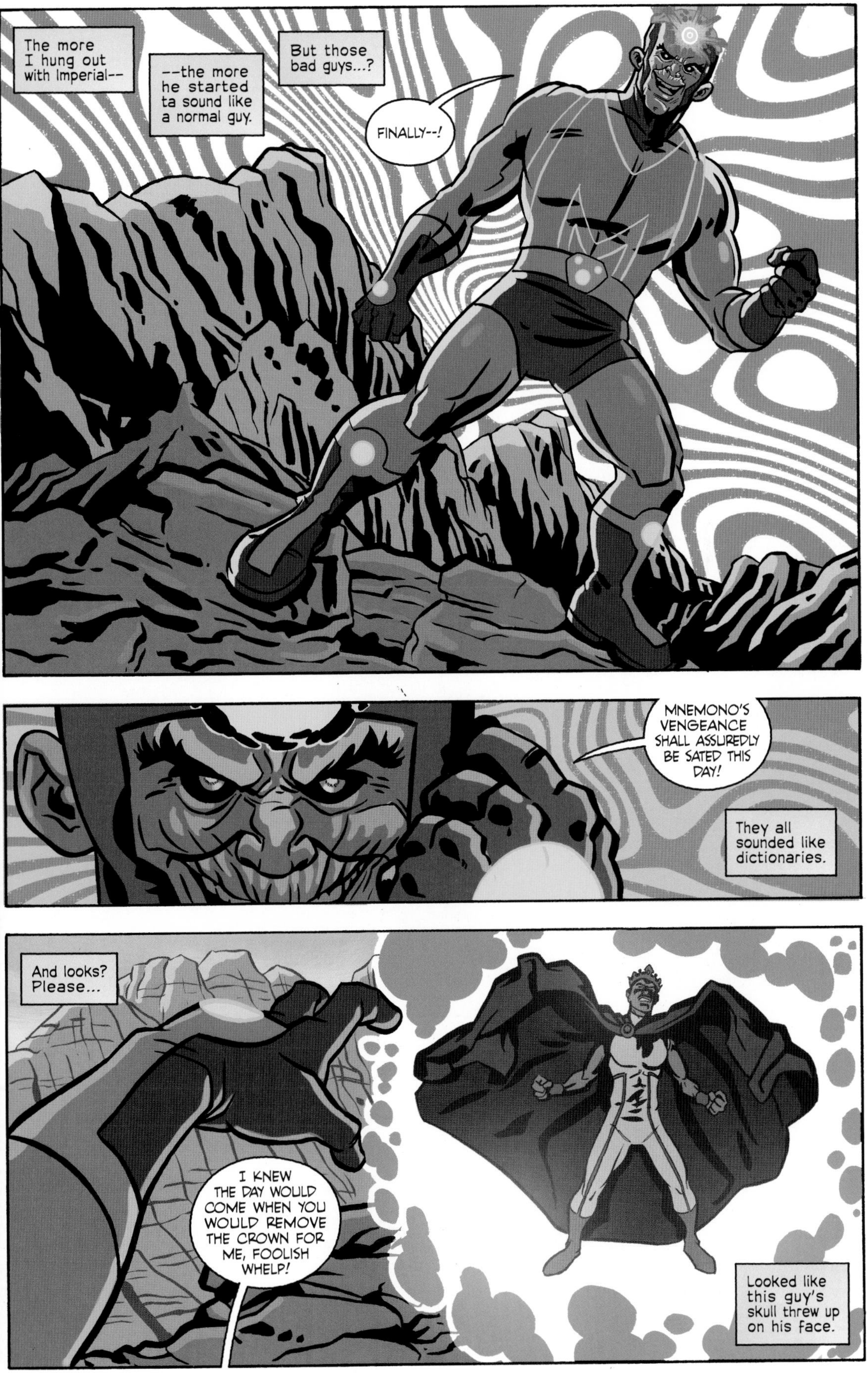
The more I hung out with Imperial--
--the more he started ta sound like a normal guy.
But those bad guys...?
FINALLY--!
MNEMONO'S VENGEANCE SHALL ASSUREDLY BE SATED THIS DAY!
They all sounded like dictionaries.
And looks? Please...
I KNEW THE DAY WOULD COME WHEN YOU WOULD REMOVE THE CROWN FOR ME, FOOLISH WHELP!
Looked like this guy's skull threw up on his face.

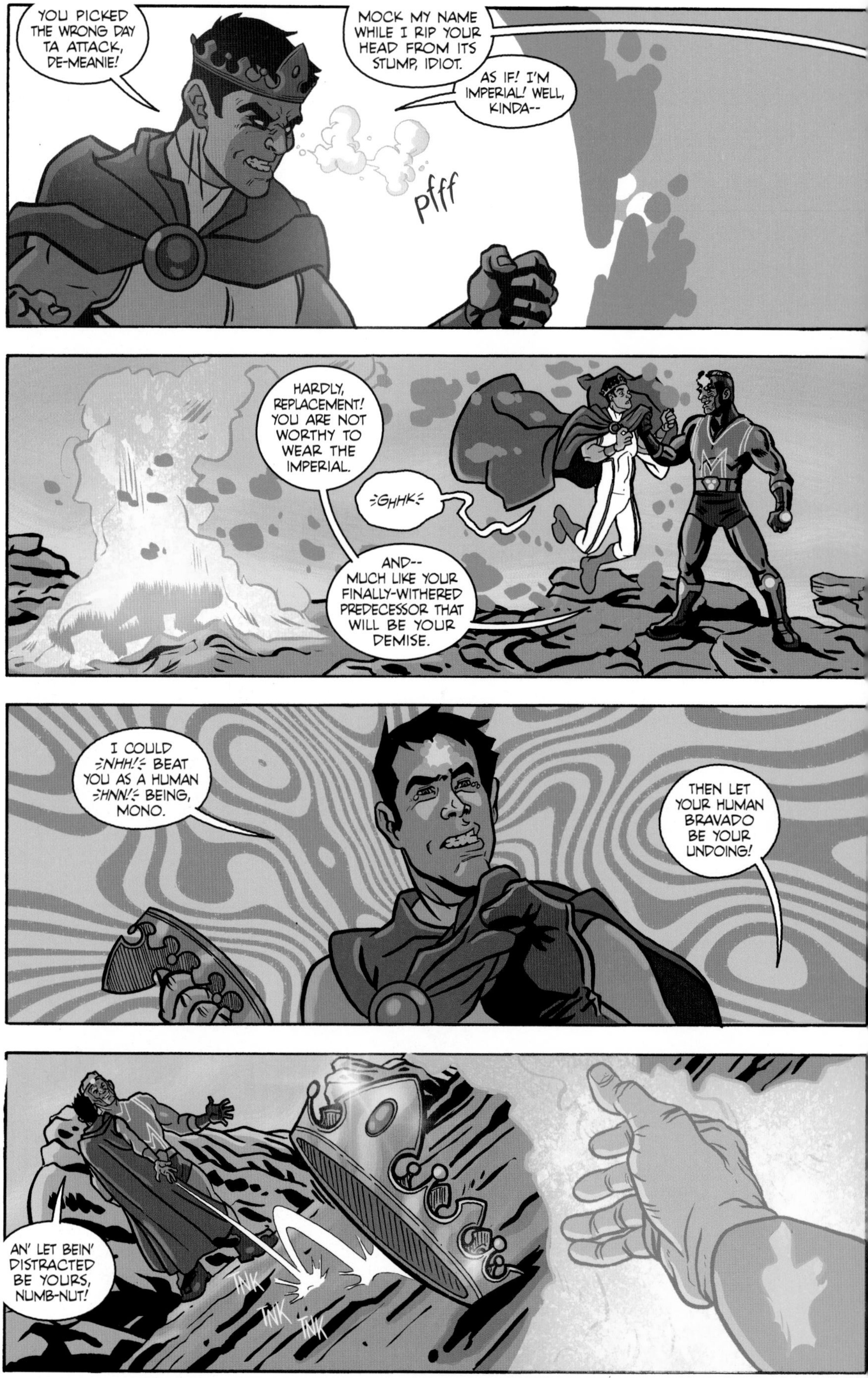
YOU PICKED THE WRONG DAY TA ATTACK, DE-MEANIE!
MOCK MY NAME WHILE I RIP YOUR HEAD FROM ITS STUMP, IDIOT.
AS IF! I'M IMPERIAL! WELL, KINDA--
pfff
HARDLY, REPLACEMENT! YOU ARE NOT WORTHY TO WEAR THE IMPERIAL.
GHHK
AND-- MUCH LIKE YOUR FINALLY-WITHERED PREDECESSOR THAT WILL BE YOUR DEMISE.
I COULD NHH! BEAT YOU AS A HUMAN HNN! BEING, MONO.
THEN LET YOUR HUMAN BRAVADO BE YOUR UNDOING!
AN' LET BEIN' DISTRACTED BE YOURS, NUMB-NUT!
TINK
TINK
TINK

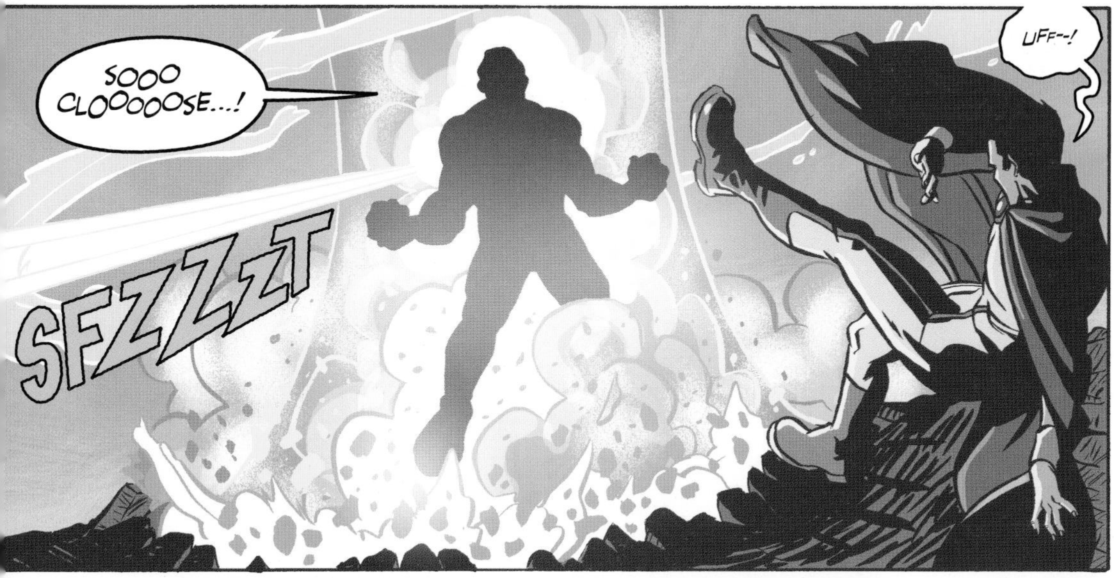
SOOO CLOOOOOSE...!
UFF--!
SFZZZZT

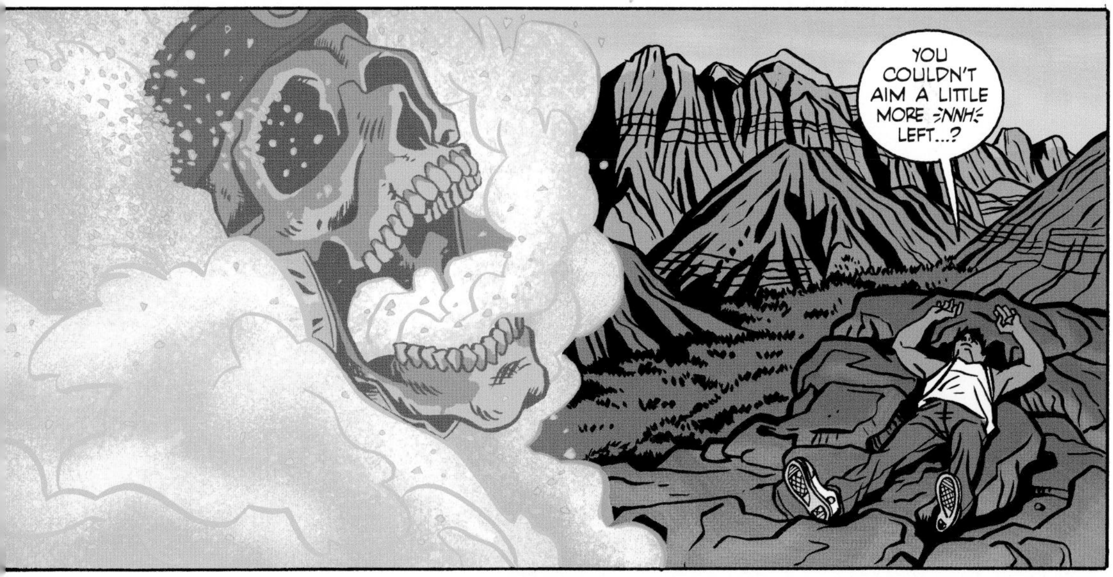
YOU COULDN'T AIM A LITTLE MORE =NNH= LEFT...?

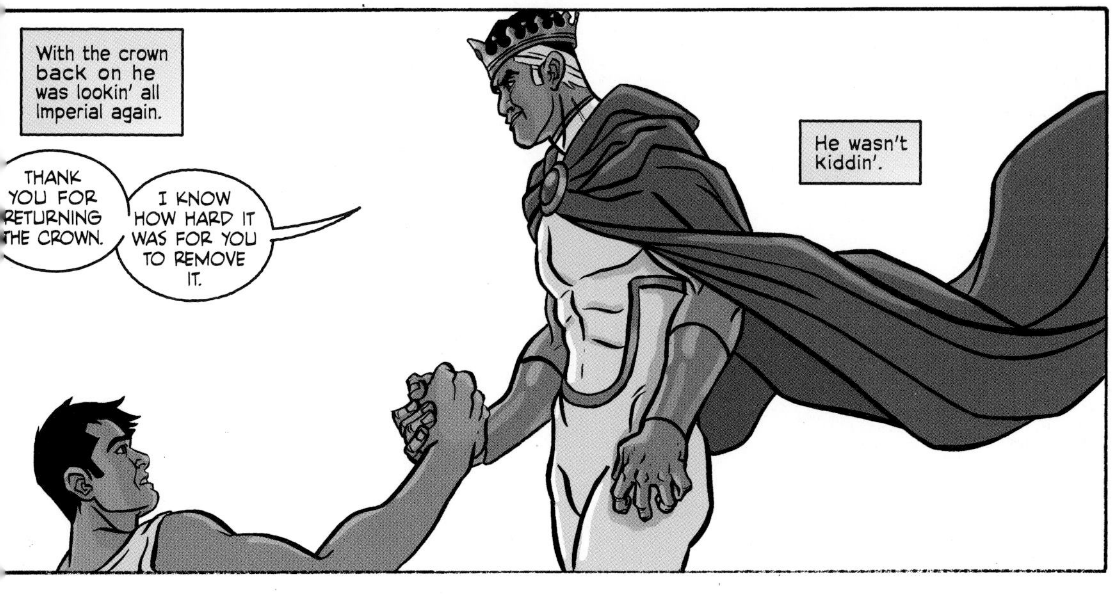
With the crown back on he was lookin' all Imperial again.
THANK YOU FOR RETURNING THE CROWN.
I KNOW HOW HARD IT WAS FOR YOU TO REMOVE IT.
He wasn't kiddin'.

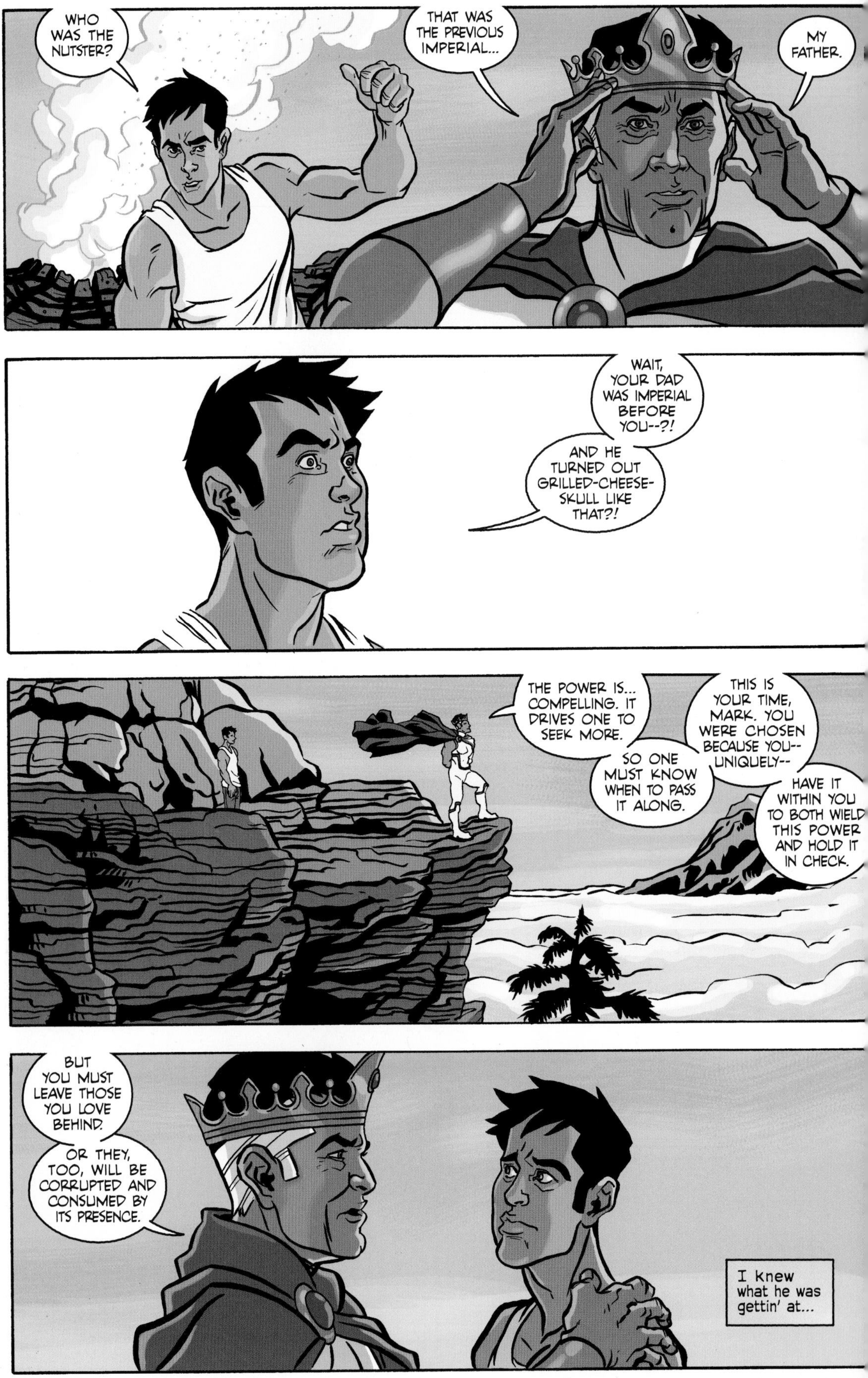
WHO WAS THE NUTSTER?
THAT WAS THE PREVIOUS IMPERIAL...
MY FATHER.
WAIT, YOUR DAD WAS IMPERIAL BEFORE YOU--?!
AND HE TURNED OUT GRILLED-CHEESE-SKULL LIKE THAT?!
THE POWER IS... COMPELLING. IT DRIVES ONE TO SEEK MORE.
SO ONE MUST KNOW WHEN TO PASS IT ALONG.
THIS IS YOUR TIME, MARK. YOU WERE CHOSEN BECAUSE YOU-- UNIQUELY--
HAVE IT WITHIN YOU TO BOTH WIELD THIS POWER AND HOLD IT IN CHECK.
BUT YOU MUST LEAVE THOSE YOU LOVE BEHIND.
OR THEY, TOO, WILL BE CORRUPTED AND CONSUMED BY ITS PRESENCE.
I knew what he was gettin' at...

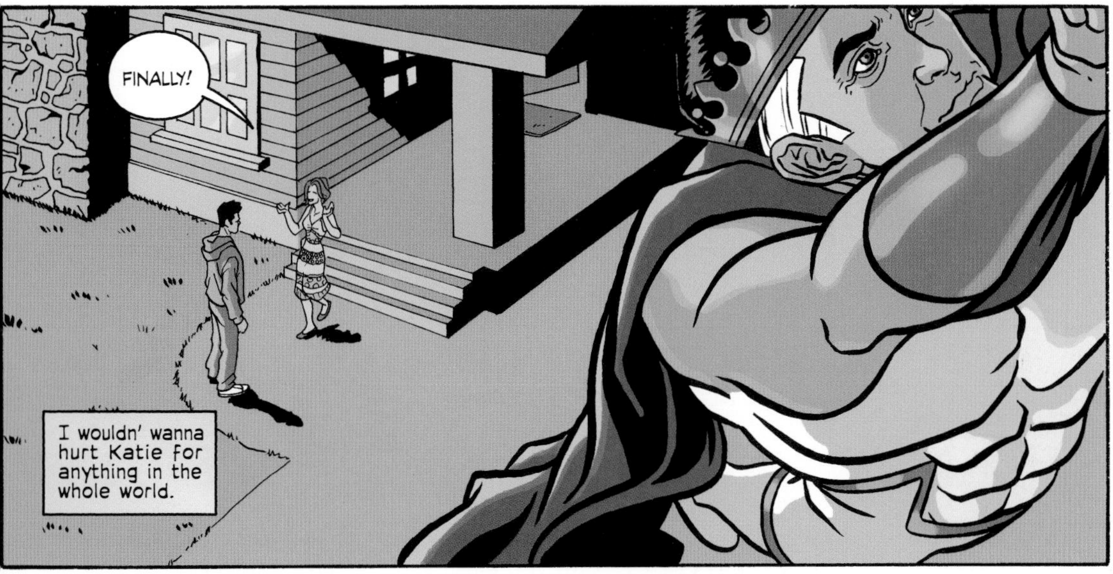
FINALLY!
I wouldn' wanna hurt Katie for anything in the whole world.

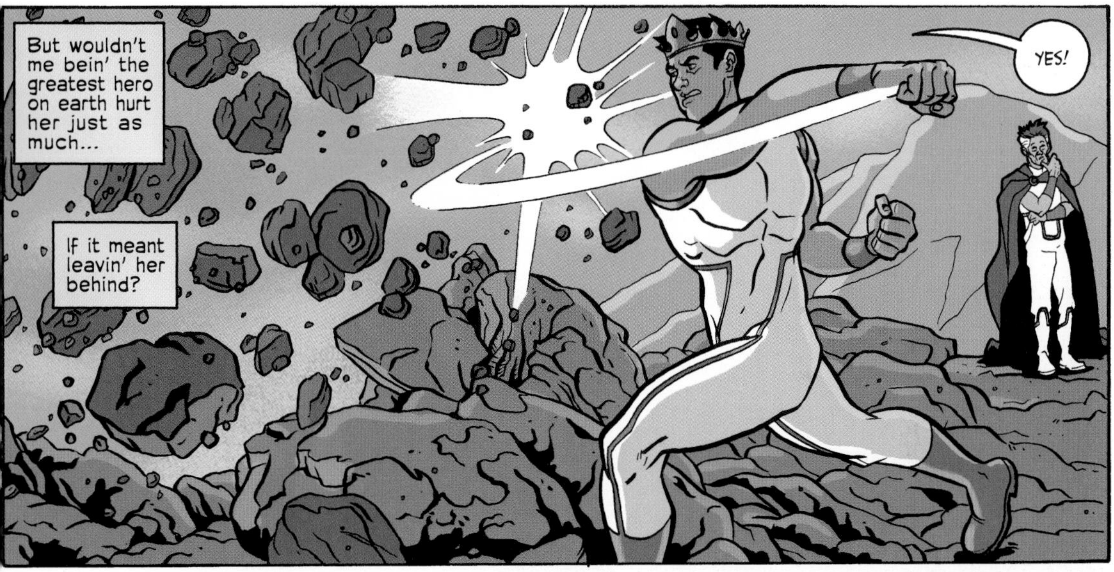
But wouldn't me bein' the greatest hero on earth hurt her just as much...
YES!
If it meant leavin' her behind?

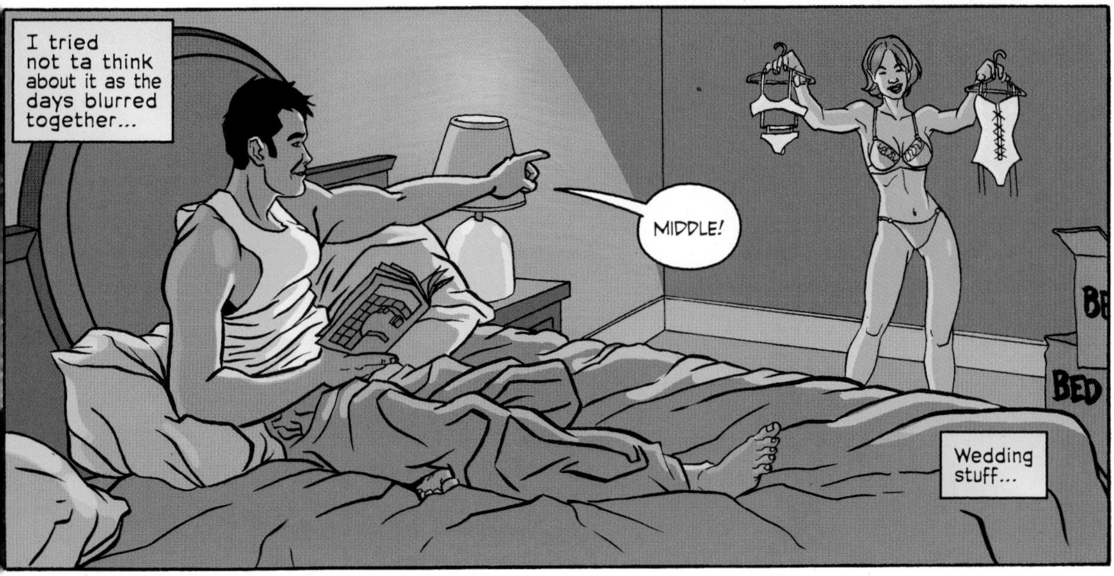
I tried not ta think about it as the days blurred together...
MIDDLE!
BED
Wedding stuff...

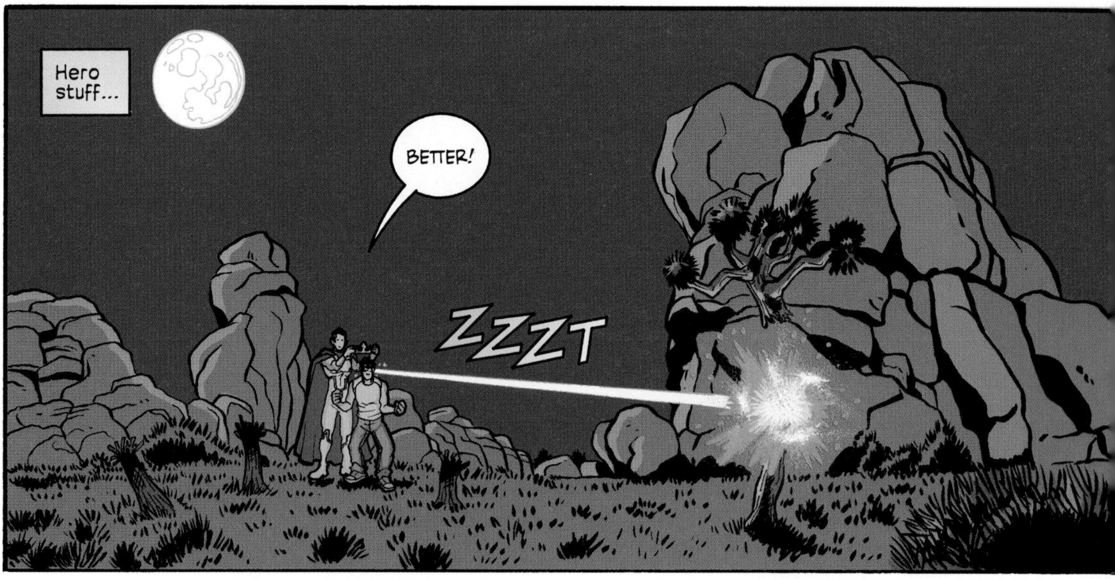
Hero stuff...
BETTER!
ZZZT

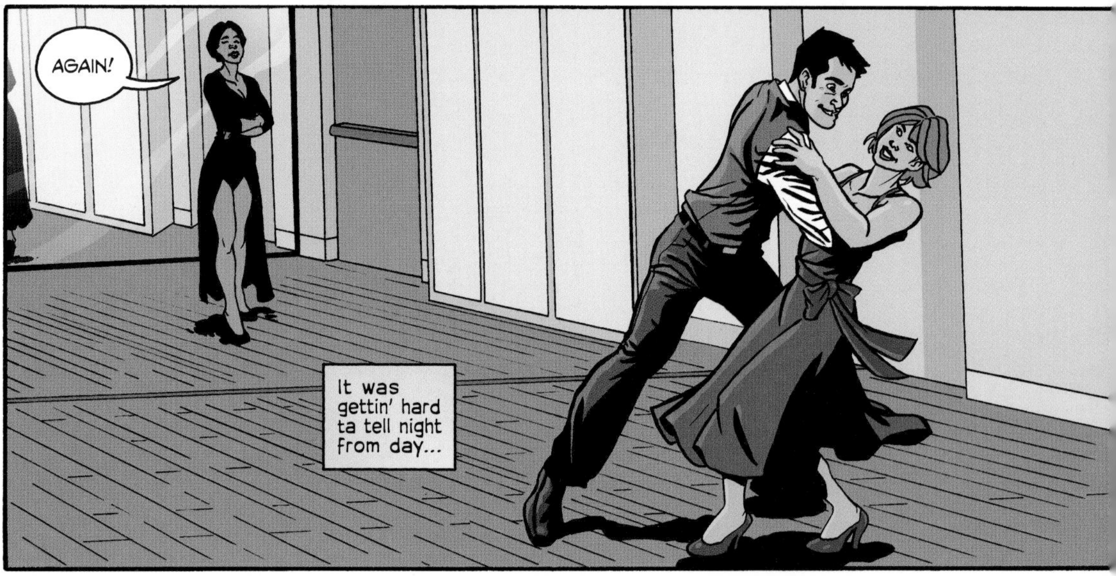
AGAIN!
It was gettin' hard ta tell night from day...

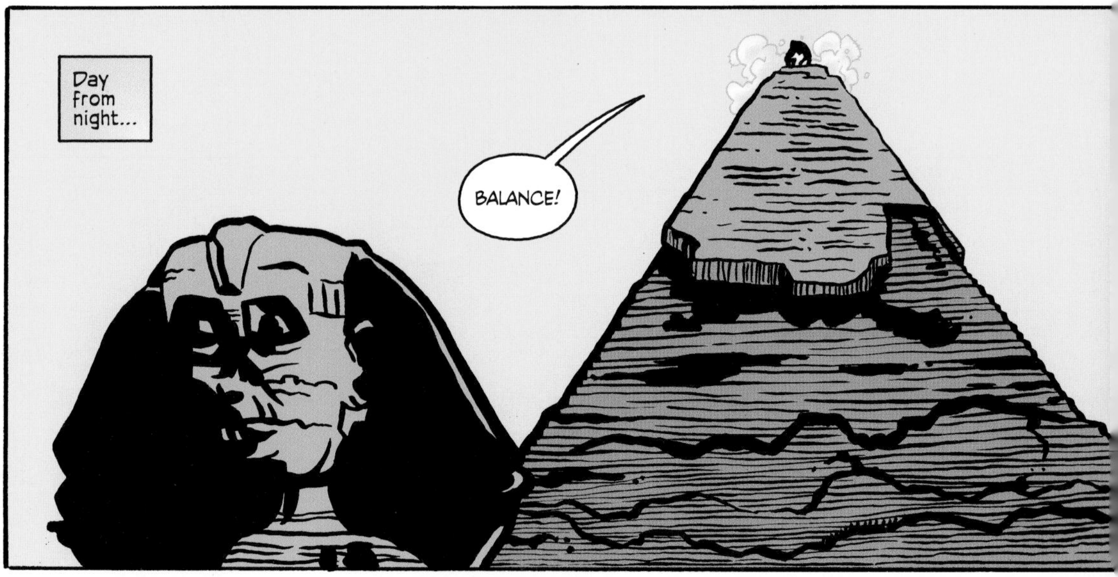
Day from night...
BALANCE!

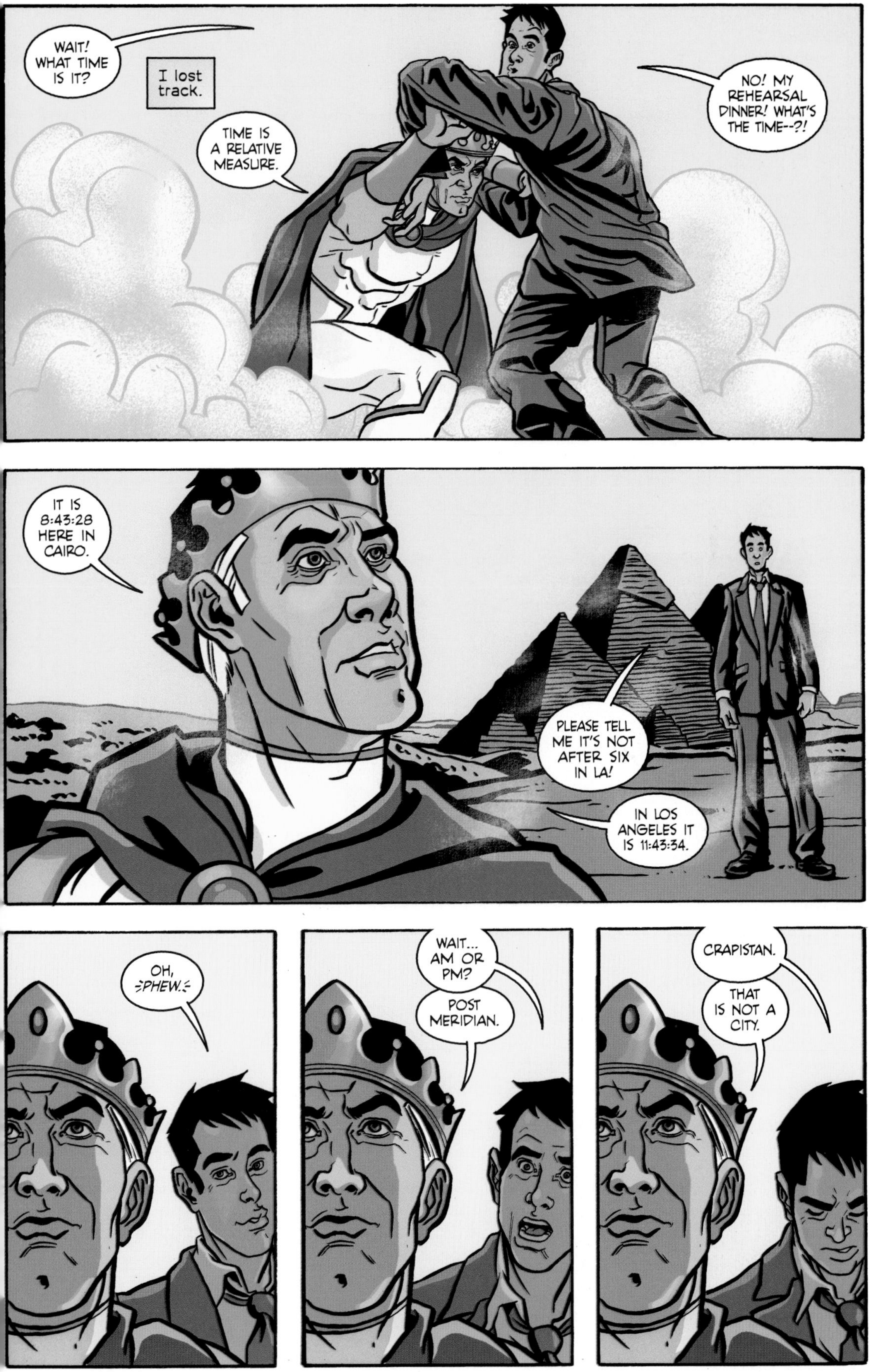
WAIT! WHAT TIME IS IT?
I lost track.
TIME IS A RELATIVE MEASURE.
NO! MY REHEARSAL DINNER! WHAT'S THE TIME--?!
IT IS 8:43:28 HERE IN CAIRO.
PLEASE TELL ME IT'S NOT AFTER SIX IN LA!
IN LOS ANGELES IT IS 11:43:34.
OH, PHEW.
WAIT... AM OR PM?
POST MERIDIAN.
CRAPISTAN.
THAT IS NOT A CITY.

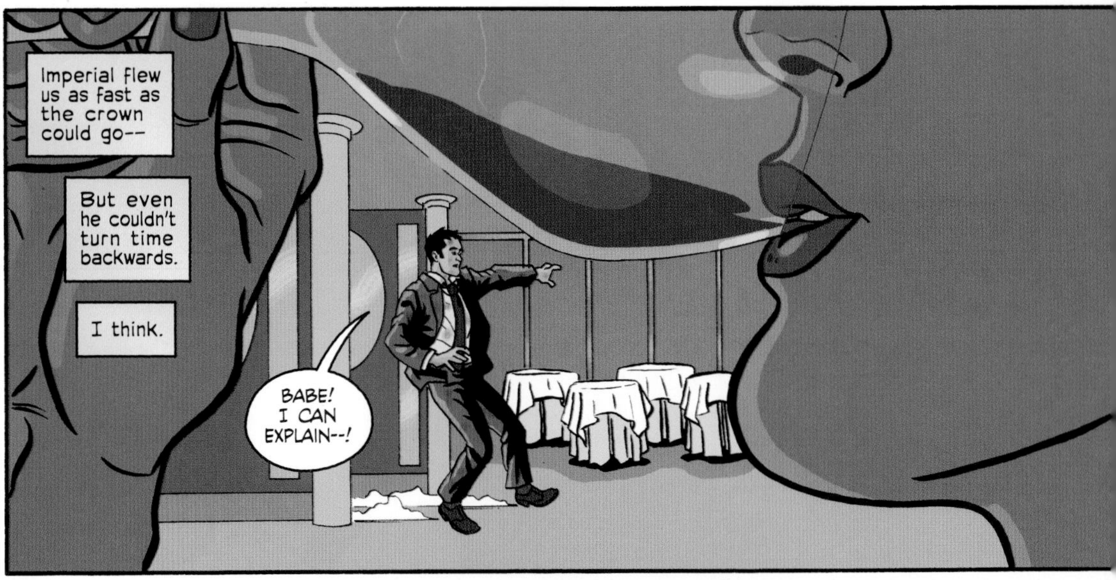
Imperial flew us as fast as the crown could go--
But even he couldn't turn time backwards.
I think.
BABE! I CAN EXPLAIN--!

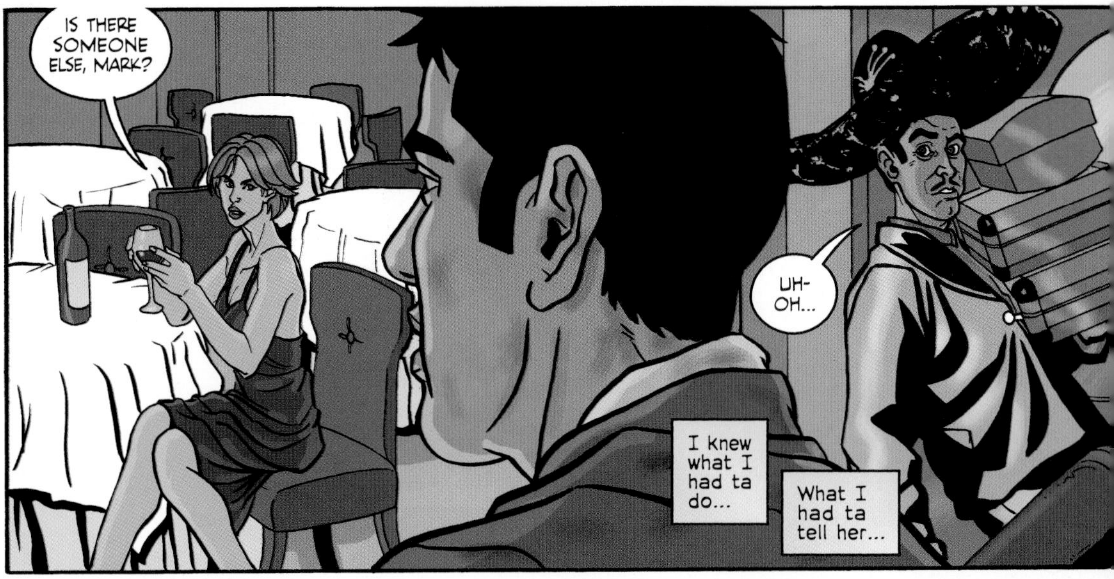
IS THERE SOMEONE ELSE, MARK?
UH-OH...
I knew what I had ta do...
What I had ta tell her...

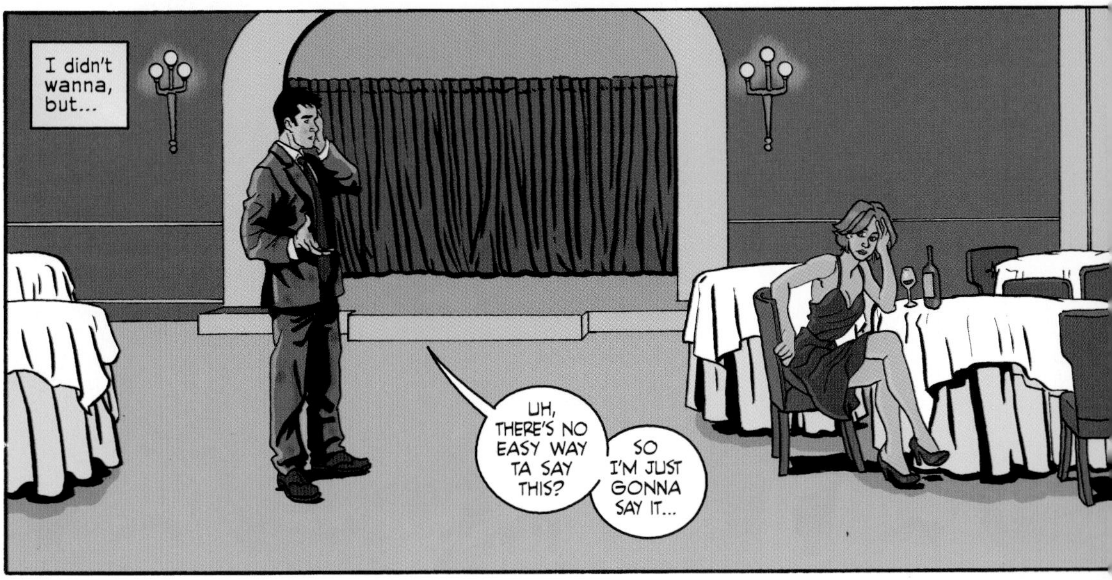
I didn't wanna, but...
UH, THERE'S NO EASY WAY TA SAY THIS?
SO I'M JUST GONNA SAY IT...

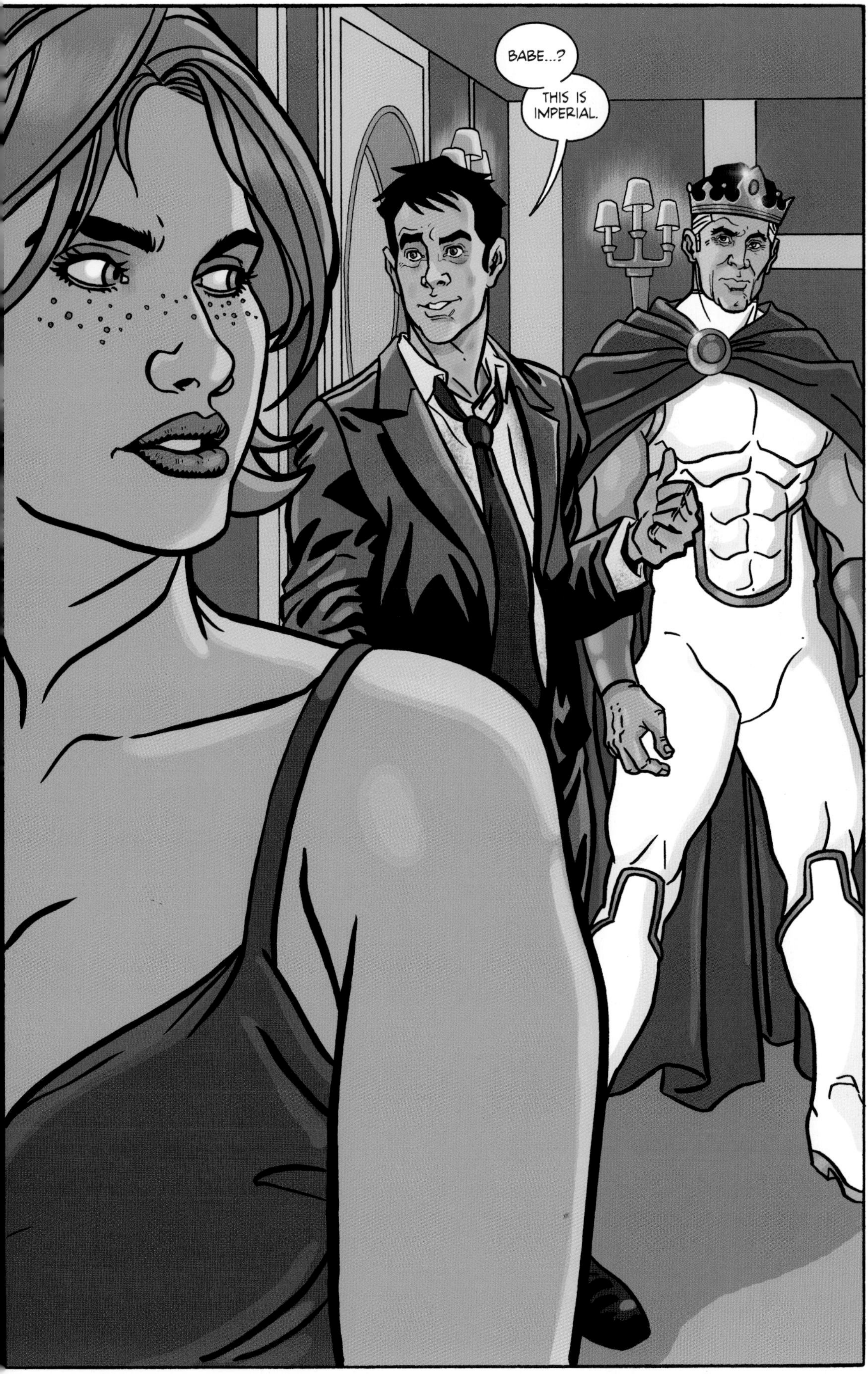
BABE...?
THIS IS IMPERIAL.

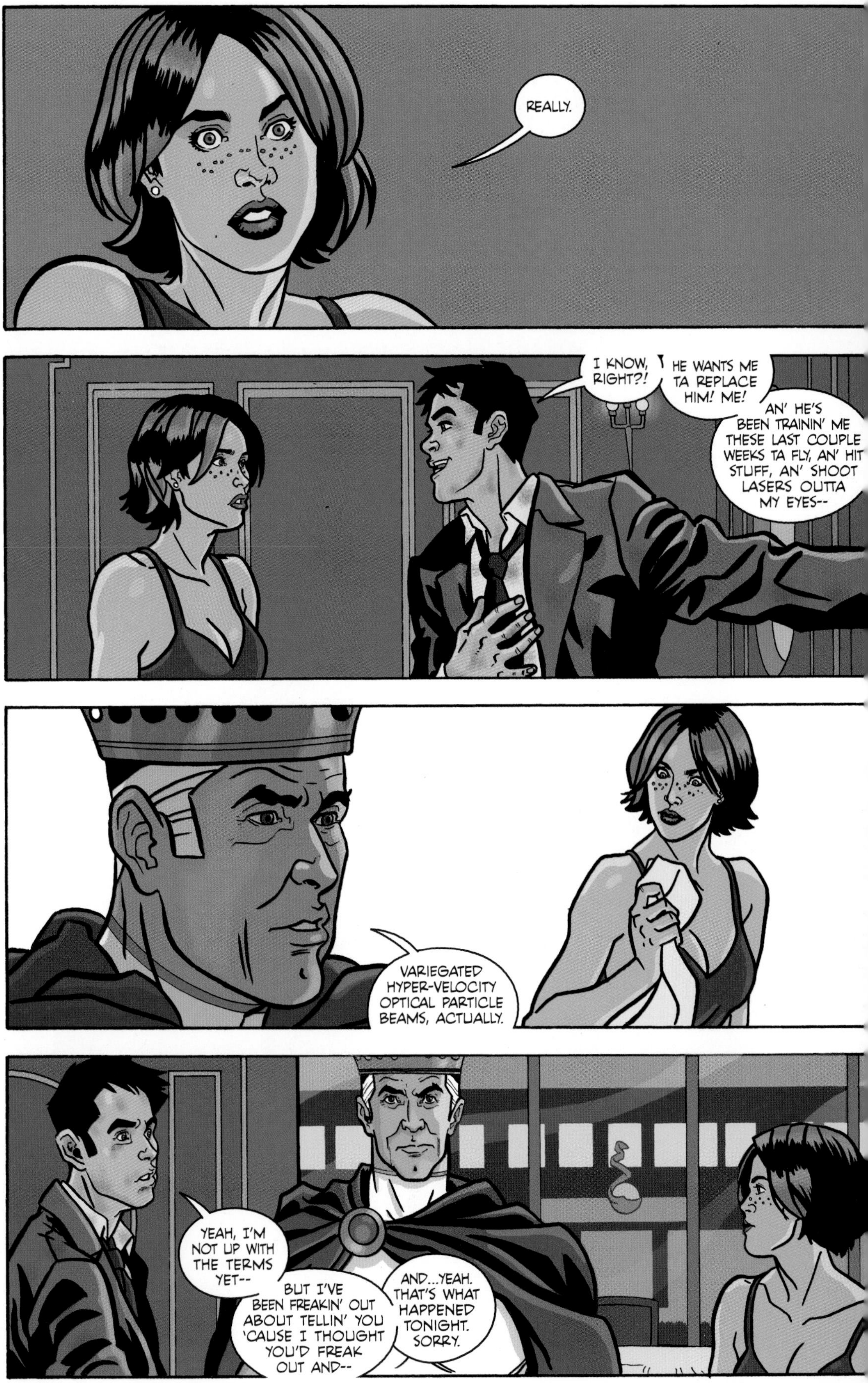
REALLY.
I KNOW, RIGHT?!
HE WANTS ME TA REPLACE HIM! ME!
AN' HE'S BEEN TRAININ' ME THESE LAST COUPLE WEEKS TA FLY, AN' HIT STUFF, AN' SHOOT LASERS OUTTA MY EYES--
VARIEGATED HYPER-VELOCITY OPTICAL PARTICLE BEAMS, ACTUALLY.
YEAH, I'M NOT UP WITH THE TERMS YET--
BUT I'VE BEEN FREAKIN' OUT ABOUT TELLIN' YOU 'CAUSE I THOUGHT YOU'D FREAK OUT AND--
AND...YEAH. THAT'S WHAT HAPPENED TONIGHT. SORRY.

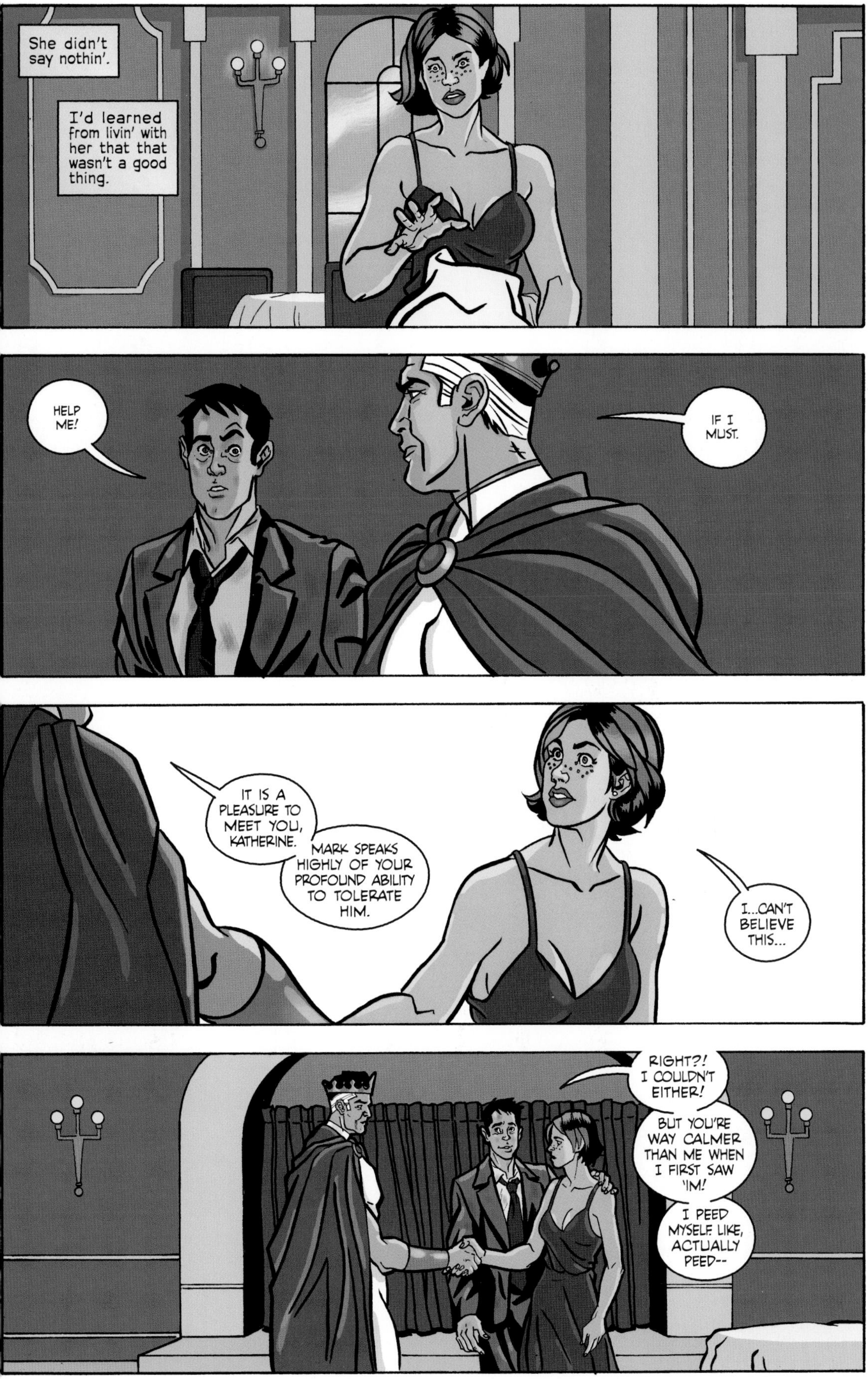
She didn't say nothin'.
I'd learned from livin' with her that that wasn't a good thing.
HELP ME!
IF I MUST.
IT IS A PLEASURE TO MEET YOU, KATHERINE.
MARK SPEAKS HIGHLY OF YOUR PROFOUND ABILITY TO TOLERATE HIM.
I...CAN'T BELIEVE THIS...
RIGHT?! I COULDN'T EITHER!
BUT YOU'RE WAY CALMER THAN ME WHEN I FIRST SAW 'IM!
I PEED MYSELF. LIKE, ACTUALLY PEED--

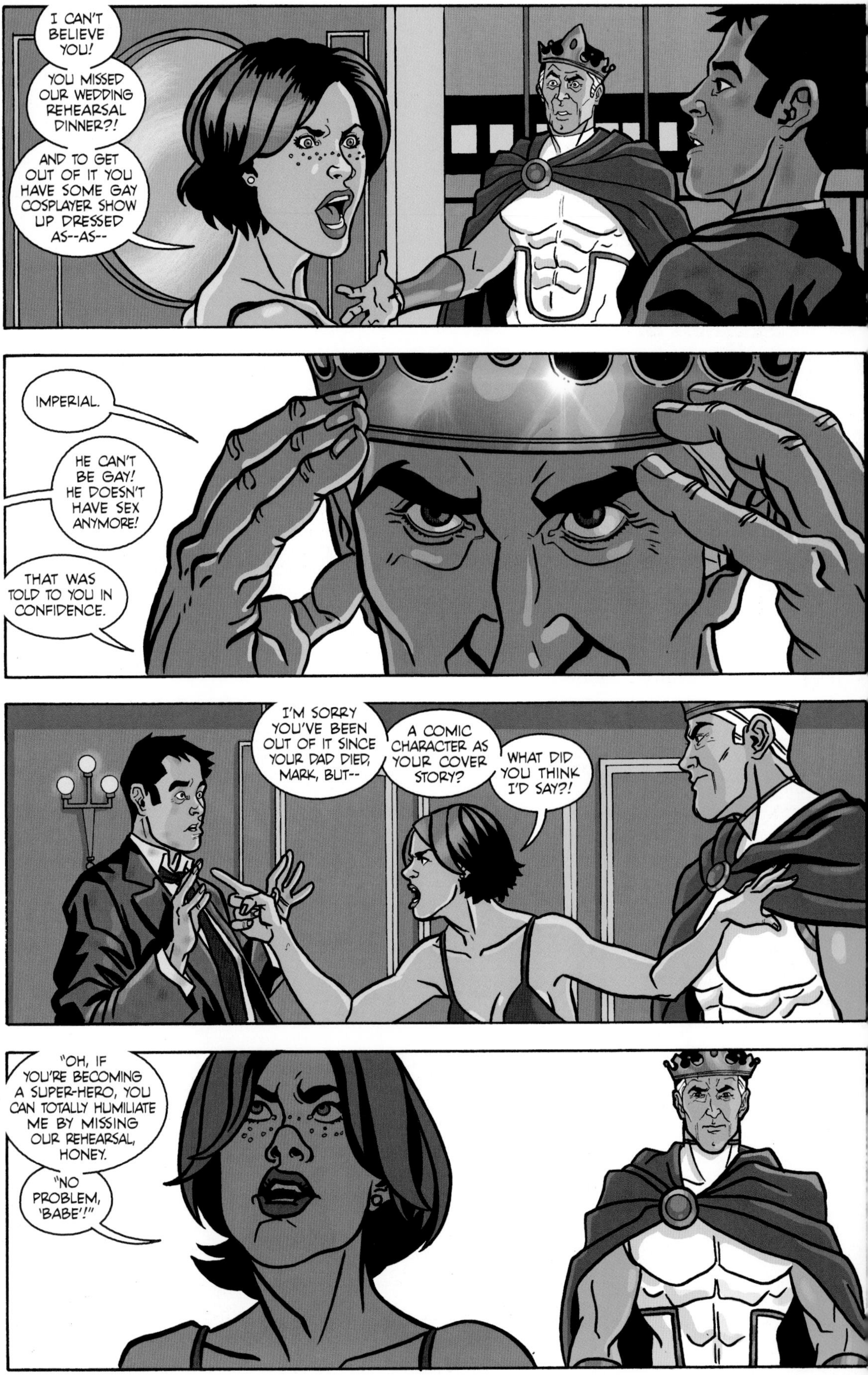
I CAN'T BELIEVE YOU!
YOU MISSED OUR WEDDING REHEARSAL DINNER?!
AND TO GET OUT OF IT YOU HAVE SOME GAY COSPLAYER SHOW UP DRESSED AS--AS--
IMPERIAL.
HE CAN'T BE GAY! HE DOESN'T HAVE SEX ANYMORE!
THAT WAS TOLD TO YOU IN CONFIDENCE.
I'M SORRY YOU'VE BEEN OUT OF IT SINCE YOUR DAD DIED, MARK, BUT--
A COMIC CHARACTER AS YOUR COVER STORY?
WHAT DID YOU THINK I'D SAY?!
"OH, IF YOU'RE BECOMING A SUPER-HERO, YOU CAN TOTALLY HUMILIATE ME BY MISSING OUR REHEARSAL, HONEY.
"NO PROBLEM, 'BABE'!"

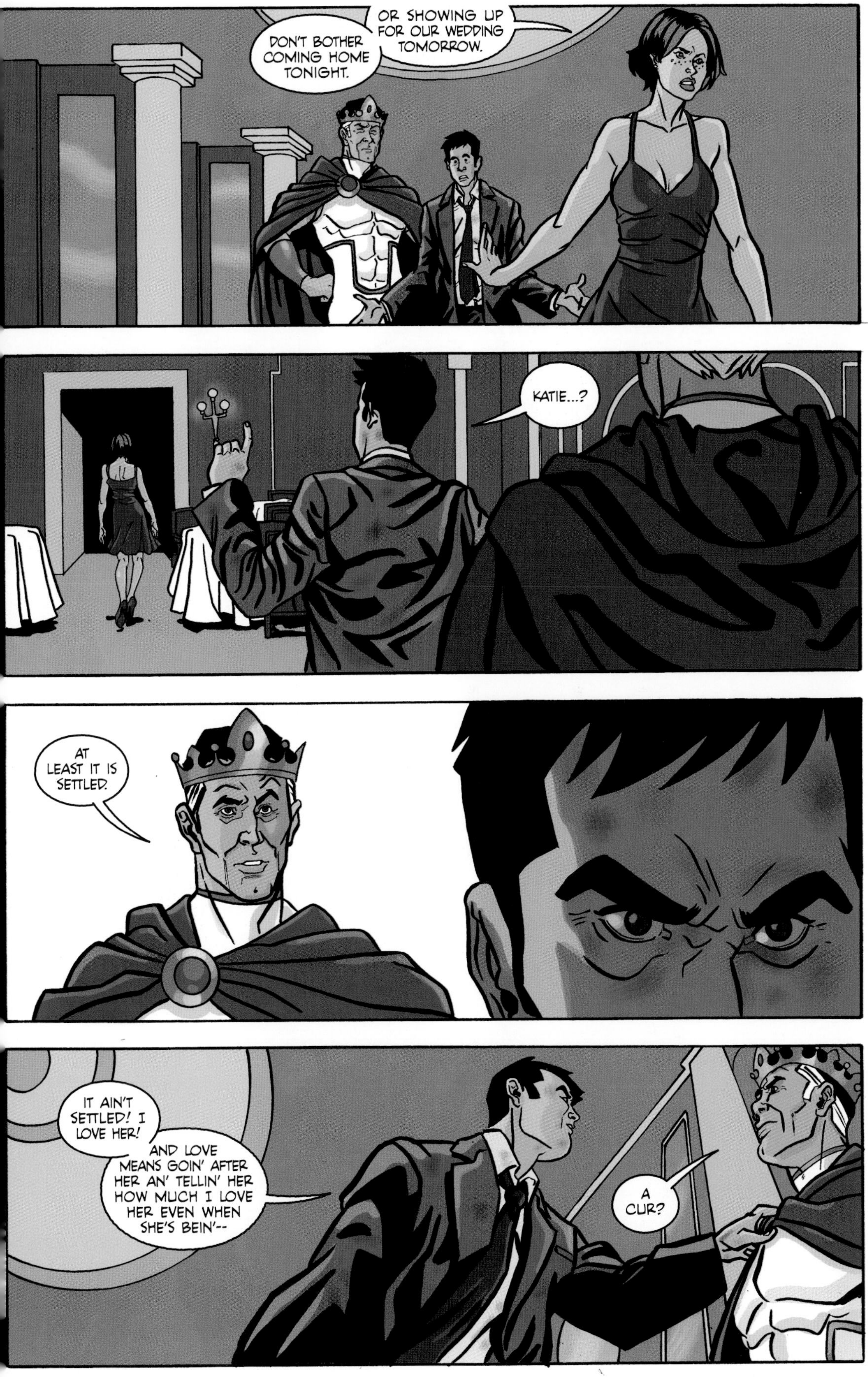
DON'T BOTHER COMING HOME TONIGHT.
OR SHOWING UP FOR OUR WEDDING TOMORROW.
KATIE...?
AT LEAST IT IS SETTLED.
IT AIN'T SETTLED! I LOVE HER!
AND LOVE MEAN'S GOIN' AFTER HER AN' TELLIN' HER HOW MUCH I LOVE HER EVEN WHEN SHE'S BEIN'--
A CUR?

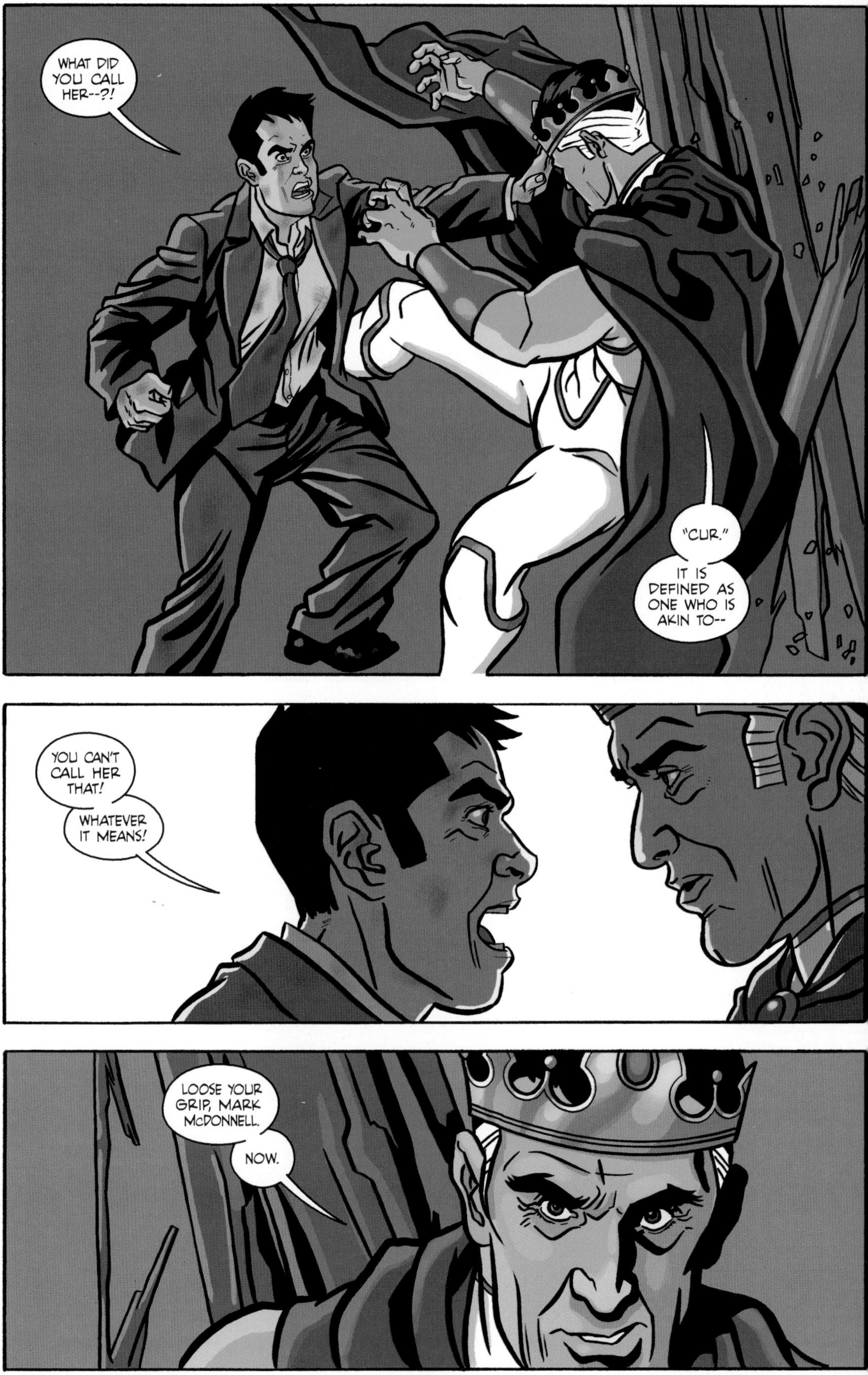
WHAT DID YOU CALL HER--?!
"CUR."
IT IS DEFINED AS ONE WHO IS AKIN TO--
YOU CAN'T CALL HER THAT!
WHATEVER IT MEANS!
LOOSE YOUR GRIP, MARK McDONNELL.
NOW.

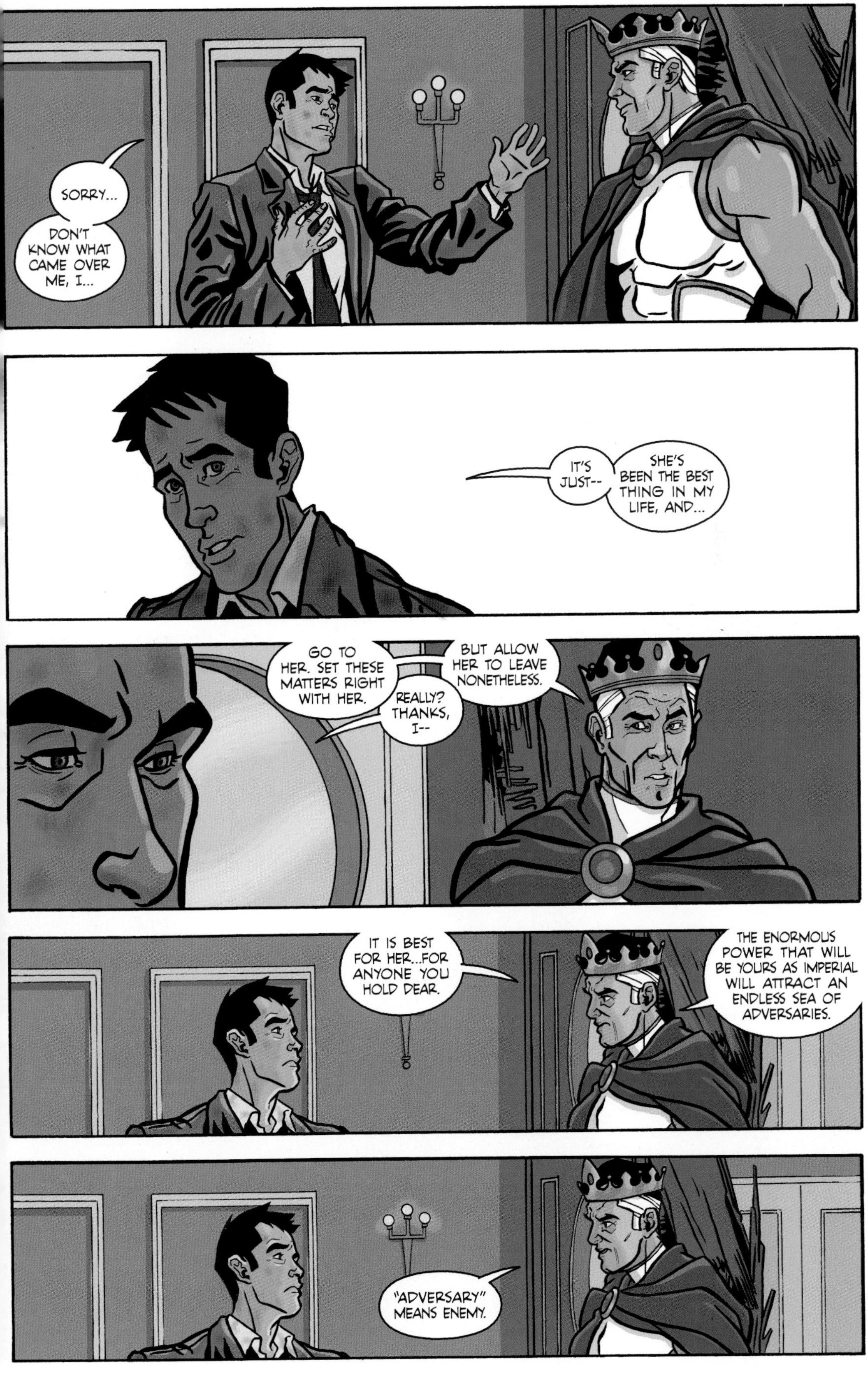
SORRY...
DON'T KNOW WHAT CAME OVER ME, I...
IT'S JUST--
SHE'S BEEN THE BEST THING IN MY LIFE, AND...
GO TO HER. SET THESE MATTERS RIGHT WITH HER.
REALLY? THANKS, I--
BUT ALLOW HER TO LEAVE NONETHELESS.
IT IS BEST FOR HER...FOR ANYONE YOU HOLD DEAR.
THE ENORMOUS POWER THAT WILL BE YOURS AS IMPERIAL WILL ATTRACT AN ENDLESS SEA OF ADVERSARIES.
"ADVERSARY" MEANS ENEMY.

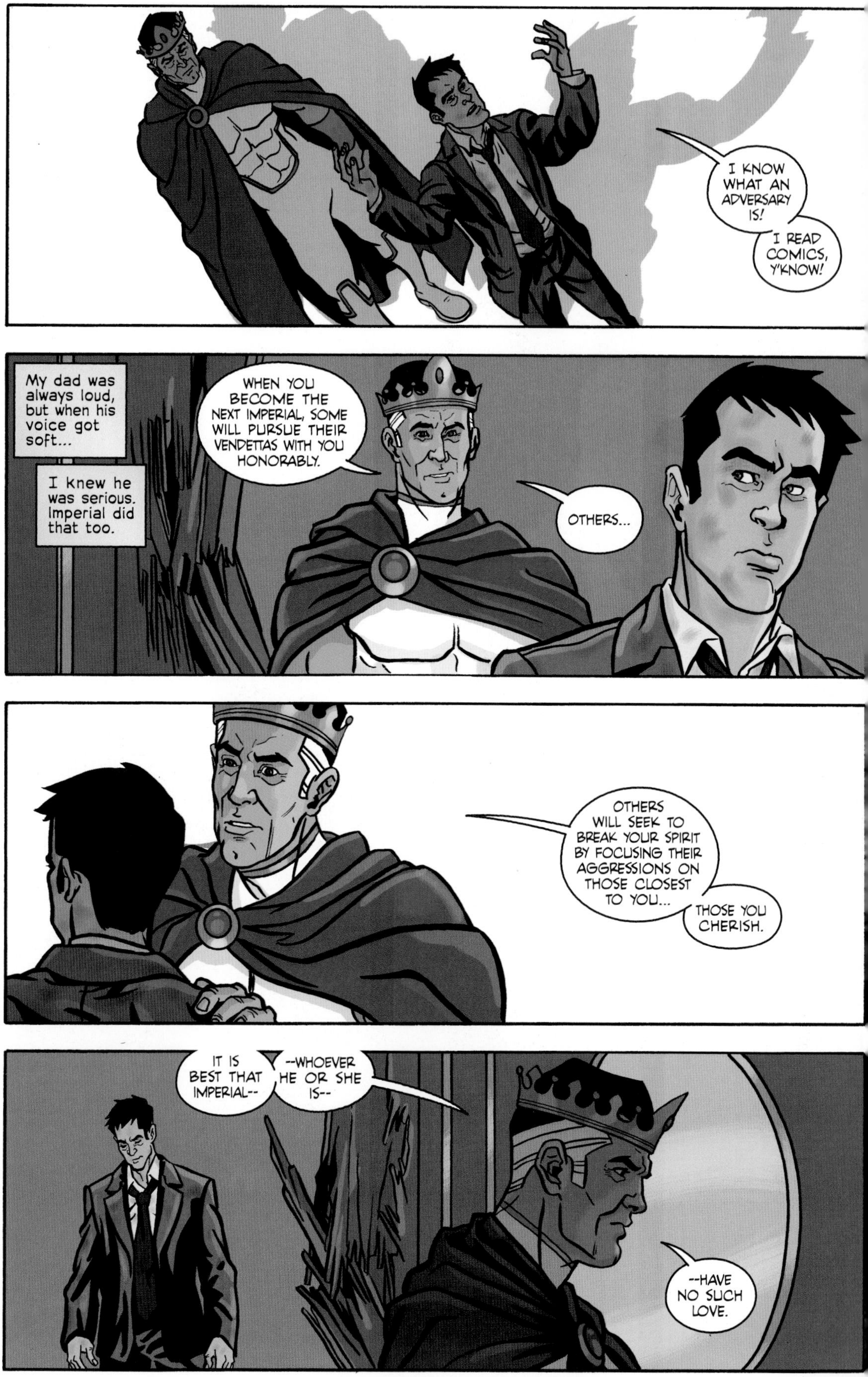
I KNOW WHAT AN ADVERSARY IS!
I READ COMICS, Y'KNOW!
My dad was always loud, but when his voice got soft...
I knew he was serious. Imperial did that too.
WHEN YOU BECOME THE NEXT IMPERIAL, SOME WILL PURSUE THEIR VENDETTAS WITH YOU HONORABLY.
OTHERS...
OTHERS WILL SEEK TO BREAK YOUR SPIRIT BY FOCUSING THEIR AGGRESSIONS ON THOSE CLOSEST TO YOU...
THOSE YOU CHERISH.
IT IS BEST THAT IMPERIAL--
--WHOEVER HE OR SHE IS--
--HAVE NO SUCH LOVE.

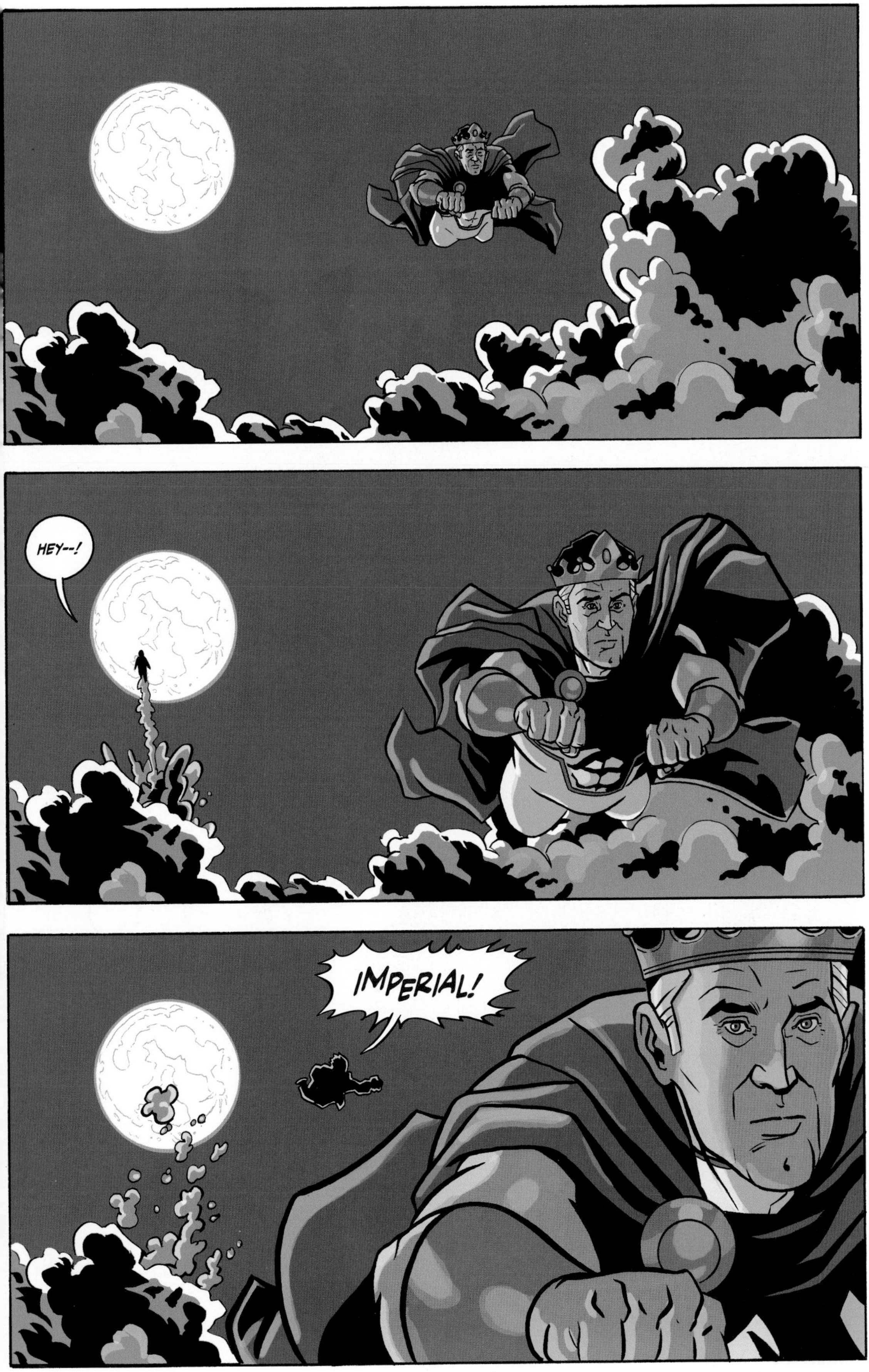
HEY--!
IMPERIAL!

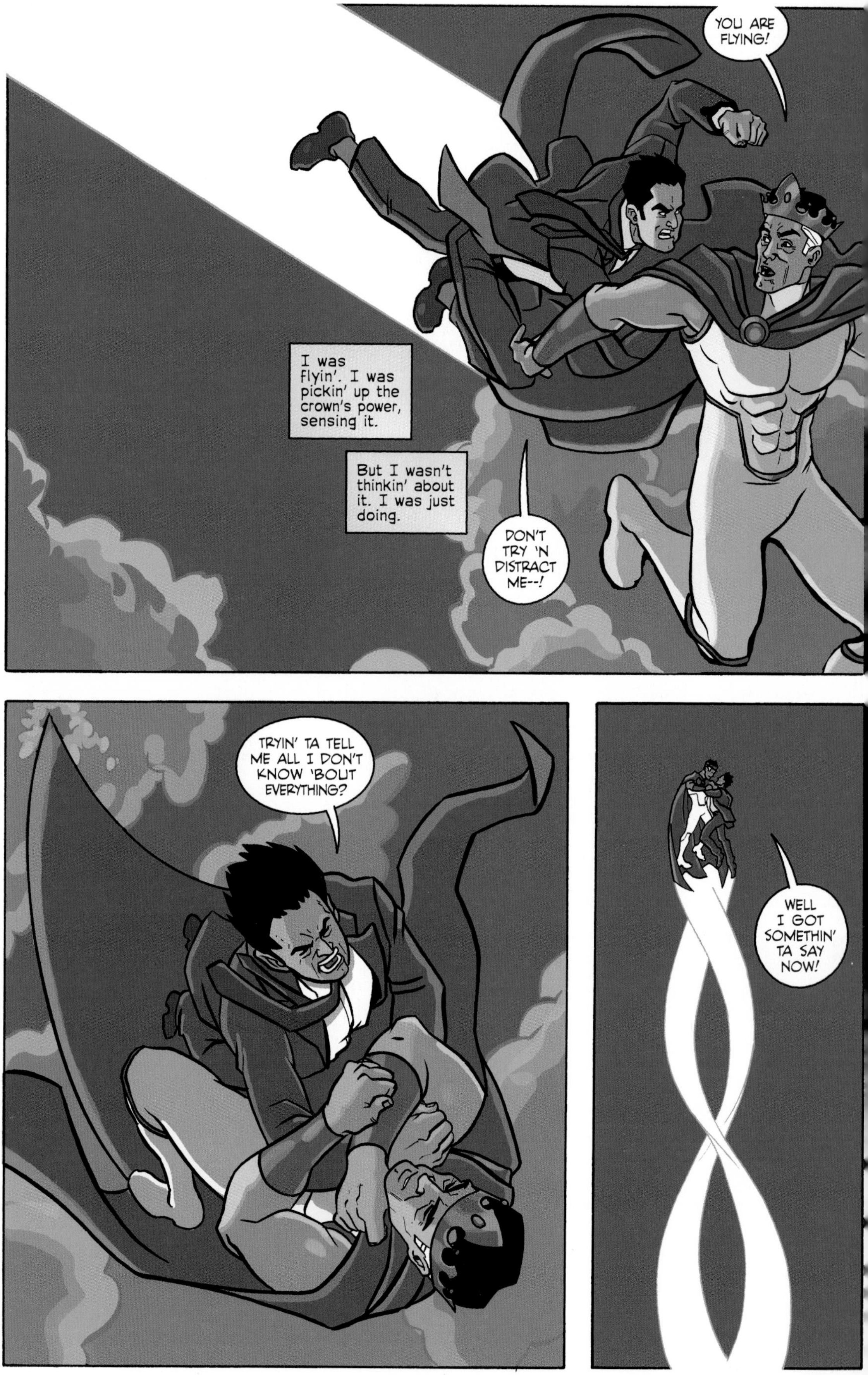
YOU ARE FLYING!
I was flyin'. I was pickin' up the crown's power, sensing it.
But I wasn't thinkin' about it. I was just doing.
DON'T TRY 'N DISTRACT ME--!
TRYIN' TA TELL ME ALL I DON'T KNOW 'BOUT EVERYTHING?
WELL I GOT SOMETHIN' TA SAY NOW!

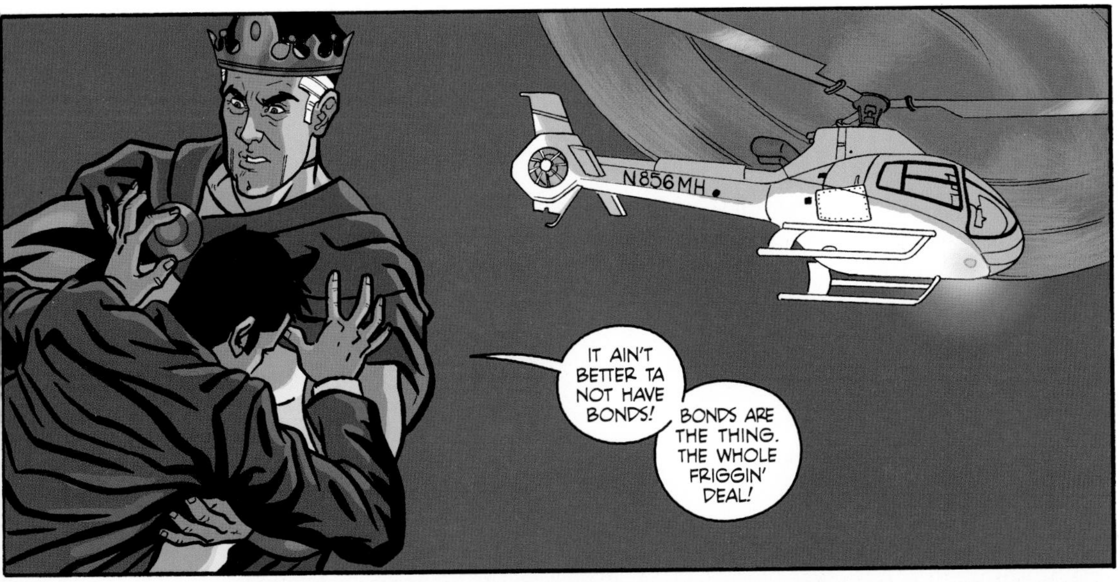
N856MH
IT AIN'T BETTER TA NOT HAVE BONDS!
BONDS ARE THE THING. THE WHOLE FRIGGIN' DEAL!

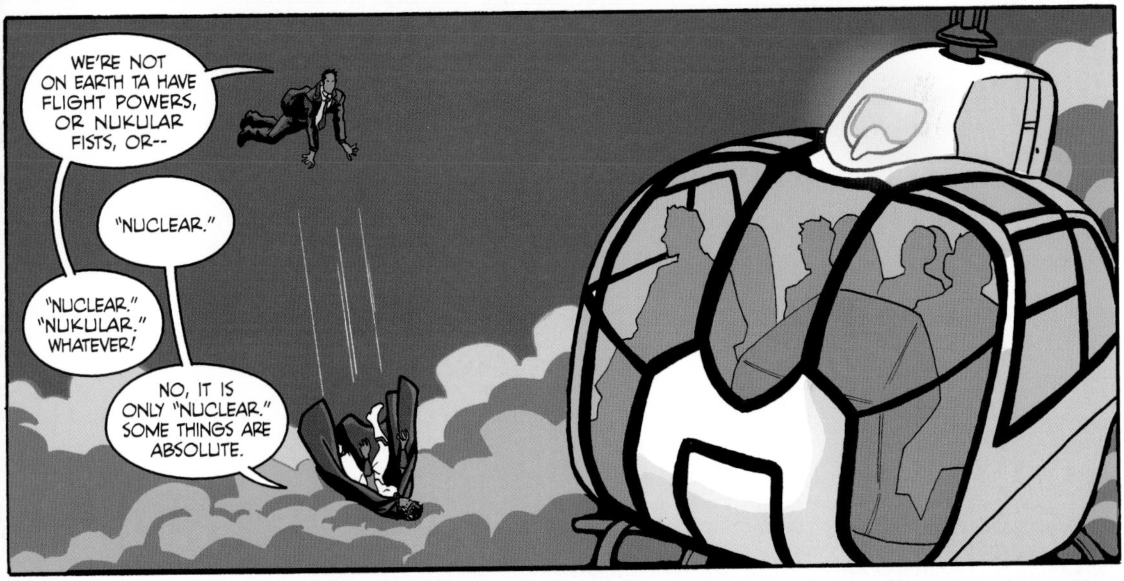
WE'RE NOT ON EARTH TA HAVE FLIGHT POWERS, OR NUKULAR FISTS, OR--
"NUCLEAR."
"NUCLEAR." "NUKULAR." WHATEVER!
NO, IT IS ONLY "NUCLEAR." SOME THINGS ARE ABSOLUTE.

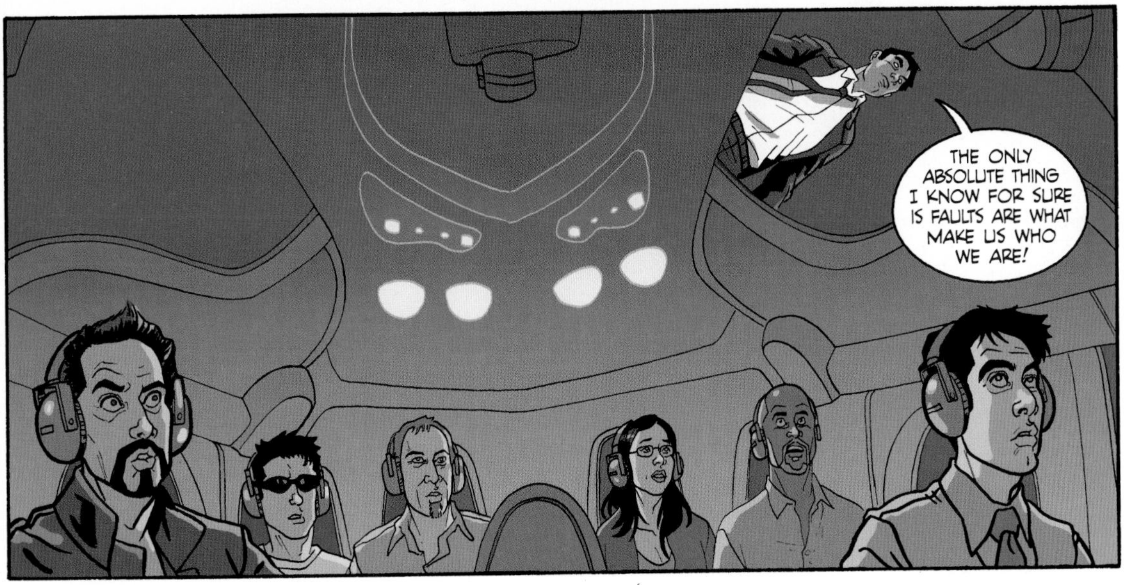
THE ONLY ABSOLUTE THING I KNOW FOR SURE IS FAULTS ARE WHAT MAKE US WHO WE ARE!

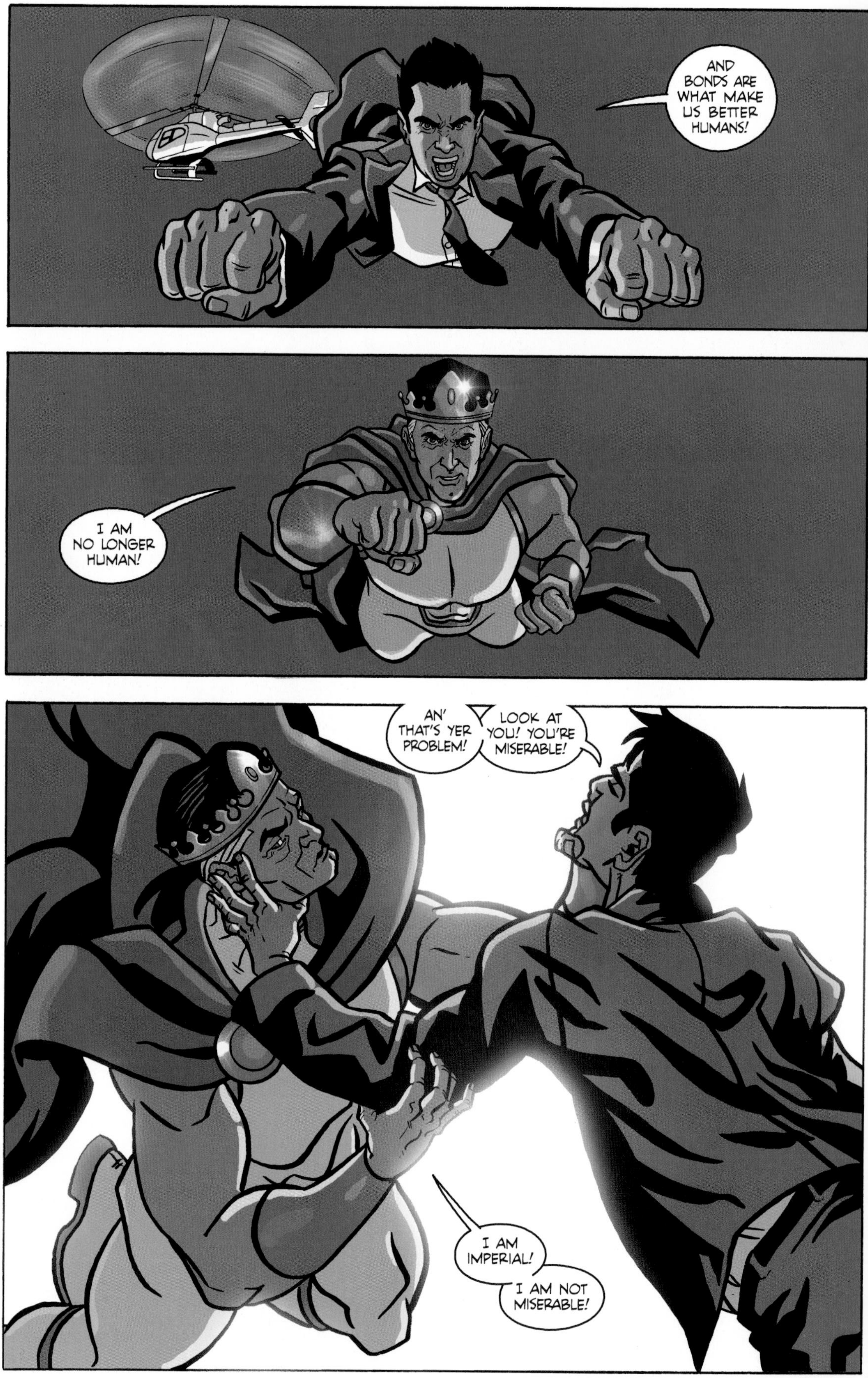
AND BONDS ARE WHAT MAKE US BETTER HUMANS!
I AM NO LONGER HUMAN!
AN' THAT'S YER PROBLEM!
LOOK AT YOU! YOU'RE MISERABLE!
I AM IMPERIAL!
I AM NOT MISERABLE!

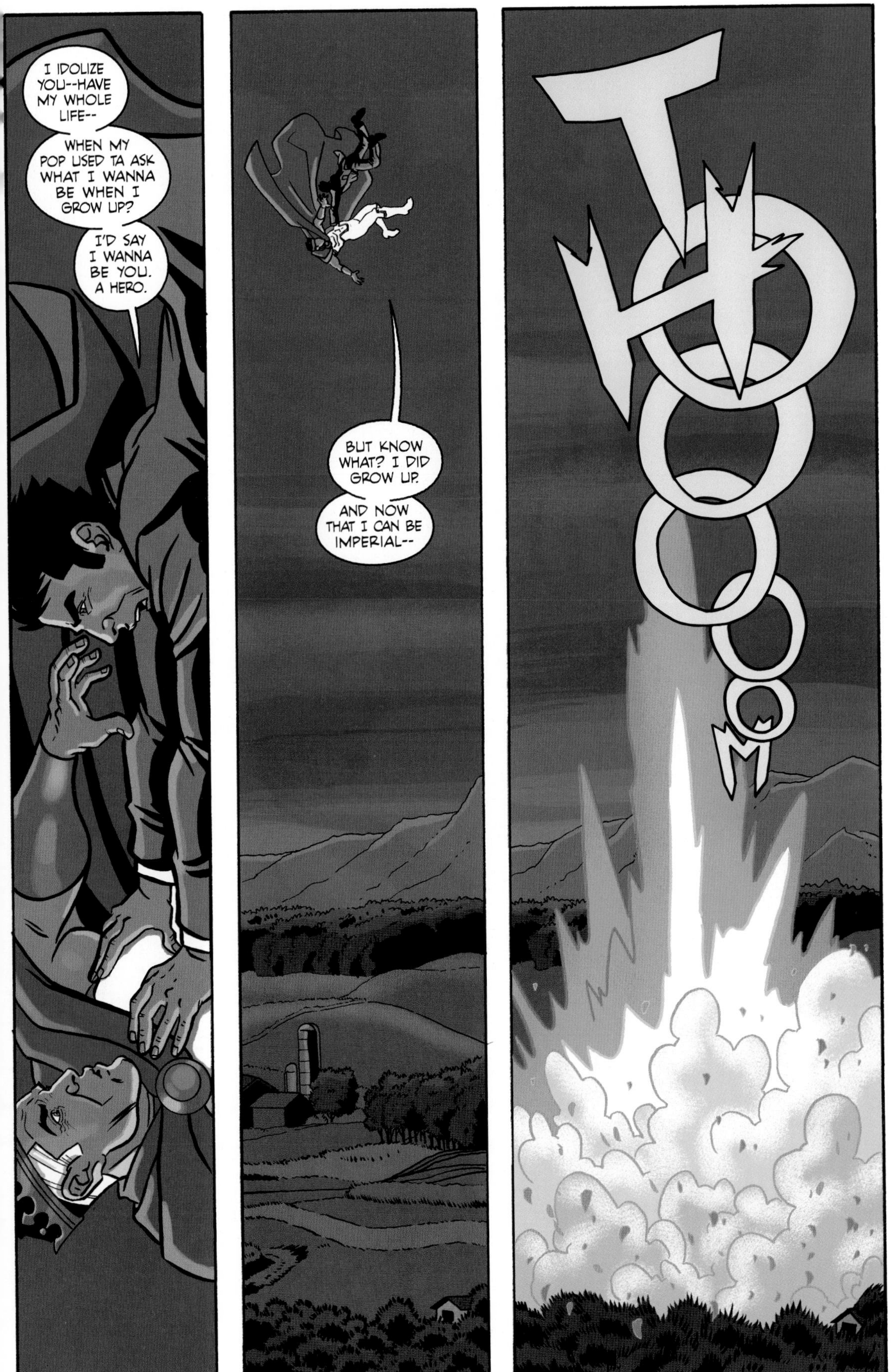
I IDOLIZE YOU--HAVE MY WHOLE LIFE--
WHEN MY POP USED TA ASK WHAT I WANNA BE WHEN I GROW UP?
I'D SAY I WANNA BE YOU. A HERO.
BUT KNOW WHAT? I DID GROW UP.
AND NOW THAT I CAN BE IMPERIAL--
THOOOOOM

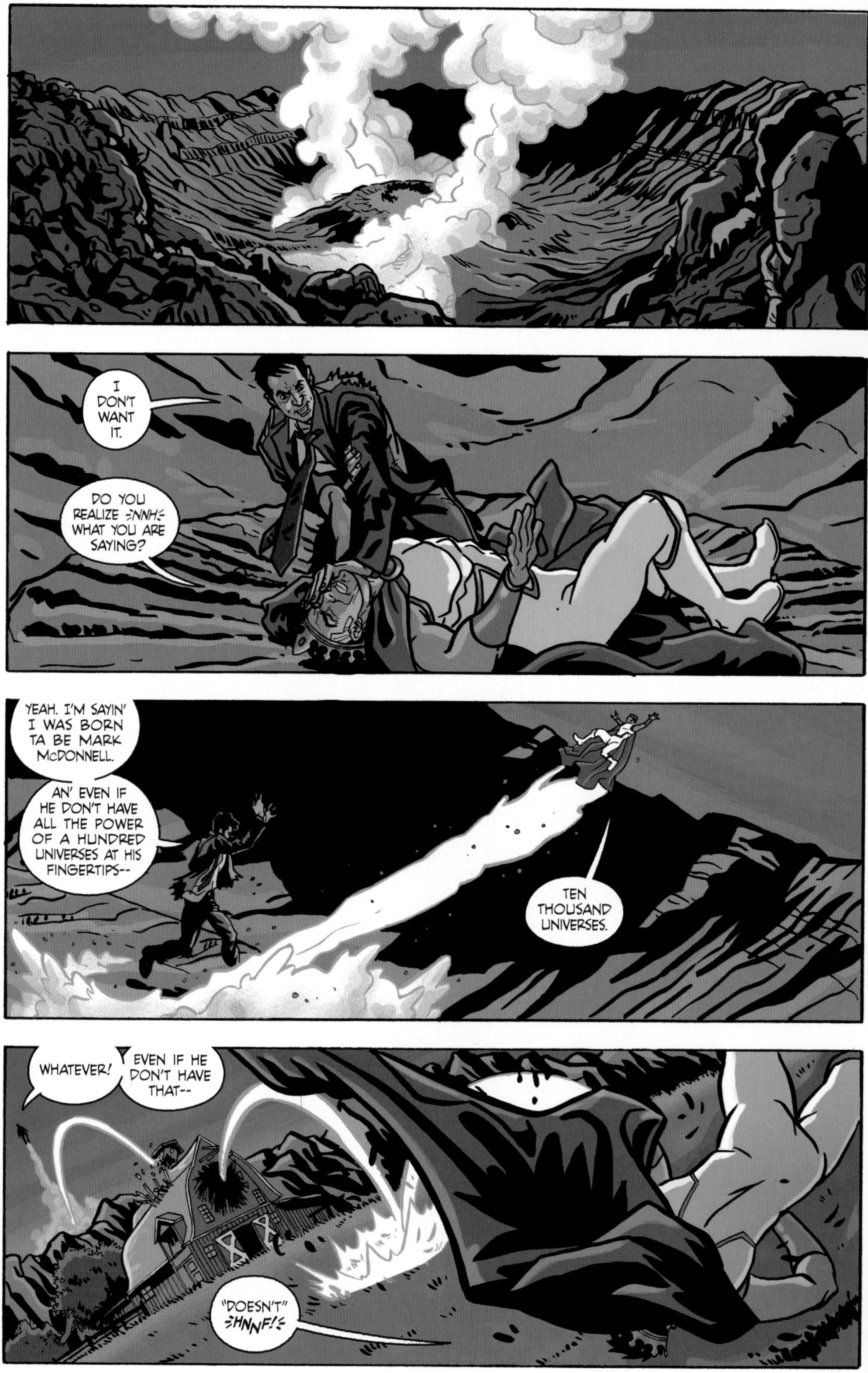

I DON'T WANT IT.
DO YOU REALIZE -NNH- WHAT YOU ARE SAYING?
YEAH. I'M SAYIN' I WAS BORN TA BE MARK McDONNELL.
AN' EVEN IF HE DON'T HAVE ALL THE POWER OF A HUNDRED UNIVERSES AT HIS FINGERTIPS--
TEN THOUSAND UNIVERSES.
WHATEVER!
EVEN IF HE DON'T HAVE THAT--
"DOESN'T" -HNNF!-

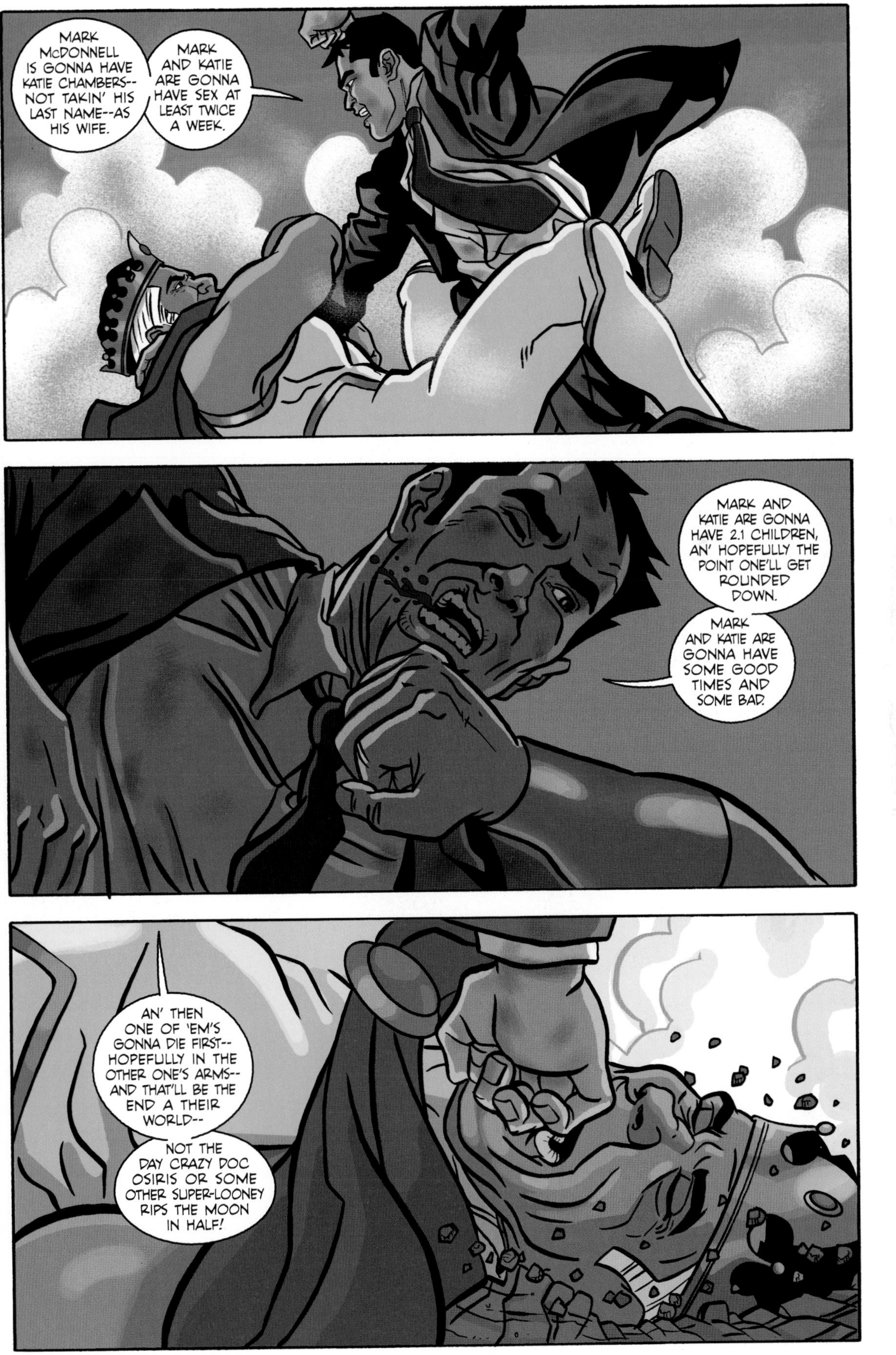
MARK McDONNELL IS GONNA HAVE KATIE CHAMBERS-- NOT TAKIN' HIS LAST NAME--AS HIS WIFE.
MARK AND KATIE ARE GONNA HAVE SEX AT LEAST TWICE A WEEK.
MARK AND KATIE ARE GONNA HAVE 2.1 CHILDREN, AN' HOPEFULLY THE POINT ONE'LL GET ROUNDED DOWN.
MARK AND KATIE ARE GONNA HAVE SOME GOOD TIMES AND SOME BAD.
AN' THEN ONE OF 'EM'S GONNA DIE FIRST-- HOPEFULLY IN THE OTHER ONE'S ARMS-- AND THAT'LL BE THE END A THEIR WORLD--
NOT THE DAY CRAZY DOC OSIRIS OR SOME OTHER SUPER-LOONEY RIPS THE MOON IN HALF!

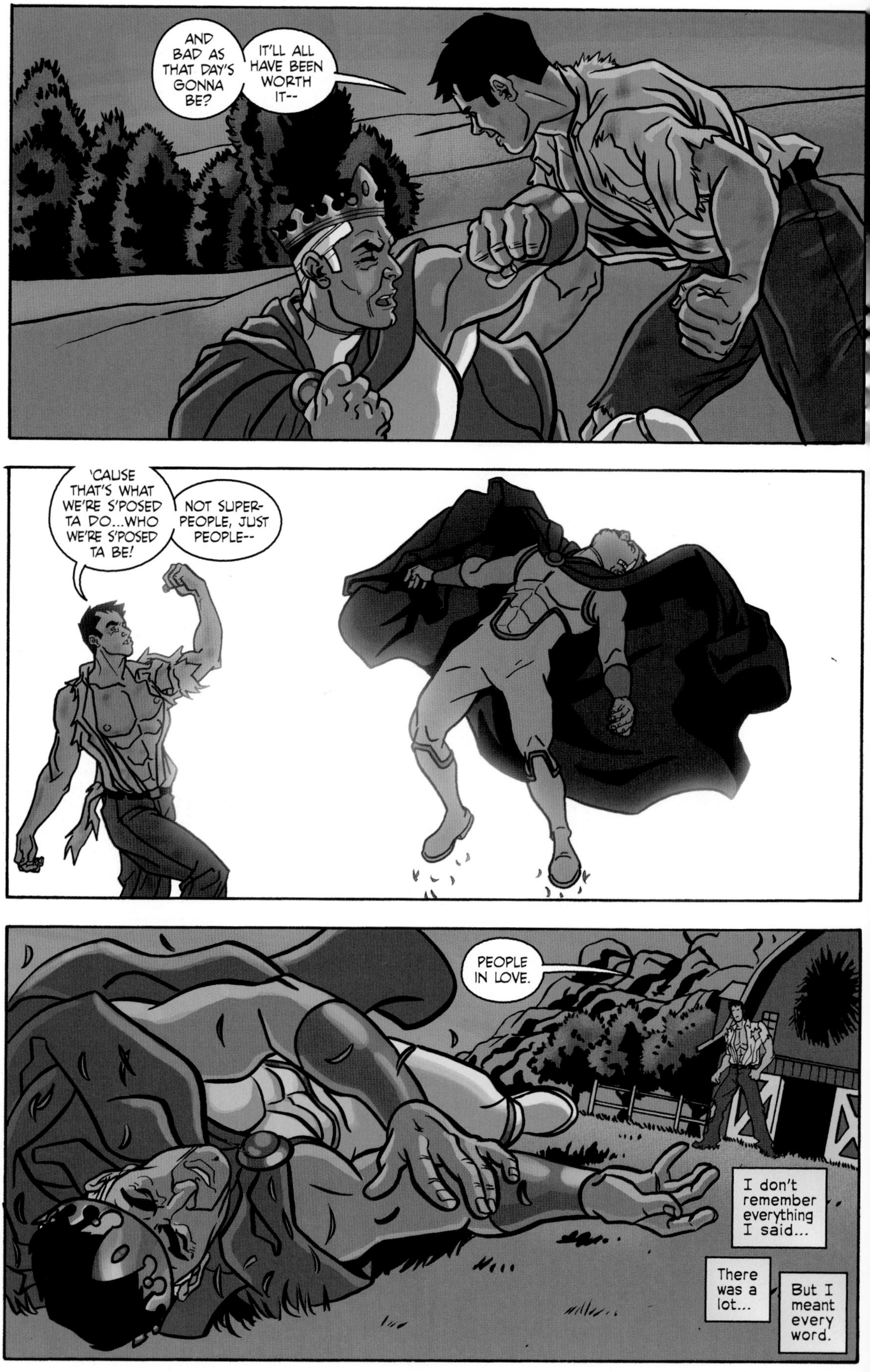
AND BAD AS THAT DAY'S GONNA BE?
IT'LL ALL HAVE BEEN WORTH IT--
'CAUSE THAT'S WHAT WE'RE S'POSED TA DO...WHO WE'RE S'POSED TA BE!
NOT SUPER-PEOPLE, JUST PEOPLE--
PEOPLE IN LOVE.
I don't remember everything I said...
There was a lot...
But I meant every word.

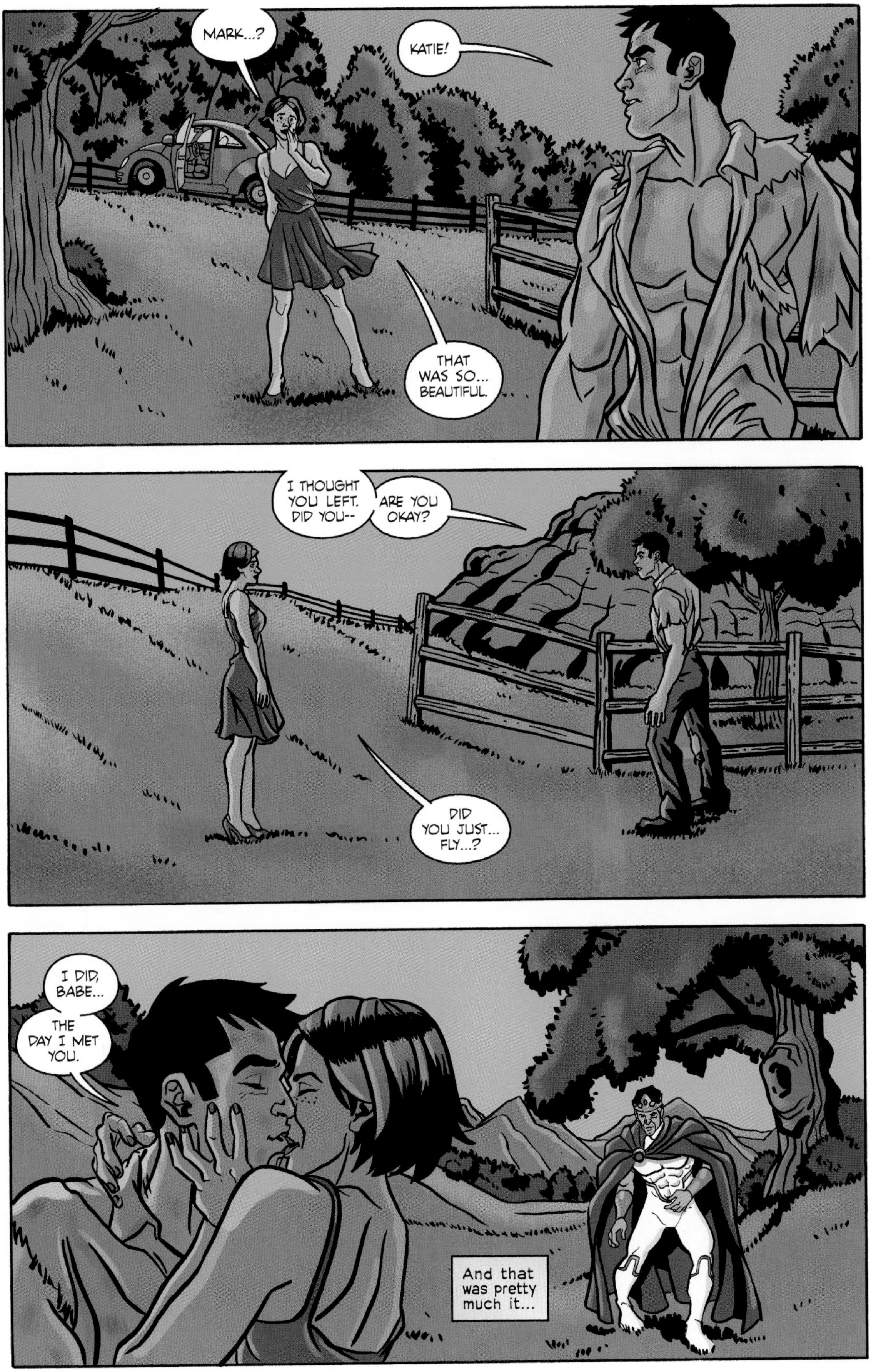
MARK...?
KATIE!
THAT WAS SO... BEAUTIFUL.
I THOUGHT YOU LEFT. DID YOU--
ARE YOU OKAY?
DID YOU JUST... FLY...?
I DID, BABE...
THE DAY I MET YOU.
And that was pretty much it...

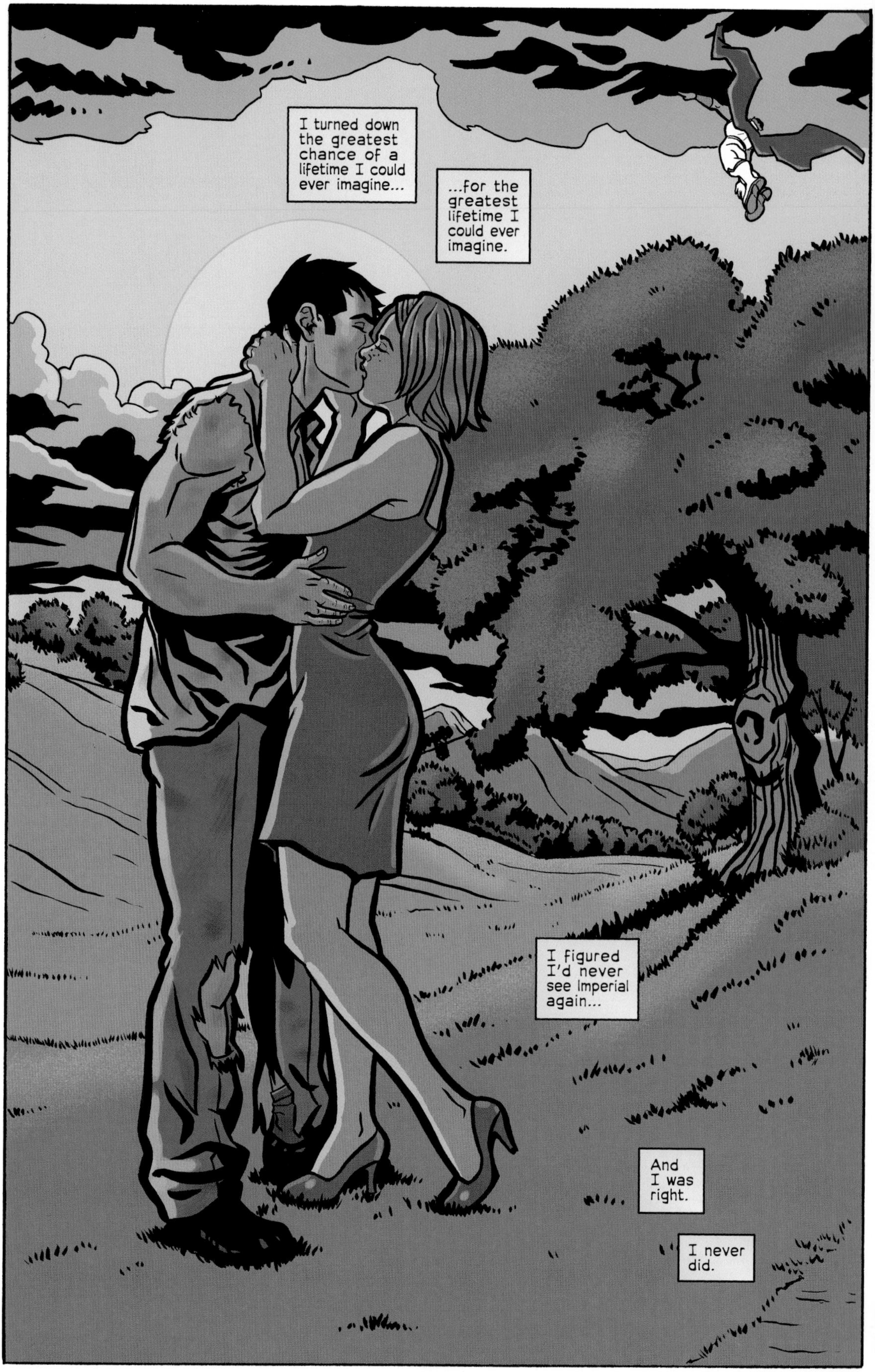
I turned down the greatest chance of a lifetime I could ever imagine...
...for the greatest lifetime I could ever imagine.
I figured I'd never see Imperial again...
And I was right.
I never did.

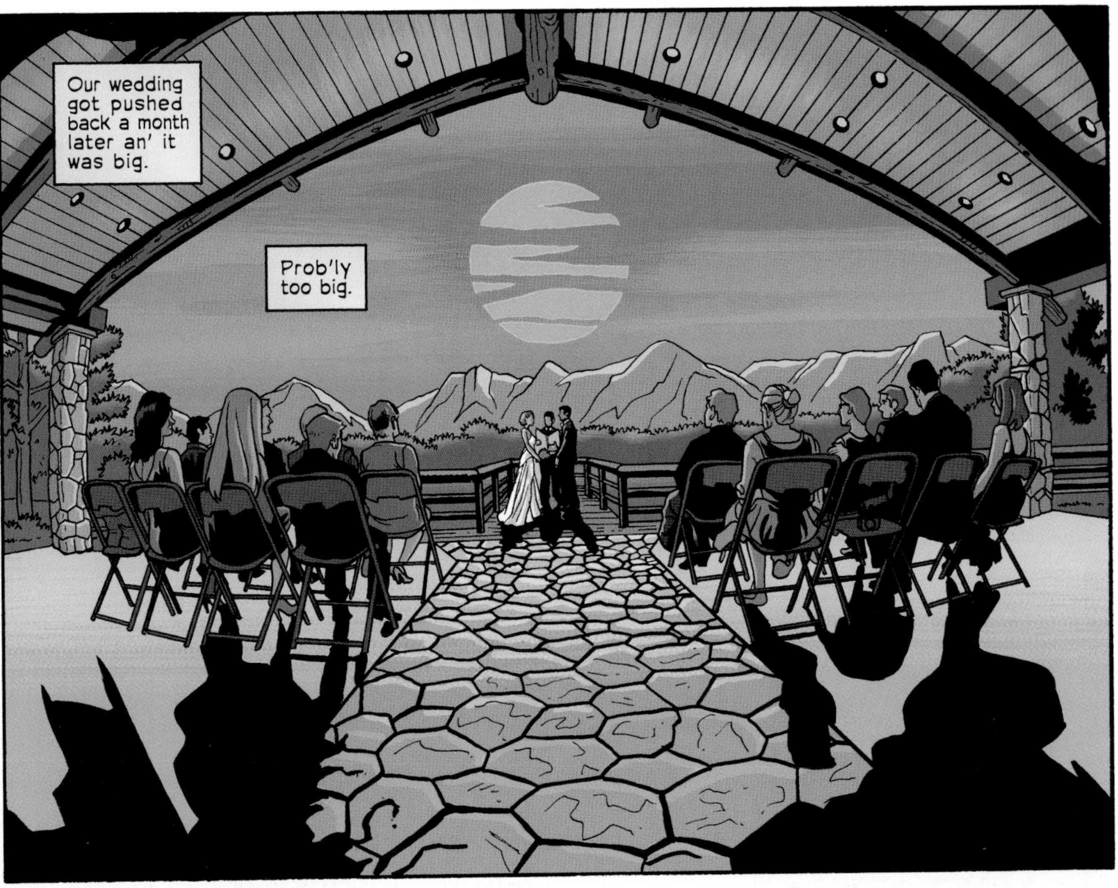

Our wedding got pushed back a month later an' it was big.
Prob'ly too big.

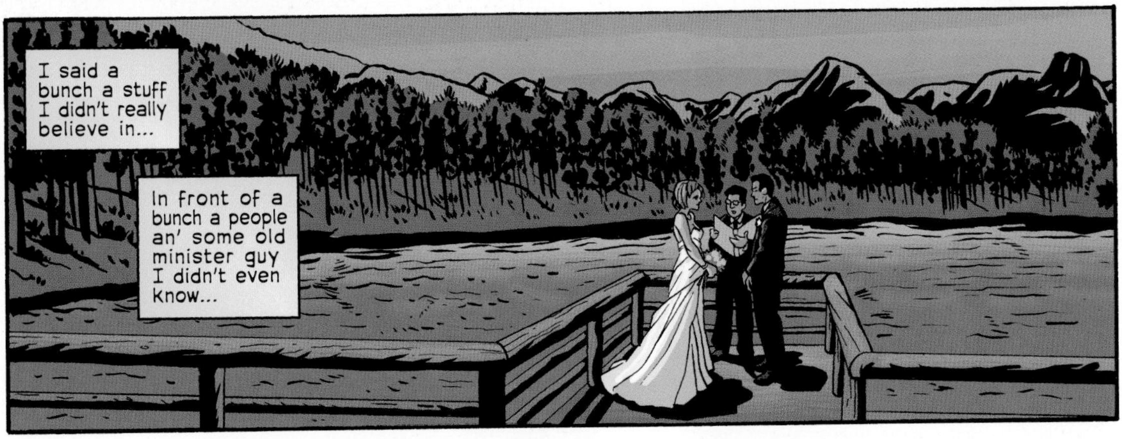

I said a bunch a stuff I didn't really believe in...
In front of a bunch a people an' some old minister guy I didn't even know...

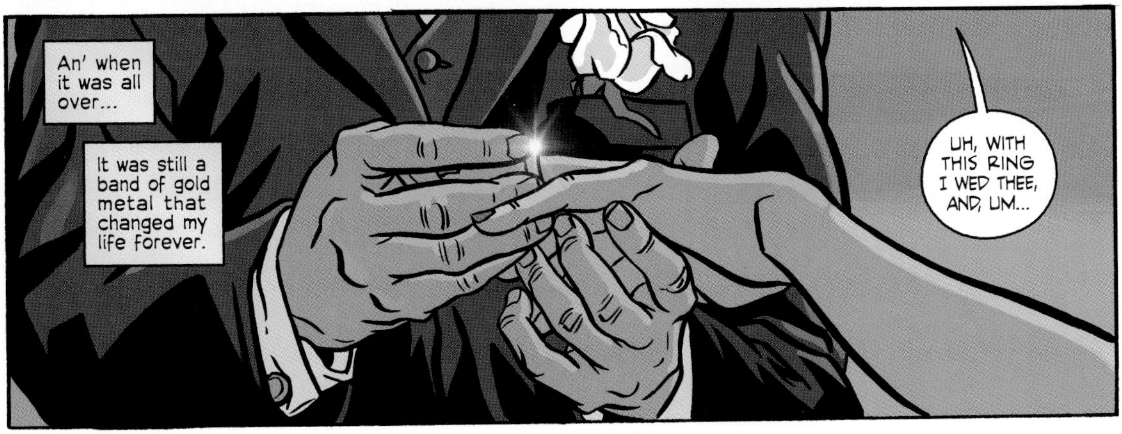

An' when it was all over...
It was still a band of gold metal that changed my life forever.
UH, WITH THIS RING I WED THEE, AND, UM...

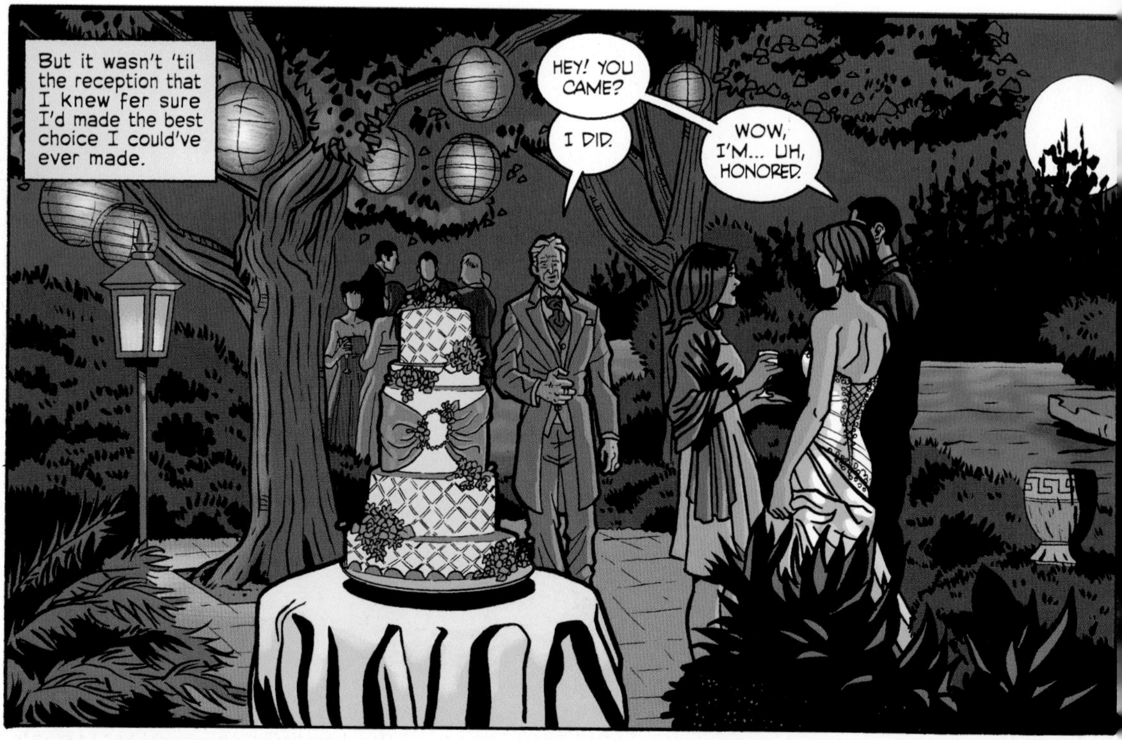
But it wasn't 'til the reception that I knew fer sure I'd made the best choice I could've ever made.
HEY! YOU CAME?
I DID.
WOW, I'M... UH, HONORED.

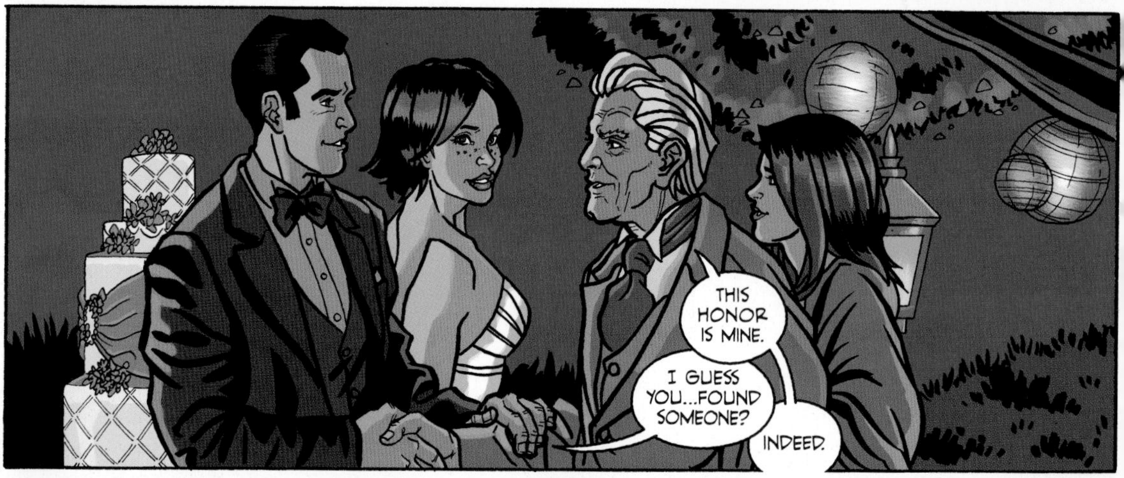
THIS HONOR IS MINE.
I GUESS YOU...FOUND SOMEONE?
INDEED.

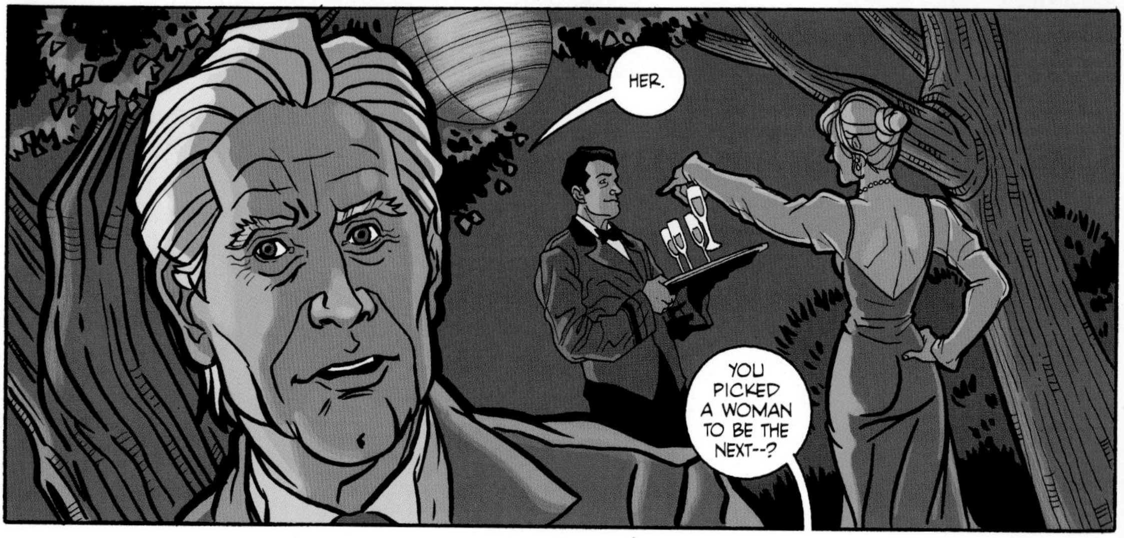
HER.
YOU PICKED A WOMAN TO BE THE NEXT--?

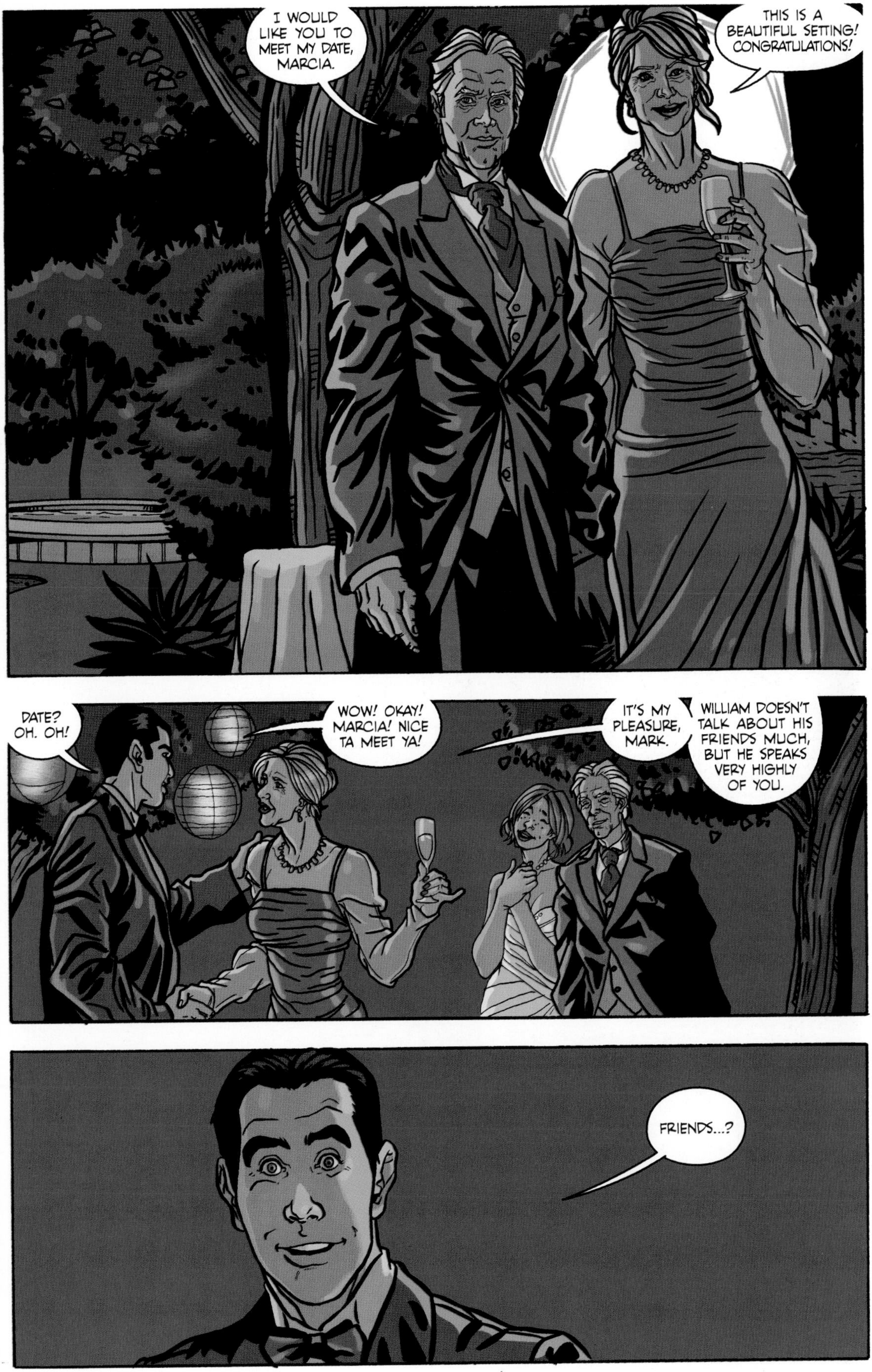
I WOULD LIKE YOU TO MEET MY DATE, MARCIA.
THIS IS A BEAUTIFUL SETTING! CONGRATULATIONS!
DATE? OH. OH!
WOW! OKAY! MARCIA! NICE TA MEET YA!
IT'S MY PLEASURE, MARK.
WILLIAM DOESN'T TALK ABOUT HIS FRIENDS MUCH, BUT HE SPEAKS VERY HIGHLY OF YOU.
FRIENDS...?

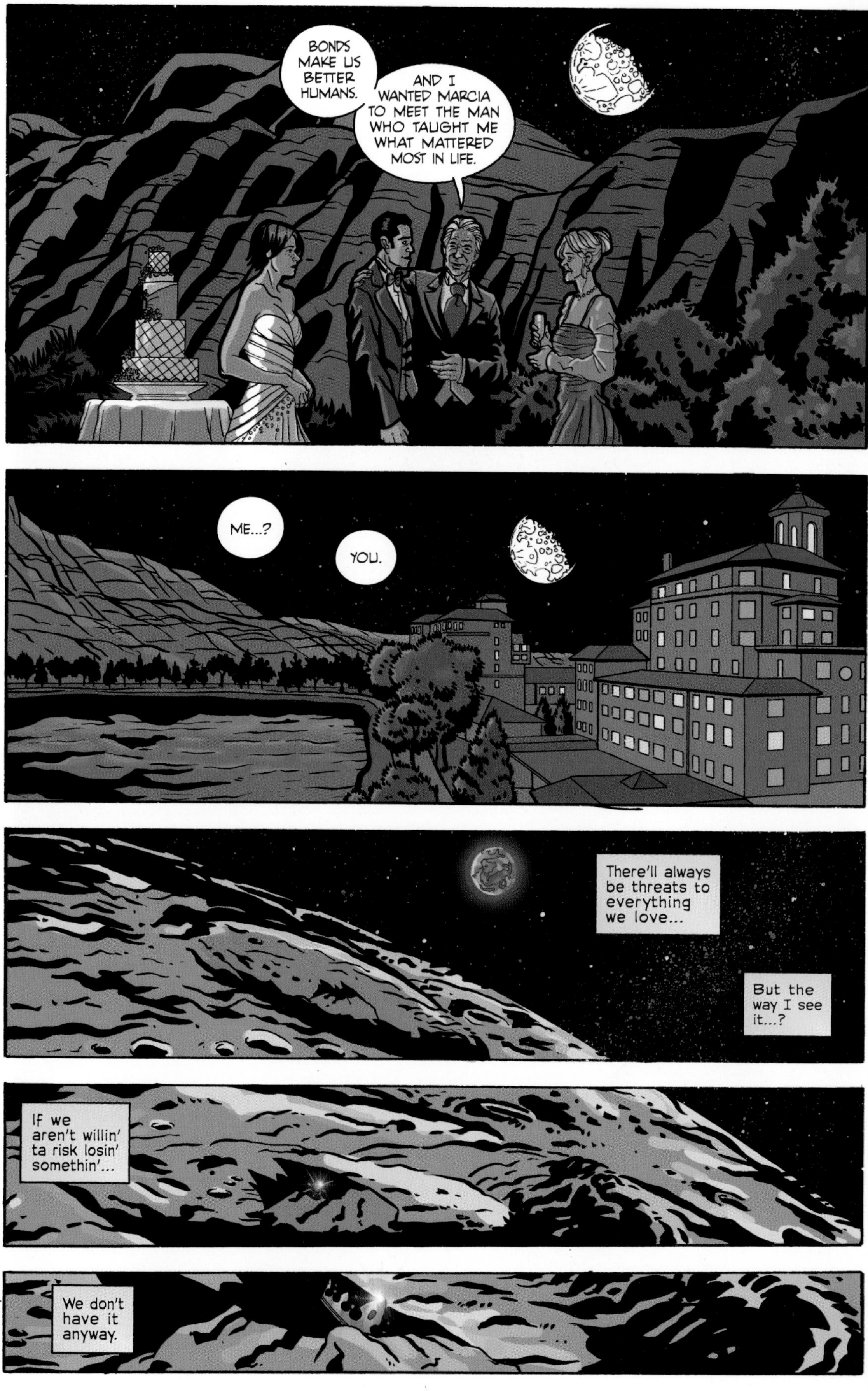
BONDS MAKE US BETTER HUMANS.
AND I WANTED MARCIA TO MEET THE MAN WHO TAUGHT ME WHAT MATTERED MOST IN LIFE.
ME...?
YOU.
There'll always be threats to everything we love...
But the way I see it...?
If we aren't willin' ta risk losin' somethin'...
We don't have it anyway.

the Artist and the Writer

on the occasion of the Artist's marriage to
his true love, Autumn Frederickson,
as photographed by
the Writer's true love, Liesel Reinhart,
just after the conclusion of
the original publication.

Mark, Katie, & Imperial first met in this Mucha-inspired pin-up from the Image Comics San Diego Comic-Con 2010 Yearbook.

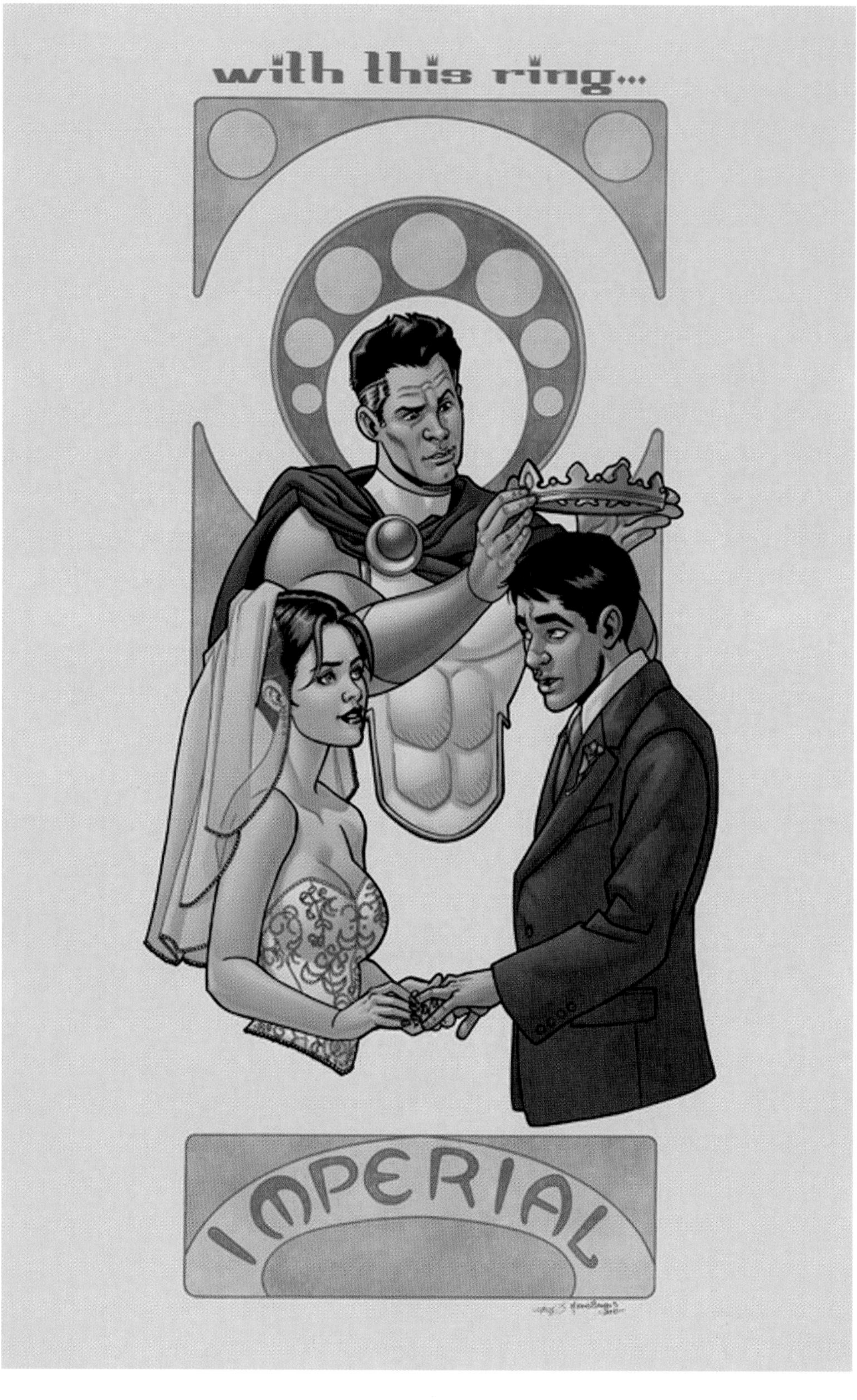
with this ring...
IMPERIAL

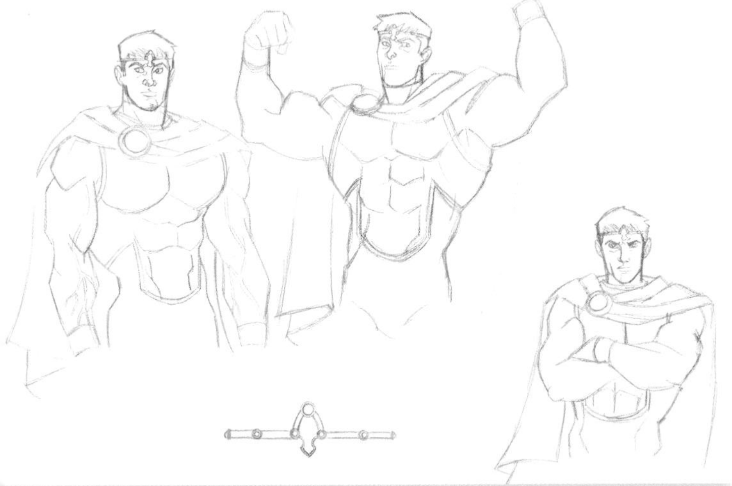

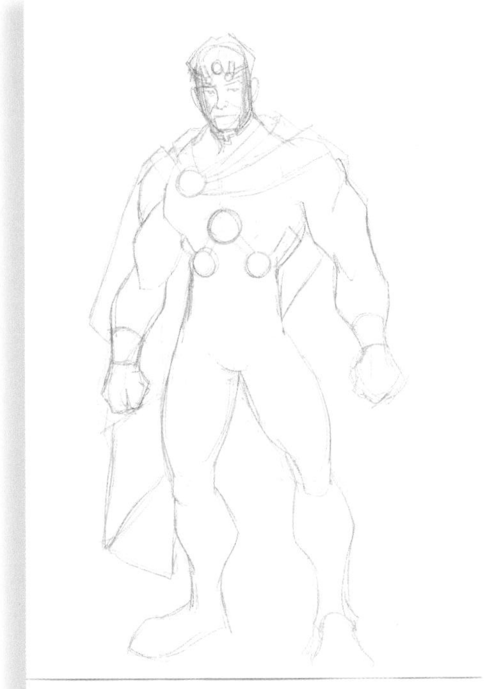

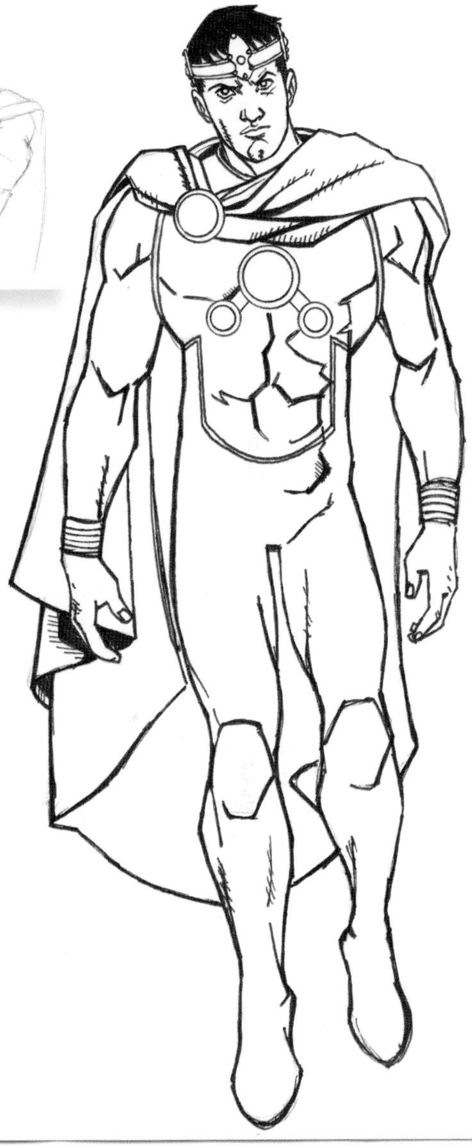

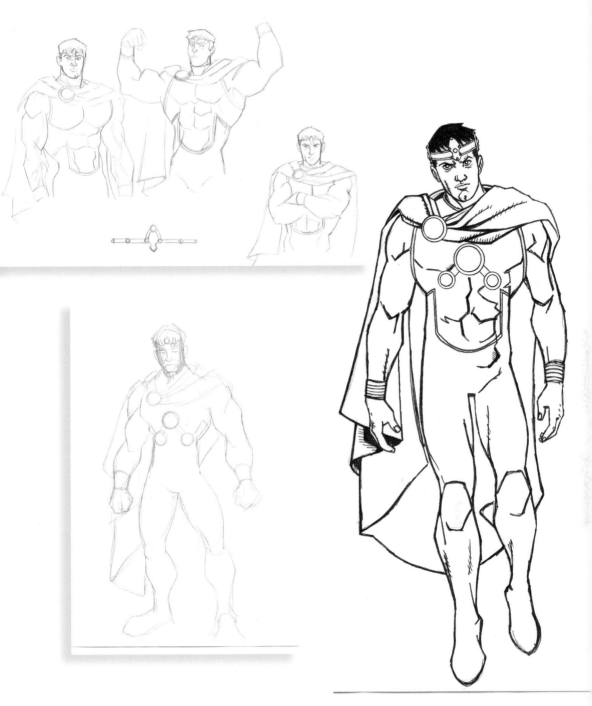

Imperial's original costume designs featured more super-heroic motifs. These were eventually dialed down to draw more attention to the crown and to fit with Mark's everyman appearance.

IMPERIAL

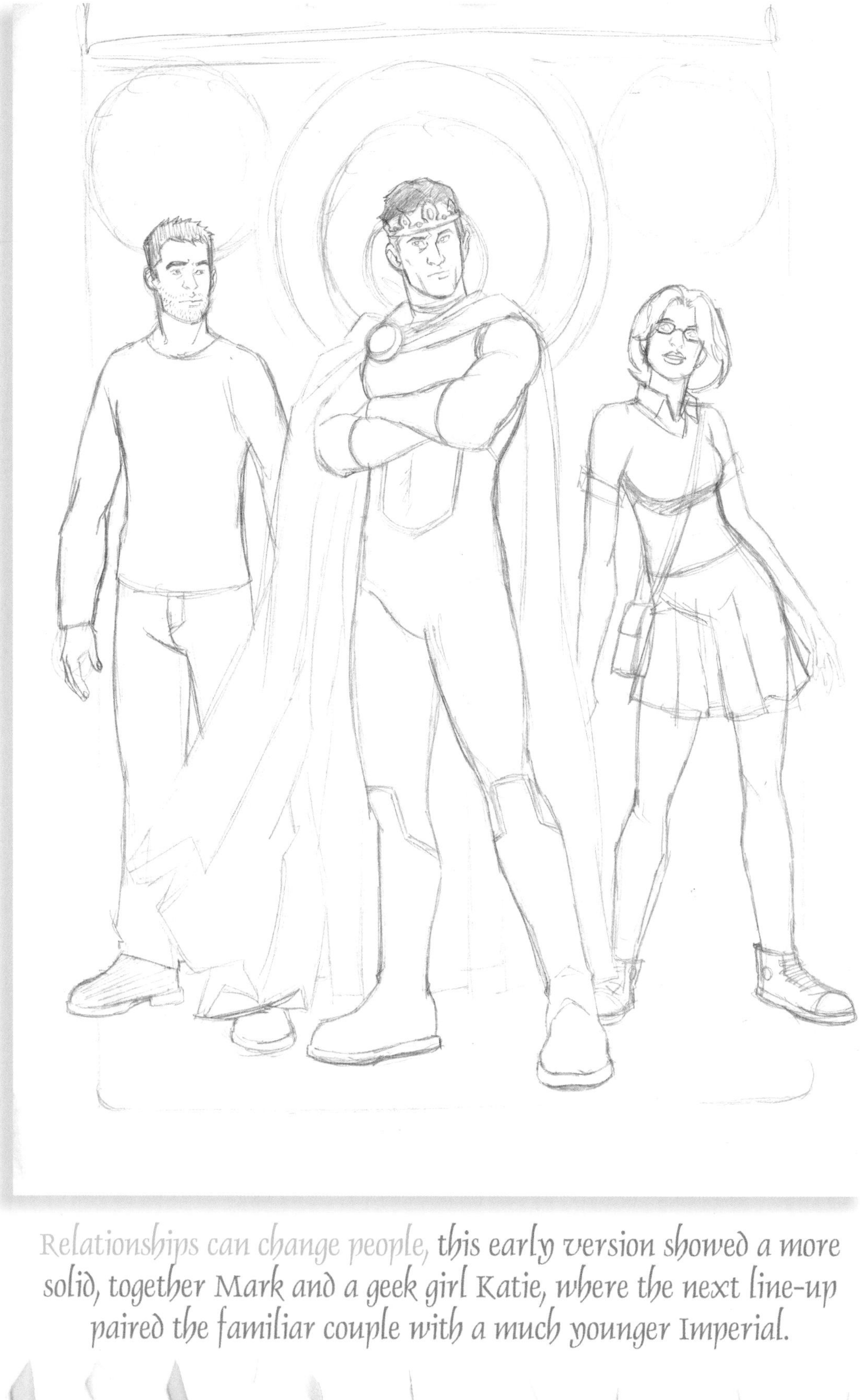

Relationships can change people, this early version showed a more solid, together Mark and a geek girl Katie, where the next line-up paired the familiar couple with a much younger Imperial.

IMPERIAL

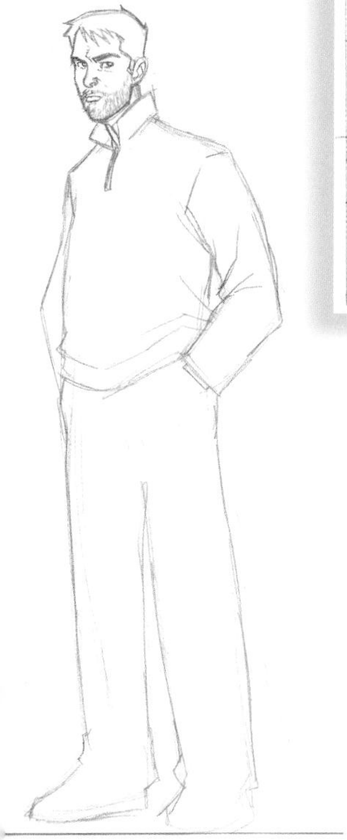

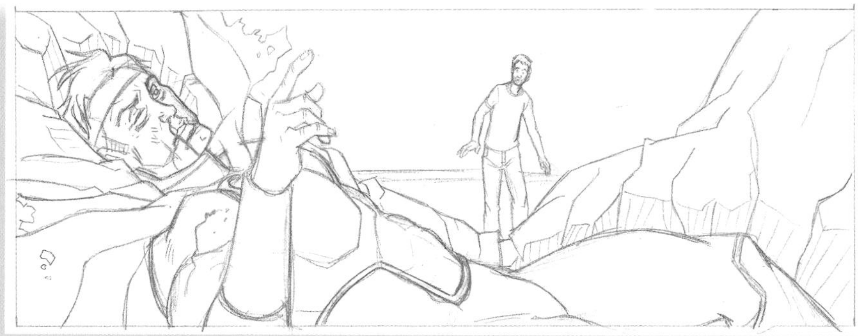

Maybe it was the stress, but Mark in the very early panel layout above seemed to put on about 50 pounds for his final look, left.

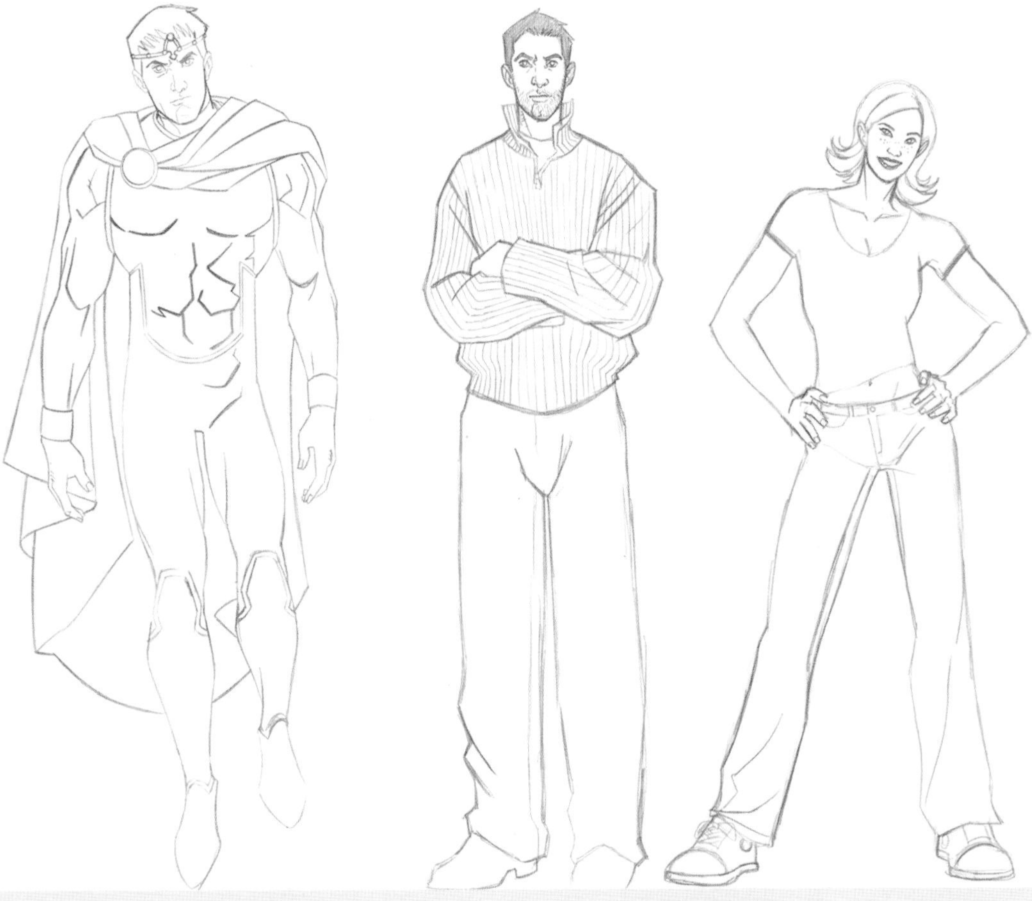

The mock IMPERIAL Comic Cover - 100% heartfelt Kirby homage - was executed in sketch before being rendered in full-size, colored, then reduced to play its part as the comic within the comic.

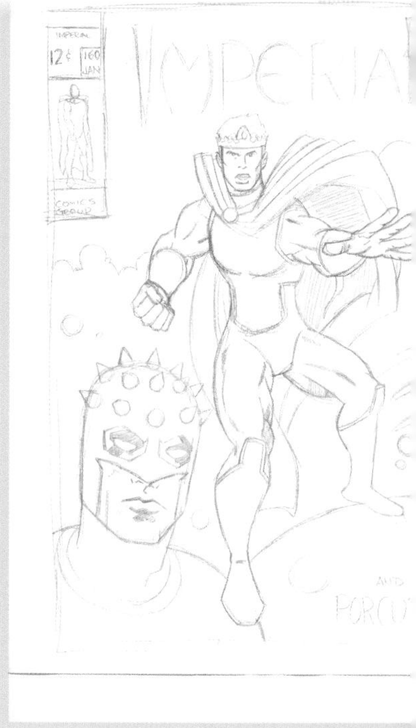
IMPERIAL
12¢
IMPERIAL
COMICS GROUP

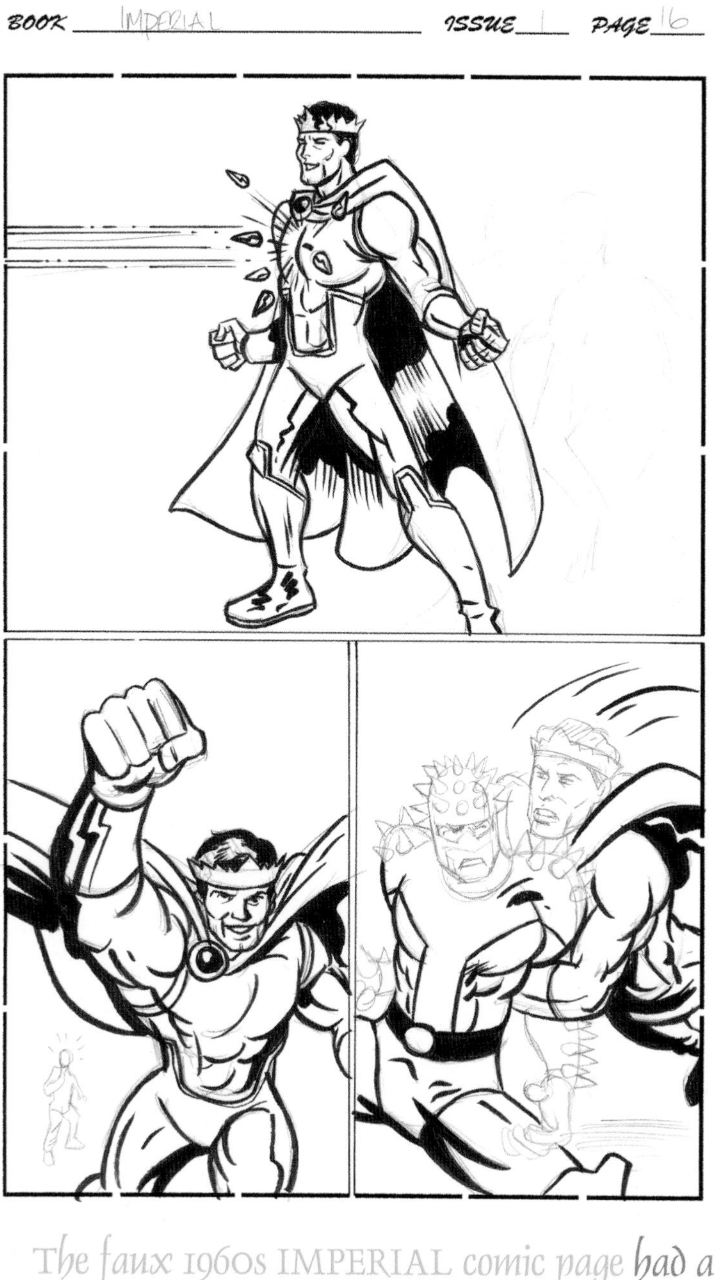
BOOK IMPERIAL
ISSUE 1
PAGE 16

The faux 1960s IMPERIAL comic page had a different staging of panel one and a variant background for panel two in this earlier draft.

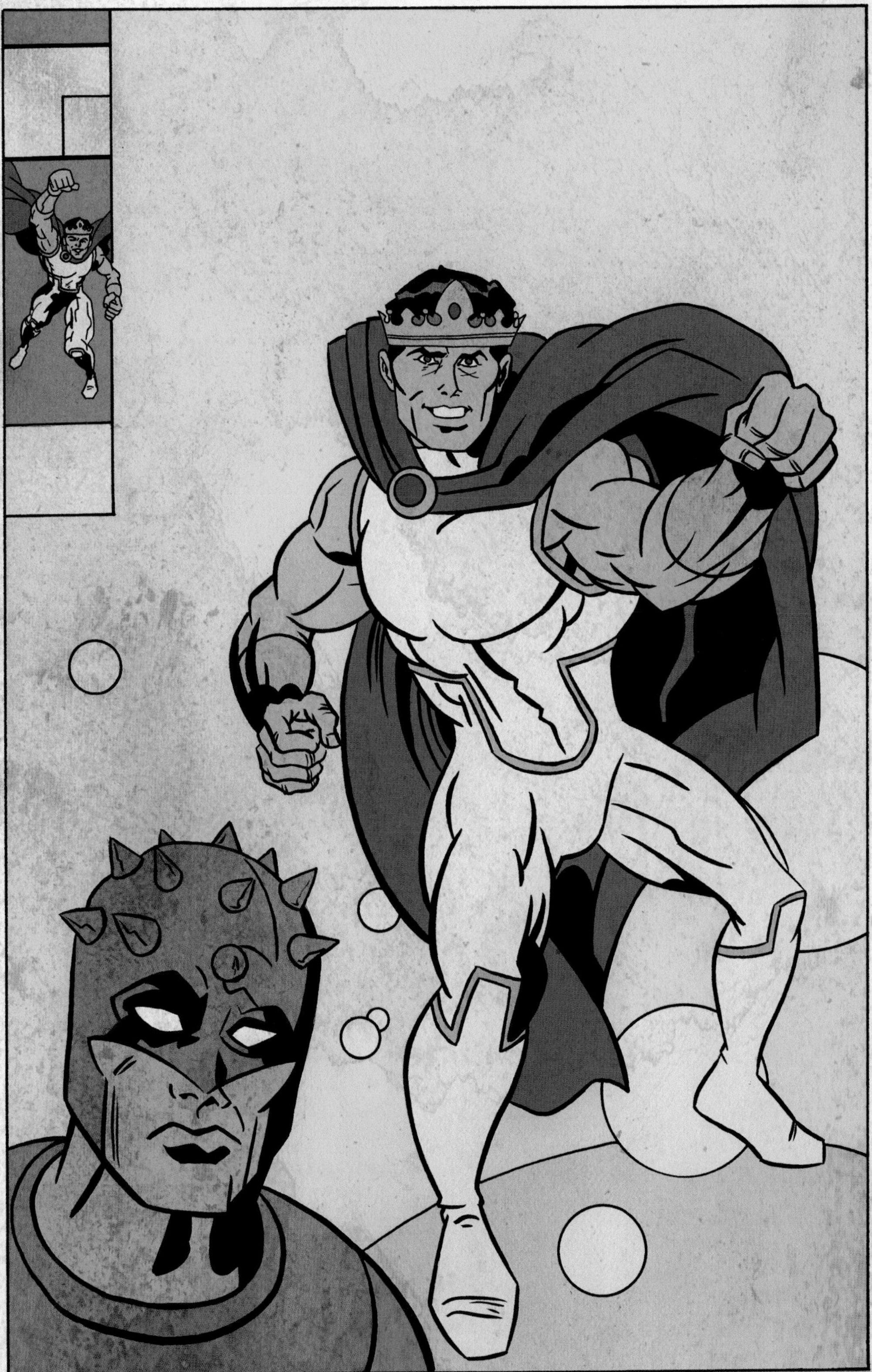

IMPERIAL

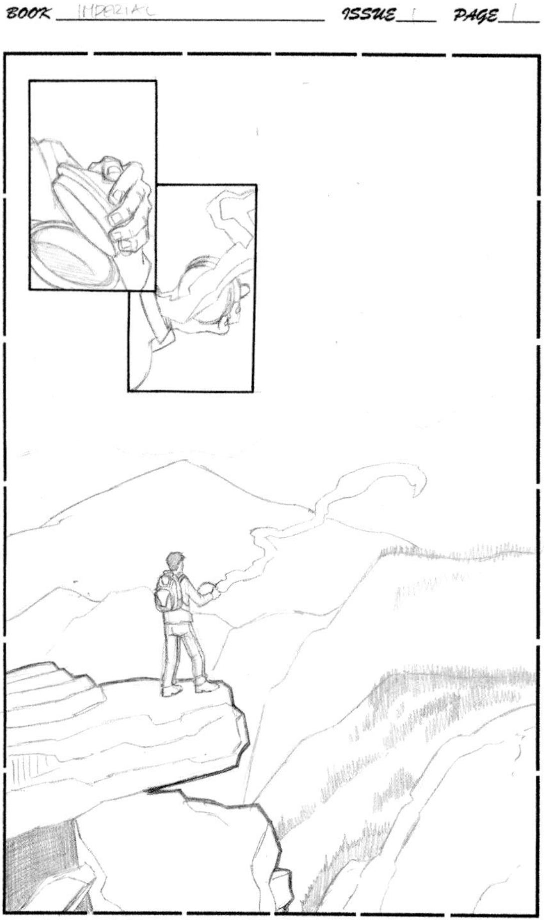
BOOK IMPERIAL ISSUE 1 PAGE 1

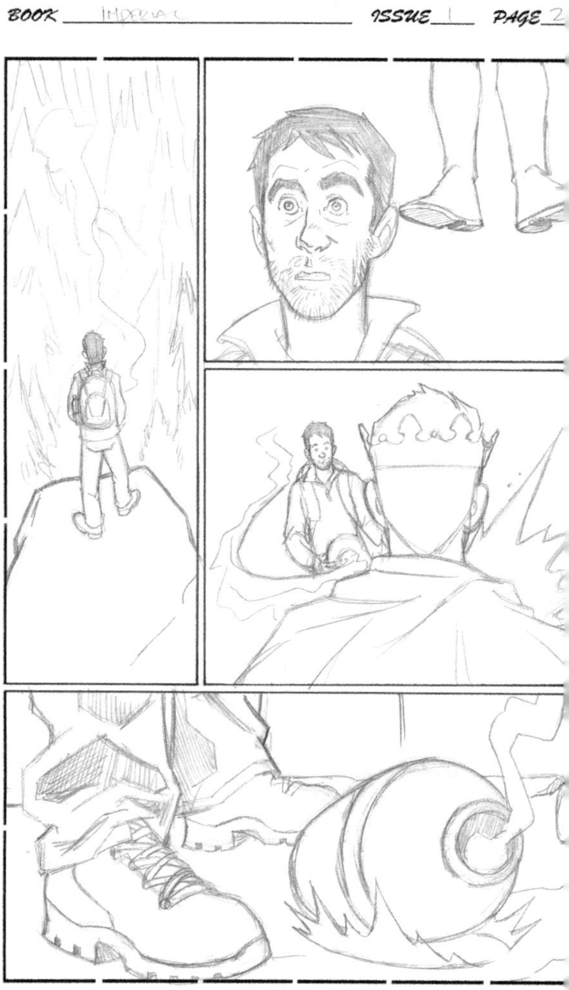
BOOK IMPERIAL ISSUE 1 PAGE 2

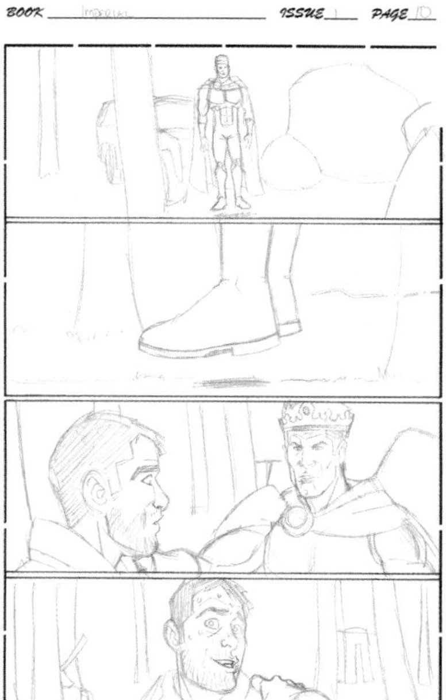
BOOK IMPERIAL ISSUE 1 PAGE 10

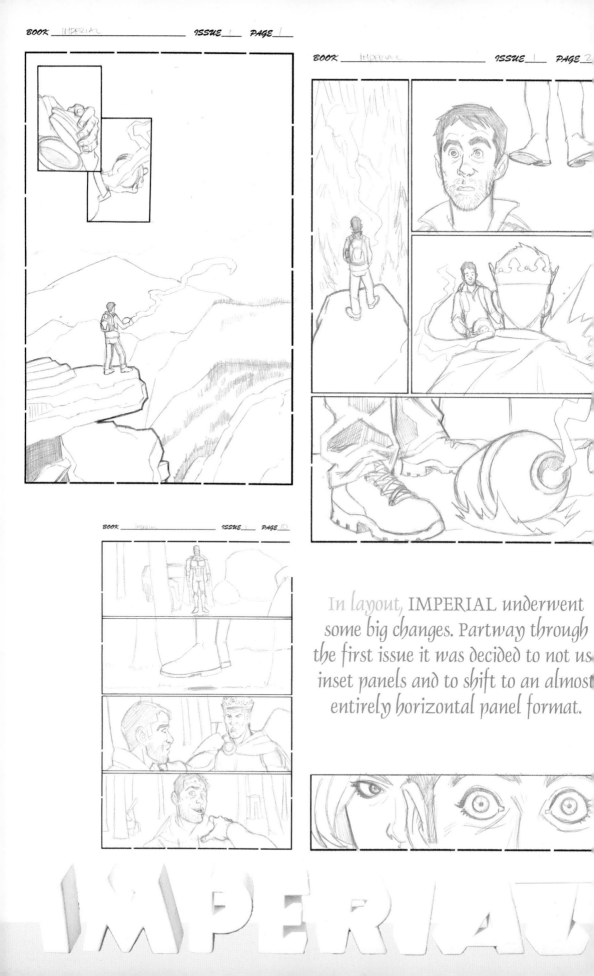

In layout, IMPERIAL underwent some big changes. Partway through the first issue it was decided to not use inset panels and to shift to an almost entirely horizontal panel format.

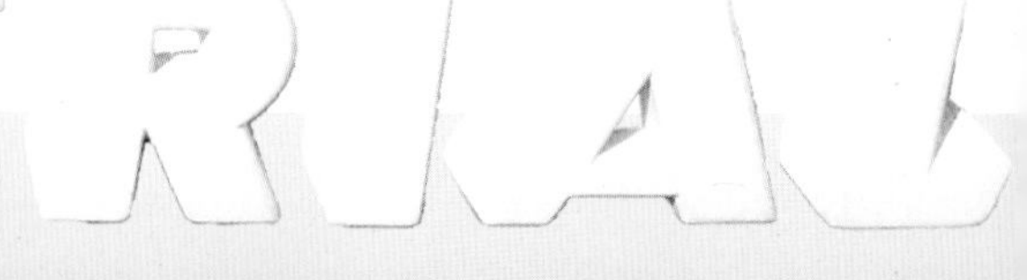

Mark's pencil pages were often testing grounds for layouts and angles that were modified for the final inked versions.

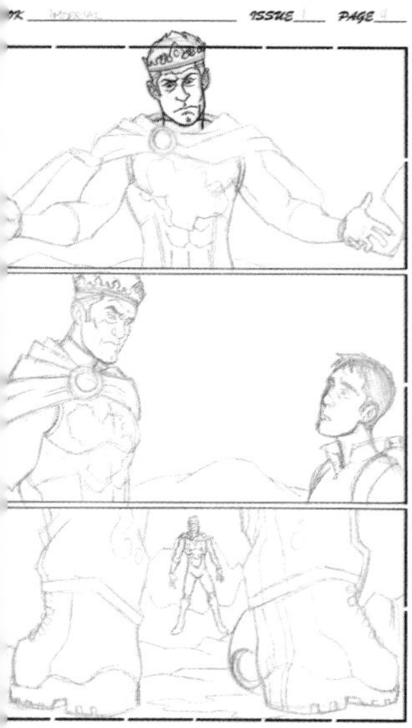

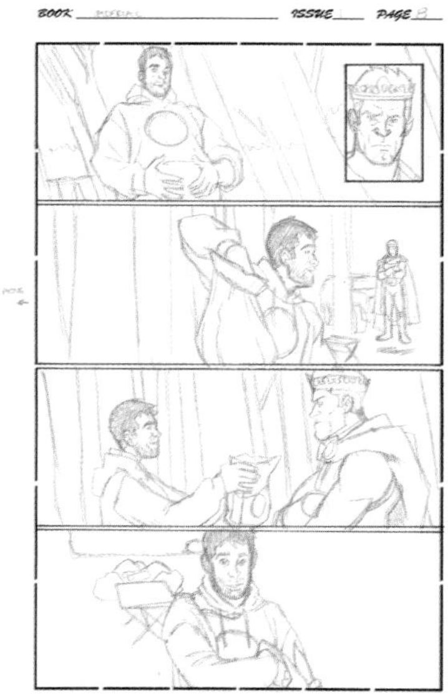

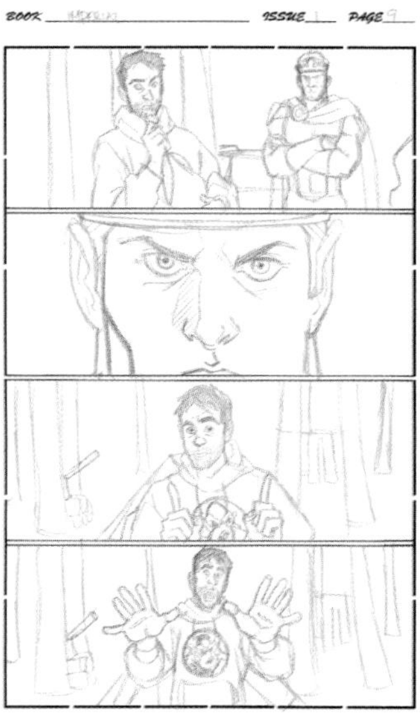

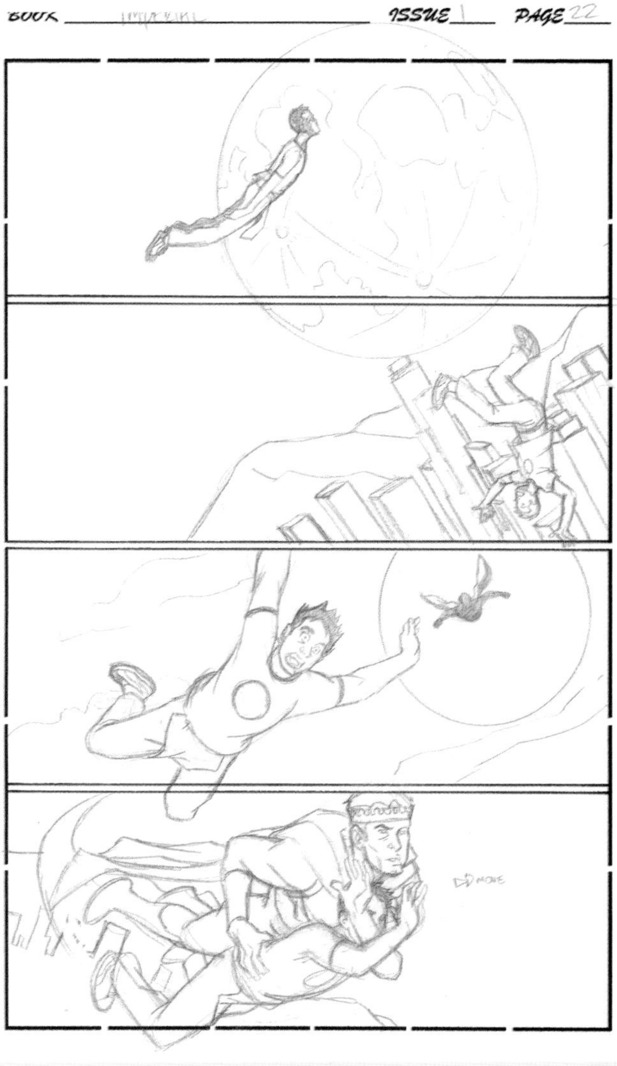

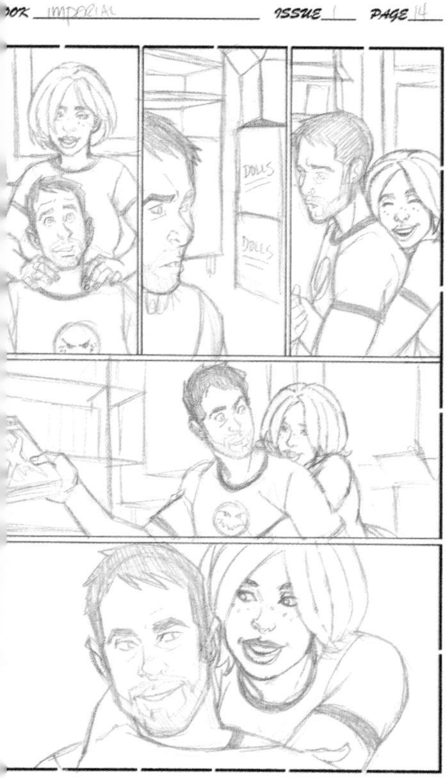

Early Cover Sketches *show some of the classic Rockwell and Leyendecker layouts Dos Santos sampled for his parodies.*

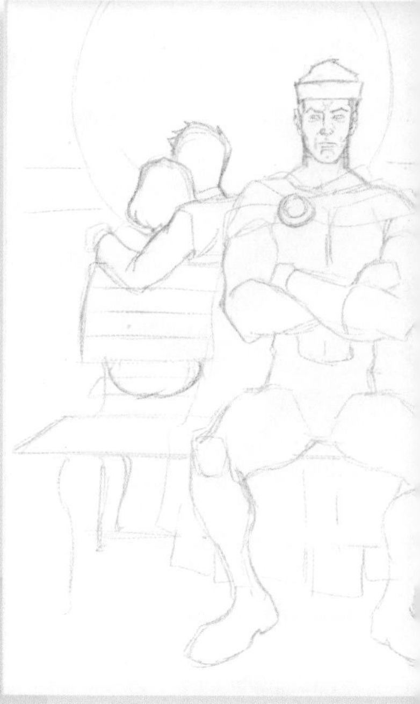

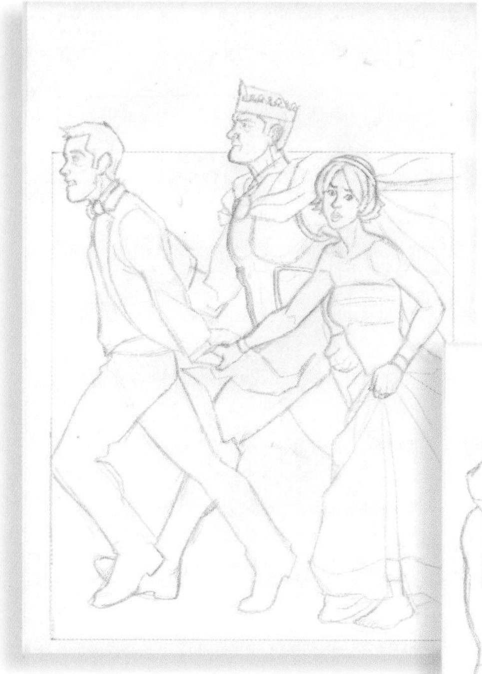

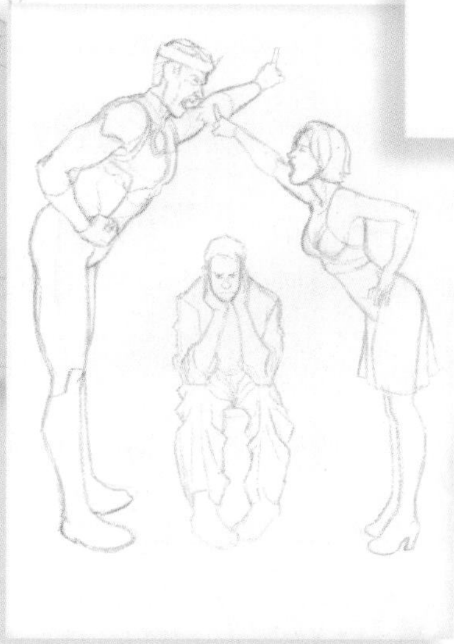

What's in a logo? IMPERIAL *was rendered in real 3-D with a set of 1930s plaster movie titling letters mounted to foam core board. The letters were lightly cleaned, straightened, and brightened in Photoshop.*

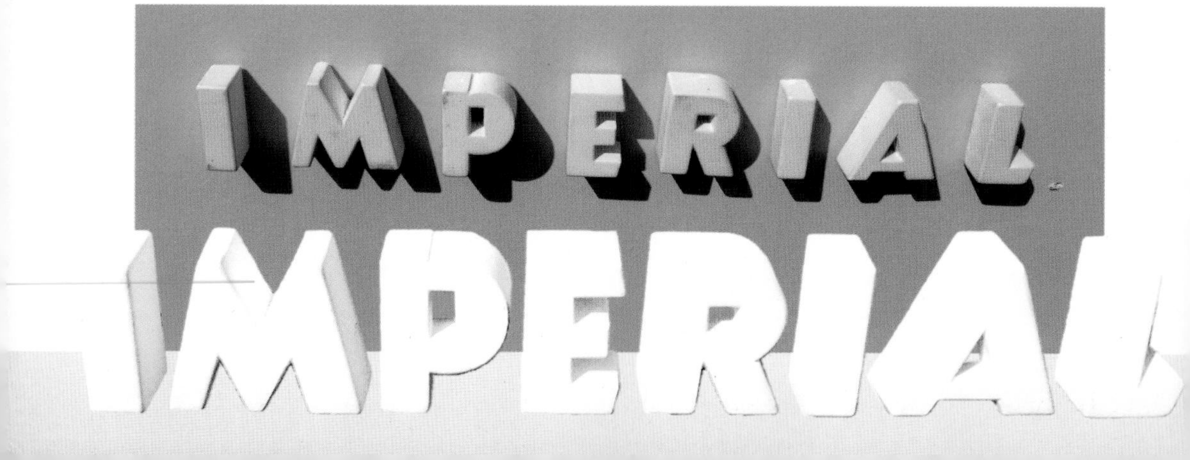
IMPERIAL
IMPERIAL

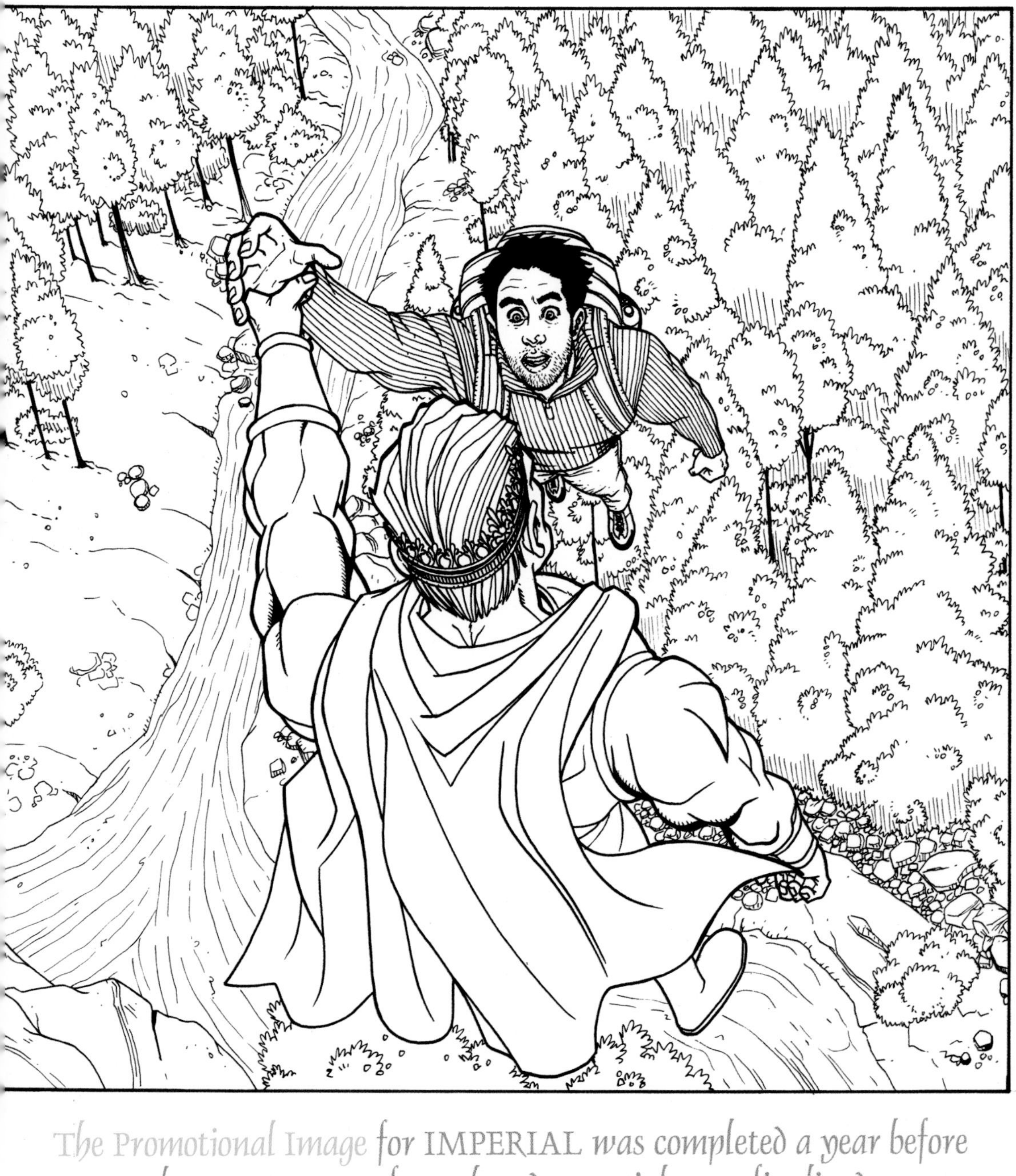

The Promotional Image for IMPERIAL was completed a year before the appearances of Mark and Imperial were finalized.

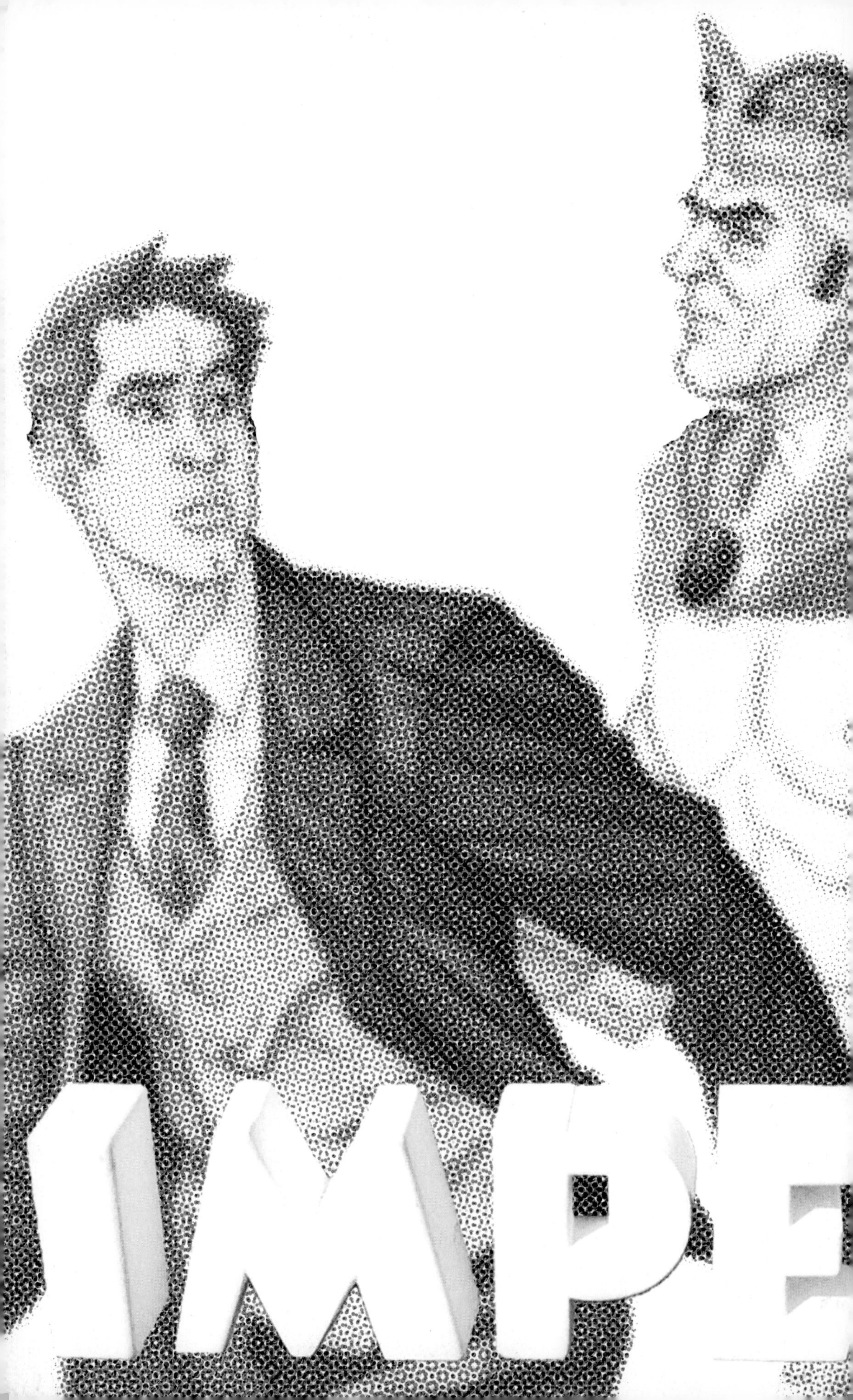